Below the town of Tyndale, the King of the Wood feels threatened. His power is waning and his minions are abandoning him. He is determined to retain control and destroy the usurper: Tom Bender. But exactly who is The King of the Wood?

Unlike previous pranks, the latest student hazing in Tom Bender's back yard proved fatal. Animals begin to obey him. Crows seem to understand what he says and pass along cryptic messages. Then everything in the garden starts to grow and keeps growing long past its natural season. Tom thinks this is wonderful until he discovers that the deck is growing too.

Brother James knows of the coming conflict. He is sure that he can defeat both the King and any human opposition. Brother James is confident he will assure the ascendance of man over nature. However, his spy in Tyndale has another target: Tom.

Praise for KING OF THE WOOD:

LONG LIVE THE KING! If you're a fan of "green men," pagan gods, cult leaders, and human sacrifices – like I am – then you're going to love THE KING OF THE WOOD! J. Edwin Buja does a great job juggling horror, drama, and even a few laughs (including some late night slapstick in a morgue). THE KING's garden is abundant. Enjoy its fruits!

– **LL Soares**, Bram Stoker-winning author of LIFE RAGE and BURIED IN BLUE CLAY

To Valerie:
hope you enjoy
a trip to the woods.
thank you.

NECON 2019

THE KING OF THE WOOD
Book one of THE WOOD

J. Edwin Buja

May 12 crows watch over you and yours

Haverhill House Publishing LLC

This is a work of fiction. Names, characters, places, and incidents are either a product of the authors' imagination or are used fictitiously. Any resemblance to actual events, locales, or persons, living or dead, is entirely coincidental.

The King of The Wood © 2019 John Edwin Buja

ISBN
978-1-949140-01-9 Hardcover
978-1-949140-02-6 Trade Paperback

Cover illustration © 2019 Neil Dring
Cover design and setup by Dyer Wilk

All rights reserved.

Haverhill House Publishing
643 E Broadway
Haverhill MA 01830-2420
www.haverhillhouse.com

For
Dianne, always

ACKNOWLEDGMENTS

I would like to thank Craig Shaw Gardner for his help and encouragement, and for making Tom less of a jerk.

Terry Fernihough has always been supportive and helpful beyond belief. I would like to give him extra thanks for letting me use him as a character though he is nothing like the Sheriff.

John McIlveen has been a friend for more years than we care to remember. We share a special bond that no soundproofing can ever hide. And thanks for taking a chance on me.

Despite what she might say, Dianne has helped keep this old thing going for longer than she realizes. And she helped a lot with the book as well. Having you in my life is the reason I have a life. Love, always.

A huge thank you to everyone at the Borderlands Bootcamp for the pain, sleepless nights, terror, and damned good lessons. If you're a survivor, you know what I mean.

Finally, to all the folks who have attended or will attend Necon, my deepest thanks and love. The friendships, guidance, encouragement, and support there are what keep me writing. Plus the scotch; we can never forget the scotch. What happens at Necon stays at Necon. But what happens at Necon is amazing and extends far beyond the confines of an annual convention.

INTRODUCTION

by
Craig Shaw Gardner

Let's get one thing out of the way right now. J. Edward Buja (CD WW) (aka "John") and I have known each other for years. We've spent many a night tossing back a drink or two (at the fabulous Necon) and solving the world's problems, (as one does while tossing back those drinks.) We're close to the same age, and like a lot of the same films. Sometimes we meet at the Fantasia film festival in Montreal and see even more movies. His hair is actually longer than mine. He's one of the world's nicest guys. He's Canadian, so that is only to be expected. He's written other things in the past, short stories and children's' books, but KING OF THE WOOD is his first book for adults. And quite a book it is.

John's first novel is something different. It plays fast and loose with genre stereotypes. It's a fantasy novel with a hearty injection of horror, with equal parts melodrama and humor thrown in. It takes place in a small town of undisclosed location. In this book, even small towns can contain world shaking events, and, as the book progresses, John takes us gradually from the "real" world into the supernatural world beyond.

The novel starts out with what appears to be a harmless prank. But that "prank" becomes something else entirely. It's, a mystery that effects the entire town. Over the course of the book, John reveals that certain characters, including the King of the Wood mentioned in the title, have histories reaching back, perhaps, to the beginning of the world. These histories find many of the characters in an ongoing conflict. In one twist after another, John shows us the scope of this battle, and how it will decide the fate of the world. It is a huge and complex story, and this book really only provides the first few pieces of the puzzle. With KING OF THE WOOD John not only presents us with a mystery; he gives us the beginnings of a fascinating and dangerous journey.

A bit of a warning here: This book is the beginning of a series, and ends with one hell of a cliff-hanger. It is certainly worth the trip. I'm already looking forward to the sequel. So what are you waiting for? Turn the next couple pages and start reading about the King.

Craig Shaw Gardner
Arlington, MA

Counting Crows	**Counting Rats**
One predicts sorrow	One is a pest
Two carry mirth	Two cause sadness
Three feel comfort	Three carry sickness
Four fear war	Four tell lies
Five warn of betrayal	Five hide deception
Six pursue wealth	Six aid a thief
Seven seek guidance	Seven fetch grief
Eight counsel caution	Eight only envy
Nine promise love	Nine can but hate
Ten lament sadness	Ten bring betrayal
Eleven bring romance	Eleven start a plague
Twelve foretell happiness	Twelve see death – today

CHAPTER ONE
THE OAK

The King of the Wood

The King of the Wood surveyed his handiwork, his art, his destiny, and he was pleased. His time had come. Again.

When he walked away the first rat crept from the shadows and began to eat.

Tom Bender

Tom Bender was not particularly surprised to see someone tied to his oak tree; he'd been expecting it for most of the month. He wasn't worried. Tom's backyard was always a few degrees warmer than the rest of the area, so it wasn't too cold outside, and the person seemed to be wearing some kind of robe for a change. Besides, the "victim" was probably still drunk. And Tom was angry about what met him in the driveway when he arrived home, so the poor slob outside would just have to be patient.

No one was able to help: the Sheriff seemed barely interested, the college denied all knowledge, and his friends were amused. The internet had yielded little – just vague references to ancient rituals involving oaks and some god that lived in the woods. The only concrete thing he discovered was that the people were tied up on the equinoxes. Today was the vernal.

Tom smiled. A rare thing when thinking about Belinda these days. Twelve years ago, he had smiled a lot.

For as long as Tom had lived in the house, pranksters from the agricultural college had been playing their jokes in his backyard. Every March and September, some hapless student, usually male, was tied naked to the oak tree during the night. Tom never heard a thing, despite being easily awakened by strange noises in his house.

Belinda had discovered the first "victim" in September twelve years ago, shortly after they had moved into the house.

"Honey, there's a naked man tied to our tree," she'd said that morning, standing at the kitchen sink washing last night's supper dishes. "He's quite well hung, too."

Tom put down his crossword puzzle, sipped his tea, and walked over to the sink. The man tied to the tree appeared to be in his late teens or early twenties. His black hair was hanging down over his face, and he was, indeed, quite naked. "It's cold out there," he said. "How can you tell?"

Belinda smacked his arm with the dish brush. "I meant the knots on the rope, you pervert. I was a Girl Scout, I can tell. I wonder what he's doing there."

The following March, there was another naked student tied to the oak.

Over the years, Tom and Belinda got used to the idea of releasing a naked student every March and September. Tom diligently copied down the mysterious words painted on them and eventually learned it was written in Middle English. It was always the same thing with a slight variation; reference to the king of the hill or the king of the wood and an exaltation to something—there was no corresponding name in his books of gods—to bring forth some kind of renewal. He didn't put much effort into finding out what it meant. It was a mystery that Tom had stopped trying to solve. The sheriff continued to show a definite lack of interest in the whole affair despite Tom's persistence. The last time Tom had enquired, the Sheriff was downright hostile.

He was hungry after his long drive so he went to the refrigerator to see if he had any leftovers, though leftovers that were more than a week old didn't seem too appealing. Unless it was pizza or pasta—pizza and pasta never went bad. The longer it was in the refrigerator, the better it got, especially lasagna. When Tom opened the refrigerator, he was greeted by half a dozen cans of Guinness and a steak that was at least an inch thick and, Tom sniffed, yes, smothered in Spanky's secret marinade. There were even a couple of baking potatoes in foil. Good old Spanky had been by last night. After the trip, it was good to be back among genuine friends.

Tom took the steak and potatoes and a can of Guinness out of the refrigerator. The barbecue had plenty of propane; Tom had filled the tank a couple of days before his trip, and Spanky would have made sure to refill it if he had used up all the gas. He set the steak and potatoes on the table and got a beer mug out of the cabinet next to the sink. Tom slowly poured the dark liquid into the mug; his mouth watered as he thought about the first swallow.

A noise distracted Tom from his task. He tried to concentrate until the last of the Guinness was properly poured into the mug, but the noise became more persistent. "What the Hell?" he said setting the can down and stopping for a moment to listen.

"Crows," he whispered. He could make out the distinct cawing of the birds coming from the backyard. There seemed to be a lot of them.

Tom walked over to the kitchen window sipping at his drink. Sure enough, there was a large number of crows gathered in groups in the back yard around and in the oak. "How many are enough for a parliament of crows? Or is it always a murder?" he mused.

Rats picked at piles of something scattered around the feet of the bound man. Tom couldn't see exactly what it was, but it must have been good because the rats were fighting each other to get at it. Four over at the compost bin seemed to be arguing over something. Tom's stomach lurched.

What the fuck are rats doing in my back yard? I keep a clean yard.

Ten crows perched on the windmill watching the rats scamper about. Six jumped about on one of the raised vegetable beds and eight stood like statues on the eastern fence.

One crow landed on the deck rail below the kitchen window and stared up at Tom; it was the biggest crow he'd ever seen. Four more landed on the rail a little apart from the big fellow.

Then a single rat climbed the oak's trunk and sat on the man's shoulder. He didn't move. Tom was astonished. He knew rats were bold, but to stand on a man seemed out of the norm. The rat nibbled at the man's neck several times then ran off with a chunk of flesh hanging from its mouth.

Tom shuddered and looked more closely at the bound man. "Oh God," he shouted when he realized that what had looked like folds of a red robe was something altogether different. He let go of the mug. It smashed on the counter. Then he vomited. Vomit, glass, and Guinness splashed out of the sink all over the counter and his pants. He turned on the cold water and splashed some over his face, bent down and sucked some water into his mouth. He rinsed out the last of the vomit.

Tom looked out the window again then shouted, "No. No. No." and vomited again. The rats ignored him but five turned and stood in a line to stare at him. The crows were galvanized into action. As one, they turned to face him then leapt from their various perches. They swooped at the feasting rats, in some cases knocking the vermin over. Quickly, the rats realized their free meal was over and scampered off towards the back fence and disappeared behind the compost bin. The crows flew over the back fence in hot pursuit.

Tom ran to the back door and pulled it open. When he stepped out to the deck an earthy smell, as if someone had been digging on a rainy day, filled his nose. All was silent, nothing moved. He stepped closer to the deck rail and when he touched it felt light-headed and tingly; the combination of no food, a little Guinness, and shock was kicking in. Reaching out, Tom grasped the rail for support and felt an electric shock go up his arm. Everything around him turned green and he slid to the deck, dead to the world.

CHAPTER TWO
THE SANCTUARY OF THE BRIDES

Sister Mary

Sister Mary walked briskly along the covered path that ran beside the Sisters' residence. A strong wind from the north was bringing heavy snow and plunging temperatures. It blew under the arches to her left and straight through her thin white habit. She shivered and pulled the garment closer about her body. She had been tempted to put on a robe beneath the habit or perhaps wrap a blanket around her because of the cold. Brother James had ordered that none of the Sisters wear anything over or beneath their habits as a sign to God that they were pure and proud to be His servants and had nothing to hide. Mary loved Brother James with all her heart and didn't want to do anything to make Him angry or think that she was not worthy of His love. Not that He ever showed the slightest bit of anger with any of the Sisters. He never raised His voice, even when Sister Rachel asked one of her incessant questions about how Brother James interpreted God's messages. Rachel was enough to strain the most patient of men, but Brother James always explained the Holy Words quietly and with complete confidence; Rachel was often taken away for special instruction. Though she knew it was a sin, Mary envied the attention her fellow sister received from Brother James. But she also knew that she was the First Bride, Brother James's favorite, pre-eminent among equals.

Mary stepped in a slush puddle and almost cursed. Her feet were numb from the cold and she wished the Sisters were allowed to wear proper winter shoes instead of the sandals they wore year-round. She quickly begged God's forgiveness for her evil thoughts and for questioning Brother James's edicts. She also asked God to give Him a special blessing as thanks for saving her. Mary owed her very existence to Brother James and His saving grace. Once in a while, during quiet moments of prayer and contemplation, she would remember some small part of her miserable life before she was called to the Church of the Immaculate Brides of Christ, before she was betrayed by those she loved and whom she thought loved her, before she became Sister Mary. These moments of remembrance grew fewer as the years passed and her life within the Sanctuary became immersed in the service of Brother James and God. Still, there were little things that made her happy—a remembered smile, a kind word. She always said a prayer after she felt these memories as thanks to God for granting her some happiness while in His service.

Approaching Brother James's manse near the gate to the Sanctuary courtyard, Mary again wondered why she had been summoned to see Him. Prayers weren't due to start for another two hours, and Brother James usually reserved this time of the afternoon for private meditation and personal prayer. It was a great privilege to be invited to join Him at this time, as she had on many occasions, but this had not been a summons to prayer. The note brought to her ten minutes ago by Sister Ruth had been terse. "Come," was all that was written. Something extremely important must be happening for Brother James to be so short. The note was added to her treasure trove of writings from her Savior: every letter, note, card, and even shopping lists that He had bestowed upon her. They were lovingly stored in a cedar chest, the one tangible reminder of her previous life, at the bottom of her bed. Brother James knew of this collection and approved. He had once written her a special letter praising her for keeping His sacred words and had given her the honored task of transcribing God's messages.

Maybe that was it—God had spoken to Brother James again and the message needed to be written down before it was forgotten. Not that He ever forgot a single one of God's words. He had an incredible memory and could recite the Holy messages flawlessly. His memory was a gift from God. Mary said another quick prayer of thanks for Brother James. She was excited now at the thought of being the first person to hear the latest Word of God. Pride was another sin, but she believed that pride in God could never be a sin. And pride in Brother James was a blessing that not enough people felt. She would do whatever she could to change that.

Reaching the front door of the massive manse and about to knock, Mary sneezed.

"God bless you, Sister Mary," said Brother James from the open door. He must have seen her coming through the snow and waited for her at the door. Such was His kindness.

Mary looked upon He whom she worshiped above all else. As happened often when she gazed upon her Savior, a tear fell from her eye. The light hanging from the foyer ceiling lit Brother James from behind so He appeared to have a halo. To her, this was no trick of the light but an earthly manifestation of His true divinity.

He was her God.

Forgetting the cold that embraced her, Mary took in the ethereal beauty of the man. His black hair waved slightly in the wind but He did not seem to notice the cold; unlike her, Brother James was not covered with goose bumps. Eyes bluer than a Greek sky in summer looked into Mary's soul and told her all was well. His full red lips split into a smile that caused her to catch her breath. Such was the comfort it radiated. He reached out a tanned and muscular arm and placed a hand on her shoulder. A jolt of excitement flowed down her spine and touched her in the most intimate places. She felt familiar stirrings.

"Come in, Sister Mary, my love," said Brother James, his voice quiet and deep and welcoming.

Mary shivered, not from the cold, but from deep-rooted desire. She loved this man and would do anything for Him. Just to be in His presence was a blessing from God. Mary hesitated as she always did before entering the manse of Brother James knowing that she was leaving the real world and all its troubles behind. Within the warmth of the manse was only love and happiness. She marveled yet again that He had deemed her worthy of such welcome.

Brother James stepped back to let her pass. He didn't remove His hand from her shoulder and His eyes never left hers. When she was inside the foyer, Brother James reached back to close the door. A breeze from somewhere within the house caught it and the door slammed, startling her. She jumped back and broke the connection with Brother James. Instantly, Mary felt as if her feet had touched the earth again. She looked down at her habit, covered with snow, and was embarrassed to be such a mess in the sight of her Lord.

"Don't worry about your appearance, Sister Mary," He said

as if reading her thoughts. "Outward appearance cannot mask inner beauty. You are always my most beautiful Bride." He reached out and wiped the snow from her habit. He got down on one knee and removed her sandals then wiped her feet dry with a towel He kept on a hook in the foyer. Shoes were not allowed in His house. He stood and caressed her face. The electric excitement flowed again and her worries slipped away like a wisp of smoke in the wind.

"Come with me to the study," said Brother James. He took her arm and guided her to the stairs. The ground floor was reserved for meetings and several of the large rooms were filled with rows of chairs and folding tables. To the left of the stairs was the chapel where Brother James conducted prayers with the Brides three times a day. Twenty Brides were in residence at this time, far more than usual, but Brother James had called many back from their missionary work in the city to wait for a looming and momentous event.

Mary wondered if He had received a message from God about whatever this event was to be. She grew anxious, nervous that she might not be able to comprehend the Word and appear foolish in the sight of Brother James and God. But He would never have called her if He did not think her capable of understanding. His faith in her was unbounded, and she praised God for it. But still, humility was a virtue, and she tried to be virtuous in all things.

Brother James walked up the stairs slowly allowing Mary to keep up with Him. Her feet were regaining their feeling and she had a little trouble keeping her balance. A few times she stumbled on the stairs but strong hands caught her and didn't let her fall. He would never ever let her fall again. She thanked God for Brother James's strength.

KING OF THE WOOD

When they reached the study, Brother James held the door open for her then followed her in. The study was lit only by the flickering light from a fire in the hearth. Shadows played across the walls. She went to sit in a large chair in front of the massive oak desk in front of the window. This was her usual seat when transcribing God's messages for Brother James.

"No, over here," said Brother James, indicating two chairs next to the fireplace. The fire radiated welcome heat. She waited for Brother James to sit in one of the wingback chairs then sat herself.

They remained silent for a few minutes. Mary stared into the fire, mesmerized by the movement of the flames and the shadows on the hearth. Usually Brother James let her know immediately if there had been a message from God. His silence now was unnerving. What could be so important that was not God's word? And what could it be that would involve her? Thinking these questions was a sin against Brother James and God. Who was she to question Their wisdom? She cleared her mind of all doubt and waited for Him to speak. He would in His own good time.

Brother James sat like a king, hands on the armrests, feet flat on the floor. Mary was aware that she was being watched and she was thankful that she pleased Him enough to earn this honor. When Brother James looked at you, saw into your soul, He knew the thing truly desired and what was best.

"Sister Mary." Her eyes were on Him. All her attention was focused on what her Savior was about to say. No sounds could penetrate her concentration, no thoughts rose to interfere with the divine Word. Brother James let a small smile escape. He knew she was rapt. "The Adversary has begun his work."

Mary jumped back in her seat, jolted by the last words she

expected to hear. Visions of flame and darkness filled her mind. She saw the damned falling into the pits of Hell to suffer eternally for denying the Word of Brother James and God. The screams of the damned echoed in her ears but were soon drowned out by the songs of praise from the saved. She saw light and the welcoming face of God, the welcoming face of Brother James. She smiled.

"I did not expect such news to make you happy, Sister Mary," He said. "Surely you do not welcome this event."

She shook her head in denial and looked at her Savior, eyes filled with ecstasy. "You misunderstand me, my Love. I smile with joy knowing that I shall be at Your side battling the evil one." She was surprised at her boldness, expecting to be at the side of One so exalted in the fight against evil. Was she worthy? "I apologize, my Love, for my presumption."

He leaned forward and touched her hand. There was the electric feeling again. In spite of the seriousness of the situation, she could feel a familiar desire welling up in her loins. She wanted to suppress it, but it felt so wonderful, especially in the presence of this man who was so much more than a man.

"You will be at my side, Sister Mary. Have no doubt about that." Brother James released her arm and sat back. He continued, "In fact, you will play a most vital role in defeating the Adversary and his damned agents."

Mary was overwhelmed and her heart almost burst with pride. That she, such a lowly and unworthy person, should play any kind of role in defeating the evil one was far beyond her wildest hopes. She had thought she might be privileged to stand with Brother James in the coming battle, but to stand at His side as, dare she think it, more than just the First Bride, perhaps even the Prime Bride, was almost more than her mind could handle.

Mary swooned and felt herself slipping from the chair.

When her eyes opened, Brother James's face was close to hers and she was in His strong arms. She smiled up at Him, unable to tear her eyes from His. They were so intense, reaching down into her soul and drawing forth such love as the world had never known. She reached up and put her arms around His strong shoulders pulling closer to Him. His bare skin felt hot and moist and she noticed that the room had grown hotter while they sat. It was like a sauna and sweat poured from her forehead and ran down her skin under her habit. Brother James's body glistened. He stood up straight setting her back on her feet but did not release her from His grip. They continued to look in each other's eyes, silent, as if waiting for the other to break the spell.

"In time," whispered Brother James, His breath hot on her. She shivered and felt a shifting in her loins, the first stirrings of an orgasm. Brother James released her and guided her back to her seat. When she was seated He went to a sideboard and poured her a glass of brandy. He held it out for her and she took it shakily. Mary could still feel the pulsing down below and was having trouble concentrating. Brother James grinned knowingly and sat.

"We have an agent watching our enemy's domain," said Brother James calmly. Mary nodded and a picture of Sister Sarah flashed into her mind. "She reports that the Adversary has taken his first step on the road to domination. He has made another sacrifice against the will of God. He has blasphemed in such a way that we cannot stand by any longer."

Mary, her composure regained, nodded. The room was silent except for the crackling of the fire; even the howling wind of the storm could not break her concentration. He paused, rose, and went to His desk where He opened a drawer and took out a file folder. He removed a photograph from the folder and stood next to her and held the photograph out for Mary to see.

When she saw who was in the photograph, she hissed and reached out to grab it. Brother James held it away from her hands and returned it to the folder. "There will be time for that later," He said, placing the folder on a side table. "For now, remember this man and the evil that was done to you at his hands."

"He will be punished?" she asked in a quiet voice. She was trying hard to calm herself but she was filled with memories of her abuser, the lies and deception she suffered because of him. She still felt the pain he inflicted on her with his guile. Her fingers felt the scars on her inner arms, the fault of the one to whom she had given her love and who had betrayed her so easily and without the slightest hint of shame. A hand slipped to her belly and through the thin fabric of her habit she could feel the most damning evidence of his betrayal, the scar from the hysterectomy that had stolen her future and destroyed her dreams.

Brother James saw what she was doing, smiled sadly and said, "Yes, I know. He stole from you that which you desired most."

"I only desire to serve You and the Lord," said Mary. There was a fervor in her eyes that Brother James knew well.

"I know, my love," He said. "But you shall be rewarded and your dream will be restored. God has spoken. You need not fear. You are a bride of Christ." Brother James paused then continued, "I sense another power in the domain of the Adversary. It's new, untested, burgeoning. We must find it and destroy it if it is not on the glorious side of Me and God.

"We are on a mission, guided by God, doing God's work. Nothing and no one will stand in Our way." He paced in front of the fire. Mary followed His every move. "You and I, together, Sister Mary, We shall lead the forces of righteousness." His voice grew deeper and more animated. She had never seen Him so inspired. Brother James's eyes were afire with religious conviction. He was sweating profusely now and every time He waved His arms to make a point, He sent droplets hissing into the fire or splashing onto Mary's upturned face. She welcomed the blessing and became aroused. The satin cloth of the habit caressed her erect nipples. Her breathing grew more rapid.

As He moved, Mary let her eyes wander for the first time, unable to resist the sight, and took in Brother James's massive chest and flat abdomen, His arms that held her so protectively, His legs like powerful tree trunks. And she saw that while He spoke, He became more excited in a physical sense. When He said, "We *will* be victorious, Sister Mary," His manhood stood fully erect and moist. Beckoning.

Brother James nodded to Sister Mary. She stood in front of Him and her hands went to the drawstring at the throat of her habit. She pulled the string and her habit fell in a pool at her feet. The heat from the blazing fire warmed her nakedness. She stared into Brother James's eyes and fell to her knees, ready to receive His Holy Communion.

CHAPTER THREE
THE KITCHEN

Tom Bender

"So, tell me again how you know nothing about that man out there," said Deputy Schofield standing with his fists on his hips. He was trying to intimidate Tom, who was seated at the kitchen table and having none of it. Schofield hadn't removed his cap or wiped his snow-covered boots when he came in the house and this bothered Tom in spite of the seriousness of the situation. Manners were important to Tom, no matter what was going on.

Tom stared blandly at the man, inhaled and replied, "Are you deaf? I told you, I don't know who he is. You saw his face. Do *you* recognize him? And I don't know where he came from, why he's there, or who did that to him." Tom's voice rose steadily as he spoke and became firmer, but he resisted shouting. While Tom stared at the deputy, he gripped the edge of the table to keep from shaking. His anger was barely below the surface, and the last thing Tom wanted to do was lash out at anyone. The deputy was only doing his job, albeit overzealously.

I will not let you get me going.

"If you don't know anything about him, why didn't you go out there and see if he was alright?" Schofield leaned in, his face only a few inches from Tom's.

Fritos. I need to see my dentist for a cleaning.

A smile crept across his face, but he checked himself. The deputy already suspected him of doing something awful, no need to prod the man with a silly grin.

"When I realized what I was looking at," said Tom evenly, "I passed out. I have a strong stomach, but that was just too much. When I woke up, I looked again and could see that there was nothing I could do."

"'Lying lips are abomination to the Lord: but they that deal truly are his delight,'" said Schofield. "You had no concern for your fellow man. Fine upstanding citizen you are."

Tom said, "I'm an atheist." He grinned when the deputy's face turned red. "Look at him," he said as he pointed to the window. "His guts are piled at his feet and tied around the tree. The rats were eating him for Christ's sake. Nobody could live through that."

Schofield's eyes nearly popped out of his head. "Blasphemer!"

"That's enough, deputy. And I'm afraid you're grievously wrong, Tom," said a voice at the back door. Sheriff Terry Finnbrough stepped into the kitchen from the deck. He wiped his feet on the doormat, took off his hat and threw it on the counter then lumbered over to the table and sat down. He looked haggard and pale. There were bags under his eyes; the usual redness of his face was gone, replaced with a pasty paleness. "According to the coroner, he was alive when he was strung up." He wiped sweat from his brow and the back of his neck with a handkerchief that he stuffed into a back pocket. His thin sandy hair was plastered to his head. "Despite the snowstorm in town, it's hot out there. Why isn't it snowing up here, Tom? You can go now, Deputy Schofield."

The deputy looked a bit flustered then said, "But I'm not finished interrogating the suspect." He paused then added, "Sir." The "sir" was dripping with disrespect. He turned to Tom. "So, I was right, he was still alive. You waited before calling us, hoping he would die. You're making up a pack of lies. 'An hypocrite with his mouth destroyeth his neighbor: but through knowledge shall the just be delivered.'"

Tom stared, trying hard not to punch the fool. He hated having Bible quotes thrown at him as if that was all that was needed to reveal the truth of a situation.

Fucking loonies.

"I said you can go now," said the Sheriff calmly.

Deputy Schofield ignored the Sheriff and continued. "Come on, Bender, I know you're hiding something. Why else would you be so nervous?"

Tom looked at the Sheriff, then at Deputy Schofield. "I need to pee."

Deputy Schofield pulled out his nightstick, said, "You dare to make light of this?" He moved towards Tom.

The Sheriff rose and stepped between the two. "That's enough, the pair of you," said the Sheriff. "Tom, go pee. Deputy, get outside and help search the yard for clues." Schofield began to protest but the Sheriff held up a hand. "I gave you an order, Deputy." The men locked eyes for a few seconds. Neither moved. "Go," said the Sheriff quietly.

Schofield holstered his nightstick, waved a finger at Tom, who was sitting again, and said, "I've got my eye on you." He left the kitchen. Tom watched the deputy through the kitchen window as he walked around the yard. The deputy seemed to go out of his way to step on the green perennials in the flowerbeds.

Four crows watched Schofield from the fence. In unison, they turned to Tom and nodded. *That didn't just happen.* "I didn't need to pee," said Tom. "That religious crap is way out of line for a cop."

"This is a murder investigation, Tom. And you are a suspect," said Terry.

Shocked, Tom felt his cheeks redden and stood. "You suspect me? But you know me. We've been friends for years. You can't possibly think I would do something like that."

Terry stepped closer and put a hand on Tom's shoulder and eased him back into his seat. The hand felt clammy, even through Tom's shirt. And Terry smelled slightly ... off. There was something buried under the cologne. Terry never wore cologne.

"Try to settle down, Tom. I know you didn't do it, but I have to go by the book here. There are rules and procedures. I can't let our friendship get in the way of that. Even Schofield has to follow procedure."

"Sorry. It's just that he gets up my nose. He's so fucking obnoxious. He makes me feel like a criminal and I haven't done anything."

"What can I say? Usually it doesn't get in the way of him doing a half decent job," said the Sheriff. "Nobody's made any complaints against him that have stuck. I know he's rough with anyone who comes in his sights, but he never crosses the line. One thing, though: if he hears anything bad about anyone, doesn't matter if it's a joke or an innocent remark or an obvious gripe, he never forgets. I try to tell him, believe half of what you see and none of what you hear. But he believes everything he hears."

"Except me saying I don't know anything about our victim out there," said Tom.

"But you do," said Terry. "I'm surprised you haven't figured it out with that huge brain of yours."

Tom stared, shaking his head. He had no idea what Terry was talking about.

"It's Gavin."

"You're kidding."

"I wouldn't make something like that up, Tom. You didn't make the connection with the town snowplow in front of your house?" Terry's voice raised a little and there was a flash of anger behind his eyes.

Tom had never seen Terry this serious. They had been friends almost from the day he'd moved into the house. "I was tired, distracted, didn't give it much thought," he said. "Sick to my stomach. It was just another person tied to the tree. Hell, you've never taken it seriously."

Terry winced. "Yes, well, maybe I was wrong. But that doesn't change the situation now. We've got a gutted man out there and I need to find out who did it."

"Sure, Terry. Sorry. But Schofield is just too much."

The Sheriff raised his hands in a gesture that said, *I give up*. He sighed. "He has absolutely no imagination; everything is guided by what he reads in that Bible of his. Granted, there's something disturbing about him, but I can't put my finger on it."

Tom guffawed, said, "Seriously? Can't put your finger on it?" He got up from the table and went to the refrigerator where he opened the freezer and asked, "Do you want anything, Terry? I've got some bourbon in here."

Terry smiled, the tension released, and said, "I'm on duty and it's a murder investigation. What do you think?"

Tom took out the bourbon and got two glasses from a cabinet. He poured two large drinks and gave one to Terry.

"Generous. Thanks," said Terry, and downed the amber liquid in one gulp. He got up and went to the sink where he washed the glass and put it on the dish rack. When Terry sat down, he took a packet of spearmint gum from his shirt pocket, offered a stick to Tom then popped a couple of sticks in his mouth. "Schofield will notice, but everyone else will pretend not to."

"Have you lost weight?" asked Tom. Terry had always been rather hefty—big-boned, he claimed—but about a year and a half ago began to pile on the pounds. Tom tried to speak to Terry about it, worried that something unpleasant might happen, but couldn't think of a way to broach the subject without offending his friend. Suddenly, a couple of months ago, Terry had spoken up about his dissatisfaction with his weight problem and had said he was going to do something about it. He hadn't revealed any specifics.

"I have," said Terry. "Thanks for noticing. I gave up chips and pop." Terry often ate a whole bag of potato chips and a two-liter bottle of Coke for lunch, every day. "It's been almost two months. I am getting tired of fresh fruit and vegetables for lunch all the time—too much green, but at least I'm regular now."

"I didn't need to know that last part," said Tom with a look of mock disgust.

Tom sipped his drink and noticed that slight earthy odor. He remembered now. It was the same as he had smelled when he went out to the deck to get a better look at ... Gavin.

"So, one more time, Tom, for me, from the top," said Terry. He took out a notebook, flipped it open, then licked the tip of his pencil and began to write.

21

"Why do you do that? Lick the pencil like that?" asked Tom. "Whenever I do it, I just get a wet pencil that doesn't write. And lead poisoning."

Terry stared at the pencil for a moment. "I saw it in a movie. The detective licked his pencil tip and caught the gangster. I thought it might help. Anyway, it's graphite. Stop changing the subject and talk."

Tom sighed deeply and had a sip of bourbon. "I was in Los Angeles for a week, left last Thursday. I got back this morning, picked up my car at the long-term parking lot at the airport, and drove home. It was snowing heavily and the idea of taking the old highway made me nervous. You know how I am with snow and freezing rain—I'm terrified I'll end up in a ditch, freezing to death. I got lost in those stupid suburbs again, couldn't see any landmarks because of the flurries. I drove very slowly and it took me about two hours to get here. When I arrived home, I discovered that someone had plowed a twenty-foot high snowdrift onto my driveway and parked a snowplow in the turnaround in front of my house.

"I was angry and was going to call the county office, but I was hungry. I got a steak and a Guinness out of the fridge. Then I heard the crows and looked outside."

"Crows?" Terry looked up from his notebook. "What about the crows?"

Tom shrugged. "They were all over the yard watching the rats. There were twenty-nine of them in assorted groups." He felt his stomach lurch when he remembered what the rats had been doing. He concentrated a moment to hold back the nausea.

"Vermin. How do you know the exact number?"

Tom grinned. He hesitated then said, "I count birds. I don't know why. Maybe trying to find a pattern in the numbers. I've done it since I was a kid."

"When did you pass out?" asked Terry. He didn't seem at all interested in Tom's explanation about the birds.

Tom saw that Terry had a strange look on his face as if he was trying to hold in his anger. *He must really be pissed about this murder.* "A bit later. I went out to get a better look. When I realized what had happened, well, you know."

Terry nodded. "How long were you out?"

"Maybe half an hour. It must have been the fatigue and hunger." He decided not to mention the silence or the smell. Or the green. "When I woke up, I called you."

Terry was writing this all down furiously in shorthand. "Did you do anything while we were on our way?"

"Yeah. I cleaned up the Guinness, glass, and puke that were all over the place from when I saw the body."

"Such a terrible waste," said Terry.

"I know," said Tom. "Even though I didn't like Gavin, it's a heck of a way to go."

"I meant the Guinness." Terry smiled. "Gavin was scum and won't be missed, except by his lowlife brother. And even then, I wonder." Terry could be a real hard case at times. "What time did you get home and when did you make the gruesome discovery?"

"Gruesome? That's a bit florid," Tom said. There was an awkward silence while Terry waited for him to continue. "Okay, I think it was about ten-thirty, maybe eleven. It was a few minutes later that I was at the sink getting a glass of water and saw him for the first time. I didn't think anything of it; you know they've been leaving people tied up to the tree for years."

"Still no idea who does it?"

"I gave up trying to find out. This new development does kind of change everything. Was there any writing on his body? There's always been before."

"None that I saw. But he was covered with blood so there might be some underneath. We'll know when he gets cleaned up at the morgue."

"Then maybe it's not students from the college after all."

"What makes you say that," asked Terry.

"Well, I don't think students are going to eviscerate someone for a hazing stunt."

Terry grinned and said, "No, that's highly unlikely. Okay, so you saw Gavin ..."

"I didn't know it was Gavin."

"Okay. You saw someone tied there and did ..."

"Nothing." He thought for a moment. "It's too warm out there."

"No kidding," said Terry. "It's snowing like a son of a gun downhill and in the city, but you've got nothing up here. And it's hot out there. What gives?"

"Well, there does seem to be a microclimate in the yard so it's a bit warmer. But that's usually during the summer. I get some snow, but not that much. Missing that storm does seem a bit odd. Not that I'm complaining; I hate this weather. But why did Gavin have to bring the snow up here with the plow? Just had to mess with me."

"Why would he do that?" asked Terry.

"I don't know. It seems so petty. But at least most of it has melted."

"Anyway, you left Gavin out there because ..."

"I was honked off about the snow in the drive and tired. I decided to let him wait. Unfair on the poor guy, but I wasn't thinking about him. And I didn't know it was Gavin, remember?

It was the crows that made me look closer. They were making a heck of a racket." Tom paused, drained the bourbon from his glass and poured himself another. "The crows chased the rats away."

"Did they?" asked Terry. He was lost in thought for a moment.

"Did you see what the rats did to him? And you say he was still alive?"

Terry put down the notebook and twirled the pencil in his fingers. Then he tapped the eraser end of the pencil on the table. He seemed nervous to Tom.

Tom had had many encounters with the O'Leary brothers, particularly Steve who ran the less reputable of the two local garages. Gavin had always been a moronic presence in the background, goading his brother with support whenever there was trouble. As much as Tom didn't like the pair, he never wanted anything like this to happen.

"Any idea how long he lived?"

"Too long, given the wounds he suffered," answered Terry. "The coroner said he thought he had only been dead a couple of hours when we arrived. The blood hadn't congealed yet, although this weird microclimate of yours may have messed up the timing."

Tom felt himself gagging and ran for the sink. He threw up the bourbon, dry heaved a few times, and washed his face with cold water. Terry remained seated watching passively while Tom cleaned himself up.

"I know you didn't have anything to do with this, Tom. Don't worry about Deputy Schofield; I'll keep him away from you. But until we find whoever did this, you'll be his number one suspect."

"Oh, joy," said Tom. "I get to look forward to the scrutiny of that idiot. He'll probably be spreading rumors about me and how I'm involved. Maybe how I'm Satan or something. Can you do anything about him?"

"I can keep him away from you officially, but when he's off duty, there's nothing I can do. I'll talk to him, warn him about slander. But I have to be careful. Most of the prominent citizens of Tyndale are in that church of his and he holds a lot of sway there. I don't need the church crowd on my back as well as the Council."

"Thanks."

Terry picked up the notebook. "I have a few more questions. Formality. Did you kill Gavin O'Leary?"

Tom was taken aback. "Of course not. I wasn't even here. You can check with the airport." There was a touch of resentment in his voice. Though he knew Terry had to ask these questions even though he knew there was no way Tom could have done anything like this, Tom couldn't help but feel a little insulted that Terry didn't just take his word for it. Tom didn't hold it against Terry, but there was still that iota of anger that his friend didn't trust him enough.

"Do you know who did it?"

"No."

"Did you have anything at all to do with this crime?"

"No."

"Can you think of any reason that this happened? Here. In your yard."

Tom hesitated a moment. He knew the O'Leary brothers had a bad reputation and wouldn't have been surprised if they were involved in organized crime. One of them could have been killed as an example to the other for what happens when you cross the mob. Tom shook his head. *I've been watching too many detective shows.*

"No."

Terry closed the flap on his notebook and put it in his shirt pocket. He took a deep breath and said, "I'm truly sorry for asking you those questions, Tom. But I had to. If I didn't, though *I* know you're innocent, someone, probably Deputy Schofield, would have accused me of not doing my job properly. And if we don't find the animal that did this, it'll be my neck in the guillotine. The Council's gonna be all over me on this. We've never had anything like this happen here. Even though we're right next to the city, the county's always been relatively crime free. Except for the O'Learys."

"I understand, Terry," said Tom. "I guess I'm still bugged at Schofield's attitude. The man is a class one dickwad."

Terry laughed and said, "Maybe I will have that second drink. I'll have to face the autopsy later. That'll be a treat."

Tom got up and poured Terry a long shot of bourbon, and another for himself. He was feeling a bit tipsy since he hadn't eaten anything since dinner last night. The peanuts served on the redeye flight from Los Angeles didn't count. *The contents may contain traces of nuts. They're fucking peanuts. Of course they contain nuts. People are stupid.* As before, Terry downed the drink in a single swallow.

"You might want to taste the stuff once in a while," said Tom.

Terry shook his head. "Can't do that. Might realize I don't like the taste and then I'd have to stop drinking."

"It's not like you've got a high-pressure job," said Tom. "What, you have to run a few speed traps for the idiots from the city, help the occasional old lady across the street, watch for jaywalking cows"

Tom saw Terry's nostrils flare a little. This was usually a sign that Terry was angry about something. Tom thought about apologizing for taking Terry's job so lightly but didn't, figuring that Terry was just under pressure because of the murder.

"Gastric ulcer. Deputy Schofield. Fred Silva," said Terry.

At the mention of the man who would be king of the county, Tom nodded. It was well known that Frederick Silva thought he owned the whole county. *Would he be king or count? Count Silva. Count Silver? Sounds like a cartoon miser.* He always stuck his nose in where it didn't belong. Silva and Tom almost came to blows a couple of times despite both being opposed to the development going on to the west of the town. Arrogant bastard was usually the first thing that came to mind when discussing Silva. *You need taking down a peg or two.*

"So, what were you doing in L.A.?" asked Terry.

Tom pondered what to tell his friend. Though Terry and Tom had been friends for years, Tom had never told Terry about his writing. Belinda had been supportive of Tom's writing but had never taken it seriously. She'd been more patronizing. It wasn't until after Belinda's illness that Tom started to write with a real passion. He used the writing to escape from Belinda's suffering and his own pain. The trip to L.A. had been about his books.

"There was a conference about databases. Very technical. Rather boring," said Tom. *Hypocrite. You expect Terry to take your word about the murder, but you can't trust him with your secret.*

At that moment, a pale-faced deputy came in the back door and said, "Sheriff, they're ready to take the body away now." The deputy hesitated a moment, as if waiting to be sent anywhere but back outside, then returned to the crime scene.

Terry got up and said, "I'd better go take a gander, though I don't need another look at Gavin. I thought car accidents were bad. By the way, the forensic boys will have to go over the house. You know, just in case Gavin was butchered in here and there are traces of blood."

He picked up his hat and as Terry walked to the door, there came a frantic pounding at the front door. Someone was shouting.

"Oh, what now?" said Tom. "Who's this idiot?"

"I'll get it," said Terry. He walked from the back door to the stairs leading down to the front door. "Maybe seeing a policeman will shut the guy up."

Tom watched Terry open the door. He groaned when he saw Frederick Silva push his way into the house. *Just what I need.*

"I demand to know what's going on," Silva bellowed. He rarely ever spoke; he always shouted as if that was the only way anyone would ever pay attention to him. Tom usually tried to ignore him. "Sheriff, I must know what's happening here."

Before Terry could say a word, Tom said, "What's going on here is private property, Mister Silva. And you're not welcome. Now get out." Tom walked over to the railing. He leaned forward and raised his eyebrows, waiting for Silva to leave.

Silva ignored Tom and repeated, "Sheriff, I demand to know what's going on." He stepped closer to Terry who was trying to suppress a grin. Tom knew Terry couldn't stand Silva and his bluster. Silva poked Terry in the chest as he said, "Sheriff, you'll tell me what's happening here. I have every right to know. I'm on the Council. You report to me."

Terry took a step back from Silva. He reached up and grabbed the hand that was prodding him. He squeezed slowly causing Silva to wince and said, "Mister Silva, this is a crime scene. I am in charge here. I'm the County Sheriff. You have no authority here." Silva tried to speak but Terry cut him off and squeezed his hand harder. "Keep quiet until I'm finished, Mister Silva. You may be on the Council, but I report to the electors as a whole, not to you specifically. And don't ever poke your finger at me again." He let go of Silva's hand. The whole time Terry's eyes had been boring into Silva's. He never blinked. Tom had seen Terry angry before and knew that when Terry stopped blinking you had better run and hide.

"Now, unless you want to face trespassing charges," Terry looked up at Tom who nodded in agreement, "you'll leave now."

Silva scowled at Tom and then Terry. "You can't do this to me, Sheriff. I own this county. You'll do as I say." He placed his arms behind his back, waiting for Terry to act. Tom saw that Silva was trying to massage some life back into his crushed hand.

Tom said, "Maybe he's right, Sheriff." Terry looked at him with astonishment, as if he couldn't believe anyone would take Silva's side. "Maybe Mister Silva should be shown what's going on."

Terry looked confused for a moment then realized what Tom was getting at. "Yes, you're right." He walked up the stairs to the living room. "This way, Mister Silva. The crime scene's out back." Terry grinned at Tom as he passed.

"Wipe your feet first, Mr. Silva," said Tom. "Mustn't forget our manners, must we?"

Silva hesitated then took off his rubber overshoes. With a smug look of triumph on his face, and his overshoes in his hands, Silva followed Terry up to the living room then through to the back door. Tom's house had a huge open space that served as a combination living room, dining room, and kitchen. The eastern wall of the room was thirty-eight feet of floor-to-ceiling bookshelves, broken only by an archway with a set of four steps that led up to a room above the garage. This room was also lined with floor-to-ceiling bookshelves.

Tom observed that Silva made sure to check out the room as he passed through. He didn't seem at all appreciative of all the books. *There's another strike against you, you illiterate bastard.* He had a policy of never inviting anyone back to the house if they weren't impressed, or at least commented on, all the books. He figured if the books made no impression, the person probably wasn't someone Tom would be interested in knowing. Terry and Spanky always made sure to go to the shelves and pull down a book and examine it whenever they came over, just to keep Tom happy, though Terry hardly read anything other than police bulletins and Spanky was mostly interested in movies.

Terry held the back door open while Silva put his overshoes on then went outside. With a last smile and a wave to Tom, Terry followed.

Tom stood at the kitchen window watching Terry guide Silva to the body. The coroner and his assistants were about to take Gavin's body down from the tree but stepped aside when the two men approached. Tom couldn't hear anything but could imagine Terry describing Gavin's wounds to the man who thought he owned the town. Silva stood there for a moment, staring at Gavin's corpse. Terry tapped him on the shoulder, pointed to the man's shoes then pulled him back. Tom saw that his uninvited guest had been standing in a puddle of Gavin's blood. *Nice one, Terry.* Silva gagged and brought his hands to his mouth. He turned quickly and ran towards the gate at the side of the house. Tom crossed to the living room windows and saw Silva running to his car. Just as he got there, he lost control and vomited into the snow in front of the plow, leaned against the machine and slipped to his knees, retching. Deputy Schofield appeared from the side of the house and went over to Silva and helped him up. Schofield took out a handkerchief and passed it to him.

Why does that not surprise me? Schofield and Silva. Schofield reports to Silva? That explains a lot.

Silva returned the soiled handkerchief to the deputy and got in his car. The driver's side window lowered and Schofield leaned in. The deputy nodded and backed away from the car. Silva's BMW nearly hit the Sheriff's cruiser when he skidded around the turnaround then sped off down the hill road. Schofield watched as Silva left then looked down at the handkerchief. He tossed it in the snow bank and returned to the backyard.

Tom returned to the kitchen window in time to see the coroner and his assistants untie Gavin from the oak. Terry and a couple of the other deputies turned away but Schofield kept watching. The coroner had trouble with one of the knots and had to cut through it with a scalpel. Dark brown liquid squirted out and showered one of the assistants. Tom looked away. He noticed the steak that he had taken out earlier. It made him gag a little to see it so he put it back in the refrigerator and went to the living room to sit down in one of the recliners. He leaned back and closed his eyes. *Will I ever eat red meat again?*

There was a noise at the back door and Tom leaned back to see Terry stick his head in the house. "We're all done here." There was a door slam at the front of the house. *Must be the meat wagon.* "The coroner and his boys cleared up as much of Gavin as they could. There are still some patches of blood around, but I think all the chunks are gone." The image of Gavin tied to the tree filled his mind. "I'll stop by later. See how you're doing." Tom waved and Terry left.

Tom lay back in the recliner and closed his eyes. He ignored the sounds of the deputies' cruisers leaving his house and moving down the hill. He tried to let sleep overcome him; the plane had been uncomfortable so sleep had eluded him during the flight. Now, all he could think about was the people who had been tied to the oak through the years. With Gavin's death, it all changed. What was really going on? Eventually, Tom began to snore.

CHAPTER FOUR
THE MORGUE

The King of the Wood

"Sweet boy, your death is meaningful on so many levels."

The King of the Wood looked down at the body of Gavin O'Leary and smiled. "But you were the most disgusting person I have ever met, and the world will be a better place without you." The King pulled back the blood-soaked sheet covering the corpse on the cold storage tray. He recoiled slightly at the sight of Gavin's eyeless face as a maggot crawled out of the dead man's nostrils. "Gross. I really must see about getting this county a better morgue. There shouldn't be maggots on the bodies when they're in storage." He gently picked the maggot off Gavin's cheek and examined it. The little white beast squirmed, trying to find its way back to its meal. He could feel its tiny heartbeat. After a few seconds he set it back on his victim's face. "I am as merciful as I am powerful. Eat, little one."

A strand of oily hair was stuck in the blood on Gavin's face and the King reached out and, in a rare moment of tenderness, pulled it off and smoothed it back. He looked at his hand and saw the oily bloody residue there and huffed. The King went to wipe his soiled hand on his trousers then thought better of it. No need to add unwanted clues, not that anyone would know it was there. He walked over to a sink by the wall and washed the mess from his hand. As he dried off, the King saw a small jar of Vick's VapoRub on the shelf above the sink; he smeared a liberal glob on his upper lip.

There was also box of latex gloves from which he helped himself to a pair and put them on as he returned to the tray. The smell from Gavin's body, a combination of blood, rot, unwashed feet, and severe body odor, was part of the natural order, something to be savored. But, though the King had a strong stomach—look at the work he had performed on Gavin in the garden—he had a very sensitive nose. Unfortunately, it was one of the job requirements he hadn't anticipated when he took over. The slightest bad smell could put him off a meal or remind him of a bad experience. This was especially true of sex, an activity he had almost forgotten about, it had been so long. *When was the last time I was offered a woman in exchange for a blessing? Eighteen something?*

Back at the tray, he stripped the sheet from Gavin and tossed it aside. A gurney stood next to the cold storage unit, an open body bag lay on top. The King moved the gurney next to the tray and prepared to slide Gavin over but a sound distracted him. The King paused and turned his head slightly, trying to hear. It had sounded like a door being opened but there shouldn't be anyone here this late; he had checked the duty schedule to be sure; the janitor had left several hours ago. It was only his own special privileges that allowed the King to be here.

"It was probably the wind, eh Gavin?" said the King.

He resumed his task. He grasped Gavin's shoulders and heaved the body onto the gurney. Unfortunately, he had forgotten to lock the gurney's wheels and it rolled a few feet when the body landed on it. The King was thrown off balance and Gavin went crashing to the floor. His internal organs, which the King had so carefully removed earlier and the coroner had placed back inside pending later examination, spilled out of Gavin's body and landed on his shoes. Blood and gore splashed over the King's trousers.

"Gosh darn it," he shouted, staring down at the mess. Overcome with rage, the King kicked the uncooperative body in the back hard enough to snap the spine with a resounding crack. "Oh, that was good," he said, staring at his hands. "The old strength is already coming back. But that doesn't help with my clothes."

Gavin lay on the floor, his back at an awkward angle and his hands seemingly reaching out for his lost insides.

The King looked around the morgue for help, not that he expected to see anyone rushing to his aid. Planning the destruction of his enemy was lonely work. He returned to the sink and used a wad of wet paper towels to wipe the mess off his trousers and shoes. His socks felt wet and the King knew something nasty had seeped into his shoes. He threw the sodden mass in a garbage can when he was satisfied that no one would notice anything wrong with his clothes. "Do you know how hard it is to get blood out of clothes?" he asked Gavin. There was no reply. "Exactly. It's very hard. This is going to cost me a lot of money at the dry cleaners. I may even have to throw the trousers and shoes in the garbage and buy new ones. Perhaps I should be doing this naked. Back to nature, you know. After all, that is what this is all about." The King noticed a plastic apron hanging on a hat rack near some lockers. "Aha," he said and went over to get it. "Even better," he said when he saw that it had sleeves and would hang down to his ankles.

Returning to the task at hand, the King bent down and lifted Gavin by the armpits. He leaned Gavin on the gurney and again it rolled away.

"I'm going to lose it," the King shouted. He dropped his burden and pulled the gurney back into position. Attempting to lock the wheels, he discovered that the lock was broken. "Does no one care about quality anymore?" Silence. "Apparently not."

He placed a foot behind one wheel then tried to lift Gavin again and was able to get the head, shoulders, and mangled torso face-down on the body bag. Keeping the gurney steady with his foot, the King crouched to grab Gavin's ankles. As he leaned forward, his foot slipped in something brown and the King fell to the floor. With a wet thump, Gavin landed on top of him.

He crawled out from under Gavin and stood. Face red with rage, his whole body shook while he tried to keep his temper under control. He paced around the morgue for a few minutes fuming then stopped and looked to the west—he had an unerring sense of direction—towards the house on the hill and raised his fist. "You'll pay for putting me through this, you poser. Don't think I'll let you die easily."

When he fell, the plastic apron had twisted around his body. The King's trousers and shirt were covered with Gavin now. The King looked down at Gavin and thought for a while. "Should I complete the ritual here?" he asked. "It's as good a place as any." He pushed the gurney away from Gavin, slid the tray back into the cold storage unit, and closed the heavy door. From a knapsack that was waiting on a table by the door, he retrieved a green robe. Quickly, the King stripped off the apron, which he rolled up and placed in a plastic garbage bag he found in a cabinet near the sink. He paused when he had his soiled clothes in his hands. In the garbage bag or back on after the ritual? *I can't be caught driving around town naked. How would that look? The ladies might like it though.* The King spread the clothes out on the autopsy table and used the spray nozzle there to rinse them off as best he could. When he was satisfied that the worst was gone, he sluiced the muck down the table gutters and into the sink drain at the head of the table. The clothes might still be wet when he left later, but at least they'd look clean. When he was finished with the clothes, he donned the robe and began to chant, circling Gavin's body as he had done at the oak. He lit the same five candles he had used earlier that day and placed them in a circle around Gavin.

"If only you knew the grandeur of your sacrifice, Gavin. You're going to help me restore life to this place. And you're going to help me stay alive. My alleged successor won't be able to stop what is beginning tonight. He'll die instead of me."

He waved an oak branch over Gavin and chanted some more.

"All those helpless animals you butchered, this is for them. All those women you watched at night while you performed your disgusting acts, this is for them. All that evil you helped your brother do at work, this atones for that. Thank you, my sweet sacrifice."

He jammed the oak branch into Gavin's chest cavity.

The King stopped and silently stared off into space. He remembered his own ascension—arriving at the grove of the old King, the headless corpses of the unlucky ones strewn about the grass. The tired look of resignation on the face of the old King as he raised his sword to face yet another challenger showed that he was ready to be replaced; the King of the Wood must be vibrant, alive to the needs of the world. The look of surprise and confusion on the old King's face as this new challenger set the harquebus on its bipod and touched flame to powder was priceless. One had to keep up with the times. Things in the world had been changing quickly but still the new King hadn't needed a Guardian or Caretaker. *Well, except for that short time with Horace. Now there was a good servant.*

And now it was his turn to fight off the challengers. But the times they were a-changing, and the King of the Wood wasn't about to succumb to the fate of his predecessors: being murdered by the next in line. No, it was time for preemptive measures, time to take the battle to the usurper, time to be proactive. Yes, that was the modern term, be proactive. It had a nice ring to it though it did sound a little pompous. *But I'm the King of the Wood. I'm allowed to be pompous. In fact, it's my duty.* He would continue to rule and no one could challenge him. He smiled, grinned widely, and started to laugh.

"What's so funny?" said a high-pitched voice from behind the King. "Who's that on the floor? Oh, fucking Christ, you're a Satanist. I got you now, you motherfucker."

The King of the Wood whirled around and set his eyes on Billy Lush, the morgue janitor. Billy stood by the main door, a look of mixed terror and glee on his face. He reached for the doorknob.

"Don't you move and watch your language," boomed the King. "Oh, that sounded regal. Didn't that sound regal? I so rarely have the opportunity to be regal." It wasn't like the old days when subjects would come to the forest and beg for good harvests and bountiful hunts and blessings. Nowadays everyone used Miracle-Gro, went to the supermarket for meat, and only wanted blessings for their favorite survivor or idol. The world was going to rot and ruin and it was high time the King of the Wood did something about it. But first, the matter at hand.

The King strode over to Billy, who had been immobilized by his mighty voice, and pulled him away from the door, throwing the little man towards the lockers. Billy hit with a crash that toppled the lockers, sending their contents sliding across the morgue floor. "What are you doing here?" the King demanded as he loomed over the man. Billy cowered trying to get away but the fallen lockers blocked his way. He bent and grasped the lapels of Billy's jacket and wrenched him to his feet then backhanded Billy across the face. He hit him again because that's what people in power do in a situation like this. "I asked you a question." He threw Billy at the autopsy table. Billy held on to the sides of the table to keep from falling again then steadied himself.

"I, I, I forgot something," he stammered quietly. "I hadda come back."

"Lies," shouted the King. "You came here to spy on me, to keep me from my work. And speak up."

Billy shook his head in denial. "No. No. No. It's true. I forgot my, forgot my ..."

Understanding dawned on the King. "You came back for Melissa, didn't you?" Billy gaped at his accuser. The little man reeked of fear. "There's no use denying it. I know you."

"No," said Billy. "You know I don't do that anymore. Not since ..."

"Since I caught you with Sara."

"It don't matter anyway," said Billy, suddenly emboldened. He stood straighter and tried to smile. "I got you, now. I seen what you were doing. I'm gonna to tell and there ain't nothing you can do about it."

The King stepped closer to Billy and whispered, "Oh, but there is. And it's 'I saw what you were doing.'" He looked into the janitor's eyes and saw his courageous front crumble to be replaced with helplessness, like a deer caught in headlights. This pathetic creature would not be a problem for the King. Billy tried to back away but the autopsy table stopped him. He slowly slid along the edge of the table, never taking his eyes off the King. There was a telephone on the desk a few feet away. If he could reach it, Billy could get help. The King saw what Billy was trying to do and rushed over to the desk and ripped the phone jack from the wall. He threw the telephone to the floor and crushed it with his foot. Shock registered on the King's face when he remembered he wasn't wearing shoes.

"It's my night for stepping on things," said the King as he limped towards Billy. "Tell me why I shouldn't step on you."

Billy looked around for help but saw there wasn't any. "I could help you. Be your sidekick, like Batman." He nodded. "Yeah, I could be Robin."

The King's mouth fell open. He couldn't believe what he was hearing. This ridiculous little man thought he could be the King's sidekick. That was the most preposterous idea since ...

"Alright," said the King. "Help me get Gavin into that body bag on the gurney."

"Why?" Billy asked.

The King glared at Billy and pointed at the body on the floor. Billy lowered his eyes and scuttled over to Gavin. He bent to grasp Gavin's shoulders but the King stopped him. "You take his ankles," he said. "I don't want to be anywhere near his feet." With a quizzical look on his face, Billy obeyed. When he bent to grab Gavin's ankles, he caught the stench coming from Gavin's feet and recoiled. "Fuck."

The King's hand swept out and smacked Billy across the side of the head. "What did I tell you about your language?"

"Sorry," said Billy meekly.

"Anyway, now you see why I'm at this end." Billy smiled tentatively, not sure how to respond.

They lifted Gavin onto the gurney and Billy shoved Gavin's feet into the body bag. "Pick up his other bits there and put them in." Billy hesitated when he saw the pile on the floor but did what was ordered. Despite what he knew about the King now, and how damning it would be if word got out about tonight's activities, Billy was clearly terrified. When the zipper on the bag was almost closed, the King stopped and asked, "Did you notice if the rest of him was in that mess?"

Billy looked confused. "What rest?"

The King looked around the morgue. "The rats took his eyes and assorted other tender parts," he said. Billy held his stomach, put a hand over his mouth, and suppressed a gag. "His tongue and genitals should be there. I'll need all that's left of him."

Billy looked more confused. "Why?"

The King was slowly losing his patience with Billy. Curtly, he said, "Because at the Shrine I need the whole offering. I will be excused for the bits the rats took. In a roundabout way, that's considered part of the offering too."

Confusion was clearly becoming Billy's natural state.

"You don't need to know any more than that, Billy. Just look in the bag and see."

Billy gingerly stuck his hands in the bag and started to fish around for the missing pieces. While Billy was occupied with Gavin's insides, the King put his clothes back on, except for the blood-soaked socks which would feel terrible and squishy in his shoes. He shivered when the wet cloth touched his body; the drive to the Shrine would be unpleasant.

When Billy found some things that were not as soft and slimy, he lifted them out and held them up for the King to see.

"Yes, good. Put them back and close him up."

"But I just got them out," Billy protested.

"Don't argue, you grotesque imbecile." The King smacked Billy across the back of the head.

The janitor looked confused again but did what the King ordered.

"Now help me get Gavin to my car. We'll put him in the trunk."

Billy pushed the gurney to the main door while the King held it open and checked to see if anyone else was foolish enough to be here tonight. No one was. They went the short distance to the building's rear door where the King had parked his car in the darkness near the wall. A streetlight across the street was burned out and had yet to be replaced but the snow was reflecting some light from the church a block away. "I'll have to see about that light," said the King. "This place has really gone to seed." Gavin was quickly bundled into the trunk and the two returned to the morgue.

"Put the gurney back where it belongs then help me clean up this mess," said the King. "There's Gavin juice all over the morgue floor and I don't want anyone to slip in it and get hurt. They might sue." Billy got a mop from next to the sink and swabbed the floor clean again; he had done the same job about three hours ago. Then he set about righting the lockers and returning their contents. There seemed to be a large number of pornographic magazines but Billy paid them no mind.

The King watched Billy from the relative comfort of the desk chair. When Billy was finished and the morgue looked as good as new, he came over and stood in front of the King. The King looked up at Billy. "Well?"

Billy said, "What's to stop me from telling everyone what I seen? You've got a body in your trunk."

The King scratched his chin and answered, "You came here for Melissa." He pointed at the cold storage unit. It had two doors. "I caught you with Sara last year. Do you think you'd last long if I told the Jamiesons what you were doing in here with their dead daughter? And she was only fourteen."

Billy's eyes widened. Jimmy Jamieson had a hunting rifle and skinning knife. "You can't say nothing," he pleaded. He grabbed the King's sleeve, momentarily distracted by the wetness he encountered there. "Please. I won't do it again." He looked over at the cold storage door behind which lay the body of thirteen-year-old Melissa Berry who had died yesterday from an allergic reaction to peanuts.

The King saw Billy was aroused in spite of his fear of exposure. "Don't worry, Billy, I genuinely have no intention of telling anyone about your hideous activities." He stood and put his left arm around Billy's shoulder then slowly led him over to the sink end of the autopsy table. "And you won't tell anyone what you saw and did here tonight either. Here, I have to show you something."

The King turned on the tap and water flowed from the spray nozzle he had used earlier. "Watch," said the King, leaning Billy over the sink, "see how the water flows." Billy was mesmerized by the swirling water. Calmly, the King brought up his right arm and drew a scalpel across Billy's throat. Billy lurched but the King tightened his grip on the dying man's shoulders preventing him from moving. A jet of blood spewed into the sink joining the water as it drained away. Billy tried to raise his arms to his wounded neck but the King held him close so he couldn't reach. He tried to speak but only a gurgle escaped his lips.

After a minute, Billy slumped forward, smashing his face into the edge of the sink. The King waited until the flow of blood from Billy's throat ceased. He propped Billy against the table and got another body bag from the cabinet. The King unfolded the bag and draped it over Billy's body like a cape and calmly placed Billy's head and arms inside. He let the body fall back to the floor then maneuvered Billy's feet and legs into the bag. When the bag was zipped shut, the King looked to see if any blood had dripped on anything. There was none.

"And it's 'saw.' What I saw."

The King made a final check of the morgue. Everything seemed to be in its proper place and there was no sign that anyone had been here tonight. The King bent and grabbed loops at the end of the body bag and dragged it out to his car. When Billy had joined Gavin in the trunk, the King drove carefully and slowly away, wishing that someone would plow the streets again. *What is this town coming to?*

He saw six crows watching from a light pole across the street and snarled, "Traitors." They took off.

CHAPTER FIVE
THE PUB

Sister Mary

"Welcome, Sister Mary," said Sister Sarah. "I trust Brother James is well."

Mary scanned the street to see if anyone was watching her. It was dark and no one appeared to be paying any attention. There was activity across the road at the bar with the ridiculous name, The Pub. Foolish people trying to be clever. She heard a door slam from somewhere above, someone leaving one of the other apartments in the house. The same person was loudly coming down the stairs that led to the door next to Sarah's. Mary had just arrived in Tyndale from the city and had made no stops where she might be remembered. "He is well, Sister, and sends His blessings. Perhaps I should come in before I'm seen."

Sarah ushered her into the tiny apartment and took her bag. As the door was closing, Mary looked back in time to see someone cross the porch and bounce down the steps to the path. She recognized Jay O'Dale. He went through the garden gate and crossed the street, obviously headed for The Pub.

Drunken fool, you'll soon feel the hand of Brother James and God. The door closed.

"This way," said Sarah and she led her colleague to the back of the apartment. "This is the spare bedroom," she said, opening the door to reveal a room barely large enough for the single bed it contained. A table with a tattered lamp was nestled between the bed and the outside wall and an old chest of drawers that looked particularly distressed was against the opposite wall. "It was originally a large closet when this house was occupied by a single family," she said while she set Mary's bag on the bed. "My room's not much larger," she added, as though ashamed at giving her guest such meager accommodations.

"As you know, our cells at the Sanctuary are smaller and more Spartan than this. We need little more than our faith to serve Brother James and God." Where she slept was unimportant when the fate of the world and the wishes of Brother James were at hand.

Sarah went back into the living room and began to tidy. She picked up a leather belt with a holster and the largest pistol Mary had ever seen and placed it inside a drawer in a sideboard. A few pamphlets were scattered on the coffee table, mostly religious tracts based on the words of Brother James, their Savior, and some of the writings of Reverend Mendax, pastor of the local church and a valuable ally.

"Would you like something to eat or drink?" asked Sarah. "It must have been a difficult journey."

This confused Mary. It was only a few miles from the Sanctuary of the Brides of Christ to Tyndale, a trip that normally took no more than half an hour. "I did get lost in the suburbs," she answered. "And then discovered that the new bridge was out. It was frustrating." She realized what Sarah was referring to and added, "No, it was not difficult. I've been on this journey for many years, waiting for the opportunity to put right the wrong that was so criminally committed all those years ago." She paused to catch her breath. "And I am an agent of Brother James and God. No difficulty, no trial, nothing is too great to suffer in Their name."

"Praise Brother James and God," said Sarah.

"And yes, I'd like some tea if it's not too much trouble."

"Not at all," said Sarah and went into the kitchen that was only an alcove off the living room with a hotplate and small refrigerator. Mary sat on the threadbare couch and picked up one of the pamphlets. She didn't need to open it to know what was written; it was one of God's messages as interpreted by her Savior and transcribed by her—she knew it by heart.

"I'll have to stay in here most of the time," said Mary. "We can't afford to let anyone see me yet. If word got back to the Adversary, it could spell disaster for our mission."

"I'll leave you a key," said Sarah from the kitchen, "in case you do need to leave for any reason. I'll stop by the grocery store in the morning and pick up some supplies. Do you have some money?"

"Yes, Brother James gave me enough to accomplish what we need for now."

"Will you be staying long?"

"Only long enough to gather information then I must return to the Sanctuary to prepare for the coming battle. The kingdom of heaven is at hand and there are those who wish to stop its arrival."

When the water had boiled, Sarah returned with two mugs of tea and a plate of shortbread cookies, Mary's favorite. They sat in silence for several minutes, sipping tea and eating cookies.

Mary asked, "Have you learned anything more about the activities of our enemy?"

It had been two weeks since Brother James had called her to His study to tell her that the Adversary was on the move. There had followed days of grueling ritual preparation for Mary's mission, rituals that had been pleasurable and painful, cleansing and purifying. She had endured everything because her only desire was to please and serve Brother James and God. Nothing else mattered—not her personal desires, fears, or apprehensions. Coming to Tyndale was a task that she never thought she would have to face but Brother James had commanded it and Mary had no choice but to obey His will. His faith in her made her weak and humble at times but also emboldened her—nothing could stop her.

Nothing.

When her preparations were complete, she had been eager to come to this hated town and do her Lord's work but He had held her back at the Sanctuary because He was receiving more messages from God and could trust no one but her to record them.

Now she was ready for whatever the Adversary threw at her.

Sarah set her mug down on the coffee table and took a moment to finish chewing. She wiped shortbread crumbs from her chin then said, "The Sheriff is a bumbling fool who thinks he knows what he's doing. It's obvious he hasn't got a clue who committed the vile act or who stole the body from the morgue." Mary nodded. She was aware of Sheriff Finnbrough and his predilection for strong drink and junk food. There was little doubt in her mind that it would lead to his untimely but not unwelcome end. Her colleague continued, "The deputy, Schofield, he's an evil man. He touches me and makes suggestions. It's horrible."

"You must be brave. He cannot hurt you while you are in the care of Brother James and God." Mary leaned over and patted Sarah's knee. "Think of the good work you are doing, Sister Sarah. Think of Brother James and His faith in you." Sarah's face lit up at the mention of the Man they both loved above all others. "His comforting arms await you when this mission from God is finished." She thought of Him, His strength, and the rapture He could provide with the gentle touch of His tongue. Mary squeezed her legs together, trying to force the growing desire from her body. Now was not the time to remember pleasures. Now was the time to think of the coming battle with the Adversary. She stood.

"Let us kneel and pray," she said to her fellow Sister. "Let us give thanks to Brother James and God and ask for Their strength in what we must do."

The two women knelt, holding hands, and bowed their heads. Sarah muttered prayers to herself, once in a while jerking her head or hand as passion took her.

Mary prayed silently, the image of her Savior filling her mind. She was distracted momentarily by the sound of something small skittering along the gutter on the porch. It sounded like birds but they shouldn't be out this late at night.

Tom Bender

"And the damn plow sat there for five days," said Tom. "It seems Gavin O'Leary was the only one who knew how to run the thing. No one at the County Office had a clue. I could ignore the police tape in the back yard, but the plow was just too much."

It had been two weeks since Tom had returned home to discover the mutilated body of Gavin O'Leary tied to his oak tree and the body had disappeared from the morgue along with Billy Lush. He had eventually been able to get the haunting image of the body out of his mind enough to get some sleep, but occasionally Tom had flashes that would distract him from whatever he was trying to do or think. The thought that a corpse was out there somewhere and might turn up on his doorstep or back at the oak sent paranoid shivers down Tom's spine. He had become nervous about opening doors and looking behind walls and bushes: you never know where Gavin might pop up. He'd done no writing and damned little database work since the discovery and he was starting to feel guilty. The college people wanted to meet with him and Spanky to discuss the work they would be doing for them, but so far, he had let his partner do all the talking. Yet another reason to feel guilty. Tom had hoped his usual Friday evening at The Pub would help clear his head.

"You should have called me to drive it," said John "Spanky" MacFarlane, Tom's best friend and business partner. He was seated across from Tom in the cubby, the Friday night gang's unofficial meeting place. The cubby was a corner of The Pub next to the bar that could seat eight comfortably on a regular night or twenty drunken revelers on those special nights when patrons wanted to welcome the new year, be patriotic, thankful, scared, or in love. It had a window to the bar that made getting drinks faster if the waitress was busy. Tom and Spanky had always tried to get the cubby when they started their Friday meetings, arriving earlier and earlier to ensure they were successful. They started arriving mid-afternoon until Nancy, the waitress, put a reserved card on the cubby table for them.

"You know how to drive a snowplow?" asked Tom. "Since when?"

Spanky brushed his hair from his forehead. He usually kept

his hair short but had been working madly trying to finish another project before starting the heavy work for the college and had neglected to make his regular visit to the barber. "Heavy lies the head that needs a cut," he said. Like Tom, Spanky often worked through the night and lost track of time. He fumbled nervously with his lighter, anxious to get outside The Pub where smokers were free to kill themselves. There were ashes on the lapels of his normally immaculate sport coat. Tom figured he must be working hard and felt another twinge of guilt about the college job. He resolved to get to work first thing in the morning.

"I use a snowblower at my parents' cottage," answered Spanky. "And I know how to drive a riding lawnmower. How much different can a plow be? Just combine the two."

Tom laughed and nodded. Ridiculous as it seemed, Spanky could probably figure out how to drive the plow. Tom never ceased to be amazed at his friend's ability to master machines. Tom was helpless and could only just put gas in his car.

"It was best to leave it for someone from the county," said Tom. "They get possessive about their toys. And they would have been terrified of getting sued if something went wrong. You could have ended up in the Nation."

"You'd think they would have come right away for it," said Jay O'Dale as he sat down with his third basket of complimentary peanuts. Jay was known to have hollow legs and was constantly challenging Tom to eating contests. Jay won most of the time, except when it came to mashed potatoes smothered in gravy and ketchup.

"They didn't need it right away," said Tom. "Since the snow melted, the town workers have been too busy trying to handle the flood waters." Temperatures in the area had risen steadily after the last major snowfall back in March. All the snow in town had melted in one day, overloading the sewer system and causing some minor flooding around town. The worst hit area had been the gated estate to the east where the Nation curved around the hills. A couple of jetties and boathouses had been washed away. The new bridge to the suburbs over the Nation River had been severely weakened by the high water level and townspeople who wanted to drive to the city had to make a ten-mile detour through the northern part of the county to the old highway—just like in the old days. No one seemed to mind too much as this meant they avoided the maze of the new suburbs and the possibility of getting lost.

It had snowed again a few times, light flurries that didn't settle. No snow had fallen on the hill.

"Hey, Tom," said Jay, "any word on our missing buddies?"

Tom gave Jay a nasty look. "I hardly think Gavin O'Leary and Billy Lush would be our buddies," he said. "Gavin was a thug and Billy is just plain …" He tried to think of the words that would explain how he felt about Billy Lush. The man always made Tom feel dirty when they met. There was something about the way Billy's fleshy lips were always moist, almost dripping with saliva like one of those bulldogs with all the jowls. "Greeby," said Tom finally. "He's greeby and I never wanted to be anywhere near him."

"Is greeby a real word?" asked Spanky. He was always looking for unusual words for when they played Scrabble at The Pub and was the king when it came to making up new, questionable words for the game. His latest triumph had been aquan; he'd had Tom convinced until a couple of days later when he remembered to consult his massive Oxford dictionary.

"I don't know," replied Tom. "It should be. It's perfect for Billy."

"Yeah," chimed in Jay. "He hung around the high school a lot." Jay taught history. "The girls were always complaining about him. He'd wear sweat pants and walk around with a boner. Try to chat up the girls, especially the young ones. The Principal chased him off all the time and was going to get a restraining order if he came back."

"They were quite the pair," said Tom. "I wonder if they were in it together, whatever it was."

"Drugs?" suggested Spanky.

"Could be," said Tom. "Anything like that come up at the school, Jay?"

"Not that I'm aware of," said Jay as he emptied a bottle of Rolling Rock. He seemed distracted by the bottle.

"Excuse me, gents," said Eddie Lycett, the bartender. He reached through the window from the bar into the cubby and placed a round of drinks on the table—another bottle of Rolling Rock for Jay, a pint of Sam Adams ale for Spanky, and a pint of Guinness for Tom. Eddie had no trouble reaching their empties and clearing them away. He also had no trouble keeping The Pub free of rowdies and troublemakers. Eddie was six feet seven inches tall and solid muscle with a scowl that could frighten a grizzly bear.

Jay picked up his new beer and examined the bottle. He ran his finger over the base. "Have you ever wondered how clean these bottles really are? I mean, I know they get sterilized and washed somehow when they're returned, but how good a job does that do?" Tom and Spanky eyed Jay warily. He had a habit of discussing thoroughly gross and disgusting topics as if they were everyday things, which, strangely, they often were. "I've seen guys use empty beer bottles for ashtrays. And some guys have peed in them. And who knows where else they may have been stuck. It makes you wonder."

"No, Jay," said Spanky, "it makes *you* wonder. I just want to enjoy my beer, which came from a keg that wasn't used as a bathroom, and not think about that."

Jay gazed at his beer bottle then took a drink. "These things just pop into my mind," he said.

"I'll pop something into your mind through your skull if you don't shut up," said Spanky.

"Boys, calm down," said Tom. "There's no reason to ... oh shit. What's he doing here?" He looked across the main room to The Pub's front door.

"Who?" asked Jay and Spanky turning to see whom Tom was talking about.

"Oh," said Spanky, "it's Deputy Tightass."

"No, it's Deputy Dipshit," said Tom.

"What about Deputy Dawg?" asked Jay.

The three men nodded in agreement. Deputy Schofield, now re-christened Deputy Dawg, had just entered The Pub and was scanning the main room. When he spotted Tom, he nodded and smiled. Schofield brought up his right hand and pointed his finger at Tom and mimed firing a pistol. *You asshole. What are you doing here?* The deputy walked to a table of young people who were trying not to be noticed. Tom guessed they were from the college, though the college students usually patronized the campus bar where things were livelier with bands, pinball machines, and video games. The Pub was the place to go if you wanted quiet and intelligent conversation, intelligent that is unless Jay was in form. Schofield had a bad reputation on campus as someone willing to break up parties and bust heads on the slightest complaint. He spoke to the students who then began fumbling in their pockets. Out came their wallets and ID. *You prick*. The deputy carefully scrutinized the proffered ID then handed it back. He smiled politely then moved to another table of young people.

"I've never seen him do that before," said Spanky. "He must be bored."

"I think it may be my fault," said Tom. "He wants me for Gavin's murder."

"I bet he thinks you stole the body, too. To perform a Satanic ritual," said Spanky. "And you probably murdered Billy when he discovered what you were doing with Gavin's body."

"Yeah, probably," said Tom.

"You sure he doesn't just want you?" said Jay. "I've heard things about him. Maybe he has a man crush on you."

Tom grimaced at the thought. "You mean like you have on Harrison Ford?"

"Hey, he's a really good actor," said Jay defensively. "I mean, if I *had* to do a guy, you know, like if I was in prison or something, I'd do him. What's wrong with that?" The others laughed.

Deputy Schofield sauntered over to their table. "Gentlemen. Having a good time?"

"Fantastic," said Spanky. "Not even the world's biggest idiot could spoil it. By the way, what do you want?"

The deputy smiled insincerely and replied, "I just want to be sure you're having a good time. You can't be too careful these days. There's a killer on the loose." He stared pointedly at Tom.

"And a body snatcher," added Tom. "Don't forget the body snatcher."

"And maybe a kidnapper," said Jay. "Don't forget Billy Lush."

"Maybe you should be out hunting for killers and body snatchers and kidnappers, oh my, instead of hassling my customers," said a female voice from behind the deputy.

Schofield stiffened and turned to face Nancy Hughes. At five feet ten in her three-inch ankle strap wedgies, the waitress was eye to eye with the deputy.

"Yeah, you berk," said Spanky quietly. "Get out of our hair."

Tom groaned. Jay was mystified and the deputy not amused.

"Well?" she asked

"'Envyings, murders, drunkenness, revelings, and such like: of the which I tell you before, as I have told you in time past, that they which do such things shall not inherit the kingdom of God.' So says the Bible. Be careful, miss," said Schofield stiffly. He gave Nancy the once over, somehow ignoring the ample bosom pushing its way out of her blouse. Her very mini mini-skirt showed off her slenderness and her long legs made longer by the ankle-strap wedgies she always wore. Nancy's long black hair was tied in a loose braid that hung over one shoulder. Schofield reached for the braid and gently lifted it over Nancy's shoulder and let it drop down her back. "I wouldn't want anything to happen to you." Schofield showed no warmth towards Nancy. He was known to have little regard for women as people and because of his religious convictions probably thought she was dressed like the Whore of Babylon.

Nancy shuddered but didn't take her eyes from his. She said, "Anyone tries to mess with me, I'll cut his balls off and ram them down his throat."

Startled, Schofield turned white then stepped back, bumped into a table behind him and knocked over a glass of beer.

Tom couldn't understand most of what was said next, the woman's accent was so strong. He did make out a few words: ferfucksakes, asshole, and dickless. They seemed appropriate for Schofield.

"OS," said Spanky.

"Obligatory Scot," replied Tom. "Bastards are everywhere."

The Pub went silent while patrons watched. Schofield stood with his mouth hanging open, unable to get a word in as the woman rose and gathered her belongings. Her tirade never ceased. Tom was sorry he hadn't noticed when she'd arrived; she had a fabulous backside. She shoved some books—*one of mine*—and papers into a knapsack then pulled on a thin windbreaker. When she moved around the table to leave, forcing the stunned deputy to get out of the way, Tom had a glimpse of her profile and felt something inside snap. *She's absolutely gorgeous.* He felt his face get warm. Butterflies began to cavort in his stomach and his peripheral vision became a deep shade of green as everything disappeared but the vision in front of him. And there was an instant stirring down below.

Waving a finger in Schofield's face, the woman said something about the criminal waste of beer and dry cleaning. With a sweep of her hand across the table, she sent a spray of beer over the crotch of Schofield's trousers. To Nancy, who had been standing by with a towel, the woman said, in surprisingly clear English, "Please excuse my language. I hope I may come back."

"Anytime," said Nancy. "Your next drink is on me." Tom silently agreed.

Then she stared directly at Tom. *Was that a flicker of recognition? No, I probably have a piece of food hanging from my chin.* His heart tried to punch its way through his chest and he forgot how to breathe. He regretted wearing tight jeans.

The woman turned away and left. When the door closed behind her, Tom's heartbeat slowed.

"Will there be anything else, Deputy?" Nancy asked.

He shook his head and quickly left The Pub. As the door

swung shut, the place erupted with laughter then cheers when Eddie shouted, "A round on the house. And that woman drinks for free from now on."

Nancy turned to Tom and said, "Was he giving you a hard time, sweetie? If he bothers you again, give me a call." She turned to clean up the spilled beer at the other table then turned back. "Call me anyway. You have my number." The three men silently watched her as she wiped up the spilled beer. She walked away with the empty glass. Tom leaned forward a little to get a look at her ankles. They were very nice.

"Wow," whispered Spanky. His voice cracked a little.

Spanky and Jay looked at Tom. "Well?" asked Jay. "Are you gonna do her? She's really hot and she wants you."

It was well known that Nancy Hughes was carrying a torch for Tom and had been for years. She was quite open about it and was always asking Tom out. Tom had gone out with her a couple of times, not because he was romantically inclined towards Nancy, but because he wanted some female companionship and Nancy was interesting. They'd had a good time, lots of conversation and laughs, but it hadn't worked. Tom made it clear he only wanted to be friends but she had wanted more, openly propositioning him on their second date. It was flattering but, try as he might, Tom couldn't warm to her suggestion. He wasn't impotent; he was, as he described it, in an emotional coma. It had been eight years since Belinda and the situation wasn't getting any better. Fear? Lack of trust? Tom asked himself over and over what the problem was. It all came down to Belinda. He had never told anyone, but he believed she had taken everything he had. Everything he was. *I'm done. Get used to it.*

Anyway, behind all the innuendo, Nancy was a truly sweet woman whom Tom sincerely wished would find Mr. Right.

Something about the quick way she looked at his friend whenever he was around told Tom she wasn't interested in him. He wanted to say, "Spanky's the one for you, Nance. You were made for each other. Stop trying to make him jealous."

"No, I'm not gonna do her," said Tom.

"Can I then?" asked Jay. "I'd club her to death with the Big Dad. I'd love to bury my face ..."

Spanky cut Jay off. "Why not?" Jay could get extremely crude at times. "She's gorgeous and she wants you. And you must need to get laid," he added quietly.

"We're just friends," answered Tom. "And I get all the sex I need."

"Yeah," said Jay, "but when was the last time there was anyone there besides you?"

"Ouch. Burn," said Eddie who was waiting at the cubby window to take their empties. He licked his index finger and drew a one in the air.

Tom's face was beet red. "Hey, it's normal, healthy even."

"You must be the healthiest guy alive," said Spanky.

"It beats being alone," said Tom. Spanky groaned.

"It's supposed to help prevent depression according to my brother," said Jay. "Oops, sorry, Tom."

Tom waved his hand. "Don't worry about it. I'm not sensitive about it anymore. Anyway, you shouldn't be talking about Nancy like that. She's a nice person, intelligent, likes old movies, and reads a lot."

Spanky watched Nancy as she moved about the main room serving customers and taking orders. "I think I'm in love," he said. "She sounds perfect for me."

I know. Tom asked, "Then why don't you ask her out? It would take the pressure off me."

"I might just, if I can get her to notice me," said Spanky. He got up. "I need a cigarette." He drained his glass, placed it on the cubby windowsill, and headed outside by way of the bathroom.

Tom and Jay talked for a few minutes. Jay was now trying to understand why any parent would use a diaper service. "Think about it: all the diapers you get have been shit in. Sure, they're clean, but would you wear a pair of my shorts if I'd shat in them?" Tom gagged and shook his head in the negative.

At that moment, Spanky came out of the bathroom and made his way between the main room tables to the front door. When he opened the door, Terry walked in. They exchanged pleasantries then Spanky went out. Tom was surprised to see him; Terry had joined the Friday night gang a few times but hadn't blended in too well. Though he hadn't been wearing his uniform, too many people had been aware of him and acted cautiously. Conversation would die down when he entered or moved through the main room, as it did now, and Terry would always watch to see who had had too much to drink and might try to drive home. Tom couldn't understand everyone's reaction to Terry; he was such a sweet guy, after all. After a few uncomfortable evenings at The Pub, Terry and Tom decided that if they wanted to have a drink together, they would go to each other's house. They had tried to meet at one of the trendy chain pubs that had popped up in the new city suburbs across the river, but the owner had followed the street naming example of the city planners. His pubs were the Maple Arms, the Birch Inn, the Beeches; neither could remember which pub was where and on what street so they gave up trying.

Terry looked around the room to see who was there then walked over to the cubby. Eddie reached through the cubby window and placed a mug of special coffee on the table. Terry thanked Eddie and took a sip after he sat. What was special about the coffee was that it was a couple of shots of bourbon. Only Eddie, Tom, and Spanky knew the truth.

Just how much do you drink, Terry? And how much on the job?

"Howdy, folks," said Terry. He was sweating even though he had just come from outside, and he reeked of cologne. There was some other familiar smell. Tom couldn't place it. Terry wasn't wearing a jacket. "I've seen unseasonable weather before, but this is ridiculous. It already feels like summer out there and it's only the end of April. My house has become a giant humidor." He liked the occasional cigar.

Tom had noticed that no one in The Pub was carrying or wearing a coat. Usually there were overcoats hung from the hooks around the room. There had been a late March-early-April blizzard in Tyndale for as long as he could remember. Except this year. Tom had worn a thin jacket and missed the cozy feel of a parka. It was nice sometimes, after a few beers, to relax into a parka that had been scrunched into the corner of the cubby bench.

"So, what brings you out on a night like this?" asked Jay.

"Hey, Terry," said Spanky when he sat down. He was the fastest smoker Tom had ever met. He had seen him light a cigarette going out the door and finish it after one extremely long draw before the door had closed. Tom leaned over and brushed ash from Spanky's lapels. Spanky was momentarily confused by the action and he checked to see if his fly was open. Tom pointed to his own lapels and made a brushing motion. Spanky shrugged, reached across the table and brushed some lint from Tom's shirt.

Nancy came by to see if they needed anything. Though she was the only waitress on duty, and Eddie took care of most of their needs, Nancy always made sure to check the cubby.

"Thanks for getting rid of that plow for me, Terry," said Tom. "I was getting kind of used to seeing it there every morning while I read the paper. I did miss it for a while." Nancy came back a few minutes later to place a round on the table. A minute later she was back with their food: Tom had a huge basket of fresh-cut wedge fries smothered in malt vinegar and ketchup; Spanky had a steak sandwich; and Jay had a bowl of curried carrot soup with fresh dill bread. Nancy looked disapprovingly at Terry then left. *Does she know about the bourbon, too?* "Any progress on the case?"

"Hardly," said Terry. "The coroner didn't have time to do a full autopsy before Gavin's body was heisted. He did get some blood and said his blood alcohol level was through the roof, so it's a wonder he was able to drive the plow to your place. I figure he put the snow on your drive to harass you. Didn't you have a beef with his brother about your car a while back?" He helped himself to one of Tom's massive fries.

"Yeah, he tried to rip me off saying I had an oil leak right after the dealership had done an oil change. I was only stopping there for gas because I forgot to fill up at my regular station and O'Leary's was still open. Gavin was there and tried to back Steve up." Tom didn't mention how he had been humiliated by O'Leary, but that was years ago, with Belinda.

"I remember," said Jay, spraying bread crumbs as he spoke. "You said you were ready to kill them. Oops. I was only joking, Sheriff. Tom said no such thing."

Terry laughed. "It's okay, Jay. Tom said the same thing to me. He's a bit headstrong but I know he wouldn't do it." He looked at Tom "Would you, Tom?" He took another fry.

Tom said, "No, no, not me. Wouldn't kill anyone. Nope." He

stopped when he realized that making jokes about a murder victim might be considered in poor taste. Except to Jay. "Schofield was here a while ago."

Terry frowned. "What did he want?" Another fry went missing.

"Whatever it was, he didn't get it," Jay said with glee. "He was checking ID and asking us questions. He was ever so polite, like a snake waiting for its chance to strike." He plopped the last bit of bread in his mouth and chewed. Tom reached over and took the empty bread plate and piled some fries on it. He slid the plate across to Terry.

"This woman with an incredible ass reamed him out in a foreign language," Jay said.

"She was Scottish," Spanky said.

"He just stood there and took it," Tom said. Thinking about the woman made him all warm inside again. "She was amazing." He stared at The Pub entrance for a few seconds, willing her to come back.

"Then Nancy chased him off," said Spanky with obvious admiration in his voice. "She threatened to cut off his balls. Do you think he has any balls?" He added a slice of dill pickle to Terry's plate of fries. If it was green, Spanky didn't eat it.

"If he does, they're made of brass," said Terry around a mouthful of potato. "Since the murder, he's been getting bolder, haranguing me about how to do my job—I can't tell you how much that annoys me. I may not have any experience with murders, but I can handle an investigation without his input. I think he's reporting to Silva, though I can't prove it yet." Tom said nothing about what he'd seen outside his house on the day of the murder. "What a pair they make. Coupla halfwits." He looked around the table. "And none of you heard me say that. Right?"

"Say what?" asked Spanky.

"Hey, Terry, when did you arrive?" asked Jay. There was an orange glob of soup on his chin. Tom threw him a napkin.

"You guys don't know anything about Billy Lush, do you? That's another dead end." Terry bit into the last fry on his plate. While he chewed, he scanned the table but everyone had finished eating now—there wasn't a scrap left anywhere, except for Spanky's unwanted steak bun. Terry pointed at it, Spanky nodded yes, and Terry tore into it. "We searched his place but all we found was some hashish and lots of photos of teenaged girls. He was pretty much a hermit so there was no one to help us with our enquiries."

"I think we all avoided him," said Jay. "Like I said before, I only saw him a few times hanging around the high school."

"Oh, well," said Terry. He finished his drink, got up and said good-bye. Nancy acknowledged him leaving then came over to the cubby. Tom watched her approach.

You really are quite gorgeous. I feel like such a heel for not being able to respond to you. But I don't need any more guilt, especially because Spanky likes you. Please try to understand. Maybe I should try explaining this to you.

"What's the point?" said Tom.

"You're thinking out loud again," said Spanky.

Tom nodded and drained his glass. "I think I'll walk home now," he said. Tom always walked to and from The Pub. It wasn't simply a matter of not driving—he liked the walk; it gave him a chance to think things through. Anyway, his house was only a couple of miles from The Pub. "I want to get an earlier start on the college project. With luck, I can blast through the weekend and get the tables created and most of the basic code finished." Spanky seemed happy about this. Jay stared at the pair, not understanding a thing they were talking about. When the two started talking databases, anyone else at the table usually tuned out until they were finished.

"I'll come out with you and have another smoke," said Spanky. He signaled to Nancy for another beer and got up.

"See you next week, Jay," said Tom.

"Yeah," replied Jay. "Watch out for used beer bottles."

Tom and Spanky headed for the door. Nancy waved good-bye to Tom and he waved back with a big smile. When they were outside, Spanky said, "I've been worried about you, Tom. Are you okay? You've been out of sorts for the past few weeks. I know the murder and everything have messed you up, but there seems to be something else going on. Is it Belinda?"

Tom remained silent for a few seconds, thinking about Spanky's questions. He couldn't isolate the problem. Sure, finding Gavin had been traumatic, but Spanky was right, there was something else. And Schofield's suspicions weren't helping matters.

"I don't know, John," he said. "There's something in here," he tapped his head, "but I don't know what it is. It's as if I'm waiting for something. Something big and I don't have a clue what's going on. I'm all butterflies inside. It's kind of exciting." He shrugged. "I'll let you know when I figure it out."

Spanky lit up. "Okay. You know where I am if you need me."

They shook hands and Tom began the walk home. It was dark but the sky was clear and full of stars. A warm breeze blew from the south.

While he walked his thoughts kept straying back to the Scottish woman. He had never seen her before and wondered if their paths would ever cross again. Probably not. He smiled sadly at the crows perched on a pickup parked on the road. There were nine of them and they were watching him.

From beneath the pickup, five pairs of red eyes also watched him.

That's odd.

CHAPTER SIX
THE POPLARS

Frederick Silva

The gentle breeze from the south did not disturb the poplars standing guard around the property. However, the aspen grove to the west of the house was in full tremble. Beneath the poplars to the south, from which the house derived its stupid name, something to be changed soon, he could see the slowly receding waters of the Nation River. When the snow melted so suddenly last week, the river burst its banks and nearly reached the edge of the trees. As it was, a large part of the lawn and the small jetty he used for his sailboat were still submerged; at least the sailboat was safe in its winter berth at the yacht club in the city. His neighbors, whose land was slightly lower in elevation than his, suffered the most damage. And there was the stench from the river slime left behind by the water. The heat wave was causing it to rot and forced everyone to keep all their windows shut.

Here and there on the grass of the grounds, patches of snow resisted the untimely thaw. Frederick Silva was not a man who tolerated anything that resisted the natural order of things. His gaze moved to the southwest, towards the hills across Cypress, the new road into town, something he had opposed because it had gained him no profit. In the hills, the home of his enemy. He couldn't see the house that rightfully belonged to him, but he knew it was there, inhabited by a fool who would soon know the true wrath of the man who knew he ruled not just the town but the whole county. And who would, one day, rule much more.

A loud knock at the study door startled him. "The gentlemen are here, sir," said Lawrence, Silva's personal secretary, in his quiet voice. No matter how much Silva abused him, Lawrence's voice never broke, never showed the slightest inkling of emotion. Lawrence had served in this capacity for thirteen years, since the death of that swine Horace. Frederick had the goods on Lawrence and thus was ensured loyalty and obedience, two things Silva valued almost as much as power and money. He knew the man hated him, but as long as the trust fund was still administered by Silva's lawyers, there was nothing the fool could do. Silva was surrounded by fools, and four more were about to enter his study.

"Show them in," Silva said impatiently; he didn't like to be kept waiting. "And Lawrence," the man turned back at the door and waited obediently. "Be sure to shine my shoes. I'm going out later." Silva searched for a reaction in his secretary's face but as usual there was nothing obvious. Perhaps there might have been the slightest flare of nostril or widening of the eyes, or even a blush that would have been visible on paler skin, but the man remained unperturbed.

"Yassir," replied Lawrence. *Was that a note of sarcasm? A mock Negro accent?* Silva was surprised at the man's audacity. He would have to think of something particularly humiliating for later; but, for the moment, the County Council required his attention.

"Gentlemen," said Lawrence holding the door open for Silva's visitors. He bowed slightly showing the men respect that, in Silva's opinion, they didn't deserve.

Mayor Geoffrey Winslow entered first, his ponderous stomach quaking. He was wiping his nose, a sign to Silva that the Mayor still had problems with a certain substance. It never occurred to him that the Mayor might simply have a cold. Fortunately for the Mayor, Silva needed his help for what was to come so the letter and incriminating photos would remain secure in the safe.

Councilman Gregory Wright followed the Mayor, a thin, weasel-like man with greasy gray hair who could have used a few of the Mayor's excess pounds. His head darted from side to side nervously, his paranoia never letting him feel at ease anywhere and rightly so. Despite his size and appearance, Wright was an animal in bed and had a weakness for unusual, some might say exotic, hookers, as could be seen in the videos Silva had acquired.

Councilman Robert Langlois was short and stocky. Quick with his fists, he needed little provocation, much to Silva's delight and expense, when confronted by a loudmouthed drunk. The death had been an unexpected bonus on a wise investment. Deputy Schofield, another of Silva's lapdogs, had been waiting for the confrontation outside the bar. He had watched patiently while Langlois tried to hide the evidence of his crime in a culvert then moved the body. When Langlois returned the following night, he had nearly had a heart attack when the body he had come to hide was gone. Only Silva and the deputy knew where the body was buried, for which information Silva had paid the deputy a handsome bonus.

And finally, there was Councilman Dennis Morisset who

thought his wife owned a successful business in the city. He had never realized that Mrs. Morisset, Silva couldn't remember the woman's first name, could forge his signature so well. The loans to start the business, all approved by Silva's business manager at the finance company, could ruin Morisset if they were all called in at the same time.

Though he was only an equal member of the Council to the public, behind the scenes he was in charge. It was so pleasant to have a cooperative Council for a change—money well-spent.

Silva took his seat behind the massive desk that dominated the room. The desk had been carved from a solid piece of the last oak felled by Silva's great grandfather, Helmut the lumber baron, when he cleared the small valley to build the town. The oak groves that dotted the valley had been ignored by the lumbermen, including Helmut, who were only interested in white pine. There had been mineral springs beneath the oak groves and Helmut had built spas and hotels for the rich city folk that needed a place to get away from the rigors of business in the city. The springs had gone dry and the hotels had fallen into disrepair but Silva still had the desk, a large portion of the property in town, and Helmut's arrogance. He poured himself a glass of Lagavulin from a decanter on the desk and sipped his drink while he left the men squirming, wondering why they had been summoned and what was going on. He never gave reasons, just orders.

The four men waited for their host to acknowledge them and perhaps offer them a drink. Silva stared at them then shouted, "Sit." Silva was mildly amused at the game of musical chairs going on in front of him as the men tried to get the best seats—the ones not directly in Silva's sight line. There were four uncomfortable chairs arrayed in front of the desk, purchased specifically because they were uncomfortable. Anyone having business with Frederick Silva would be eager to close a deal or agree to unfavorable terms in an effort to escape the agony of the chairs. Mayor Winslow never had a problem with the chairs as his ample bulk provided sufficient padding to protect his posterior. Besides, he thought he was immune to Silva's power. Wright, on the other hand, was quite bony and was fidgeting from the moment he sat thanks to his hemorrhoids—information from yet another source in Silva's pay, Doctor McMullin.

Silva remained silent letting them stew in their own paranoia and suspicion. He could tell they were relieved to see each other but still wary—a meeting alone with Frederick Silva could mean the loss of a sum of money or threats against business and family. Though a blackmailer, Silva had a code by which he operated: he never let anyone else know what he knew. Information was for his own private consumption and use. The victim could know Silva knew, but everyone else had to be kept at a disadvantage. The men would feel secure that Silva would keep their secrets from their colleagues.

For the lawyers, Wright and Langlois, a meeting with their client often resulted in having to deal with the degenerates whom Silva wanted cleared of whatever charges had been laid. Both men were well-acquainted with Gavin O'Leary though neither knew why Silva helped the pervert—and it was best not to ask. His recent death had relieved both men.

The Mayor sneezed into a handkerchief and was about to speak. Silva silenced him with a look and shuffled some papers around on his desk. The papers were irrelevant to this evening's meeting, but they had the desired effect—they made the men nervous about their contents.

Silva took a deep breath and said, "You're here today

because it's time to put my plans in motion. I've waited long enough, tried other means, and I'm fed up with the lack of results." The men clearly had no idea what he was talking about. "The development project," he said when he read the confusion on their faces.

No one reacted at first but slowly the men's faces revealed dawning comprehension then disbelief that he was bringing this topic up again. The Mayor chuckled. "Frederick," he said. "When you brought that up several years ago, I thought it was just a whim, a fantasy. We can't go back to the old days." He looked to the others for support. No one said anything; they knew better than to cross the man in front of them when he had an idea in his head. It was best to let the Mayor take all the heat.

"Shut up, you fat moron. I didn't get you elected so you could get in my way. You're there to do what I tell you when I tell you."

The Mayor sputtered and said, "Look, Frederick, you can't talk to me that way. I'm not your lackey. None of us are. We were elected by the people of this county, not you." He looked to the others for support but they only stared at their laps.

"You think so?" Silva opened a drawer and took out a small plastic bag which he tossed on the desk in front of the Mayor. Winslow's face went red when he recognized the powder in the baggie. He reached for it then pulled back. Sweat began to bead on his forehead. Silva rose and strutted over to the window where he pretended to be engrossed with something outside. The sun was setting and shadows crept across the garden.

There was movement in the shadow of the poplars near the river but Silva could not see clearly what it was because it was too far away. Probably the gardener clearing away the debris from the flood. *I'll dismiss him tomorrow; that job should have been finished last week.*

Silva walked quietly to a spot behind where the men sat. He put his hand on Winslow's shoulder and bent so his mouth was close to Winslow's ear and whispered, "Winslow, I own your connection, I own you." The redness on the Mayor's face extended to his neck. He used his handkerchief to wipe sweat from his face, leaving a glob of green slime on one cheek. He didn't seem to notice.

Silva moved along the line to Wright where he kept his voice uncharacteristically low and said. "Wright, does the name Naomi mean anything to you? Has your wife met it?" Wright's face cracked and a tear rolled down his cheek as his situation sank in. He brought his hands to his face and quietly sobbed. Silva thought about the video of Wright and the beautiful Naomi, not quite a woman but more of a man than Wright would ever be.

Langlois was grinning at Wright's discomfort but the grin quickly disappeared when Silva smiled and quietly said, "Langlois, last March outside the Crown and Anchor bar?" Horror spread across the man's face and he gasped, "How?" then fell silent.

Morisset was shaking. Silva had spoken so softly that he hadn't been able to hear a word said but he knew it had to be bad. "Morisset, I can foreclose on the loans anytime I want." Morisset looked confused.

When he was finished, Silva returned to the window and waited. He could see their reflections in the windowpanes while they looked at each other and then at the floor, probably realizing that they were together in a hopeless situation. Only Morisset did not appear totally beaten.

Silva whirled suddenly, his face twisted with rage. "Do any of you have anything to say?" he screamed. Spittle flew from his mouth and splattered on the desk. A drop hit the Mayor in the face. No one moved.

Morisset raised his hand like a nervous schoolboy. "What loans?" he asked.

"The ones your wife took out to finance her idiotic store in the city. I did it as a personal favor to her, among other things." He rubbed an itch in his crotch—let the man think the worst. "She hasn't made a *proper* payment yet."

Morisset's face showed confusion then understanding then disgust. "But I thought …" he started.

Silva smiled. "You thought it was solely your wife's business, but your signature appears on the loan agreement. You really should be careful what you sign, Dennis, especially when a woman has her face buried in your lap. And she is a master forger to boot." Morisset's eyes flared when it was clear he remembered the event and he started to rise from his chair, obviously angry at what Silva had said about his wife and still with an air of disgust about him. Common sense and self-preservation got the better of him and he sat back down.

Silva returned to his chair. He enjoyed a sip of whiskey, savoring the smoky aftertaste, and waited. Breaking the silence, the Mayor said, "What do you want us to do?"

Silva smiled at the men; he felt no pity for any fool who could be caught so easily. He had never let himself be trapped by anyone, even by Marie and her bitch friend. They had tried, helped by that scum on the hill, but ultimately failed because he, Frederick Silva, was the better man. And now it was time to act.

"Gentlemen," Silva began, "I have set things in motion. You don't need to know the details, just the parts you will play." Silva got up and paced behind the desk. He was at his best when lecturing to underlings, pacing made it easier for him to think. "I want to reopen the spas and hotels that my great grandfather founded."

"You're crazy," said Gregory Wright. "There's no ..." Before he could finish, Silva rushed around the desk and pushed hard on Wright's shoulders forcing the man and his chair to fall backwards. When Wright tried to get up, Silva grabbed the shocked councilman by the lapels and pulled him to his feet. The other men also stood, unsure what to do, ready to help their colleague, but not ready to cross Silva. Wright tried to breathe but his suit coat was constricting his chest and Silva was not letting go. He started to panic, tried to swat Silva's hands away, but to no avail. Silva gazed into Wright's eyes for a moment longer then shoved him away. Wright went sailing backwards over his fallen chair and landed on his back near the study door. Langlois ran to help him but stopped when Silva boomed, "Leave him." Wright slowly got up, breathing hard and shaking. He steadied himself against the bookshelves that lined the study walls. His eyes never left the floor.

Silva ran a hand through his mussed hair and said, "Yes there is. I know it." He looked at the other men. "Anyone else have any objections?" No one spoke. "There's a spring at the base of Horace's Hill, behind the bakery. I want approval for my development plans and then I want the land expropriated for the project."

Langlois shook his head. "But that would mean the Knudson's would lose their bakery—it's been in their family for fifty years. And Tom Bender owns the rest ..."

"No one gives a damn about a bakery," Winslow butted in. "And Bender doesn't own the rest of the land. It's federal land."

Silva glared at Langlois. He wanted to hit the man for what he had just said but didn't want to give anything away. Uncle Horace had arranged to have only a small portion of the hill around the house sold. The rest of the land—from the top of the hill down to Hill Road and the bakery in the north, south and east to the river, and west for almost two miles—had been held in trust. If any relative of Horace, who was a conservationist and hated all his living relatives, proved worthy, he or she would inherit the land after thirteen years. If not, the land would revert to the current owner of the hilltop lot—Tom Bender. Until now, only Silva and Langlois, whose late father had been Horace's lawyer, knew about the trust, which had run out a few months ago. Everyone else thought it was public land held by the federal government. Silva had ordered Langlois to delay informing Bender about his windfall to give him time to prevent the loss of his legacy. If he couldn't inherit, then he'd get the land by default. "I know and I don't care," said Silva. "I want that land and I want those people out of there. I don't care who owns it. And I want them out by the end of the year."

"Why not just buy them out?" asked Winslow. "You can afford it."

Silva bristled at the Mayor's audacity. Suggesting a course of action for him was an outrage and Silva wanted to hit the man. But he kept his rage in check; he couldn't let anyone know of his financial problems. It was bad enough people had found out thirteen years ago after Horace died—and he was sure it was that swine Bender who had told everyone; how the man had discovered the details of the bad investments that Silva's stockbroker had failed to disclose, he couldn't fathom. He had only found out the details from the bank manager thanks to Steve O'Leary's heavy hand with a ball-peen hammer, but he'd prove it someday—however, if anyone knew now, it could spell disaster. His plans were in motion and nothing could get in their way. Through gritted teeth he said, "No. I want it done this way."

"It could be done," said Morisset. "We'll do it with taxes. Reassess then audit them, say they owe far more than they could ever pay." Silva liked the sound of a toady and Dennis Morisset was the king of toadies.

"Listen," said Silva. He paced again. "This town was once a prosperous place. The upper crust came here regularly for the summer season to get away from the scum and rabble that were invading the city. The hotels were always full and businesses flourished. The spas attracted the unhealthy rich from across the country; some even came from Europe during their grand tours." Silva's eyes lit up while he spoke. He remembered the stories his father had told him of life as a boy during the heyday of the town. "We can have that again. Rejuvenate the area. We can get rid of the riffraff that infest this town. Scum like the O'Learys and the Knudsons and Bender. This is our town, we can take it back."

"And get rich while doing it," said Wright.

"Richer, don't you mean," said Morisset with a smile. "As always, your plans are brilliant, Mr. Silva."

"Of course they are, you idiot," said Silva dismissively. Morisset looked hurt. Silva took something rolled up from a shelf and spread it out on the desk. The four men got up to get a better look at what Silva was now examining—an ordinance map of the town and county. Silva pointed to a spot on the map marked with an X. "That is the location of the spring my men found last summer. As you can see, it's just up Horace's Hill from the bakery. I understand Knudson uses the spring water for his baking; it's supposed to make everything taste better."

"It does," said Mayor Winslow. "Their éclairs are something special. Why just the other day ..."

Silva cut him off with "Shut up about pastries. We're here to discuss money."

"I was just saying," said the Mayor.

"Beer," said Langlois. "I could use the spring water for beer. Reopen the Nation Brewery. This time it could be a success, what with all the microbreweries opening up around the country."

Silva waited for the man to finish then said, "No. We take this land," he indicated the area on the map around the bakery and to the west, "and use it to build spas. Up here," he pointed to the top of Horace's Hill where a large house was shown, "we build a new grand hotel. Something from the turn of the century with large balconies and walks, a patio overlooking the forest and the hills. A place for rich patrons. It will be the rebirth of this town."

"Tom Bender's not going to like this," said Langlois. "You remember how he reacted when you tried to buy the house shortly after he and that wife of his, what was her name? Nice tits and an ass to die for? After they moved in."

"Belinda," said Morisset. "Tits forever."

"Shut up," bellowed Silva. "I don't want to hear any more of this foul talk. One more word from either one of you about anything other than my plans and I'll have you thrown out of the house."

The men apologized. Silva stood for a moment calming himself. He knew it was no secret that he had had a thing for Belinda Bender and that she had rebuffed him on more than one occasion. It was widely believed that this obsession had led to the crumbling of Silva's marriage, though no one knew for certain what had happened. There were suspicions that no one spoke of for fear of facing Silva's wrath and lawyers. And he let them keep on suspecting; better to think that whore of a wife ran away because of an affair than let the truth come out. Sometimes the wrong information was as profitable as dirty little secrets. Still, it was a failure that he hadn't been able to buy the woman's favors.

"Is there enough room at the top of the hill for a hotel?" asked Mayor Winslow in an effort to change the subject. Silva's face was quite red and the Mayor knew that the man might lose control if he didn't calm down. Robert Langlois wasn't the only Councilman known for his short temper. "I mean, there's just a house up there right now. There can't be that much more space."

Silva looked over at the Mayor and tapped the map. "As you can see here, if you can read a map, the top of the hill is much larger than it appears. The house only occupies about a tenth of the available space. Old Horace didn't want neighbors so he built his house in the most awkward spot. The trees up there hide a lot. You can see from the other side of the river, get a better idea of the sheer size of the hill. I doubt if Bender has ever bothered to explore the whole thing." Silva's voice showed irritation at the thought of the interloper who had stolen his heritage. It didn't matter that he and Uncle Horace had hated each other, he—Frederick—should have inherited all of Horace's property, especially the house on the hill. He looked at the men who were intently studying the ordinance map as if they understood what it meant and could barely disguise his contempt for them. He could scarcely credit that they believed his ridiculous plans. His contempt for these fools was boundless.

Suddenly, Silva could not stand the sight of them. The presence of these creatures was an affront to his sensibilities. He strode over to a bell pull near the fireplace and yanked hard on it. "Get out," he shouted. The men looked up, confused. "I said, get out. I don't want you here anymore. Leave." The study door opened and Lawrence entered; his jacket was off; his sleeves were rolled up and he had his left hand in a black shoe. He seemed a little distracted by something at the window while he waited for instructions from Silva. Silva let the smallest grin cross his lips when he spied the shoe and said, "Escort this lot out of here. Quickly." Lawrence nodded and motioned towards the door; the men moved silently out of the room. They knew better than to argue.

When Lawrence had shut the door, Silva refilled his whiskey glass and returned to the window. He shut off the light so he could see outside. The sounds of shouting from the foyer amused him; the Councilmen and the Mayor were taking their frustrations with Silva out on Lawrence. Good. That boy needed some discipline.

The sun had completely set now. Through the trees at the end of the garden, Silva could see the distant lights of the city across the Nation. The wind was picking up and an errant strand of ivy scraped the window in front of Silva. He'd have to speak to the new gardener about removing the stuff. Something dark dropped from the roof above and swooped past the window then blended with the shadows of the aspen grove. Silva thought he heard cawing but decided it was just more cackling from the hall as his guests continued to complain about their treatment.

Sister Mary

Mary pulled the hood of the sweatshirt back over her head. It had caught on the low limb of a tree when she dove for cover. Someone, most likely the vile Frederick Silva, had looked out the window as she was running. The man hadn't rushed away, so Mary assumed she hadn't been seen. Still, she waited for several minutes in the shrubs listening for the wail of an approaching siren. When there appeared to be no imminent danger, she got up, ran for the side of the house and hid amongst the rose bushes there. She hoped there was no one near any of the windows to hear the sloshing of her boots. Sarah had not warned her that the area had been flooded so when she scaled the wall that surrounded the estates and jumped down, Mary had been unprepared for the small lake that waited for her. The water was about a foot deep and quite cold despite the warmth of the evening. Wading towards the distant house, she had barked her shin on something hard and sharp. Closer examination showed the thing to be an iron bench lying on its side. Mary then realized that she wasn't in a shallow lake, but on a partly submerged lawn. By the time she reached the poplars along the southern edge of the house's main garden, the ground had become drier but was still spongy. Several times Mary's boots sank in mud past her ankles filling them with the foul-smelling sludge that covered everything.

Now, whenever she moved, her boots squished and splashed making her fearful of revealing herself. To be found out this early in the battle would be a disaster and could ruin Brother James's plans, not that Mary could see any possible way that His plans could be ruined, they were so brilliant. However, she was on a mission and His righteousness would protect her from harm and discovery.

When she was about to move along the wall, a light came on inside the house. Its beam shone through the window above her and cast shadows on the lawn. Mary pressed as close to the wall as she could and waited for whomever it was to leave. The light went off quickly and she relaxed a little. As silently as her sodden boots would allow, she crept along the wall until she was outside the window through which she had seen her quarry. Ever so slowly, Mary inched forward to peer inside. There were heavy curtains on the windows, pulled to the side, which provided some cover for her. Through a crack in the curtains, she could see the men inside. Silva was strutting about in that way of his and the others seemed to be afraid. His voice, never much below a shout, could be heard through the heavy panes of the window, though it was muffled and impossible to understand individual words.

The men were all looking at something Silva was pointing at on the huge desk. Emboldened by her faith in Brother James and His protection and faith in her, Mary stood to get a better view. She could see that they were inspecting a map. Good. This might provide the information Brother James needed to combat the Adversary, give a clue as to his location. Silva had something to do with it but they had no way of getting close to the man without raising suspicions. Sarah could help but even her resources were limited unless she played along with Deputy Schofield. Though many of the sisters had done worse, the thought of having to be with such a disgusting individual, someone so devoid of conscience or soul, was almost too much to bear. However, if it was necessary, Sarah was ready to do the deed. Brother James had to know what the Adversary's plans were before He could mount a successful counterattack.

It took all of Mary's concentration to recognize the basic shapes on the map—it was the hill with the big house. She shuddered. What did that place have to do with the Adversary's plans? Brother James had briefed her about the possibilities at the church or the old factory, not the house on the hill. This changed everything.

Mary decided that she had learned all she could by peering through windows and decided to return to Sarah's apartment to think. She would need to contact Brother James for advice. Sudden warmth spread through her as she thought of her Savior. For a moment her mind filled with images of Brother James as

He loomed over her, about to use His tongue or fingers to bring her to ecstasy. Mary smiled and her hand slipped down to her thigh.

A shout woke her from the distraction. Silva was waving his hand about as the men backed away from him. Mary saw a door open and a middle-aged black man walked in. Lawrence the lackey, subservient as ever. He pretended to be friendly but was as ready as any man to betray a trust. He appeared to look directly at Mary and she backed away from the window.

Heart beating wildly, Mary ran through the shadows then across the lawn. She no longer cared if anyone heard the noise of her boots. When she reached the estate wall, she scaled it, wishing she had climbed it here where it was dry rather than further along. A boxwood hedge lined the road about three feet from the wall. Mary thought this an odd lapse for something that was supposed to provide security for the residents of the estate. As she was now, intruders could hide between the hedge and the wall to watch for passing patrol cars or to catch their breath after a run.

While she sat, several cars emerged from the estate gates about five hundred yards to the north along the road. These must be Silva's dismissed guests Mary thought. When the cars were no longer in sight, she pulled the hood back and stepped through the hedge. A quick jaunt across the road took her to a path that led through the woods to the downtown area. Sarah's house was just a few blocks away.

Much as she wanted to be a part of Brother James's plans, Mary hated being in Tyndale. She hated the town, hated everyone in it, but most of all, hated herself for allowing it to cause doubt about Brother James. She resolved to do penance when she got back to Sarah's. Her fellow sister would be more than willing to help with the flagellation.

Lawrence Burke

Lawrence shut and locked the door, closed his eyes, and listened to Silva drive away in his BMW. The house seemed to breathe a sigh of relief now that its master was gone; a heavy weight had been lifted from the atmosphere. Lawrence walked directly into the study and over to the decanter of Scotch. He took one of the glasses on the tray there and poured himself a generous drink— why there were four glasses, he didn't know; Silva never ever offered anyone else anything. The decanter would be replenished soon enough, not that Silva would have noticed the level of liquid. Despite his attention to business details, Silva was useless when it came to running the house; hence some of his recent financial problems. The economic collapse had distracted the man from the needs of the house; consequently, simple repairs to the roof had been ignored until the situation had become dire and terribly expensive.

Lawrence sat in the chair behind the desk and put his feet up. It was as much of a sign of disrespect as he could muster. Once in a while he would let something slip, like he had earlier with the "Yassir" comment, but for the most part, he retained remarkable control over his emotions. Lawrence Burke had been in service to the Silva family for twenty-six years, since he graduated from college and was taken on as personal secretary by Horace. The years with Horace had been happy ones, full of excitement and good works. Horace had been a kind man, generous to a fault and not at all like any of the rest of the family. The Silva's were well known for their ferocity in business, never ones to let something as useless as sentiment or friendship get in the way of profit. Horace had tried to change that when he inherited the family business from his father. He had funded a town library, built a new wing on the hospital, and covered most of the cost of the new gymnasium for the high school. All this had happened during the happy years after Lawrence joined him. By the time Lawrence lost his wife and daughter, Horace was sick with the cancer that would soon kill him, but he still had enough fight left in him to keep his nephew at bay.

From the first day Lawrence went to work for Horace, he came into conflict with Frederick. Frederick was cut from the same cloth as most of the Silva men, heartless, selfish, and arrogant. He wanted the family business that his own father would have inherited if he hadn't been killed in a railroad accident. When they first met, Frederick had referred to Lawrence with a racial epithet he had long thought fallen into disuse except by the KKK. The secretary had remained calm and let slide the ignorance of the nephew, but their relationship had been tarnished from that moment. Frederick badgered Horace interminably, with Lawrence acting as a buffer between the two and suffering the brunt of the rage.

When Horace had finally died, Lawrence was forced to continue his position with the gleeful heir due to an amendment to the trust fund Frederick had been able to get the dying man to approve. Kindly old Horace had thought he was assuring his faithful secretary of permanent employment when in reality he had doomed him to a life of abuse and servitude. However, Lawrence endured because he could never have afforded the private nurse and full-time care Luana had required since the accident. Lawrence lived in hope that one day his daughter might recover her mental capacity, despite what the doctors said about how long she had been under water. She was the only reason he tolerated his situation.

When he finished his drink, he wiped the glass with a handkerchief—let the boss drink from a dirty glass, a petty thing to be sure—and replaced it on the tray. He got up to close the curtains and when he looked outside, he remembered the figure he had seen earlier when he had entered the room to remove the guests. *Could it have been her? After all this time, was she back? And why?* Since she was lurking outside Silva's home, it could only mean something bad for the arrogant bastard. Good.

Lawrence pulled the curtains shut then went to a section of shelves near the middle of the west wall of the study. He took a few books from a shelf and reached in probing for the latch. There was a quiet click and the section of shelves swung on a pivot. He walked through the door into a small room full of filing cabinets. The secret room had been discovered a few months ago while dusting; Horace never had any need for these kinds of secrets. Nephew Frederick, however, was full of secrets, and so was this room. All of the information the blackmailer had gathered from his various sources were stored in these files, and there were hundreds of them. Whenever he had the chance, usually when Silva was out on one of his late-night jaunts, Lawrence would sneak in here and search for anything that could help him and Luana be free of the evil in this house.

So far, he had come up with a lot of interesting facts about various townspeople and the behind the scenes dealings of the town of Tyndale. Lawrence knew there had to be something here in all these thousands of pages that could bring down Frederick Silva.

Soon. Soon I'll have what I need to take you down and free myself and this town from you and your evil.

He took a file with a tab that read Land Trust from a drawer and began to read.

CHAPTER SEVEN
THE GARAGE

Tom Bender

Tom knew what he was doing was wrong and stupid and unnecessary, but he was helpless. It was as if he was outside of his body, watching while he slowly approached disaster, unable to intervene, unable to avoid the inevitable.

For years he had been wracked with guilt and the most trivial thing could send him deep into a funk that would obsess him for weeks. He felt guilty about Belinda, about Spanky, about Nancy, about Spanky and Nancy. Even for thinking bad things about Silva and Schofield. The list went on and on. But right now, he felt most guilty about Gavin.

His mind was cluttered with questions he couldn't answer: What did Gavin's death have to do with all those students that had been tied up over the years? Were they even students? *Am I in danger?* Though logic told Tom he had nothing at all to do with Gavin's death, he couldn't shake the feeling that somehow, he *was* responsible. Gavin was killed in Tom's back yard, tied with his own intestines to Tom's oak tree. *Why would the killer choose my house as the location for whatever is going on?* As far as he knew, he had no enemies. Sure, some people didn't like him much, Silva and Schofield came to mind first, but Tom couldn't believe that either hated him enough to violate his home in such a way. *There I go being self-centered again. Why do I always think of the murder in terms of how it violated my home? What about how it violated Gavin?*

Tom had spoken to Terry about Gavin and found little that could explain what had happened. The O'Leary brothers were known to have questionable ethics and be on the shady side. Why be nice about it? They're crooks. They were suspected of being the major drug suppliers in town, though Terry had only been able to catch Gavin with a couple of joints "for personal use." Not worth pursuing according to Terry. It was clear that Steve O'Leary was the mastermind, Gavin being little more than a moronic toady to his brother. Terry had looked into the O'Leary's background and discovered Steve had been brilliant in high school. The problem was, he was a lazy and had spent most of his time cutting class and waiting for Gavin to steal lunch money for cigarettes. There was a wedding that went bad, after which Steve seemed worse than ever. The garage had been an inheritance from Steve's father. The man had overcome his laziness and worked hard at running the business and had done quite well.

Steve's bad reputation and apparent lack of interest had caused a steady decline in the number of customers at the garage. Terry maintained Steve kept only enough customers to make the garage business look legitimate. It had become nothing more than a front for Steve's criminal activities. Now if only Terry could figure out what those activities were, he'd be all set. Tom couldn't understand why Terry didn't just set Schofield on him;

there'd be answers in no time. *Ah, fuck, another reason to feel guilty: doubting Terry's ability to do his job.*

Steve was always immaculately dressed, the perfect gentleman, polite to all with whom he had dealings. It confused Tom to no end. While attempting to rip him off over an alleged oil leak, the crook had treated him with the utmost respect. He should have been a car salesman.

Tom stepped to the side of the road when, despite the music from his iPod, he heard a car with a defective muffler approaching from downhill. He was distracted by the seven crows that appeared to be following him. Impossible. Now they were swooping around him as if in a panic. He stopped to watch and wonder. As a result, he didn't pay attention when a car passed going up the hill. Nor did he think anything of it a minute later when the car returned from the hilltop, where the only house was his own, and slowly passed him again. The crows were still going crazy. He coughed when he walked into the black cloud of exhaust the car left in its wake.

Tom felt hot and sweaty. It was early April and the weather felt like a sunbaked July. The temperatures had been rising steadily for the last month. And the rain only seemed to fall on the hill, something that was probably the result of an overactive imagination.

Or global warming.

When he left the house, he hadn't taken into account the heat and the distance to the garage. Tom had worn a sweatshirt under his jacket as well as a regular shirt for his outing and was paying for the mistake now. Sweat trickled down the inside of the shirt, and his feet seemed to slide in his socks whenever he took a step. Normally fastidious, he felt extremely untidy and dirty now. Taking off the jacket and sweatshirt would be awkward because he'd have to carry them with him anyway.

He was startled by the sudden silence when the music stopped. He was shocked to see that he had been so deep in thought he had walked all the way down Hill Road to Mott Street, then along Mott past the edges of the downtown district. He had passed the high school at the corner of Silva Avenue, along which stood the Sheriff's office.

Looking up, he saw he was on Trinity Street which became the old highway to the city, not far from O'Leary's garage. The garage was in what Tom still thought of as the seedy outskirts of town, not that the town was big enough to have a seedy part. Across the street sat the railroad tracks and the abandoned Trinity box factory.

Tom stopped in front of the bar that Gavin had been known to frequent and immediately felt nervous, which added to the discomfort from the heat. Tom looked cautiously at the bar, nervous in case some rowdy patron took offense and came to sort him out. Its walls were covered with asphalt shingles that looked like bricks; they were ripped and falling off in several places. The windows were filthy and flyblown, their screens torn and hanging out of their frames. A couple of signs sparked now and again, advertising some cheap local brew that Tom remembered as little more than flavored water. "Try refreshing Nation beer! Brewed with all of nature's goodness!" the ads had said. Except taste. Terry said there was always some kind of trouble there, fights over drugs or bootleg cigarettes and liquor, gambling, prostitution, underage drinking, rat fighting.

Perched on the limb of a dead tree next to the bar were six crows, all watching him. "Lost someone?" The crows turned to stare at O'Leary's garage.

Tom followed their gaze. Movement at the corner of his

vision and the sound of a chugging engine distracted him. He saw the last two feet of the hood of a black car slowly backing through a cloud of exhaust into a lane between two of the factory buildings across Trinity Street. That looked like a police car. *Lunch? Surveillance on the bar, looking for criminal activity?*

Now, as he neared O'Leary's garage, he remembered how Belinda had had some fun at his expense and humiliated him in front of O'Leary. He felt angry, angry that he had let someone treat him with such callousness and casual indifference; angrier that he had seemed powerless to do anything about it. He also regretted his decision to come here even more now that he was this close, but as long as he had come this far, he might as well go through with it. Guilt made you do stupid things sometimes. Stupid things like taking the blame for someone else's bad behavior or trying to apologize to a thug for something you didn't do.

When he crossed the road, he surveyed the street laid out before him. Trinity was littered with empty beer and soda cans, paper, broken cardboard boxes, and even a few condoms. Burst trash bags were piled in front of the few rundown houses dotted along the street, their contents sending out an almost tangible aroma. The huge lot of O'Leary's Garage nestled among the trees at the edge of the woods was a surprisingly clean place compared to the surrounding neighborhood. The two gas pumps out front shone and there was no trash anywhere. Next to the open bay doors stood several trashcans, each labeled with its contents: empty oil cans, soiled rags, paper and boxes, and assorted car parts. Tom looked in the bays and could see no one about, no cars were waiting for service. The office to the left of the bays was also empty, except for about two years' worth of old Penthouse centerfolds on the walls. *I remember you. And you.*

Oh, and especially you. The cash register on the counter outside the office didn't have a key visible, so Tom assumed it was locked. He called out, "Hello," but when there was no answer, he walked back out of the garage and over to the parking lot next to it. Five cars in various states of decay lined the garage wall. None looked like they would ever be on the road again. Tom went through the parking lot to the back of the garage. When he got closer to the back, he could hear some movement, as if someone were dragging something heavy along the ground.

When he rounded the corner, Tom was surprised to see no one. The back of the garage was piled with neatly stacked wooden pallets, oil drums, milk crates, and paint cans. There wasn't the tiniest piece of litter anywhere, not even discarded gum. *For a creep, this guy is incredibly tidy. Almost as good as me.* Two more cars sat near the trees rusting away. An old pickup truck that looked like it must have been built in the thirties or forties was up on blocks. *Cool.* Tom was mildly impressed by the truck

A noise from behind a low shed under the trees caught his attention. He walked towards the shed, called, "Hello," again, but there was still no response. Someone said something that sounded like a curse and he was sure it was Steve O'Leary. He quietly followed a path around the back of the shed. For some reason, Tom wanted to be cautious here. Something felt a little off. Confusion filled his mind when he peeked around the corner. In a clearing in the woods, Steve O'Leary, clad in clean overalls, was leaning an oil drum over a pit. Black liquid, oil Tom guessed judging by the consistency of it, gushed from a hole in the top of the drum. *Must be a holding tank for used oil. Seems like a lot for a small garage.* He coughed to get the man's attention.

Steve O'Leary jumped at the sound of the cough and almost

lost his grip on the drum. Some oil splashed on his work boots and overalls when he jerked up to see who was there. "Damn," he said. Glowering at Tom, O'Leary stood the drum up and screwed on a cap. He picked up a rag from a pile on a small wooden stool and wiped the oil off his boots. When as much oil as possible had been removed, he folded the soiled rag, placed it on top of the drum, then marched past Tom without a word or glance.

Disconcerted, Tom followed O'Leary into the garage through a back door. The mechanic went straight to the office where he sat down at the desk, which Tom now noticed was as neat and orderly as his own, and removed his boots and overalls. He took a pair of expensive looking running shoes from a cabinet behind him and put them on. The boots, still dripping a little oil, went into a plastic bag, the overalls into a hamper. "I'll have to get those cleaned," he said. "It's murder getting oil out." While Tom waited silently, O'Leary went into a washroom at the back of the office. He heard the sounds of running water and hands being washed. O'Leary exited the washroom with a handful of paper towels. Carefully scanning the office floor, he wiped up every drop of oil he could find. He left the office and walked to the back door, again wiping up any oil spots he saw. "Okay, I get the point," Tom wanted to say. When he was satisfied, O'Leary dropped the oily paper towels in a trash can near the back door and returned to the office.

O'Leary sat in his chair, leaned forward on the desk, clasped his hands together and asked, "What do you want?" He smiled coldly up at Tom.

Tom hesitated, not sure how to explain why he was here. He scratched the back of his head, itchy from sweat. "I don't really know," he began.

"Fine then," said O'Leary. "You can leave now. I have a lot of work to do. You're wasting my time, unless you know anything about fixing cars." He grinned and moved to get up.

Tom gazed into the bays wondering what O'Leary was talking about. No one had put any cars there in the last five minutes. In fact, it looked as if there hadn't been any cars in the garage for weeks, or even months. The concrete floor was spotless with not a trace of oil or the garage grunge he was used to seeing. The floor even had a shine from the high gloss floor paint that had been applied to it. Tools were placed neatly on wall racks and all the drawers of the large red toolboxes were closed. Even the worktables looked as if they had been scrubbed recently.

"I wanted to express my condolences about Gavin," Tom said quickly. "What happened to him, it was done in my back yard."

O'Leary sat back down and stared at Tom who stared back not knowing what to say. O'Leary reached for a pack of butterscotch Life Savers on the desk. He offered the pack to his guest, who declined, then slowly removed one and popped it in his mouth. He silently pointed to a dish of wrapped mints on the desk, again Tom declined. Steve leaned back in his chair, red leather Tom noticed for the first time, Queen Anne style. *I'm starting to like this guy's taste. Am I insane?* O'Leary sucked on the candy, moving it from cheek to cheek, clacking it across his teeth, all the time waiting for his visitor to continue. "So?"

"Well, I don't know. I somehow feel responsible." Tom looked for a chair. He felt clumsy standing there being stared at and thought sitting down would make things easier, felt like he was in the Principal's office. "I mean, I didn't do it, but it was my back yard." Sweat trickled down his back again and his face felt hot. He wanted to be anywhere but here. And he felt the need to use the washroom; he didn't want to ask O'Leary if he could use his. After the oil cleanup display, he figured O'Leary would be as fanatical as Tom about strangers using his bathroom. He tried to distract himself: *Think about something else. Not about how much I want a drink of water. Stupid guilt, stupid decision. This is pointless.*

O'Leary stared some more. After more awkward silence, he said, "I know you didn't kill Gavin. He was a bully and had a big mouth. He couldn't keep out of trouble." This was a surprising admission though the truth was hard to deny. He got up and walked around the desk. Standing in front of Tom, he said, "And I know you couldn't have had anything to do with it. You may be big, but you're soft. You're the kind of man Gavin would eat for breakfast. A sissy." He took another Life Saver from the pack then continued, "And I know you didn't have anything to do with his body disappearing from the morgue. You're the kind of guy who would puke at the sight of blood."

Tom was stunned not so much by what O'Leary had said, but by the fact that he had said it at all; it was an assault on his manhood, something at which this man was extremely good. Any feeling of warmth Tom may have felt towards Steve O'Leary evaporated at once. Even more ill at ease now because he knew that O'Leary was right about him, and sure now that coming had been a mistake, Tom turned to leave. He wanted to defend himself—*you have no idea what I can tolerate you smug asshole*—but couldn't garner the energy.

"Thank you for your concern and condolences," said O'Leary before Tom left the office. "I really do appreciate them." He seemed genuine.

Tom looked back to see O'Leary smiling at him. He rushed through the garage and out the front door. Walking briskly down Trinity Street to Mott Street, Tom heard someone running over the road at the factory. He ignored it and walked faster, the urge to pee driven away slightly by his quickened pace. *Eventually, I'll be running. Can't go in that grotty bar. There's a bathroom at the diner across from the high school. It's private.* When he turned up Mott, a car started over the road. Whoever was driving accelerated too fast and sent a spray of gravel bouncing off the corrugated steel walls of the factory. Tom paused while the car approached, thoughts of bathrooms pushed aside for a moment. The car's defective muffler sounded vaguely familiar. It slowed when it passed him, a patrol car with a smiling Deputy Schofield at the wheel.

Across Mott, he saw nine crows perched on the crossbeams of a telephone pole. They were staring down at him. Nine rats at the edge of the alley also stared at him. He walked past them and all their heads turned in unison, following his progress up the street. They never made a sound.

Deputy Schofield

Deputy Paul Schofield, he hated the name, he hated the mother who had named him after one of her favorite actors—he claimed he was named after a saint, and he hated most people, turned the police cruiser into the parking lot of the Good Eats diner and backed into a parking spot near the dumpster at the rear. At this time of the day, the trees from the hill provided shade that would help conceal the car. He didn't think he needed to hide; Bender knew he was following him now—that slow drive by had been stupid but it had been worth it to see the look on the fool's face. Everyone knew Bender killed Gavin O'Leary they just refused to admit it because they were taken in by his charm. Some charm. Schofield knew about what Bender had done to his wife, knew what he had done to Silva's wife, and so knew he was capable of anything, even a grotesque murder. And body snatching wouldn't be out of the question, either. *Now I just have to find proof.*

Figuring Bender would take quite a while to get here, assuming he was heading home after whatever business he had with that crook O'Leary, the deputy went into the diner to get a cup of coffee and a doughnut. When he went through the door, the chatter in the diner stopped and a few people looked up to watch him walk to the counter. Most of the patrons kept their heads down, concentrating extra hard on their meals and drinks. Schofield liked this reaction; it showed that people feared him, because they should. They all had something to hide and eventually, through God's grace, he would find out what it was and make them pay. It was his God-given mission on earth.

The owner, a short round man with a tiny moustache and the unlikely name of Antoine Good, had the deputy's coffee and Boston cream, fresh from Knudson's, ready by the time he got to the counter. As usual, Good refused to accept any money from the deputy, claiming it was his small way of repaying the hard work done by the Sheriff's department. Schofield knew better; the Sheriff and the whore deputy never got freebies at the diner, he had checked. Antoine was up to no good. He chuckled at his little joke and was pleased to see a couple of nervous looks pass between the people at the counter. *That's right, fear me. Fear God.* Walking away from the counter, scanning the patrons for signs of their sins, he muttered under his breath, "Yes, 'Fear God, and keep his commandments: for this is the whole duty of man. For God shall bring every work into judgment, with every secret thing, whether it be good, or whether it be evil.'"

He returned to the cruiser to wait for his quarry.

As he set his coffee on the dashboard and opened the bag that held his treat, Tom Bender ran into the diner. The deputy was surprised to see him here so soon. It should have taken the man at least another ten minutes to get here. What could he be up to? Schofield decided to wait and see what Bender did. The windows of the diner extended along the northern wall almost to the back of the building. He could see inside and spotted Bender at the counter having an animated conversation with Good. Almost immediately, Bender rushed to the back of the diner and disappeared through a door that led to the public washrooms. Meeting your connection? Here of all places?

In a couple of minutes, enough time for the deputy to finish the doughnut, Bender exited the washroom area. He returned to the counter where he picked up a cup of something and a bag of something. Could Good be the connection? He waited a minute after Bender left the diner then started the cruiser's engine. The muffler coughed a couple of times and sending a cloud of black exhaust into the air; the deputy didn't care. The car had needed a new muffler for months but he felt it was more important to repair the ills of the world than a vehicle. Putting the car in gear, he slowly moved towards Mott Street. When he reached the sidewalk, the deputy paused and looked up the road, the direction Bender had taken. There he was, walking along, drinking his drink.

Cruising along Mott at well below the speed limit, the deputy soon caught up to his quarry. When he passed, like he had done earlier, he looked over at Bender and smiled and waved. Bender did not seem amused and spat onto the sidewalk. The deputy thought for a moment about giving the man a ticket for spitting in public but decided against it because it would more than likely annoy the Sheriff who was probably in Bender's pocket.

At Hill Road, Schofield turned left then pulled into the small parking lot at Knudson's Bakery. He stayed in the cruiser and watched Bender come up Mott. He saw shadows move across the town. The clouds were gathering over the hill as they had done almost every day for more than a month. Bender reached Hill then turned right to head up to his house, looked up at the threatening sky, and started to run. *Get soaked. Not that anything short of baptism into God's holy family would cleanse your evil soul.*

There was no more need to follow him. Schofield thought about going into Knudson's to get one of those incredible éclairs but passed on the idea when he remembered that it wasn't Saturday. Anyway, the owner never gave him freebies. Ollie Knudson didn't seem afraid of him and that was just wrong. He'd get something on the baker one of these days. God and Silva would provide.

For now, Deputy Schofield took a clipboard from the passenger seat and started to write his reports. The first was for his boss, that incompetent fool Sheriff Finnbrough. This report would detail his activities while tailing the suspect Bender. The second report was for his other, real boss, Frederick Silva. Though members of the same church, where everyone was an equal, outside of the church they had a lucrative relationship. Schofield got the dirt, Silva used it. And Schofield's dirt was going to make Silva's plans come to pass and carry the church to new heights of glory.

Nothing could stop them now.

Raindrops spattered on the windshield. For a few minutes, he couldn't see anything for the rain. Then it stopped abruptly. Across the street, in the fairgrounds parking lot, it was perfectly dry. It was as if someone had drawn a line down the middle of

Hill Road to delineate the limit of the rainfall.

God works in mysterious and bewildering ways. But it is not my place to question you, oh Lord. I await your righteous direction to smite our enemies.

Also, across the street, nine crows were perched on a fence. For the briefest moment, he felt as if he was the subject of their scrutiny but knew this was a flight of fancy. God's creatures did not intimidate Paul Schofield.

CHAPTER EIGHT
THE PIT

Steve O'Leary

Gravel chattering against the steel walls of the factory distracted Steve from going over Bender's visit. He listened carefully and heard the familiar chugging of a defective muffler. *What are you doing around here?* The Sheriff often posted his men on surveillance outside the bar down the road because of the petty crime and rat fights–savages–but it was unusual for any police to be hanging around in the middle of the afternoon.

What he needed to do right now was stay out of trouble. There were too many questions being asked. "Thanks, Gavin," he said to one of the Penthouse centerfolds on the wall. He got up and went along the wall taking down the offensive pictures, careful to remove the staples that held them in place. He liked seeing naked women as much as the next guy, but this was too much. They had only stayed because Gavin insisted they made the garage look more legitimate. As if he even knew what the word meant. Moron. When he had all the centerfolds down, he scrunched them up and tossed them in the wastebasket next to his desk. Thinking better of it, he took them out, smoothed out and folded them neatly. Picking up a letter opener, he slowly scanned every inch of the now empty wall for errant staples. He found a couple, removed them, picked up the centerfolds and walked out to the trash bins in front of the garage where he dropped the staples in with the cans and the centerfolds in with the paper. Steve laughed at himself when the contradiction hit him; he was so careful about recycling yet was able to conduct his illegal operations without a shred of conscience. *I am complicated. That's what makes me so irresistible to the ladies.*

He was about to return to the office when he looked at the factory over the road. Down near an alley between two of the buildings, traces of black exhaust still hung in the warm air. "Yep, Schofield," he said. Could this have anything to do with the disappearance of his brother's body? Steve didn't think so. He'd heard that Schofield suspected Bender of killing Gavin, a ridiculous idea because, despite what he'd said to the man a couple of minutes ago, O'Leary thought Bender was a decent person, too upstanding to do anything outside the law. The only thing he deserved was the grief Steve gave him over his utter lack of knowledge about cars; all in fun, of course. He waited by the pumps for a few minutes, just to make sure, took out a pack of cherry Life Savers and popped the last one in his mouth, and thought back to the first time he met Bender. His car, that big old Galaxy, had needed to have its carburetor adjusted. Steve had been happy to do the job once he had spotted the delectable Mrs. Bender and her mini skirt in the car. Little did they realize that he'd been able to see the whole show in the reflection of the office window when she'd hiked her skirt for her husband. The image of the woman's incredibly gorgeous ass had stayed in his mind for days. If only she'd stayed around long enough for him to work his magic; he'd have had a piece of that ass.

Gavin had almost ruined everything, jacking off at the cash register like that. "I never could control that side of you, you perv," he said quietly. He remembered swatting his brother upside the head for getting spunk all over the counter. Gavin had been good muscle whenever it was needed but his overriding libido had caused too much trouble. It had taken a lot of money to keep the O'Leary name out of the Peeping Tom investigation and now he was indebted to Silva. Even as a kid, Gavin had always had his hand in his pants or around the neck of some hapless animal. And his non-existent sense of personal hygiene had been revolting. Good riddance to bad rubbish. Try as he might, Steve couldn't feel the tiniest bit of remorse about his sibling's murder and disappearance. Oddly, this bothered him, as if brotherly love should have been a part of his make-up but was sadly lacking. *Oh, well.*

When he'd finished the candy, he returned to the office where he placed the empty candy wrapper in the wastebasket. He put on a fresh pair of overalls then sat and took a clean pair of work boots from the cabinet behind the desk. There was no way he'd put the oil-stained boots back on. Damn Bender for making him soil them; he was always so careful with the waste. After he put them on, he returned his runners to the cabinet and placed the plastic bag with the soiled boots in a cardboard box on the desk as a reminder to take them to the cleaners later today. For now, there was work to be finished.

Steve closed and securely locked the two large bay doors. There was no point leaving them open as temptation for another nosy person to accidentally discover what he was doing out back. At the office door, he turned the Open sign to Closed, locked that door, and headed out the back way.

When he got to the shed, he paused for a moment, unsure whether to finish with the oil drum or sort out the stuff he had hidden inside this morning. The oil drum he decided—might as well get one job finished at a time. This made him think of his brother again. The idiot could barely finish any task without wandering off to read a porno magazine or watch some mindless sitcom on the tube. Screw him. Life would be so much simpler with that clown out of the way. Steve decided he would like to thank whoever it was that killed Gavin, that is, right before he gutted the person himself. Family honor and all.

Back at the pit behind the shed, he put on the work gloves and maneuvered the oil drum to the concrete edge of the pit. The pit was about twelve by twelve feet across and originally fifteen feet deep. It had been the basement of a storage building for something or other, part of the box factory. To Steve, it looked more the size of a jail cell than a storeroom. A fire had reduced the building to ash and left a gaping hole near the trees. When Steve's father purchased the land to build his gas station, he boarded over the hole, leaving a trap door through which he dumped the garage's garbage. Eventually, by the time Steve inherited the place, the makeshift roof had collapsed on the decades' worth of refuse. Steve had built a new lid for the pit and continued to use it for a garbage dump.

When the recycling craze hit, Steve found a new use for the hole in the ground. He had carefully sorted out the years of accumulated trash and sent the recyclables off to wherever they went. He'd made a little extra money selling the old Coke bottles to collectors on e-Bay; his father had been a Coke fanatic, often downing a dozen bottles in a day. Steve missed guzzling Coke and cream soda from a real glass bottle, ice cold from the old chest cooler that had sat inside the garage next to the cash register. It had been a sad day when it was replaced with an upright can dispenser. The rest of the garbage went into bags and off to the dump. The garage had always had lots of toxic waste—used motor oil, transmission and brake fluid, dirty turpentine—but it had been difficult to get rid of the stuff. Throwing it out with the curbside trash was a possibility but there was just too much of it so it went to an expensive plant in the city for disposal. Eventually, Steve hit upon the idea of dumping it in the old basement. He blocked the drain with cement, never wondering why it had been there in the first place but glad it was, otherwise sorting the trash would have been a nasty job, and checked the concrete to make sure it was watertight. Then he started to fill the pit.

Realizing how much money he was saving by dumping waste into the pit and stuffing old tires in a small cave he found about twenty yards into the woods, Steve decided to make some extra cash. Soon he began to take toxic waste and tires from other businesses in the county, having told the owners he had a contract with a processing plant in the city and could get them a decent rate. The money paid out by the businesses went in his pocket and the used oil, paint, and whatever else went into the pit while the tires created homes for things with too many legs in the cave.

He had been filling the pit for about ten years now. The black lake had slowly risen until it was almost at the top. A couple of years ago it had stopped rising. Steve suspected the concrete had cracked somewhere down there but he wasn't about to go down and find the leak. The ground around the pit didn't show any signs of a leak and the trees that grew a couple of feet back of the pit and up the hill didn't seem to be adversely affected. He assumed there was another cave or something under the ground and the toxic sludge was simply draining into it—a bonus that allowed him to keep going with this sideline long after the pit should have been full.

Steve uncapped the drum and poured out the remainder of its contents. He liked the sound the oil made as it sloshed into the black mass below, somehow soft and welcoming, and was fascinated by the eddies and currents moving beneath the surface. At times, when he was feeling bored, he would sit at the edge of the pit with a sandwich and imagine what kind of life might exist within an oily black lake like the one below or at the bottom of the ocean: giant squid, blind fish preyed upon by sleek white sharks only concerned with their next meal—something like himself.

When the drum was empty, he recapped it and used a dolly to move it to the back of the garage, where it would be picked up at the end of the week. There were five more empty oil drums awaiting pickup. One job down, one to go.

The cloths he had used to wipe down the drum went into a bin inside the back door of the garage. It was almost full and would be sent off to the cleaners tomorrow. Feeling dirty, Steve ached to get to the washroom to clean up, however a car pulled into the garage parking lot and a second later a car door slammed. "Christ, what now?" he muttered. He went back out to see who was here to annoy him. He smiled when he saw the shiny blue BMW. Silva had parked discreetly next to one of the wrecks; no one passing on Trinity would be able to see the car. Silva was nowhere in sight. Steve went to check the car to see if it was locked—Silva was a fanatic about his car and would never venture far without setting the Club on the steering wheel and activating the car's security system. As he bent down to look in the passenger side window, Silva sat up and looked like he nearly had a heart attack when he saw Steve's face through the glass. When he had regained his composure, he got out of the car.

"Good afternoon, Mister Silva," said Steve, hesitating before extending his hand in welcome; there wasn't that much oil on it. Silva ignored it. "And how are you this fine day? Well, I hope." Silva said nothing and looked around the lot to as if expecting someone else to be there. "I'm alone," added Steve as he popped a peppermint Life Saver in his mouth. He offered the pack to Silva who looked at it as if his mother had just been insulted. *Do you even have a mother? After all, you are such a reptile to deal with.* "What can I do for you?" The scent of English Leather was heavy on the air; the man had no idea about moderation.

Silva stared for a moment, perhaps assessing him, though Steve couldn't imagine why. "Bender was here. What did he want?"

Steve pondered how to answer the question. It was none of this arrogant asshole's business, but he had to be careful around this man. He decided to be honest, for a change. "He came to offer his condolences for my brother and see if there was anything he could do. I thought it rather decent of him, don't you agree?" He showed Silva the winning smile that always got him in good with the women of Tyndale.

Silva spat and said, "There's nothing decent about that swine. As far as I'm concerned, he's responsible for your brother's death."

Steve resisted the temptation to look down at the ground where the man had spat. His stomach lurched at the thought of the gob of saliva waiting to be stepped on and tracked into the garage. He had strict rules about that kind of thing and had reproached Gavin many times for just such a lapse in good taste and manners. "I'll grant you that's a possibility, albeit a slim one.

Bender doesn't have the fortitude to do something like that to anyone. I would imagine he even has trouble swatting flies and mosquitoes." He chuckled at the image of Bender trying to catch a fly and release it outside. "His heart's too good."

Silva looked at him as if he was out of his mind. His cheeks reddened and he got angry. "Don't you dare suggest that I'm wrong about that ... that ... creature. He's responsible for everything that goes wrong in this town."

Maybe for everything that goes wrong for you. Though how he does it, I can't imagine. He wondered why the richest man in town was so obsessed by someone so inoffensive. Everyone in town knew about Silva's attempts to buy out the Benders when they had purchased the house on the hill; it had been good for some laughs at the various bars Steve frequented. But that had been ages ago; surely the man was over it by now.

Or could it have something to do with Marie, Silva's long-lost wife? Steve remembered the time the two of them had performed for Silva. Marie had been reluctant at first, distracted by the sound of the video recorder, but had gradually come around, pardon the pun, as he worked on her. For a woman twenty, maybe thirty years older than him, she had been a spitfire, one of the best times he'd had. And Silva had paid him well. He felt himself getting hard but the thought of the disgusting thing on the asphalt soon put a stop to that.

Steve turned to walk to the back of the garage. He didn't want anyone passing on Trinity to see him talking to Silva—he had a reputation to maintain, not much of a one mind you, but one he cherished, nonetheless. Silva followed. While they walked, Steve asked, "Forgetting Bender for the time being, what can I do for you today, sir?" He was always especially polite to Silva despite his almost overwhelming desire to rip out the man's throat. He didn't want to look back at the asphalt. He truly didn't but it was so hard to resist.

Silva took a couple of seconds to regain his composure. More often these days, his obsession with revenge on Bender was getting the better of him. O'Leary had seen too many displays of near insane ranting recently to be comfortable with his situation. As soon as possible, he would be severing all connections with Silva, decent blackmail money or not.

When they reached the back door of the garage, Steve paused to see if his guest wanted to go inside where it would be more private. Apparently not, because Silva began speaking straight away. "The members of the Council, and others, are acting upon my wishes. Soon, events will be set in motion that will completely change everything. I'll be on top again, in charge as I'm supposed to be. I'll be prepared to reward those loyal to me handsomely." He looked into O'Leary's eyes and set a hand on his shoulder, a friendly gesture from just about anyone else, but a sign of power from this man. *Don't touch me*, Steve screamed in his head; he hated being touched. "Can I count on you, O'Leary? Are you with me in this?"

Steve also hated being called by his last name, it was so rude. Call me Steve or call me Mister O'Leary, but never just use my last name. With all the sincerity he could muster, he said, "Of course I'm with you, sir. This town needs a shakeup and you're just the man to do it. I'm there until the bitter end." He smiled his best smile, showing his perfect white teeth. He watched for Silva's reaction and remembered Marie's taste, trying to corrupt this moment as best he could.

Silva beamed, evidently clueless. "Good. I need you to do a few things for me. When does the Mayor pick up his next, what do you call it? Score?"

"Tomorrow," answered Steve. "I was about to prepare it when you arrived."

"Excellent" Silva rubbed his hands together. O'Leary stifled a laugh. This was too much like an old movie with the insane bad guy. All Silva needed was a top hat and cape to go with that stupid goatee of his. "Put him off for a few days. Tell him your supplier ran out. Make something up."

Steve wasn't sure where this was going. He said, "I can say there was a major bust in the city. All my connections have to lay low for a couple of days. He'll wait. He trusts me."

Silva nodded. "He knows you work for me." O'Leary raised an eyebrow. This was new and he wasn't sure that he liked it. His link to Silva was supposed to be anonymous or at least discreet. The man continued, "He'll think I had something to do with it because he tried to cross me a while ago. He'll view it as payback for being disloyal. And he's absolutely correct." He waved a finger in the air. "But there's more ..."

Steve pretended to cough and pulled out a handkerchief to hide the unstoppable grin on his face. Had this man been watching old movies to get his dialogue? Next thing you know, he'll be doing a Snidely Whiplash laugh while tying some helpless girl to the railroad tracks, not that any trains ever came through here these days. When he had himself control again, he put away the handkerchief and told himself to be serious, which only made him want to break down laughing. He could feel the strain in his jaw while he maintained a straight face.

Snidely went on, "I want you to add some arsenic to the package. You've got some, I assume. Or you know where to get it."

What the fuck are you playing at? He nodded and said, "I keep some around for the rats. We don't get many, I keep a clean establishment. You know, it's not that hard to keep the place clean. I know you might think, sure, it's easy, he doesn't have any business anyway. But I tell you, this place can get turned into a heap in an instant." He snapped his fingers. "And the rats. Christ, they're huge. I don't know what they eat around here, maybe a deer or two, but ... Son of a bitch, there are three of them." The rats stared at him then ran off. He noticed the blank expression on the other man's face. "Sorry. When I get to talking about keeping the place clean, I tend to go on." There was still no expression on Silva's face. *Boy, I've pissed you off, haven't I?*

"Are you quite finished," asked Silva through gritted teeth. He wanted to explode, Steve could tell, but didn't dare here. Anyone could be walking by.

"Given the size of the Mayor's habit, he should be frantic by the time he gets his next supply. He'll probably go for an extra-large snort right away. Do you want me to put enough in to kill him or just to make him sick?" Steve was surprised at how easily he talked about killing someone. He'd never been much for violence; Gavin had always done all the dirty work and had enjoyed it. Killing someone was a big step. The urge had been coming on him for a while. His temper had been flaring lately and he'd almost hit a couple of drunks in the city last week when they'd objected to him picking up their wives. The nerve of them; their wives had been quite willing. He needed to get away, collect his thoughts, regroup and start over. Maybe somewhere warm, though it was getting pretty warm around here of late. Santa Fe. He'd always wanted to go to Santa Fe, had read about it in a thriller a few years ago. Yes, as soon as he was done with the mayor business and whatever Silva was planning, he'd head off to Santa Fe for some rest and relaxation. Something distracted him. Silva had said something.

"Sorry, what was that?"

Silva was annoyed. He tried to make his eyes look menacing but all he did was squint. *Ming the Merciless, that's who you are.* Steve stifled another guffaw with a cough. *Shave that head and you're perfect.* Ming went on, "I said, I don't want him dead just yet. I want him scared. I want him ready to do whatever I say because he knows I can get to him."

"No problem, sir," said Steve. He looked over to the parking lot, hoping Silva would take the hint and leave. This was becoming tiresome and Steve wanted to get into the bathroom and clean up; his fingers still felt a little oily from the work gloves.

Silva took the hint. Without a word, he returned to his car and drove off.

Steve went into the garage, washed his hands then put on a clean pair of work gloves. He picked up a clean cloth from the pile on the workbench next to the back door and returned to the spot in the parking lot where Silva had been disgusting and surveyed the asphalt for the nauseating expectoration. When he spied the offending mass, he carefully crouched and, trying not to look at it, cautiously wiped it up with the cloth. Holding it gingerly between finger and thumb, he deposited the cloth in the bin near the door. Then he got a couple of clean cloths and dropped them on top of the pile in the bin to hide the fouled one he had just used. He thought for a second about getting some disinfectant and pouring it on the asphalt but decided that might be taking things too far, even for him. Maybe.

In the washroom, his hands and forearms heavily soaped, Steve tried to imagine Santa Fe. But it was impossible. He dried his hands and pulled on the pair of yellow rubber gloves that always sat at the ready next to the sink. Picking up a mop and a bottle of Lysol, he headed out to the parking lot, cursing those two stupid girls who sat on either side of him in grade nine. Everyone else in the class had avoided the cafeteria food, especially the macaroni and cheese, before biology class but not these two winners. When they saw the dissected frogs and vomited, he was caught in the middle and scarred for life.

John "Spanky" McFarlane

"Are you sure he was following you?" asked Spanky. He was sitting at his office desk, feet up, a bottle of Rolling Rock within easy reach on an old CD used as a coaster. His small apartment, the attic space of a detached garage a block away from The Pub, was sufficient for his needs, which were few—beer, a computer, a big screen TV, and a massive shelving unit full of almost two thousand videos, DVDs, and Blu-Rays.

Milk crates served as shelves for hundreds of issues of Entertainment Weekly, Empire, Premiere, Psychotronic Video, and other assorted movie magazines. The bed was a fold out couch rescued from Tom and Belinda's basement in the distant past when she had had one of her frequent "let's clear everything out and start over" decorating spells. The kitchen was an alcove with a full-sized stove and refrigerator, the former rarely ever used because he ate so often at The Pub, and the latter full of Rolling Rock and Sam Adams ale. The Rolling Rock was a fine substitute for the nasty water in the apartment. The bathroom lived behind a curtain at the back of the apartment; it had a shower stall, an old porcelain receptacle, and a stainless-steel bar sink. A stack of recent, well-thumbed Marvel comics sat on a stool next to the throne, ready to entertain. To say Spanky had an office was an exaggeration but one that he liked. An old door covered with a sheet of plexiglass resting on more milk crates served as his desk and was home to his computer and library of database and programming manuals. The office itself was the desk and an outrageously expensive chair that was so comfortable, Spanky hardly ever left it. Yet he remained thin as a rail.

The War of the Worlds–the original–played silently on the big TV. Spanky could program, watch a movie, and conduct a conversation simultaneously and never miss a beat, a talent he knew Tom shared but not to such perfection.

He swallowed the last of his beer and said, "Sorry, Tom, I missed that. The Martians are in Miamah."

"I said, I'm sure Deputy Dawg was following me. He was hanging around the old factory, watching me while I was talking to O'Leary. Then waiting for me at Good's, and then again at Knudson's. I don't know what to do about it," said Tom at the other end of the phone.

"Call Terry and complain," said Spanky. "Get him to do his job for once and call off his dog."

"That's unfair," answered Tom. "Terry told me he ordered Schofield to back off. I guess the guy won't listen." Tom always defended Terry, a trait Spanky admired, but there was still something about the Sheriff that rubbed him the wrong way, like wet denim on inner thighs.

"No way. If Terry ordered him to stop tailing you, he would have. Did you ever think maybe Terry's got the idiot following you so he'd be out of his hair? Having Deputy Dawg on *your* ass instead of his own would make Terry's investigation go a whole lot smoother, don't you think?"

Tom said, "I suppose that makes sense in a twisted, only you could come up with something like that, sort of way. I'll let it go for now. Talk to Terry if Dawg gets persistent."

KING OF THE WOOD

Spanky stared at the beer bottle sitting on the coaster then said, "Could you believe Jay on Friday? I think he outdid himself."

"No kidding," said Tom. "I mean, have you ever wiped your ass, had the paper stick, and got a handful of shit?"

Spanky said nothing.

Tom said quietly, "Oh, God, you, too."

Spanky said nothing again.

"Where does he come up with these things?" asked Tom.

"I don't want to know," replied Spanky. "Remember that thing about using a urinal while wearing shorts?" He shuddered and reached over to the refrigerator to get another beer. This one he poured into a mug. The bottle joined its brothers in the Rolling Rock case next to the desk. A resounding fart reverberated in the leather of the chair.

"I heard that," said Tom. "And so did the neighbors. They're complaining again."

"You don't have any neighbors."

"The Knudsons down the hill. You're souring the éclairs."

"Shut up, 'kay."

"Look, um, I'm going to blitz the college code later. I know I haven't been pulling my weight lately. There's no excuse, just a lot of explanations you don't need to hear. Ten days and we should be ready to present something to the administration." He paused, waiting for a response. "Are you still there?"

Spanky burped and said, "Yeah. I thought I heard something outside. Sorry about that." He had a sip of beer. "Don't worry about the project; it'll get done with plenty of time to spare. I've gone over everything, so that should take care of most of the input problems. But you know they'll come up with more requirements at the last minute."

Tom chuckled and said, "Such is the nature of our work. I'll call you in a couple of days and let you know how it's going. Bye." The line went dead.

Spanky set the phone back in its cradle and listened for a few seconds. It certainly did sound like someone was outside. It couldn't be the Wainwrights, they were on a cruise and not due back for another week. He got up and put on the pair of jeans lying on the couch. Slowly, he went to the front door and drew back the lace curtain that covered the window. He saw a face, screamed and jumped back.

There was a knock at the door.

When his heart slowed enough, Spanky opened the door. "You nearly gave me a heart attack, creeping around like that. It's been a long time. Too long. What can I do for you?"

Lawrence Burke said, "I'm sorry. I'm trying to be unobtrusive but your girly scream isn't helping. Do you think the neighbors heard?"

"Doesn't matter, they're used to it. Enter, freely and of your own will."

Lawrence entered, removed his coat, and sat on the couch. Spanky went to the refrigerator and took out two bottles of Sam Adams, gave one to his guest. Sitting in his office chair and instantly wanting to take a nap, *damn it's comfortable*, Spanky said, "What's up? You're the last person I expected to see here." He watched Lawrence squirm, apparently uncomfortable about something. Consorting with the enemy, maybe? Or at least the enemy's friend.

"I have some information for your friend, Tom Bender. I'd like you to pass it along." He took a rolled-up envelope from inside his coat.

"Why don't you give it to him yourself? You know where he lives."

"And you know my employer." He looked towards the door as if expecting Silva to come through it at any second. "If he had any idea what I'm doing, well, the costs to me would be insurmountable."

"What? You'd lose your job," said Spanky. "How bad could that be? The guy's a total creep."

Lawrence smiled sadly and said, "It's my daughter I'm worried about. I can't risk her. You know that."

Spanky felt like an idiot, felt his face redden with embarrassment. He was well aware of what had happened to Luana Burke, had been the one to pull her from the submerged car. Such a beautiful girl, such a tragic waste. He'd never been satisfied that Celine Burke had lost control of the car and driven into the Nation. She had been one of the most careful drivers he'd ever known, cautious to a fault. He still felts pangs of guilt that he hadn't been able to get her out of the car even though the coroner said she'd been killed instantly by the impact. Spanky spent every possible hour at the funeral home, supporting Lawrence who had few friends in the town. They became close despite the age difference but lost contact once Silva began to exercise his financial muscle.

At least Luana had been saved, not that it had done much good. Her brain had been starved for oxygen; now she was little more than a vegetable. Spanky tried to visit her many times, bring her stuffed animals and treats from the bakery, but Silva made it clear he was trespassing on his property. Lawrence was devoted to her. For him to risk her well-being, the situation must be serious. "What do you want me to do?"

"Take this," he handed Spanky the envelope. "It contains copies of documents relating to Horace's Hill and Horace's will. Tom will be interested in the information they hold. He recently became the largest landowner in the county."

Spanky dumped the contents in his lap and thumbed through the pages of legal documents. None jumped out and said, "Read me!" so he put them back and asked, "Silva is trying to hide this from Tom? Why?"

Lawrence drained his beer and handed the empty to Spanky who went to the refrigerator for refills. "Silva wants the land for himself, obviously. He resents Tom for not selling it to him twelve years ago. Resents hardly describes it. Silva has a pathological hate on for Tom. It's quite the sight when he gets going. One day he's going to burst a blood vessel."

Spanky laughed. "That I'd like to see. Silva has been lording over the town for as long as I can remember. I'd love to see him brought down a peg or two. Or three."

"I agree. But we have to be careful. If he finds out what I've done, Luana could be at risk."

"So, what can we do to cover you and protect her?"

Lawrence took a slip of paper from his vest pocket and handed it to Spanky. "That's the access code for the county records. You should be able to get into them from here. That code gives you full administrative access to everything. Take this." He handed across a sheet of paper with two columns of small print. "These are names of pieces of property, companies, and transaction dates, all the information you need. Check it yourself then give it to Tom. That way, it will look like you found it without any help." He chugged the last of his second beer and stood. "Be careful, John. Silva is a vicious and vindictive man. He'll destroy you and anyone you care about if he finds out about this."

Spanky shook Lawrence's hand. "You're the one taking the risks, and Luana. I won't let anything happen to either of you."

KING OF THE WOOD

He led Lawrence to the door, opened it, and checked outside. The coast was clear.

Before he left, Lawrence turned and asked, "Have you ever thought about moving into a real apartment instead of this pit? You can afford it."

Spanky laughed. "It serves my needs. Maybe one day, if I ever meet someone to share my space with." He thought of Nancy Hughes and sighed.

"Ask her," said Lawrence. "Take care." He went down the steps quickly and disappeared into the shadows at the side of the house. Something flew over him. Bats, he guessed except they were too big, and there were five of them, whatever they were.

Anxious to learn more about Tom's windfall, Spanky stripped off his jeans and went straight to the computer and got online. In a minute, he was on the county server and accessing all kinds of juicy bits of information. The printer next to the computer worked overtime spitting out page after page of deeds, land transfers, tax rolls, and assorted other documents relevant to Tom and Horace's Hill. There was so much information he knew it would take him days, even weeks to sift through it all and make it presentable to Tom. But Tom was his friend and they would do anything for each other. And it would be a chance to stick it to the lord of the county.

Out of curiosity, Spanky began to search for items related to people he knew. It was slightly unethical, but he would never let anyone know what he found out. If there was one thing Spanky was proud of, it was his discretion. He had never spoken to anyone about Tom and what effect Belinda's illness had had on his friend. And he was the only person that Steve O'Leary had trusted with the truth about the aborted wedding sixteen years ago. No one gave him the benefit of the doubt. Except Spanky.

121

Over a bottle of bourbon, Steve had poured his heart out to his old friend but secured a promise that the truth would never be revealed. Unbelievably, he still felt something for his ex-fiancé and didn't want her to get hurt. Unable to trust anyone anymore, Steve had cut his confidant off and gone on a rampage of seducing women without conscience. It pained him but Spanky remained silent, grieving for the friendship that had been killed by two betrayers and never giving up hope that Steve might come around one day.

Spanky's insatiable quest for knowledge, and a new access to information was irresistible. After a couple of hours of boring research, something jumped out at him.

"Now why would you want to buy an old factory?" He printed a copy of the deed to the land and placed it in a folder. This could be useful if he could ever figure out what to do with it.

When he was finished, Spanky shut down the computer and leaned back the chair. Time for another movie. He got up and slipped The List of Adrian Messenger into the machine. With another beer at the ready, Spanky got lost in a world of intrigue and deception.

CHAPTER NINE
THE GARDEN

Tom Bender

Tom shut off the iPod and set the headphones on the hook at the side of his desk. He backed up his work then shut the laptop lid. He pushed it out of the way and grabbed the ever-present yellow pad to add more notes as a reminder for when he started work again later today. Assorted scattered papers and diagrams were gathered up and stacked neatly, and other clutter was tidied. Satisfied that everything was in its proper place and the desktop was clear, he got up and pulled aside the heavy curtains on the office window. Only when the burning sun blinded him did he realize it was daytime, early morning from the look of it. Tom had been keeping tech hours since he got back from the garage, barely noticing the passage of time as lines of code poured out of his head. Tea had kept him going throughout, literally forcing him to get up and go to the bathroom several times. He ate when the hunger pangs grew too annoying to ignore, mostly chips and stale doughnuts and chocolate—high tech health food. He'd soon make up for letting Spanky do so much of the groundwork on the revamped college application; they had decided to try and sell versions of it to businesses and other schools. He had no idea what day of the week it was, or how much of the month had slipped away.

Tom stared absently at his front yard, scratching an itch in his crotch. The thousands of crocuses he had planted over the years were in bloom and the daffodils and jonquils seemed thicker and larger than usual. Randomly planted tulips were in flower everywhere in the yard and the phlox was in full bloom. The rose bushes along the roadside were thick with leaves and buds. Here and there, a splash of bright red reminded him that he had not finished deadheading the roses in the fall; he'd clip the rosehips later in the day, maybe experiment with rosehip tea, unless they needed to be fresh and not over-wintered. The mulch in the flowerbeds, usually excellent at keeping down the weeds, was alive with growth, both weeds and sprouting flowers. *I've got my work cut out for me.* Daylilies and tiger lilies along the edges of the turnaround were lush green and had flower stalks that were at least two feet tall, and a couple of irises had burst into color. The narrow grass paths between the flower beds, all that remained of the huge front lawn, needed cutting, and were full of blooming dandelions to boot. The grass that he could see along Hill Road before it disappeared down the slope was almost solid yellow with dandelion blooms. If they all came to seed at the same time, and the wind was right, there would be enough seed parachutes to blanket the suburbs. At least it would add some color.

Tom sat and put his feet up on a rolling file cabinet. After a long and burdensome winter, it was a pleasure and relief to see the green again. He hated winter and its foul weather, had often thought of moving to a sunnier climate where there was no snow or freezing rain or sub-zero temperatures. Somehow though, he just never got up the energy to do anything about it. He was too comfortable in his home and too lazy to move. It took far less effort to bitch and complain about the weather than to do something about it.

The south-facing window afforded him a panoramic vista of the distant city and its encroaching suburbs. But something, just out of reach, disturbed him about the view. The new leaves of a honey locust tree partially blocked the view of the taller city buildings far to the southwest. A gray haze hung over the city giving it a mirage-like appearance. Sadly, it was all too real. From the south bank of the Nation, the suburbs stretched for mile upon mile to the city. The blues and grays of the houses blended to give the area a uniform dullness. There was an occasional swatch of green; a lone tree spared the crunch of a developer's bulldozer, more a whim than any sort of plan to maintain green space.

He thought of Frederick Silva. They had been enemies almost from the moment Tom and Belinda had arrived in town. Silva tried to buy them out but Belinda had seen him off quickly. They hadn't needed the money because Belinda's mother's estate provided enough to pay for the house.

He thought about taking a shower since he'd been working at the computer for the last twelve hours and felt grotty. A quick nap would be a good idea, too. Then he thought about the garden. He should get out there and start clearing away the winter garbage and the remains of last fall's dead foliage. The vegetable beds needed to be turned so he could lay in some manure and peat moss and to encourage any weed seeds to grow so they could be pulled before planting started. And it wouldn't be too early to put in some root vegetables and lettuce and spinach. Tom's garden usually kept The Pub gang supplied with fresh greens for most of the summer and early fall. Weeding and garden work always relaxed Tom and allowed him to think through things that were bothering him. If he'd been able to get out into the garden earlier, he would have been able to talk himself out of acting like a complete idiot at O'Leary's Garage.

After changing into an old pair of jeans that he used for garden work, and putting on a pair of socks, something he only wore if he had to, Tom went out onto the deck to see how much work lay ahead of him in the back yard. When he stepped through the back door, Tom noticed that the deck seemed cleaner than usual. He hadn't power washed the deck boards for a couple of years and the accumulation of dirt and grime was turning the wood black. However, now the boards seemed quite light, almost their natural wood color. The green from the pressure treating process was long gone. Then the rustling of leaves caught Tom's attention. He looked up.

"Holy crap."

The oak was in full leaf and swayed in the warm and gentle breeze. The birch trees by the back fence were also covered with leaves, as were the fruit trees along the eastern side of the garden and the chestnut on the west. The fruit trees were also covered with blossoms. Even the trees beyond the fence had some leaves, though in the distance Tom could see that the trees on the surrounding hills and in town were still bare.

Then Tom looked down and nearly fell over. Everywhere was lush green. All the clematis were in full bloom, covering the fence with swaths of purple, lavender, blue, burgundy, and red. The kiwis were growing vigorously, new vines swaying in the breeze trying to find something to curl around. As with the front yard, the daffodils and tulips were blooming like gangbusters. The perennials, geraniums and dahlias, lilies and hostas, were thick with green. The yuccas had two-foot flower stalks. From between the slats on the compost box, Tom recognized potato plants and the vines of some kind of squash. The rhubarb was out of control. The sight made Tom think of rhubarb and custard. "I'm hungry," he said. All the beds, whether covered with mulch or left bare, were carpeted with weeds, many almost a foot tall. The grass looked as if it hadn't been cut for months.

"I must have been working really hard," said Tom to a pair of mourning doves that were watching him warily from the side of one of the beds. He moved to lean on the deck rail and the doves flew off in a panic over the fence and into the woods on the slope. "It's impossible." He leaned forward so he could see through the large window at the back of the garage. There was a calendar hanging on the side of a shelf just inside but he thought he must have forgotten to change the month when he saw that it showed April.

He stepped down to the lowest section of the deck where he saw that the annual geraniums in the pots there were growing. They should have died off over the winter. *Could they have seeded themselves? I need to check on that.* Tom suddenly felt as if someone or something was watching him. He looked across the fence but could see no one trying to hide in the trees. A slight movement to his left caught his attention. A robin stared at him. This wasn't that unusual. In the spring there were usually several baby robins bobbing around waiting for their parents to feed them. Though wary of Tom, they didn't panic at the sight of him like the doves. However, this robin was on the deck rail not two feet from him and didn't look like it was going to move. Then he saw another baby robin a few inches away from the first.

The closest robin cheeped. This seemed to be a signal. The

whole back yard erupted with birdsong. There were sparrows on every tree branch, along the top of the fence, gathered around the bird pond Tom had made with an old mixing bowl. All were watching him. Blackbirds hopping across the vegetable beds all seemed to be heading for him. "The Birds. I've got to run," he said quietly so as not to disturb his feathered visitors. "Where are the seagulls? Where's Tippi Hedren?" As suddenly as they started, all went silent. The weirdest sight, though, was a gathering of twenty-five albino sparrows at the foot of the oak. He assumed they were sparrows because they were the same shape and size as the sparrows everywhere else. The odd thing about them was the thin line of red that ran up their breasts. They were completely motionless, staring at him with those dark eyes, their beaks moving but making no sound.

Tom turned and was startled by four crows sitting on the gutter above his head. They too stared down at him.

A slight chittering caught his attention and he turned towards the sound. Eight rats watched him from the base of the back fence. Five more sat on top, also watching.

He slowly inched his way to the back door, slid it open and darted inside, slamming it shut behind him. He looked out the kitchen window and watched while the birds slowly left the backyard. Only the albino sparrows remained, still noiselessly watching him. The rats stayed for a moment, looking confused as if they didn't know what to do, that is, if rats can look confused, then ran off. He could hear the crows running along the gutter towards the back door. Then they hopped down to the deck rail just outside the door where they looked into the kitchen. Tom waved to them. They bowed then took off and followed the rest of the birds into the trees on the other side of the fence.

"What the Hell was that all about?" he asked his reflection in the window. Then he remembered the crows from the day of the murder; they had acted weird, too.

He went to the refrigerator to get a drink of water. The calendar on the wall next to the fridge showed April. Forgetting about his drink, he ran to the phone and called Spanky.

"Yeah, Tom," said a sleepy voice at the other end of the line. "What's up?"

"What's the date?"

"Don't' you have a calendar there?"

"There was a power failure and it went off. I need to reset it."

Silence. "Sure." There was a rustling as Spanky moved papers around on his desk. Unlike Tom, Spanky was rather disorganized. He had no problem finding anything; it was just buried under mounds of other stuff. "Here 'tis. It's the twenty-third."

"Of what?"

"April."

"Oh, shit."

"What?"

"There's something weird going on over here."

"Weirder than a guy strung up by his innards?"

Tom paused for a moment. "Yeah."

"Need help?"

"I don't know."

"I can be there in five or ten minutes."

"Which?"

"Depends on whether I put some clothes on." Spanky always worked naked, claimed it freed his mind to concentrate on the problem at hand. Tom never sat in Spanky's office chair.

"By all that's holy, put some clothes on. But there's no rush. It's not going anywhere. Why don't you pick up …" A sound from the front of the house distracted Tom. It was the low rumbling of a car muffler. "Son of a bitch."

"Pick up son of a bitch? You want me to get Deputy Dawg?"

"You're psychic. I can hear his car out front. He's checking up on me again." Tom sighed. The sound of the defective muffler had become a regular interruption over the past ten days, though he hadn't let it take him away from his work. If the deputy wanted to waste his time hanging around outside his house, fine, but don't expect to be able to use the bathroom. "I'm going to call Terry and file a complaint about this idiot. Why don't you pick up a couple of steaks and come over this afternoon? I think we've done enough work for a while."

"So, you don't need me right now?"

"No, it's okay. Just a momentary panic."

"Give me a little extra time. I've got some stuff to show you. I think you'll be pleasantly surprised."

"It's not more nude photos of old college chums, is it? I had enough of that last time."

"No. No," protested Spanky. "This time it's really important."

"You've got a key, let yourself in. I'm going to work on code for a while," he said. *I don't think I can face the garden yet.*

They hung up. Tom called Terry to talk about Deputy Schofield. As he waited for someone at the Sheriff's office to answer, he heard a noise at the kitchen window. One of the albino sparrows fluttered at the sill trying to get a foothold. Clawhold? This one seemed to have a redder breast than the others. Then he saw the crows were back on the deck rail, eleven this time. They watched him again, heads occasionally bobbing as if they were having a conversation about what he was doing.

Someone answered the phone to take his mind off the weirdness outside but Terry was out.

"I don't see what's so special," said Spanky shortly after he arrived. "Your garden is always lush and green." He poured some vinegar into the mixture in the bowl then stirred it a few times with a wooden spoon. A quick dip of a finger to check the taste, then he put the steaks in the marinade one at a time, being sure to cover them completely with the dark sauce.

Tom watched his friend prepare the meat, trying to see how much of each ingredient he added, knowing he would never get it to come out as good. "It's too early in the season for all this growth. And the flowers don't all bloom at the same time. It's weird."

"But your garden is always weird. Didn't you still have carrots or something last November?" Spanky put the bowl with the steaks in the refrigerator and said, "We should leave them about an hour before we cook them. Are the potatoes ready?"

"Yeah, I'd forgotten about them. Having fresh vegetables seems so natural now, I didn't think about how late everything grows. Now that you mention it, the growing season up here has been getting longer. There's never been anything this early before, but when I first started growing stuff, I think it was done by early October or something," said Tom while he wrapped some potatoes in foil for the barbecue and placed them on a platter. "Do I have some kind of mutant garden, do you think?"

"No, not the garden. It's you that's the mutant."

"What's this stuff you wanted to show me?"

"Sit down and I'll explain everything."

When they were seated at the kitchen table, each with a fresh drink, Spanky got nervous. "First, you're going to kill me, but I haven't done any work on the application for a couple of weeks."

Tom nearly spat out his Guinness. Here he was feeling guilty about letting his friend do all the work and the guy had been goofing off. He wanted to get angry but it was impossible to get angry with Spanky—the guy was just so damned decent. Tom tried to frown when he looked his friend in the eye and said, "Splain."

"It was all for you." Spanky told him about the visit from Lawrence and the necessity for secrecy. He opened the briefcase which had confused Tom when he arrived because Spanky never used a briefcase—all his notes were carried in a huge loose pile, without so much as a rubber band around the sheaf of papers. Apparently, this was how Spanky had been since high school; no binders, duo-tangs, folders, nothing but a big pile of papers waiting for some joker to knock them flying. It had never happened, and he claimed he had never lost a single sheet and knew exactly where everything was. Tom believed him. Spanky passed across printouts of deeds and assorted other documents while he related his efforts to research the facts about Horace's Hill and the old man's will. Tom didn't interrupt, tempted as he was, and let his friend finish the story. "It's taken me the last eleven days to sort it all out. You wouldn't believe the trouble I had accessing some of those files; the lawyers are getting smarter but they can't stop me when I want to know something. Nothing can stop me. Nothing, I tell you."

"The lyrics to 'Louie Louie.'"

"You vicious bastard."

"But it's true."

"I'm not stopped. I'm just taking a long break between research attempts."

"It's been six years."

"A relatively short time, considering how long the song's been around."

"You're stopped. Admit it."

"No."

"Admit it."

"No. No. No. And once more, no. Now fuck off, 'kay."

Spanky's eyes bulged and his face was red; it was so easy to get him stirred up. Tom waited while his friend calmed down.

"So, there you have it, Tom," said Spanky as if his abilities had never been questioned. "You now own the whole of the hill, down to the bakery and where Hill Road curves east. And down to the edge of the swamp. And then there's all that forested area on the other side of Hill Road, almost all the way to the old ranger tower."

"I still don't' understand, John. How can this be? It's too incredible." He got up and paced around the kitchen. "It doesn't make any sense."

Spanky pulled out a sheet of paper and tapped it. "This explains the gist of the will. Horace hated Frederick Silva with a passion. The last thing he wanted was for his asshole nephew to get control of the forest. He figured the guy would clear cut it and put in a golf course or sell it off for as much money as possible. Silva had to prove that he deserved to inherit the land."

"But how could he prove that?" asked Tom, still confused.

Spanky waved the paper. "That's where it gets interesting. Horace specified a number of conditions. Things like planting a certain number of trees, seeing that designated areas of land around Tyndale were preserved in as close to their natural states possible. Losing out to the developers on the other side of the Nation was the biggest blow." Tom smiled at the reminder of his alliance with Silva. "When that green space went to Hell, something that Horace had worked hard with his friends in the city to establish, Silva pretty much lost all hope for inheriting."

"But he didn't seem all that broken up about losing," said

J. Edwin Buja

Tom. "I remember he made a lot of noise then went away. If so much was at stake, wouldn't he have gone ballistic at the time?"

"Yeah," said Spanky. He drained his beer then got another from the refrigerator and continued, "He had it both ways. His company held the mortgages on several of the estates. When the developers bought them, Silva made a killing. He also owned the land they built the new road and the bridge on. There was no way he could lose."

"But what about Horace's Hill? Hold on." Tom went out to the deck, looked around nervously for birds and when he saw none fired up the barbecue. He put the foil-wrapped potatoes on and shut the lid. When he returned to the kitchen, he set the timer on the stove to give him notice when to put the steaks on. Spanky would cook the meat.

When Tom sat again, Spanky went on, "From what Lawrence told me, and what I could gather from my research, Silva was counting on two things. First, you would have no idea about the conditions of the will and wouldn't make any claims when the trust ran out. Second, none of Horace's lawyers are still alive and Silva has the new lawyers in the bag."

"The one thing he didn't count on was the disloyalty of an employee."

Spanky bristled a little at that. "Careful, Tom. Lawrence is not disloyal. He's a good man who doesn't want to see Silva get away with anymore crap. He's looking out for you."

"But why? He doesn't know me. Doesn't owe me a thing."

Spanky shrugged. "Lawrence wants to see justice done. Silva treats him like shit and has him over a barrel." He explained about Luana.

"Christ, the risk he's taking. Is there anything I can do?"

"Just keep quiet and never mention his name. You found out

about this from me, which is true. My story is that I was testing a search program and got lucky. It's farfetched, but most people won't know that. They think computers are magic."

"You mean they're not?" Tom sipped his Guinness.

"You realize you're rich now, don't you? You're the biggest landowner in the county. You practically own the county."

"I'm rich."

"Yes."

"Richer than you."

"Thanks for reminding me."

"I own the county."

"Virtually."

"I'm like, the Count or the Earl, like royalty."

"Could be."

"Bow down, knave. Obey me."

"I'm a socialist. I don't believe in the class system."

"I'll make you my head servant, pay you well."

"No thanks."

"You dare to refuse?"

"Too little too late. Down with upper-class oppressors."

"You want the vote?"

"Representation by population."

"I'll have you thrown in prison or shot."

"I'll get Jay and start a revolution. Off with your head, you aristocratic bastard."

"That's not nice."

"You were turning into Silva."

"I don't have a goatee."

"Thank fuck for that. You'd look ridiculous."

The timer on the stove went off.

"Time to cook." Spanky got the steaks out of the refrigerator and went out to the barbecue. "Tom," he shouted a minute later. "Get out here."

Tom jumped up and joined his friend on the deck. "What is it?"

Spanky pointed with the barbecue tongs. The birds were back. The albino sparrows perched in a line on the lowest limb of the oak. Blackbirds filled the trees. A hawk seemed to be eying the steaks as they sizzled on the barbecue. There were now five crows staring down at the men from the roof of the observatory room over the garage.

"Should I be scared?" asked Spanky holding the tongs in front of him, ready to swat attacking birds out of the air. He looked brave and formidable except for the oven mitts.

Tom stayed silent, trying to think what to do. He stepped to the railing and in a steady voice said to the birds, "Leave us alone please. We want to eat in peace."

As one, the birds took off and flew into the woods that surrounded the house.

Tom and Spanky looked at each other, back at the disappearing birds, and then darted into the house.

When the door was locked, Spanky asked, "How did you do that?"

Tom shook, his mind reeled at what he had just witnessed. "I don't know, man. This day is too much. I'm suddenly rich. Now I'm fucking Doctor Doolittle."

"Well, not quite," said Spanky. "The birds didn't talk to you." He checked outside to see if it was all clear. "Did they?"

"I was too rattled to notice. Better check those steaks. Let's not ruin dinner."

Cautiously, they went back outside. While Spanky flipped the steaks, Tom stood guard, cricket bat at the ready to defend his friend if any of the birds came back.

"I don't know why you're so afraid of the little birds," said Tom. "You're used to small peckers."

"Shut up, 'kay."

The rest of the evening passed without any weirdness and Spanky left after dark. He took a flashlight, "Just to be safe, you know. There might be coyotes in the woods."

"Or small birds?"

Spanky glared at Tom.

After a good night's sleep, Tom went to his desk and lost himself in work. Several hours later, he finished typing a query, hit the Test button and waited while the computer did its work. Three seconds later the screen froze again. He pounded his fist on the desk, nearly knocking over the cup of tea perched precariously at the edge. Suddenly feeling thirsty, he took a sip and grimaced—the tea was cold as ice. *How long ago did I make this?* Setting the cup back on the desk, Tom pulled a yellow pad closer and made some notes. He unfroze the screen then rewrote the query. The screen froze but it took longer this time. "Progress," he muttered.

He removed the headphones he always wore when writing code. The playlist had finished an hour ago and he had been too absorbed in his work to notice the silence. Tom changed to a new playlist then went into the kitchen to brew up a fresh pot of tea.

All the blinds in the house were closed so he couldn't see the activity in his back yard. The muffled sound of birdsong didn't register in his preoccupied mind because he always played his music loud enough to drown out any other sound. The warmth of the house went unnoticed because he was so used to it and his feet weren't cold. His thoughts were of nothing more than queries, statements, queries, that woman, queries, and more

queries.
What woman?

CHAPTER TEN
THE SHRINE

The King of the Wood

"It's just a little bit further up here," said the King. "Be careful. We wouldn't want you to get hurt now, would we?" Gregory Wright struggled to free his wrists. The bonds were tied tightly, as tightly as the King could tie things with his mind. He winced as the shoeless man tried to walk normally; his feet were bloody from the sharp rocks and twigs on the path.

The poor fool had been so trusting, seeing a friend come to his aid when his car broke down on the old highway. The offer of a ride home had been expected and accepted happily. The blow to the back of the head, however, had been a complete surprise. When the King had reached the new bridge to the suburbs, he had parked his car behind some heavy machinery still being used to repair the bridge. The damage after the flooding last month was more extensive than anyone thought and the unions were dragging the work out for as long as possible. Someone on the County Council was making a killing. Speaking of which, someone on the County Council was going to be a killing.

After checking to be sure there were no workmen about, it was a Sunday and there shouldn't have been but best to be safe, the King dragged his semi-conscious captive from the back seat. The councilor was a small man so it was easy to manhandle him over one shoulder and carry him into the woods that bordered the swamp. It was a little awkward carrying a man and a knapsack full of supplies but difficulties were to be expected when one was trying to fix the world. Once they were well within the trees and away from any prying eyes that might pass on the highway, Wright was dropped on the ground. While Wright shook his cloudy head trying to figure out what had happened to him and where he was, the King said, "Take your shoes and socks off. I don't want you trying to run away." He ordered a willow to drop some whip-like branches and bind the man's wrists. Sweat rolled down his forehead as he concentrated on what used to be easy—willows were always most cooperative. Something was wrong here but would soon be set right by Wright. Satisfied that his prisoner couldn't free himself, and a little tired from the exertion, he said, "Sorry about the knock on the noggin but I couldn't afford to let you see where we were going. I'm sure you understand." The little man did not answer. When Wright was bound, the King guided him through the woods to the edge of the swamp. They stopped while he carefully checked along the edges of the water and out to the hummocks to see if anyone, particularly that irritating Ravenscroft woman, was out exploring this morning. No one was. And there was no sign of the enemy, no feeling of fuzzy power that was a danger to the King.

Now, the King paused for a moment and looked around. "Where are all the birds and wild beasts?" he asked. "They should be flocking to me for instructions." He shrugged. "Must be that the presence of the enemy has scared them off. At least my rats are here."

Twelve rats sat on a rock near the water waiting to do the King's bidding.

With a jab to Wright's ribs, they set off along the edge of the swamp until they came to a thick stand of arbor-vitae, the limbs of which were so entwined they formed a solid wall of branches. The rats scurried alongside the pair keeping watch. A trickle of water ran along the ground from behind the trees into the swamp. The King waved his hand several times and had to empty his mind of all but the trees before the limbs slowly parted to reveal a path that ran alongside the rivulet and up the hillside. As some leaves were crushed by the moving branches, an odor of tansy wafted over the men. Breathing hard from the effort, he said, "Spectacular trees, aren't they? Did you know they can live up to three hundred years? But that's nothing compared to a redwood." He waited for Wright to respond and grew annoyed when the man showed no sign of appreciating nature's wonders.

The King huffed and went on, "That stream is from the same source that Ollie Knudson uses for his baking. Have you ever tried his wares?" The little man nodded; he had a sad look on his face as if he realized he would never eat anything from the bakery again. "There's a deep underground reservoir that feeds the springs around here. The water's pure and tastes wonderful, unlike that filth from the Nation. It's a crime what's happened to so many rivers. But that's all going to change, isn't it?" The King pushed Wright through the break in the trees then sighed as he waved his hand to close the limbs. For a moment, everything went black and he thought he might lose consciousness. When the arbor-vitae had entwined their branches again, it was impossible to see anything of the swamp that now lay beyond the trees. He turned to see Wright staring at him, mouth hanging open in awe.

"It's a pretty good power to have, you know," he said in his friendliest voice. "A necessity when you have to move quickly through the woods. I must look a sight. I do seem to be a bit rusty, though. Must be getting old." He snickered. "A while back, while I was trying to follow that Ravenscroft woman and the enemy, I couldn't force the bushes apart fast enough to let me through. I actually had to crawl in the dirt. Me. Can you imagine it?" The King could see that Wright had absolutely no idea what he was talking about. "Ravenscroft was out in the swamp. You should have seen her sitting out there on a rock having lunch."

Seeing the confusion on his prisoner's face, the King said, "You have no idea who I'm talking about, do you? No matter. That foul-mouthed woman isn't important. The enemy is simply a pig." He thought for a moment then added, "A perfect naiad, if you believe in such things. Do you believe in anything, Gregory?"

Wright tripped over a fallen branch and landed hard on his face. Blood spurted from his nose and covered the front of his suit. The King helped him stand. "It's just up here a ways," he said. "How's the noodle? Still sore? What about the hands? Are they numb from being tied? Your feet must be in agony. Not to worry, it won't be much longer." Wright remained silent. They walked another twenty feet along the path then halted before an opening in the hillside.

"Through here," said the King. He shoved his prisoner into the cave entrance. "I think this was once used by the local Indians as a home. I found some stone tools further in. Not interested in the history of the area, Gregory? That surprises me. Naturally, I thought everyone would find history fascinating. I'm just a novice, but I'm learning. I suppose I should have paid more attention over the years. But life, family, work, it all distracted me. Well, not the family part, and I really don't have much of a life." He waited for a reaction then prodded Wright in the shoulder. "That was a joke. I don't have much of a life? I am life. Get it? Oh, well." The King took a flashlight from his knapsack and turned it on. The cave walls showed evidence of being worked with chisels; perhaps the Indians had tried to widen the cave. "I think this might have been used as a storage area."

They walked for quite a while, the cave twisted and turned and generally went up, and Wright stumbled many times when his bloodied feet slipped on rocks and outcroppings. By the time they reached the main part of the cave, Wright's suit was covered with gray dust and dirt, and blood.

"Here we are," said the King with obvious pride. He left Wright standing in the middle of the cavern, took a barbecue lighter from the knapsack then went around lighting torches that were jammed into crevices at various heights along the wall. "You know, we used to be able to do this with a snap of the fingers." He snapped his fingers near an unlit torch. There was a tiny flicker but nothing else. "Over the years, since humanity discovered fire, the ability atrophied. It's not something you need when you have electricity or one of these." He held up the lighter. "Wonderful devices, these. They even negate the need for matches."

Wright looked around the cave and his eyes widened. Whimpering, he back-peddled until he tripped on one of the branches on the cavern floor. His head smacked into the cave wall and he went down, unconscious once again.

"Nitwit," said the King. He finished lighting the torches and put the lighter back in his knapsack then went over to see how the fallen man was doing. The pulse was strong and fast, breathing steady. There was a nasty wet stain down the front of

Wright's trousers. *Not another one. Can't any of these people control their bladders when they get a fright?* He took hold of the willow bindings around the unconscious man's wrists and dragged him to the center of the cave. There, growing out of the rock was a yew about seven feet tall and six inches thick; its roots had pierced the bare rock. About five feet up, a silver spike protruded from the trunk. The King got Wright to his feet and leaned him against the yew then shackled his wrists. The shackles were attached to iron chains wrapped around the yew's leafless branches. *Glad I'm not one of those supernatural beasties that's allergic to iron.* Stepping back, he gave his captive the once over. "You know, Gregory, hanging like that, you make quite the fetching damsel in distress." No reaction. "Only kidding. You know, trying to lighten the mood. Serious times and all."

Wright moaned. The King slapped his face. "Wake up, Gregory." Another slap, another moan. "Wakey wakey." Slap, moan. "Come on, my lad. You've got a date with destiny."

The shackled man opened his eyes a little but kept them focused on the ground and said, "Don't want to see," and then turned his head. The King took hold of Wright's chin and yanked his face forward.

"You'll look at me when I speak to you, Gregory," said the King quietly. "There's so much I wish to narrate. Do you know how hard it is, being the one in charge and having no one with whom to speak?" Wright tried to turn his head away again but the King's grip was firm. "Pay attention, Gregory. This is like one of those movies where the bad guy has the hero tied up and reveals everything before attempting to kill the good guy." He laughed. "Except, in this case, you're not the hero, and I'm not going to attempt to kill. You're really going to die. There's no escape. No one knows you're here. No one is searching for you, and even if they were, we're well hidden. And you're too cowardly to try and escape anyway. Sad really. Where are all the heroes?"

Wright's eyes were wide open now, the horror clear in his face. He said, "You're not really going to kill me, are you? I mean, we've been friends for years. Please."

The King shook his head in pity. "You're so naïve. We were never friends. How could that be possible? I am so far above you in every way. I can't have friends, not in my position. No, I simply had to use you to get where I needed to be and to acquire those things I needed to accomplish my goals." Leaning in closer, he whispered, "You are most definitely going to die, Gregory, and, I'm sorry, but it's going to be quite painful, too."

Hopelessness spread across the man's face as the realization that his captor was deadly serious sank in. Wright's bladder let go again then his bowels. "Please, please, don't kill me," he cried. Tears rolled down his cheeks and his nose ran.

The King backed away. He looked skyward and asked, "Can no one around here die with dignity?"

"I don't deserve this," said Wright, spraying the King with spittle. "I helped you; you can't do this to me."

Anger flashed in the King's eyes. "Shut up," he shouted and smacked his captive across the face. "I don't want to hear any more of this pleading and begging. It's so undignified." He concentrated on Wright's face for a moment, watching the man's eyes as they rapidly moved about. "I never noticed that before. You have nystagmus. I always thought you were just nervous and paranoid. Fascinating." He sounded almost friendly.

Wright picked up on the friendly tone in the King's voice and pleaded again, "Please let me go. I won't say anything."

The King whispered into Wright's ear, "Sorry, Gregory. You

mistake natural curiosity for compassion. In this business, you can't afford to be compassionate. Now shut up." With that, he shoved Wright against the silver spike. Wright's mouth opened wide in surprise at the sudden pain of the metal piercing his flesh and lung. When he tried to scream, the King grasped the protruding tongue, sliced it off with a knife he had pulled from his belt, slashing Wright's lips at the same time. He threw the lump of meat over his back. Smiling, he said, "Now I can expound in peace."

Gasping, Wright tried to scream again but the only sound to escape his shredded lips was a series of grunts. His head drooped forward and blood poured from his wounded mouth, soaking the front of his suit. He sobbed and yanked at his chains, tried to wriggle free of the spike but it held him fast. When the King tapped him on the shoulder, Wright tried to look away but couldn't resist and gazed into the man's grinning face.

"Paying attention now? Good. Welcome to my nidus. You might think of it as my den, my sanctuary, my nest. It's truly a shrine. To me. To my power. To my destiny. Not to be narcissistic, but I am going to rule the world. Again. You're going to help in your own small and bloody way, as have our friends here." He waved his hand around the cave indicating the bodies propped up along the walls, held against outcroppings of rock by a web of tree roots. Most were extremely decayed with only a few leathery flaps of skin and hair and cartilage still attached to the bones. Two had fallen free of their bonds and were piles of bones on the cave floor. The two directly in front of Wright were quite fresh, covered with masses of writhing maggots. "Allow me to introduce the newest members of our little family." He walked over to the fresh corpses and indicated one that was clad in overalls. It was the only body that showed any evidence of having been clothed. "This is Billy Lush. You may have been familiar with him. Morgue attendant, scumbag, pedophile, necrophiliac. And this," he said pointing to the rotting corpse next to Billy, "is the infamous Gavin O'Leary." He scratched his nose. "Does the smell offend you? It does me. That's why the balsam branches are all over the floor. Nature's own air freshener." He clapped his hands.

Wright found some strength and tugged mightily at the shackles that were binding him but the spike in his back still held him in place. There was a loud crack and a grunt of pain escaped from his bloody lips. He stopped struggling and his head slumped down. The spike forced him to remain standing though it was evident his legs could barely hold the weight of his body. The King approached him, curious about what had broken.

"My, oh my, dear Gregory. You've snapped one of your wrists. I congratulate you on your efforts. Who'd have thought there would be that much strength in that negligible little body of yours?" He gently stroked the man's injured wrist as if trying to ease the pain. "Dear boy, please don't try to make this any more painful than it already is." He returned to the wall of corpses. "Now here," he continued, patting a body that was little more than bones and cartilage, "is our first lady, if you can call her that. I seem to recall she was the fourth or fifth sacrifice." A large flap of skin with a barely legible tattoo of the name Darla hung from one shoulder. "A fine specimen she was. Fought like an Amazon. Had a mouth you would not believe; could have put a trucker to shame—Ravenscroft rather reminds me of her, though she's somehow less coarse. There was something compelling about her. I have to admit, I sacrificed her while I was inside her." He looked up at the roof of the cave, thinking. "Yes, that *was* the last time I ever did it." He went to a section of the cave wall where a low ledge jutted out and sat. Gesturing towards the other bodies arrayed along the wall, he said, "The rest are less memorable. All gathered and sacrificed as part of the ritual to restore all my powers. They've been allowed to wither away over the millennia. My predecessors didn't try very hard when the enemy began to gather followers and gain strength. Idiots and their namby-pamby 'let's all get along' ways." He wagged a finger at Wright who was no longer paying him any attention. "You don't retain power by being nice. You know what I mean?"

The King stood and paced around the cave. "I mean, look at the work I've done here. Twelve years of sacrifices, regular as clockwork. Hang them naked from the holy tree then gut them in the Shrine. It all adds to the powers that reside here." He indicated the cave. "Something to do with a confluence of ley lines, I understand. Don't ask me to explain." He shook his head sadly. "I just wish you lot hadn't started the whole blood sacrifice thing. Now, it's the only way these rituals work."

He stopped speaking to adjust some bones on one of the hanging skeletons. An arm had fallen to the cave floor. The King picked it up and tried to reattach it to the rest of the body. When he could see no way to accomplish this, he impatiently thrust the humerus through the ribcage. The hand dangled from some cartilage and seemed to be waving goodbye while the King walked away.

"And now the enemy has come here. How he found me, I don't know, but he does have acolytes everywhere. Millions of them. Ridiculous people who preach the superiority of man and their so-called god. As if man is superior to anything. Such a misuse of the gifts that were given." He quickly stepped over to Wright who had drifted into unconsciousness and lifted the man's face. A moan escaped his lips and some more blood spurted but he didn't acknowledge the presence of the King. "Your kind is just part of the plan. Nothing special. Not better than any of the other animals." He let Wright's head fall with a thump against his chest. "And he has the gall to call himself the Spirit of Humanity. He's corrupt. And he's corrupted the earth for far too long. That's about to change.

"And don't get me started on that poser up above us. Thinks he can waltz into my domain and murder me just because fate wills it. Bah. He doesn't stand a chance. You know why? Because I'm stronger. I'm the strongest King there is, was, ever will be. And no one or thing, poser or so-called Spirit of Humanity, can hurt me. Hah."

The King paused, staring down at his feet, breathing hard. After a minute, he raised his head and looked at his captive. Nodding, he went to stand in front of the bound man. "It's time," he said quietly. "This time, the sacrifice is directed right at the usurper above. I'm going to break him. Destroy him. Give him no reason to live." He picked up an oak branch lying next to the stake and waved it while he paced around the perimeter of the cave, chanting all the way. When he was in front of his sacrifice again, he dropped the branch and held the knife up high.

Wright was conscious again, sobbing, twisting his head from side to side as if that would deny what was coming. The King smiled warmly and said, "It'll all be over soon. Just remember, you're part of something wonderful. The rekindling of the earth."

Using the knife, he cut away Wright's clothes, surprised to find a bra and lace panties. "Goodness, you are a strange one, Gregory. And a real damsel in distress. No wonder you didn't laugh at my joke." When the man was naked, the King placed the knife against Wright's lower torso, just above where his pubic hair would have ended if it hadn't been shaved off. He slowly pushed the blade in. Wright grunted, tried to back away from the blade but that only forced his body further onto the silver spike. Appalled at the anguish on Wright's face, the King ripped the knife upwards as quickly as he could until it met resistance at the ribcage. Expending more effort, he sawed the knife through the ribs until the blade reached the bottom of Wright's throat then tossed it away. He reached inside the gash with both hands and pulled hard, ripping Wright's abdomen apart with a loud wet crack. Viscera landed with a splash all over the King's shoes. He jumped away.

"Oh, by all that's natural. Why? Why does that always happen to me?" He stomped around the cave; a loop of intestine caught on a bootlace flopped behind him leaving a red trail. "I'm supposed to get naked before I do this." He turned to face his gutted captive. "It's your fault," he shouted. "You distracted me by making me think of my nemesis." He lunged back at the bleeding mess hanging from the tree and lashed out, punching the torn torso, slapping the head. Then he took the head in his hands and wrenched it from the body, launched it at the cave wall where it ricocheted with a dull thud and bounced off one of the skeletons, shattering it and sending bones sliding to the floor behind its root bindings. The King yanked the arms and tore them from the shackles, leaving the bloody stumps of hands behind. He threw the body to the floor and stomped on it until it was flat. Covered from head to foot in blood and gore, the King stopped raging, his anger spent. Surveying the carnage, shocked by what he had done, he quietly said, "What have I become?" and stumbled over to the stone ledge where he sat down. He rubbed the palms of his hands on the cave wall in an attempt to clean off the blood. "What have you done to me?"

The King sat silently for a while, his head hanging down. "How much longer? When is this going to end?" He looked up at the ceiling of the cave, tried to see through the rock and earth into the house far above. "And you're not helping, you know."

Wright's head stared blankly at him from where it rested on a pile of bones and balsam branches. Feeling better, the King said, "Bender might resist, but it's all for naught. In a nanosecond, that buffoon will be a quivering mass begging to be put down. And I'll be the one to do it. You watch, see if I'm right, Wright. Hah."

Tom Bender

Tom read the note from Professor Ravenscroft again, though by now he had it memorized.

> *Mr. Bender:*
>
> *I teach botany at Tyndale College and am very interested in the incredible growth that is occurring around your home. Would it be at all possible for me to investigate more thoroughly? Please. I assure you, I will not be a pest or cause any harm to your fantastic garden. If you would be willing to allow me access, please contact me at the number below. And do you have a chestnut tree?*
>
> *Thank you.*
> *Professor C. Ravenscroft*

The professor had left it wedged in his front door sometime last Saturday while he worked on code. As usual the loud music playing through his headphones made him oblivious to the world. *Damn.*

He'd tried calling the college last Saturday afternoon on the off chance the professor might be there, but when he had only reached an answering machine, he was surprised to hear a woman's voice. He tried to leave a message but her heavy Scottish accent threw him. Then he remembered the woman from The Pub, the one who had shown up Deputy Schofield. *What are the odds of there being two Scottish women in town?* Excited by the chance that the two women were the same person, he tried to leave a message but every time he did, he sounded over-eager or just plain creepy.

Trying the Botany department office, he got another answering machine. Damned things with their silly messages or never-ending jokes or jingles should be outlawed. Never-ending options that never take you to a real person, only to frustration, should be a crime punishable by death. And whose idea was it anyway to play music when you got put on hold? Don't these people realize that no matter what music you choose, but especially if it's country, you're going to offend the person at the other end? Or was that the idea in the first place? Piss them off with music so they'll hang up and stop bothering you. Especially when you're trying to get hold of a beautiful woman. *I hope. Was that her I bumped into a Knudson's the other day?*

Tom gave up. *I should have waited until Monday. Now I've shot my wad on phone nerve.* He felt embarrassed now. There's no way the professor would even think about getting back to him after his fumbling.

He put the note down and had a sip of Guinness, his first in a long time. The local store had run out of the heavenly brew for a few weeks and he'd been too lazy, or not desperate enough, to drive into the city for a new supply. "I need a break," he said to his computer, got up from his chair, and carried his drink into the living room. There, he sat in one of the recliners and stared out the window. Things were growing out of control but he tried not to think about it too much. He'd weeded as best he could, a long and arduous task given the incredible growth happening in back. The compost bins were overflowing already. And the weeds just seemed to grow back faster, bigger, and more robust than ever.

Now if the professor would just call back, *as if*, she could give him a rational explanation for what's going on. *Because I surely need some rationality in my life.*

"And let's not forget Spanky. Fine friend he turned out to be. Here I am living the quiet life only pissing off a few people like Silva, and along comes Spanky with a bombshell. So I own most of the county." *I'm talking to myself out loud again. At least no one's here to hear me.* "Holy fucking shit," he muttered. "What next?" He drained the can and got up to get a refill in the kitchen. "Restless," he said to no one.

As he leaned over to drop the can in the recycling bin under the sink, a memory rushed to the front of his mind sending him reeling with dizziness. He sank to his knees, tried to reach out for the counter, missed it, and slipped to the floor on all fours. Shaking his head, Tom tried to stand, felt the dizziness sweep over him again, and sat back down against a cabinet.

What he remembered was how it had been when he had returned from that last business trip to Atlanta. It was the height of summer and he'd been away for a month, an unusually long time, but the client had been paying and the money was obscenely good. The writing hadn't taken off yet. He and Belinda had last spoken five days ago, so when she hadn't answered the phone for two days, he figured she must be a little miffed with him for being gone so long. But it couldn't be helped—the business depended on it and she had agreed to it. As he drove up to the house, he could see Belinda sitting at the living room window, staring out at the turnaround. Tom put the car in the garage, shut the door, and went to open the door that led from the garage to the kitchen. When he turned the knob, he found the door was locked, not an unusual thing, but why hadn't Belinda unlocked it for him when she saw the car arrive? He knocked on the door and waited but she didn't come. He knocked again thinking that she must have gone to the bathroom. He knocked a third time but she still didn't respond. Frustrated and in need of the bathroom, Tom dropped the groceries, threw up the garage door so hard it bounced back on its track and crashed shut almost taking off his head as he ducked under it. He stormed around to the front. That door was locked, too, and Tom had forgotten his house key when he left a month ago.

    He pounded on the front door and waited, jumping around a bit because the need was getting worse. Still no answer. He stepped back into the front yard and, sure enough, there was Belinda still at the window. Furious now, he leapt up and slapped the palm of his hand on the window pane. Belinda was startled and gave him a nasty look. *Don't you fucking be mad at me, bitch.* He immediately regretted thinking it. Pee need makes you think and do the damndest things. She got up and went to the door. As soon as it opened, Tom rushed in, yanked off his shoes, no knots for once, and decided to skip his ritual.

    As much as Tom usually needed to use the bathroom when he got home from anywhere, he preferred to be completely ready first. Belinda was used to this and always liked to make fun of him as he hurried to remove his shoes, put away whatever groceries he had brought home, empty his pockets, and remove the remainder of his clothes, either folding them neatly and putting them away, or bunching them up and tossing them in the laundry basket. Find something to read or a crossword puzzle if he expected to be sitting for a while. All the time jumping around, desperate to go. Finally, ready to burst, he would rush into the bathroom, often to find Belinda sitting on the throne with a big gotcha smile on her face.

Today was different. Belinda just stood by the door silently. Tom leaned in to kiss her but she backed away. Already annoyed, his mind swimming, Tom made a face, *suit yourself,* and ran up the stairs. The groceries in the garage could wait; today's emergency was too great. In the bathroom, Tom only tore off his socks, threw them at the laundry basket then stood at the toilet. Relief flowed through him, out of him.

When he was finished, Tom wasn't surprised to see Belinda standing at the bathroom door staring at him. What was unexpected was that her cheeks were wet with tears.

Tom hated to see Belinda cry, it broke his heart. At the sink, while he quickly washed his hands, he felt the last drop leak out. *Damn it, why now?* Feeling uncomfortable with the small spot of wetness down below, he went to Belinda, put his arms around her and pulled her in close. "What's the matter?" he whispered into her ear. Her hair was matted and smelled funny, as if she hadn't washed it for several days. She was careful about her hair, washed it almost every day. And there seemed to be a slight body odor and her clothes felt clammy.

Belinda cried into Tom's shoulder for a few minutes. When she stopped, Tom led her into the bedroom where he sat her down on the bed. He sat next to her, feeling a little uncomfortable having just spent half a day traveling without the opportunity to have a shower. And there was the drop. Try as he might to concentrate, thoughts of getting clean kept creeping into his head. "What happened?" he asked.

Belinda wiped tears from her eyes and softly said, "I lost the baby, Tom."

Tom couldn't believe what he was hearing. "What baby? Since when were you pregnant?"

She pushed away from him a little and looked at his face. "My period was late before you left, you remember." Tom didn't. Since going off birth control pills, Belinda's periods had become almost random. "While you were away, I saw the doctor and was tested. It was positive. We were going to have a baby."

Tom's face flushed and he began to feel hot, the onset of severe guilt and shame. They had spoken many times about Belinda going off the pill, more for safety's sake than any desire to have children. Neither had wanted children when they got married, him because he had a weak stomach for things like spitting up and diapers and just didn't like babies, and Belinda because of her abusive mother.

"Are you sure?" he asked. "The test couldn't have been wrong? What did the doctor say?" Tom's mind was full of questions, like did the condom break, and one in particular that he didn't want to ask: Is this why you never wanted me to get a vasectomy?

Belinda shook her head. "He confirmed it. Oh, Tom, it was wonderful. I was going to be a mother. I was going to be the best mom you ever saw, make up for what that bitch did to me." Her face brightened a little. "I wanted to call you at the hotel in Atlanta, but I decided to wait and surprise you when you got home." Tom waited for more. "Four days ago, while I was on the toilet, the baby came out." She started crying again.

Tom drew her closer and hugged her, stroked her stiff hair. "You should have called me. I would have come home."

"But you didn't," she said. "I had to wait four days for you to come back. You never even called."

"I did call, you didn't answer. I left messages, sent emails. Did you check the email? I must have sent a dozen to you."

She ignored what he was saying. "I needed you here, Tom. Why weren't you here?" She punched him hard in the chest.

"I didn't know." He hoped it didn't sound as lame to Belinda as it did to him. "Are you absolutely sure you were pregnant? Could it have been something else?"

Belinda pushed him away and stood. She walked to the bedroom door, shaking. Turning to face him, she said, "What do you know about it? You're a man. How could you possibly know what my body was doing?"

Tom got up and went to her, his mind a mass of confusion. He felt self-conscious about being dirty, not that anyone but him could tell. Also, he hadn't seen Belinda for a month and couldn't help feeling just the tiniest bit horny. He tried to suppress the feelings, knowing this was the worst possible time to try and get Belinda to have sex. "I'm sorry, sweetheart. I guess I was trying to be too logical about it. I don't know anything about women and their bodies." He reached for her but she didn't move.

For the next few minutes they stood silently in the bedroom. Tom had trouble focusing. He felt devastated for Belinda and the loss she must feel, yet a small, selfish part of him was relieved. He absolutely did not want children, had grown accustomed to a childfree lifestyle, and couldn't imagine having another person in their house. It was hard enough when people came to visit for a week or two. Of course, if she had been pregnant, he would have been overjoyed. He hoped. He simply didn't know. Every thought he had contributed another brick of guilt to burden him. He knew he had to be careful with what he said to his wife at this sensitive time. Belinda was going through her own emotional battle. She looked from side to side, mumbled to herself, and nodded several times. Tom was about to say something when she spoke.

"We can try again," she said. She took Tom by the arm and led him to the bed, started to unzip his fly. "Right now," she continued as she pulled off her sweater. She wasn't wearing anything underneath it. Tom was knocked back by the smell that came from Belinda's semi-naked body. He could see dirt and grime in the wrinkles at her armpits. She must not have bathed since the miscarriage.

"Can you? So soon after, you know," asked Tom, all thoughts of sex having been chased from his mind by guilt and bad smells. "Maybe we should wait."

Belinda stopped undressing and thought for a moment. "You don't want me?" she asked. This was the last thing he expected to hear. "I'm not good enough for you now? Am I damaged goods? Am I dirty?"

Before Tom could stop himself, he said, "Well, you are a bit ripe. When was the last time you had a shower and washed your hair?" He wanted to slap himself but she did it for him.

Her face was red with rage. "You son of a bitch. I've just been through Hell and you're more concerned about personal hygiene?" She grabbed her sweater and quickly pulled it on then ran from the room. Tom followed but Belinda went into the bathroom and locked the door.

"Come on, honey, let's talk about this." There was only silence from the other side of the door. Tom waited. After ten minutes, he returned to the bedroom to get some clean clothes and went to the bathroom in the basement to use the shower stall.

Things could only get worse.

They never had sex again.

Sitting in the kitchen now, Tom asked, "What the fuck brought that up after all this time?" He tried to stand but suddenly felt terribly weak, not just in his body but also his mind. It wasn't that he couldn't get up; he couldn't face the idea of getting up. "What's going on?"

And then it hit him.

Loneliness.

Utter unbearable loneliness.

The dam burst and memories of abandonment flooded in. He felt his throat constrict and his eyes started to burn. "No," he tried to resist. "Why?" A tear trickled down his cheek.

He'd never been able to maintain long-term relationships. His family had moved many times when he was growing up, always far enough away that he never saw his friends again. He never forgot them but he never tried to contact them either. For most of his early years, he had been the perpetual new kid at school, never accepted as part of the group, not that he cared that much about the group, always cut off. It didn't help that he was smart, always in the top five in the class; this just made him more hated by the dumb ones in the in-crowd who always seemed to be bigger than him and more aggressive.

High school had been Hell, hanging out with the few other guys who were shunned, who didn't play sports, or an instrument, who liked books and movies, who had acne and didn't have the nerve to ask out girls. And when they did ask out a girl, the answer was usually a guffaw, sometimes with actual honest to god spit in the eye, or a look of such unbelievable disgust. And yes, he'd had a few fantasies about machine guns and grenades in the gym, the site of some of his worst humiliations. Winning the essay contest and receiving the award on stage in front of the whole student body had been the ultimate; the only academic award amongst all the jocks. He could still hear the laughter and jeers.

Never asked to dance, or chosen for a team, or invited to parties, he had existed in his youth as an outsider looking in on a world that refused to welcome him.

There had been a few girlfriends later, disasters all, never lasting more than a couple of weeks. All allowed to fade away, no breakups, no sorrowful goodbyes, just apathy. But he never had the guts to approach the ladies, much less sleep with them. He always came home to nothing.

Tom had always dreamed of meeting his soul mate, had fantasized so much that he was sure she was a real person, out there somewhere waiting for him to sweep her off her feet. The ideal of her helped him get through high school, at home, the world drowned out by the loud music in his headphones, living in a place where he mattered, where he didn't avoid attending the prom for fear of being humiliated, where he was a hero, loved and wanted by all the girls. His older cousin introduced him to the rock music of the sixties and seventies and though he loved the heavy stuff, he always drifted towards the slower, romantic tunes of Free, Led Zeppelin, Rod Stewart, and the Beatles, thinking about the girl he knew must be out there somewhere. He'd written about her, escaping into stories, the genesis of his current career; she even became the main character in many of his stories, and in two of the novels he had written in the last few years.

And then there was Belinda: the prettiest girl at college, exotic and tempting with her long black hair and tight clothes. He'd made a point of hanging around outside the classrooms he knew she'd be entering just to get a look at her, see how short her skirt was today. They'd finally met in the cafeteria when she'd dropped an open carton of chocolate milk in his lap as she'd passed. Three months later, they were married. Belinda's family had objected. Her father had taken Tom aside to explain that Belinda had problems but he would never be specific, so Tom ignored him. He was a good man, Belinda's father, just not forthcoming. Her mother had committed suicide years before Tom came on the scene and Belinda never talked about the woman. Tom's own family had missed the wedding because a vacation in Hawaii couldn't be cancelled, adding to his feeling of alienation.

The first years of their marriage had been wonderful, fun and full of adventure. Totally in love, accepting each other for the incredible people they were. No secrets. No guilt. They lived together in a tiny apartment while both finished college. Tom freelanced for the local paper and Belinda tutored for some of the rich kids in her old neighborhood. They got by. After college, Tom discovered computers, took to them like a fish to water, and lucked into a high-paying high-tech job. Still, the volatility of the high-tech workplace and the constant job changes did little to stabilize his life.

Then Belinda's mother's will had finally been sorted out and they came into enough cash to buy the house in Tyndale.

Four years later, Belinda was gone.

Since that time, he had lived in the house alone, virtually a hermit. Friends came by occasionally, and for a while he went to The Pub regularly, but for the most part, he maintained a solitary existence. He had never discussed how he felt about Belinda with anyone. At the time, as good a friend as Spanky was, and as supportive as he had been for the whole length of Belinda's illness, he simply wasn't the kind of friend to whom Tom could open up. Tom had always had trouble discussing his innermost feelings with anyone, felt embarrassed or ashamed by some of the things he thought, the burden of guilt he carried. Then Belinda had come into his life and he'd been able to unburden his soul, shake off the guilt he had felt through high school and college about abandoned friends and dumped girlfriends who were as messed up as him.

Eight years later and here he was, sitting on his kitchen floor, overwhelmed by the realization that his life was one long smelly piece of shit.

To this day, he could feel isolated in a crowd. Sometimes, at The Pub, he felt like an intruder. He hadn't been born and raised in Tyndale like Spanky, Jay, and Terry, wasn't part of the town. He was grudgingly accepted, tolerated because it amused the others. They were being kind to poor pathetic Tom.

His shirt was saturated with tears that freely dripped from his cheeks. He was wracked with deep, earth-shattering sobs, had cried out loud in a way he hadn't since an accident when he was six. Resting his head on his knees, he let despair take him away, gave up resisting the loneliness and the guilt. Everything bad was his fault and his alone. Not his parents. Not Belinda.

Him.

It all came down to him.

Everyone would be so much better off if he simply left, removed himself from their lives.

But how?

Did he get rid of all of Belinda's medication? Was there any morphine? No, too much risk of hurling everything up and becoming a vegetable in hospital sucking food from a tube.

Slashing the wrists? Too painful and messy. How could anyone do that?

Hanging? Undignified and painful and it would probably take too long.

Jumping off something high? It would be interesting to watch the ground rush closer. Forget it.

I don't own a gun. Damn.

The car? Run the car in the garage and let the exhaust quietly take him away. No pain, no worries.

"That's it," he said and climbed to his feet. Resolved to end his problems, Tom suddenly felt strong again.

A noise at the back door distracted him.

Two crows tapped at the glass. He walked over. The crows stepped away from the door and flew up to the deck rail where nine other crows waited. The birds stood in a line, never taking their eyes from Tom. He slowly slid the door open and stepped outside.

The birds didn't move.

He looked out at the garden. There were birds on every branch of every tree and all over the ground: the albino sparrows, finches, doves, house martins. Even the hummingbirds were still. Sitting on the top of the fence were squirrels and chipmunks. And he had never seen as many mice as he could see staring at him from the compost bins.

All were watching him, silent. He went down the deck steps, and to the gravel path. Rank upon rank of insects covered the path: centipedes, crickets, beetles, flies, ants, and so many spiders Tom's skin crawled. Frogs and toads stood at the edge of the grass.

Still, every creature remained motionless. On the deck rail by the path, twelve crows stood, their eyes fixed on him. He raised a hand, expecting the birds to fly off in a panic. They didn't.

Ever so slowly, he inched towards the birds, his hand still out.

The closest crow, a little larger than the rest, black as night, stepped towards Tom and rested its beak in the palm of his hand. He brought his other hand up and stroked the bird's head, saying, "Hello, you. Nice to meet you." The other crows moved closer, leaning their heads in. Tom stroked each bird in turn.

He moved along the gravel path, the mass of insects moved aside for him, and walked towards the oak. None of the birds moved, even the mourning doves, the most amusingly skittish birds he had ever seen.

"Well," he said, "how about a tune?" Instantly, the garden was filled with birdsong. Though all the birds sang different melodies, they blended to create the sweetest sound Tom had ever heard. The chattering rodents provided a nice backbeat, and the frogs and toads threw in the bass. Crickets and cicadas were the horn section. He smiled and his heart seemed to swell. A robin leapt from a low branch on the oak and landed on his shoulder. It nuzzled his neck, made him laugh as its feathers tickled his skin.

Tom felt something. He couldn't quite put his finger on it, but it made him feel good, made all thoughts of harming himself dissipate. Unable to resist, he started to giggle then laugh. He walked to the arbor at the back fence and sat on the bench there. The birds never stopped their singing, never took their eyes from him.

Smiling, Tom enjoyed the show, understanding dawning. The feeling, deep down, long forgotten.

Belonging.

His tears were of joy, now.

CHAPTER ELEVEN
THE BEDS

Tom Bender

Tom crawled out from under a rose bush then picked some thorns from his shirt sleeve. It was always fun crawling into the middle of a rose bush to prune dead growth at the center. But this year, it was different. Everything looked healthy and was heavy with blooms. There were no dead branches from last year to prune.

At least there weren't any of those honking great brown spiders hanging about right now. And they refused to stay in one place in the garden; their webs were usually everywhere: in the trees, in bushes, on the deck railings, under the eavestrough, next to the front door. Always lurking, waiting to bite off a limb or two. *Bastards.* Spiders usually didn't bother him much as long as they stayed far enough away, but these brutes were huge and extra ugly with their fat spotted bodies and long legs. It was as if a new species took over the garden every couple of years. First had been the hairy wolf spiders with the brown racing stripes on their backs. They had blended in with the old carpeting on the basement floor and made for many a shiver when Tom was sorting through boxes down there. Next were spiders that looked like the wolf spiders but were smooth-bodied and didn't have the stripes. Then there were the silver-green garden spiders with their long black legs—he actually touched one of them, a feat of unbelievable bravery. And now the fat brown orb-spinning bastards had arrived. He shivered at the thought. It had taken Tom a lot of years to overcome his fear of spiders; he no longer ran like some little girl whenever one of the eight-legged nasties crossed his path, but they still weren't his favorite thing in the garden. He unconsciously rubbed the inside of his left leg where a crescent scar covered a small hollow spot caused by a Daddy Longlegs that had attacked him in the garden when he was six. The thing had been lurking on a wall in the garden shed, waiting for unsuspecting boys to get within reach of its evil jaws. Running away in fright carrying a broken rake handle that played the part of a rifle in his games was bad enough. Tossing the handle away then landing on it as it bounced off the concrete walk was worse. The hole in his leg had been an inch across and about an inch deep, with chunks of fat hanging out, and had hardly hurt or bled until he went running for help. Even today, Tom's buttocks clenched at the memory of how close the wood had come to penetrating higher up his leg, or maybe his genitals, or perhaps worse. *Could there be anything worse than punctured genitals?* Tom smacked the side of his head to stop thinking about it. Damned spiders. He took a sip of water from the bottle that he always kept at his side when gardening. The water was still cold enough even though it had been hours since the ice in it had melted.

    Only a week had passed since Tom called Terry to speak with him about Deputy Schofield's harassment. When Tom called the

Sheriff's office that morning, the dispatcher, Deputy Nye, said Terry was out of town on official business. Tom figured his friend was away consulting with other law enforcement authorities about the murder and disappearances though why they couldn't come to Tyndale was a mystery. He had no reason to distrust Terry or question his handling of the investigation but he still bristled when he remembered how he had been interrogated after the murder. Terry had been a little standoffish the last time he saw him, but Tom attributed that to pressure from the County Council to solve Gavin's murder and find the missing men. So far as Tom knew, there were no clues and no suspects, in spite of what Deputy Dawg believed. The deputy had dutifully appeared almost daily—whenever Tom happened to notice, the headphones cut him off from a lot—driving up Hill Road slowly then pausing for anywhere from a few minutes to an hour in the turnaround. Tom was amazed that the man hadn't replaced the muffler on the police cruiser. At least that way, he would have some chance of surprising Tom at whatever nefarious activity he was suspected of being engaged upon. At first Tom had gone to the front door and used his binoculars to stare out at Schofield, playing a waiting game until the deputy was intimidated enough to leave. After a few days, Tom decided to ignore his regular visitor altogether. He did, however, play one nasty trick on the deputy. Tom spread glass from some broken mason jars along the side of the turnaround where he knew his sentinel liked to park and watch. He had the satisfaction of watching Deputy Dawg sitting frustrated as he waited for a tow after two of the cruiser's tires punctured. It may have been petty revenge, but it felt good to Tom. For a short while. Until the guilt set in like a familiar itch. Oddly, he felt most guilty about the cruiser. Tom had a bad habit of apologizing to inanimate objects when he bumped into them or they suffered because of his actions. It must be the Canadian in him.

In the weeks since he had discovered the lush growth in his gardens, Tom's ideas about plants and gardening had not only been turned upside down, they were doing somersaults. He wondered why Professor Ravenscroft hadn't returned his calls. Perhaps whatever was happening wasn't all that special. Perhaps it was a crank note. No, that couldn't be it. She was real, had a voice. A rather interesting voice now that you mention it. What would she make of the birds? They still watched him from the trees, seemed to follow him wherever he went. The crows were the strangest. He read that they were supposed to be intelligent, but that still didn't explain their current behavior. Whenever he went in a building, a group of crows, most often nine but sometimes four or eleven, would perch on the roof and look around. They resembled a criminal's henchmen, standing guard while their boss conducted his business, always looking in every direction, checking for danger. Weird as it was, Tom felt somehow more secure and safer. He had his own personal muscle. Maybe he should sic them on Schofield, have the birds peck his kneecaps and warn him off. No, that felt wrong; a gross misuse of power.

At first, he had prepared the yard for planting by weeding in May. With each passing year, it seemed he could start sooner. Last year the ground had been workable at the beginning of March. This year he hadn't paid attention to the garden to notice when it was ready—too much computer work with Spanky.

The front yard had not needed as much work as the back because it was all perennials and bulbs. The weeds had been a pain, but only for a short while. Tom hadn't even considered doing anything about the dandelions that were running amok out front. The wide swath of yellow looked beautiful against the dull backdrop of the suburbs and city. Tom found weeding relaxing. Crawling around the yards on his hands and knees, getting his fingers into the soil to get roots, filling his large bucket with weeds for the compost bin, were sometimes hard work, but he was able to think. He often had inspirations when he was stuck on a database problem, and the plots to two of his novels had had breakthroughs while he was pulling out dandelions. It had taken Tom two days to clear both the front and back yards of weeds. Weeds. Where were they now? He had fully expected to have to weed again within a week. No matter how careful he was, and he was careful, he always missed either some small plant hidden under another plant or one too small to bother with. However, it had been weeks since he had last pulled a weed and the yards were still free of unwanted growth. The vegetables and flowers were doing gangbusters, but there wasn't a weed in sight. It was as if the garden knew exactly what Tom wanted to grow and, based on what he had pulled and dumped in the compost bin, refused to let anything else come up. Uncanny.

Today, as it had been for months, the backyard felt like a greenhouse. The heat was consistent—always about eighty-five degrees with little or no variation day to day. Even at night the temperature rarely dropped below eighty. The heavy heat, the nineties and hundreds, usually didn't hit until August. Tom was sweating profusely even though he had done little yard work, his shirt was soaked, and the front of his jeans looked like he had wet himself. Tom was about to pick up his unnecessary pruning tools when he heard a sound like a sharp intake of breath from somewhere near the house on the other side of the yard. He looked up from the rose bush to see the startled face of Terry through the lattice atop the garden gate.

Terry quickly held up a box from Knudsen's Bakery, probably something baked fresh that morning. Tom's mouth watered, he'd forgotten to eat again. He crossed the yard and unlatched the gate. Terry came into the yard without a word, gave Tom the once over then pointed up to the back door and, when Tom had nodded okay, walked up the deck and into the house. He was astounded at how his friend's appearance had changed since he last saw him. There were bags under his eyes and his face was ashen, his hair a little greasy where it stuck out from under his hat; and the uniform didn't sit as well on his body. He'd lost a Hell of a lot of weight. That can't be good even if he had needed to lose a few pounds. *And you smell bad, too.*

Being Sheriff, Terry took pride in appearing fresh and crisp at all times to give the impression that he was in charge and on the ball. Now, he seemed a little sloppy. There were sweat stains at the armpits of his shirt and his trousers needed ironing. His boots, usually polished to a mirror shine, were scuffed and muddy. *Must be the pressure from Gavin's murder and Billy's disappearance.* And now Councilor Wright was missing, too.

Guilt tried to take its usual place at the forefront of his mind, but he pushed it aside easily. He had nothing to feel guilty about, not even Belinda. Amazing how it could be flushed out with simple birdsong—a sort of mental enema, a high colonic of the mind. "Eeyuk," he said. He felt gratitude and astonishment that Terry had taken the time to come and talk to him about something as minor as Schofield hanging around while there was a real crime wave happening out there.

Tom went into the garage to clean the dirt off his hands and clothes, anticipating the tea and goodies waiting for him in the kitchen. Terry knew where everything was and usually had a pot on the boil before Tom could stop him. Terry was a drinkaholic—

KING OF THE WOOD

he put away large quantities of anything in sight, tea, coffee, bourbon, beer, soda. It seemed harmless enough, except maybe for the booze, but it did make it difficult for Terry to be on patrol for long. Stakeouts were a bitch; Terry refused to use the milk carton method favored by many cops. Not that there was ever much need for stakeouts in Tyndale. He did know the location of every bathroom in town, but he claimed it was undignified for the Sheriff to be in the bathroom constantly. Fortunately, Terry had Deputy Schofield to do most of the patrol work.

This brought Tom back to the reason for the Sheriff's visit. And pastries might not be enough to make Tom nicer about it. He felt a momentary twinge of guilt, but a wild canary swooped by cheeping and took the guilt with it. Terry meant well and Tom didn't want to belittle him for an act of kindness. Tom had plenty of experience at being rebuffed for trying to make a kind gesture. *Thanks, Belinda.* He'd have to walk a fine line between demanding that Schofield be told to back off and understanding the pressure on Terry to deal with all the shit that had been coming down for the last month.

When Tom got inside the house, he found Terry sitting at the kitchen table eating an éclair oozing with crème and chocolate and sipping a mug of steaming tea. There was no coffee at the house because it did strange things to his insides if he drank too much of it. He enjoyed the occasional coffee after a meal at a restaurant, but that was about it.

"That was a quick out of town visit," said Tom.

Terry looked puzzled for a second then said, "I saved you some," holding the bakery box up to Tom. "Gastronomic delights. Eat enough of these and I'll be obese before I know it."

"That'll be the day. Have you lost weight?"

"Not that I know of."

Tom took the box. "Generous of you," he said. "I figured whatever they were you would have scarfed them all down by now." He reached in the box and stuck his finger through an éclair. "Oops." He placed the éclair on a plate, licked his finger clean then washed it off at the sink. "I always do that. Why can't I reach into a box of éclairs and not stick my finger through one?"

"It's something to do with genetics obviously. Guys obsess about packing as much stuff as possible into a small space," said Terry. He took another éclair from the box, not stabbing his finger through it. "I've observed it with you many times. You're probably more in touch with your feminine side."

"You're making that up," said Tom around a mouthful of crème.

"Probably," replied Terry, "but it sounds genuine."

"Not to a woman, I don't think," said Tom. "Belinda would have torn you a new one if you had said something like that to her," he added, surprising himself with the mention of her. He was also surprised that, for the first time since he couldn't remember when, he didn't feel sad, guilty, or angry at her. *About time.*

"Ouch," said Terry. "Or she would have come up with something equally as ridiculous." He drained his tea and poured a fresh cup from the teapot on the table.

"And what's packing got to do with sticking your finger in pastries?" asked Tom.

"Pack boxes. Pack of cigarettes. A cigarette after sex. Foreplay. Sticking your finger in something soft and tasty. Éclairs. Simple."

"Right." Terry's logic was often lost on Tom but rarely ever led to sex.

"You still doing okay? Alone, I mean. With no woman."

"Thanks for the reminder," Tom said through a sigh. Terry nearly always asked this when they were alone. Despite their friendship, Tom couldn't reveal his inner feelings. Belinda had been the only one with whom he had let down his guard and look what that got him. He felt his throat constrict as he came over all lonely and empty and had to concentrate hard not to gag on his éclair. But at least it wasn't because of Belinda. He chewed slowly, more than usual for a pastry, swallowed carefully then took a sip of tea to wash it down. He could feel his eyes getting wet so he faked a cough and said, "Went down the wrong hole." Closing his eyes for a moment, he waited for the feeling to pass. *Now what? Maybe I do need a woman. That one from The Pub. Wow! That's a new one.* Tom didn't know whether to be overjoyed or horrified at the sudden realization.

Tom saw Terry smiling sadly at him, knowing full well he was being lied to. He knew Terry wouldn't press him about Belinda, but he also knew his friend wouldn't give up asking. Annoying as the questions were, Tom appreciated this concern.

Terry took another éclair out of the box, bit half of it off and placed the rest on his plate. He pushed the box back over to Tom, a sign that he had had enough cakes for now. It was up to Tom to get as many éclairs in as possible before Terry's appetite kicked in again. He was surprised to see there were still five éclairs left, Terry usually didn't bring that many; he must have had some idea about the seriousness of what Tom was going to say. He quickly ate one before Terry changed his mind.

Before Tom could speak, Terry said, "Deputy Nye told me why you called." Tom had a picture of the dispatcher flash in his mind—a small woman with a perpetual frown, he knew she didn't like Deputy Schofield and would have been sure to pass along Tom's complaint. "I spoke to Deputy Schofield and told him to back off. He protested, claiming he was conducting a legitimate investigation but the onus was on him to show me something and he couldn't offer any proof or the slightest bit of evidence showing you as a suspect."

"There couldn't be any evidence," said Tom. "My alibi is rock solid and ..."

Terry cut him off. "Actually, your alibi isn't rock solid. I checked with the airline. You did arrive when you said, but we only have your word that it took you as long as you said to get home."

Tom was shocked by what Terry was saying. Didn't he trust him?

"I drove the route you took from the airport to here," said Terry. "It took me forty-five minutes. You claim it took you almost two hours because of the bad weather and getting lost."

"I don't claim anything," said Tom slowly. "It did take me two hours and I did get lost. You know what those suburbs are like. I can't believe I was stupid enough to go in there again."

After all the trees in the greenbelt had been hacked down to make way for houses, some wag who worked for the developers thought it would be a good idea to name the new subdivisions after the trees. Hence there were now Elm Heights, Maple Vale, Birch Dale, Beech Heights, and Poplar Heights. The land was only slightly hilly, there were no real heights, but pretension won out. That wouldn't have been much of a problem, except the street names were so similar: Maple, Beech, Elm, Poplar, and Birch Lanes, Streets, Ways, Crescents, Boulevards, Roads, Closes, and Privates. The issue was they were all over the place. The Elm Heights streets weren't all Elms. As a result, because there were only about six different house styles used, and all the roads twisted and turned to follow the contours of the land, it was extremely easy to get lost. You could never remember if Elm Road met Maple Lane or Maple Boulevard, and was that in Elm Heights or Maple Dale or Vale? Tom's house on the hill acted as a landmark; most people could focus on it and just head in that general direction. The new bridge across the Nation was only a mile or so upriver from Tom's house. Many of the townspeople, Tom included, stuck with the old highway that ran far to the east of the suburbs. It took a bit longer to get to town, but no one ever got lost going that way. On the day Tom returned from his trip to Los Angeles, there had been snow squalls that had made it impossible to see ten feet ahead on the road, let alone to the house on the hill.

"I believe you, Tom," said Terry. He placed a hand on Tom's arm as if to assure him. Tom's eyes were drawn to the hand and he was appalled at what he saw: the nails were yellowed and bitten, the cuticles torn, the skin dry and cracked and peeling off at the thumb, and covered with liver spots. It looked like the hand of an old man. "It's just that the coroner said that the obscenity committed on Gavin could have been done just before you say you got home. Someone who doesn't know you as well as me, like Schofield, could figure you were lying about getting lost. Then you would have had enough time to kill Gavin and say you passed out. You see what I'm getting at?"

"Yeah." Tom got up and went to the sink to clean his plate. His appetite had vanished. "I see you're saying I am a suspect. It's been months, Terry. Why did you wait so long to say anything?" Terry said nothing. "Should you be here talking to me like this? Do I need to get a lawyer?" Tom had trouble looking at Terry. He knew the Sheriff—at this moment Tom couldn't think of Terry as his friend—was only doing his job, just as he had been when he questioned Tom the day of the murder, but it still rankled. Tom knew he was innocent, why couldn't Terry see that too?

Terry stood. "Look, Tom, don't let our friendship obscure the fact that I have an obligation to do my job. I know you didn't do it, but like I said before, the County Council is all over me on this. Odious as it seems to you, I have to cover my backside, even if it gets you annoyed."

"Annoyed barely describes how I feel, Terry," said Tom curtly. "I want Schofield to stop following me or I'll seek legal advice regarding harassment."

Terry was breathing hard and sweating as if talking was physically draining. Tom could see his friend was trying hard to rein in his temper. But who was he mad at? Tom or Deputy Schofield? "Like I told you, Tom, Schofield's been instructed to keep away from you. I expect him to obey me but I can't do anything about him when he's off duty, so maybe that's where your harassment might be. But please, don't think the department is after you. On my oath, it's just one persistent idiot. If that's not good enough, you could ask for an ombudsman to look into it."

There was pleading in Terry's eyes. Tom felt bad for giving his friend such a hard time. Terry must be under tremendous pressure to solve the crimes; his reputation was on the line. The least Tom could do was cut him some slack. He walked over to Terry and put his hand on the man's shoulder. It was uncomfortably bony, making Tom wonder if there truly was some kind of sickness there. "Buddy, I know it's not your fault. Don't ever think I blame you for this. You just take care of yourself, don't worry about me." He sat down. Terry picked up the bakery box, fished out the last éclair and sat.

"Schofield's a dork. Let's leave it at that. I know you don't need me getting on your case while you're trying to play detective," said Tom.

"Play? You think I'm playing, you fool," answered Terry with a terrible attempt at an Inspector Clouseau accent. "You be careful or I'll break out my official Dick Tracy detective's blackjack and beat a confession from you. Or maybe I'll set my minky on you."

"Minky? What's a minky?"

They both started laughing.

The tension broken, Tom leaned back in his chair. "What do you know about gardening?" he asked.

"It begins with a G?" said Terry. "There's green stuff involved, and you seem to enjoy it."

"Let me show you something," said Tom. He got up and walked to the back door. "Come outside."

Terry grabbed his hat from the counter and followed Tom out onto the deck.

"Did you notice anything odd when you arrived?" asked Tom.

"Odd as in a little bit strange, or odd as in outré?"

He stared at Terry for a second before answering, "Just odd."

"Can't say that I did," replied Terry. He looked out at the garden. "Wait a minute, something doesn't look right." He examined the garden for a few seconds then said, "I can't see what it is, but there's definitely something off here. Did you add some new beds?"

Tom said, "You don't see what's unusual about the garden?" He waited for Terry to answer. Terry remained silent, his jaw set. Tom knew he was getting impatient with all the questions so he asked, "What's the date?"

Terry thought for a moment then answered curtly, "The sixth of June. D-Day, I think. So?"

"So," said Tom pointing to the garden. "How much should the

garden have grown by now?"

Terry looked confused. "Tommy, Tommy, quite contrary, how does your garden grow? How the dickens should I know? You're the gardening expert. You tell me." He seemed irritated now.

"Even someone with a brown thumb like you should see that there shouldn't be this much already." Tom stepped down to the bottom deck then onto the gravel path. He walked to a vegetable bed. Terry followed him. Tom stooped, pulled out an onion, and held it up to Terry. "See?"

Terry said quickly, "It's an onion. It's red and round and looks tasty. Again, so? What's your point?"

"I planted it in May." When Terry shrugged, Tom continued, "I planted almost everything in May. Onions usually take at least a couple of months before they're anywhere near ready to pick. This one looks like it's been in the ground for five or six months." Tom pointed to a line of tall green plants coming up alongside the row of radishes. "See those? They're carrots. And those are parsnips. Neither should be ready until September or October. Over here," he stepped over to the next bed, "is my third load of lettuce, and Swiss chard, and spinach." Plants about ten inches high were growing in neat rows in the beds. "I planted that last week. And I've already had four crops of radishes."

Terry nodded. "So, you've got a successful garden. No big deal. You always have a successful garden. Did you plant any okra?"

"What?" Tom shook his head. "You don't understand."

"Obviously," said Terry. He had that hooded look so often seen on Schofield that said, stop fucking with me or I'll kill you right now.

Amused, Tom went on, "This shouldn't be happening. At least

KING OF THE WOOD

not yet. The greens shouldn't show for at least a month. It's only been taking a week." He spread his arms wide. "The whole garden has gone crazy. Flowers that should only just be coming up have grown, bloomed and dropped their petals. The tulips and daffodils were gone before I even noticed them. Now they're coming up again. It looks like September here. It's only June. Doesn't that strike you as odd?"

Terry looked bewildered. "I guess I just don't see what the big deal is. You've always been able to grow stuff here earlier than the rest of the town. You said you have an oasis because of all the trees and the fence and raised beds and stuff. It creates a microclimate. So, it's a little bit earlier this year."

"A microclimate doesn't account for this," said Tom.

"What are you saying? That there's some kind of magic going on here? What? Voodoo, obeah?"

Tom rolled his eyes and said, "Okay, so you're up to 'O' in the dictionary."

"Oui," replied Terry.

"Look, I don't know if there's anything supernatural going on. I doubt it. Come here." He walked to the back fence and climbed up on a park bench that sat under a trellis arch. Terry climbed up next to him. Through a space in the fence, they could see into the woods on the hill. "Look."

Terry looked. There were rampant weeds for about fifteen feet then trees. "What am I looking at," he asked. "I see trees and weeds."

Tom let out a breath. "Yes, you see trees, full of leaves. And that's all you see. Solid green. Those trees have been like that since May, I think. I didn't spot it at first so the time's a little vague. But you should still be able to see part way down the hill. You should be able to see the church steeple, and the fire tower, and the box factory. Can you see the birds?"

Terry looked again. "Holy liftin'." The trees were full of birds, all silently regarding the two men. There were sparrows and robins, blue jays and cardinals, pairs of mourning doves, wild canaries and finches, four and twenty blackbirds all in a row. From the tops of the trees, hawks looked down at them. None of the birds moved except for the albino sparrows; they appeared nervous. There were no crows. Here and there, squatting on low branches, squirrels and chipmunks also watched, unafraid of the predators above. The heads of rabbits and groundhogs popped through the weeds. And the air was alive with insects: hundreds of butterflies—all colors of the rainbow, clouds of midges, and swarms of bees and wasps and hornets, all keeping a respectful and non-threatening distance. He turned to face Tom, his face contorted with anger. Tom backed away, upset and shocked.

"What's going on, Tom?" snapped Terry as he stepped down from the bench. "That's too odd for words, those creatures. What are you up to?"

His friend's attitude confused him. Quickly, he answered, "I don't have the faintest idea. Whenever I'm working out here, the birds stand and watch. They don't seem afraid of me. Heck, the crows let me pet them and the blue jays even take peanuts from my hand. And here's another thing." He decided not to mention the way the birds took orders from him; that would have sounded too bizarre. More bizarre was how mosquitoes didn't bite and bees and wasps didn't sting; and spiders made their webs well-away from anywhere he worked. Tom sat on the bench and pointed to the flower bed next to it. "No weeds. Anything I pull, it doesn't grow back. Not even dandelions. And you know how hard they are to kill. Leave a chunk of root, and the whole thing comes back."

"And you're complaining?" asked Terry with disbelief. He was sounding more like Schofield all the time. "Sounds like a gardener's dream come true."

"Yeah," said Tom. "But it's creeping me out. And what's weirder, last month, the further away from the house you got, the less fast things were growing. When you got to the other side of Hill Road, everything was normal. It was the same out front, the rapid growth started to taper off as you got down to the road. On the other side of the road, at the edge of the cliff, everything was normal."

"You say was," said Terry, bouncing from foot to foot, obviously impatient to get away. Maybe nervous about the birds. Or in need of a pee?

"Yeah," replied Tom. "That was last month. Didn't you see, further into town, how much thicker and lush everything is. Along Hill Road, you can barely see ten feet into the woods for all the shrubs and weeds. And the grass is growing faster. Surely someone has said something. You must have noticed."

"Can't say as I have," said Terry. "Been quite occupied with the cases and all."

It started to rain. Tom and Terry looked up at the sky. There were heavy clouds overhead that seemed to be centered on the town. All around, over the city and the far away hills, the sky was a clear and brilliant blue.

"It's rained every day for months," said Tom. "Always on the hill and Tyndale, never on the city."

"Again, can't say that I've noticed," replied Terry. "It's probably what's causing the accelerated growth. Anyway, I have to get back to work." Terry walked towards the garden gate by the garage. Tom went after him.

"There's one more thing," said Tom as he stopped beneath

the oak at the spot where Gavin's body had been strung up. "Look at this." He tapped the trunk of the oak.

"Now what am I looking at besides a tree?" He huffed and stood with hands on hips waiting for Tom's answer. Now it was Tom who was impatient for Terry to leave.

Tom tapped the bark and drew his index finger around a slight bump. "This is where that silver spike was driven into the tree. The one Gavin was impaled on. You took it away with his body."

Terry looked closer at the spot Tom was indicating. "There's no sign that anything was there," he said. "Are you sure this is the same spot?"

"If there was more than one oak, I might think I was confused, but this is the only oak in the garden. It's the only one on the hill."

"I guess the spike didn't do as much damage as you thought," said Terry. He shrugged and walked away. When he got to the gate, he stopped and turned around. "Don't worry about what's happening, Tom." His voice was calmer, more like the normal Terry. "Maybe the weather's been odd for this time of year. We had the longest May heat wave I've ever experienced. That's probably what's caused everything to grow so fast. And we're having a wet spring. It's just nature playing with your head. There's nothing occult going on, no omnipotent power trying to change the world." He smiled.

Tom followed Terry through the paved courtyard at the side of the garage. He tripped on a brick that had heaved up sometime during the winter.

"You should fix that," said Terry. "Someone could sue you for negligence."

Tom looked around the courtyard. There were several more bricks heaved out of line. "Five years and none ever moved," he said. "I didn't notice these bricks before today. Why now?"

Terry said, "Get your nose out of the books and start seeing the world."

While Terry walked back to his cruiser, Tom asked, "How do you explain the birds?"

Terry stopped, thought a moment, and said, "Now, they're out to get you. You can't trust those oscine little beggars. Watch your head or you'll be covered in bird poop."

Tom laughed and said, "Yeah, like Mel Brooks in High Anxiety." Terry didn't react and walked away. "Anyway, there's a professor from the college interested in what's going on. I'm waiting to hear back from her."

Terry stopped and turned to Tom. "She got a name?" he asked brusquely.

Tom nodded, wishing he hadn't brought up the professor "Yeah. Ravenscroft. She sounds Scottish."

"What does she have to say about it all?" The tone of his voice was unpleasant, like he was interrogating a felon.

"Nothing yet, I haven't actually spoken to her, just left messages." He wanted Terry to leave, stop all the questions and the mood swings; this was none of Terry's business, he decided.

"Watch her," said Terry. "She's trouble."

Curious now, Tom asked, "In what way?"

"Woman's got a mouth on her. Had Schofield in tears, if you can believe it. Claims to have had some trouble in the swamp a while back. She's not worth your time. Trust me."

With a tip of his hat, Terry got in his cruiser and drove away.

Tom shrugged then went to pick up the pruning shears he had left next to the rose bush when Terry had arrived. When he got to the rose, he noticed that the birds were now sitting on the fence and in the trees around the perimeter of the yard. They were still and silent, as if waiting for something. Under the oak, the albino sparrows stood in a line. Tom counted them quickly and saw that there were now twenty-six. Nine crows came from over the house and landed on the deck rail not far from him. Six more flew in a couple of seconds later and perched on the trellis over the bench. He smiled, waved and asked, "Where have you been?" The crows all turned to face the courtyard. "Didn't like my visitor?" The crows abruptly faced Tom and if crows could look angry, these did. "Sorry about that," he said, then added, "It's okay, you can go now." The birds took off in a cacophony of song and disappeared over the trees on the slope. Two crows remained. "Hello, Heckle and Jeckle," said Tom and he started to laugh when they nodded to him.

"I'll never get used to that," he said to the decorative stone face of the Green Man that was staring at him from amongst the leaves and vines of clematis. The face seemed to be grinning but Tom knew that was impossible. But so was everything else that was happening.

Steve O'Leary

"Stupid cat," said Steve. He struggled to get the lip of the dolly under the oil drum. The cat arrived at the garage earlier this afternoon, mewing loudly enough to get him to leave the accounts he was working on in the office and see what all the fuss was about. There, squatting next to one of the gas pumps was a ginger cat, wet from the rain and covered in mud. His heart, hardened by the loss of his fiancé all those years ago and the subsequent misuse of any married or attached woman he could find, melted when he saw the pathetic creature shiver. When he stepped closer, the cat looked up at him, expectantly it seemed, but didn't move. It shivered again. Steve bent and picked the animal up with both hands, careful to hold it away from his clean clothes. The cat squirmed trying to turn around. Steve turned it so he could see its face and it mewed at him and tried to lick his hand. His stomach lurched at the thought of getting kitty spit on his skin but the feeling went away quickly enough when the thing started to purr.

"So, cat, where'd you come from?" he asked. It mewed in reply. "Best get you cleaned up a little, hadn't we?"

He took the cat to a sink at the back of the garage and set it down. There was no way he was going to take this filthy thing into the washroom in back of his office. He washed his hands thoroughly and put on a pair of yellow rubber gloves and an apron then put a plug in the sink and turned on the water. "Glad I got this type of faucet, eh cat. One handle and ..." The cat attempted to flee the warm water cascading on it but Steve held it down. "Don't worry, cat. I'm only going to wash the crud off you." He said this with as soothing a voice as he could muster, somewhere between pretending to admire a target's pictures of her children and reassuring said target that her husband would never find out. He stroked the cat's head with one hand while the other held its body under the water. When there was enough water in the sink, he shut off the faucet and scooped some hand soap from the jar on the shelf above the sink. The cat stopped trying to get out of the water and sat there looking dejected as if waiting for the next insult in its already miserable life. Steve lathered up the soap and worked it into the cat's fur. Still the cat didn't resist.

"Good cat," Steve cooed. "We'll have you clean in no time." When the water was a grayish brown from the sludge that had been embedded in the cat's fur, he ran the water again to rinse the little creature clean. He lifted the cat out of the sink and set it on the counter then wrapped a cleaning cloth around it. "You wait there while I clean the sink." Using powder cleanser and a scrub brush, he washed the muddy residue from the sink, shined the faucet then dried the bowl with a towel. When he was satisfied with the job, he turned his attention back to the cat, which hadn't moved while he was cleaning.

"Good cat," he said as he rubbed the beast with the towel. When it was fairly dry, he carried it, again careful to keep it away from the apron, into the office. Rummaging through a drawer in his desk, he found a comb, never used, still in its cellophane wrapper. This he used to smooth the cat's fur and remove any tangles caused by the mud and a sad life. The cat never stopped purring. "I can't keep calling you cat, can I cat? You need a name if you're going to be around here for a while." He had already decided to keep the cat as a companion for a while. It would be better company than Gavin ever was; at least it wouldn't be jerking off whenever it saw a good-looking woman. Or would it? He didn't know anything about cats. He could learn.

When its fur was smooth and tangle-free, Steve tossed the comb in the garbage pail next to the desk. The cat began to swat at his sleeve when he moved so he moved more, amused by the playfulness of the animal. He'd never had pets when he was younger—Gavin always killed them before anyone could grow too attached to them—so this was a new experience for him. Remembering something he had read somewhere, he took a piece of string from a drawer and dragged it across the desktop. The cat went berserk trying to catch it and Steve was almost paralyzed with laughter.

"Okay, cat, I'm going to call you Stringer. Come on, catch the string." He played with the cat for a while then noticed a shadow pass over the front of the garage. He looked up to see that it was getting a bit darker outside. "What the? What the heck time is it?" Checking his watch, he saw that it was now past six. He'd been playing with the cat for almost two hours. "Damn, I've got work to do." He looked at the cat sitting on his desk patiently waiting for him to start the string game again. "No can do, Stringer. I have to get some stuff done."

Steve got up and took a broken-down box from a closet near the washroom. He assembled the box, taped the bottom, and set it on the floor. It looked bare so he got some cleaning cloths from the bin in the garage and tossed them in. "That looks sort of comfortable," he said. When he set Stringer in the box, the cat immediately crawled under the cloths and wrapped itself in them. "You wait here while I go do what I need to do." He removed the apron and replaced the rubber gloves with a clean pair of heavy-duty leather work gloves.

There were three drums of old oil waiting out back of the garage to be dumped into the pit. It usually didn't take Steve long to do the dumping but he had wanted to be on the prowl early tonight. He'd heard that there was a hen party going on at the country club and he figured there'd be some easy conquests there. That was one of the perks of working for Silva, a free country club membership and a kind of legitimacy with the rich crowd. Many of the wives there liked the idea of slumming with someone who actually got his hands dirty doing real work. Not that Steve's hands were ever dirty any more.

When the first oil drum was on the dolly, he heaved back and pushed the load forward. Approaching the shed, the going seemed to get more difficult. By the time he reached the side of the shed, it was taking every ounce of strength he had to push the dolly.

"What the heck is going on?" he asked. "Am I going soft?"

He pushed harder and found that the dolly had to be almost perpendicular to the ground to get enough leverage to move. He decided to stand the dolly up to see if one of its wheels was sticking and almost lost the load when the dolly tipped sideways. The oil drum fell against the side of the shed. The thought of a possible rupture and the mess the oil would make made Steve move like lightning to catch it before it fell. Sweating profusely in the heat and needing to catch his breath, he leaned against the shed wall. There, he noticed that the path was out of kilter or something. He couldn't quite put his finger on what was wrong.

Making sure the drum wouldn't move, Steve walked to the area of asphalt behind the garage and gazed back towards the shed. Sure enough, there appeared to be a bit of an incline where there hadn't been one before. "What? That's impossible." He moved closer to the shed and saw that the paving stones on the path were definitely no longer entirely horizontal. And they were heaving out of the gravel, too. Now that he looked closer, even the shed seemed to be tilted forward towards the garage a little. He walked around the structure to the trees and saw that there was a slight incline here as well.

Curious, Steve followed the path to the pit. Everything appeared normal at first glance but closer inspection showed that something was seriously wrong back here. By looking at the trees that surrounded the pit, he could see that the whole area had raised up, possibly about a foot. The trail leading through the woods to the back of that dive down the road should have been flat; it now dipped about fifty feet from the pit. And the pit itself was different. Where before the walls of the pit went about six inches above the ground, now they looked like they were maybe a foot above the ground. And they were cracked along the top, far more than normal. Lifting the wooden trapdoor at the edge of the pit, Steve crouched to look at the walls inside. In the fading sunlight light and darkness under the makeshift roof, he could make out larger cracks in the concrete. The level of liquid in the pit appeared to have dropped but it was too hard to tell in the bad light.

Leaving the trapdoor open, he walked towards the cave where he dumped the old tires. The trail here didn't dip but ran straight to the cave entrance just like it always did. The only odd thing was that the ground, usually moist and spongy under the canopy of trees, was rock solid, as if it was drying out. In fact, here and there were small cracks in the dried dirt. At the cave mouth, all appeared normal again. Steve checked the ground around the entrance and found nothing unusual. He climbed the side of the hill next to the entrance, went up about fifty feet, and saw nothing but pine trees. When he was about to turn to go back and finish dumping the oil, something odd caught his attention. He stood for a few seconds trying to figure out what it was. Something didn't look right. He felt nervous.

"Nothing's going to jump out and bite you," he said quietly to reassure himself. *Stop acting like a scared little boy. There's nothing wrong.* Not able to see what was bothering him about the landscape, he walked back down the slope. A noise to his right, a crow taking off from a tree limb, made him look that way and he saw what had been bothering him.

For about a hundred yards, all the pines were tilted at an odd angle. Instead of going straight up like they normally did, they were tilting away. At about a distance of a hundred yards, Steve could see the trees were still standing straight. He slowly turned one hundred and eighty degrees and saw that it was the same wherever he looked. The trees near the cave mouth were now tilting away from the entrance.

"This isn't good. Trees don't tilt that quickly."

Walking cautiously in the direction the trees were leaning, he felt the ground change. Though he was on the side of the hill walking parallel to the bottom, Steve could tell that he was going down. Then he saw there was a definite demarcation line where the pines stopped tilting. Moving into the still upright trees, he stopped and looked back. He was shocked to see what seemed to be a small hill growing out of the side of the larger hill. He was sure this was something new because he had been walking in these woods for years, since he was a kid and needed to get away for some peace and quiet. There was no way this small hill had been here before last week, the last time he had gone for a walk. The pines on this hill were dropping their needles and the other trees were rapidly losing leaves as he watched. Even the bushes were thinning. All the vegetation looked sickly.

"What the heck is happening here?"

He followed the base of the small hill as it went up the larger hill then curved back around and down to a spot about a hundred yards from the cave entrance. At the foot of the hill, the incline around the pit area went in a slightly curved line towards Trinity Street. He walked along the line, seeing that the pit area was in fact raised about a little more than two feet above the surrounding ground. The trees and bushes on the higher ground were tilting outward a little, too, but not as much as up the hill. *Probably because of the incline of the hill itself.* Eventually, he arrived at the west side of the shed. It, too, was tilting. It hadn't been his imagination.

He took a handkerchief from the back pocket of his trousers and wiped the sweat from his forehead. Folding the handkerchief, he hesitated, not knowing what to do with it. It was soiled now and couldn't go back in his pocket. He felt sweat roll down the inside of his thigh to his knee then down to the top of his sock. Steve shuddered, realized that his clothes needed cleaning anyway and stuffed the used handkerchief into his back pocket.

Everything appeared to be centered on the pit and the cave entrance.

"Weird," said Steve. He fished a mint from his trouser pocket, wiped it on the sleeve of his overalls then removed its wrapping and popped it in his mouth. The wrapping went back in his pocket. Sucking on the candy, he thought about what he had seen and tried to rationalize it.

Could it be earth heaving from the winter frost? It's a little late in the season and it's a heck of a big heave, but why not? Maybe there was an earthquake no one noticed and a fault line moved. Fine, except what fault line had anyone ever heard of that ran in a circle?

"What to do? What to do?" He thought for a few seconds then said, "Work, clean, and screw," and forgot about the bump in the hill. He had other priorities.

Working quickly, Steve hauled the oil drums to the pit, pulling them up the incline, and emptied them. When he was finished, he stacked the drums with the others that were waiting to be picked up by their owners and went to the washroom to clean up. He rinsed off as best he could without a shower, tossed the soiled clothes into a laundry bag, and put on some clean clothes that would suffice until he could get home, get showered, and put on some proper clean things.

He was about to leave the office when a mewing caught his ear and he remembered Stringer. The cat looked up at him from its bed in the cardboard box and purred as soon as it saw him. He petted its head and lifted the box.

"I guess you can stay on the porch at my place for tonight but tomorrow, I'm making you a proper home here. You can keep the mice down and be company for me. How's that sound?"

Stringer mewed and purred some more.

Steve got in his car and drove away while seven crows watched from the roof of the garage.

CHAPTER TWELVE
THE CHURCH

Frederick Silva

"Brother Frederick, sir, it's so good to see you."

Silva's nostrils flared at the greeting. *I cannot stomach this "Brother" garbage.*

Reverend Mendax stuck out his sweaty hand and grasped Silva's, shaking it vigorously. Silva marveled again at the pastor's luxuriously long, black hair; his sideburns and eyebrows showed no traces of gray either. He was perfectly coifed, not a single hair out of place, though a warm breeze and high humidity tried their best to dislodge something but couldn't match the wonders of styling gel and hair spray. The hair was in stark contrast to the white suit which reflected the morning sun into Silva's eyes, forcing him to squint. The only flaw in the picture was the pale blue shirt and silk tie; usually they were a perfect match but today the shades were slightly off. Mendax was at least as old as him—they had known each other for almost forty years—yet while Silva showed his age, *gracefully*, the reverend seemed the picture of youth. That is, until you looked closely at his eyes. If the eyes truly were the windows to the soul, then Reverend Mendax's was old, indeed. The pastor leaned in close and whispered into Silva's ear so quietly he could hardly be heard, "I must speak to you after the service. There seems to be a problem with the church accounts." His breath smelled of wintergreen.

Maintaining a smile despite his mind doing back-flips, Silva replied calmly, "Of course, Reverend. I'm sure you're mistaken though. I went over the books myself two weeks ago and everything was in order." He kept his usually booming voice low; the reverend wore a lapel microphone for his services and there was no way to be sure it wasn't turned on now. The last thing anyone, especially Silva, wanted was for the whole congregation to hear that there were questions about the books. Heavens, people might stop tithing. He squeezed the man's hand hard, an unconscious reaction to being caught in the act. His creative accounting had been a work of art; the church didn't use fancy financial systems but relied on a simple system of entering each member's contributions on a weekly basis and totaling the amount. It was tedious work because there were so many members—some even came from the city, but Silva didn't mind because he found the extra funds useful; and, to be honest, taking the money was both fun and habit-forming. There was so much money coming in, almost all from the tithing of the congregation, that it was easy to skim what he wished off the top. Luckily for him, most of Tyndale's elite were members of the Church of the Divine Word of God; and many left healthy bequests in the hope of smoothing their way into heaven. Silva chuckled to himself at the thought of how he was double-dipping from the rich: extorting money to keep their secrets and taking a percentage of their tithes. It was only fair—he was the master of the county after all.

KING OF THE WOOD

"Is something funny, Brother Frederick?" asked Reverend Mendax. He tried to look imposing but the way his jug ears stuck out of the mass of black hair spoiled the picture.

Silva composed himself and scowled. "There's nothing funny about implications of wrong-doing with the church's accounts, Reverend," he whispered. "Please keep your voice down. The last thing you need is someone overhearing us and spreading unwarranted rumors. Slander is such a nasty thing to deal with in court." Toss the accusations back at your accuser; throw them off guard and onto the defensive. He'd always found this to be an effective way to derail any criticism of his actions.

The pastor backed away, a look of anguish on his face; he knew full well what Silva could do to him if he weren't careful. "No, no, no, please, Brother Frederick," he sputtered, clutching his Bible as if it would protect him. A few congregants peered over to see what the fuss was all about. They weren't used to their pastor showing so much animation away from the pulpit. Mendax acknowledged them and smiled reassuringly then said, "I wasn't accusing you of anything, sir. I merely wished to have some clarification on a few points." Silva could tell Mendax was hoping to have mollified him so he decided to make the fool pay for questioning his honesty and kept the scowl on his face. Plus, it was all he could do not to smack this moron in the face. "You know I am not an accountant. I have no head for numbers. If there is anything amiss, I'm sure I'm not the one responsible." Mendax was sweating now and pulled a handkerchief from the breast pocket of his suit to wipe his brow. The morning was already stiflingly hot and most of the men entering the church had forgone the usual Sunday attire of suits and ties. The women were all in their Sunday best, as they should be, following their husbands into the church, eyes cast down. Mendax tugged on his jacket, adjusted his tie though it was perfect, and casually checked his fly. Silva almost smiled at the recollection of the service the reverend had performed with his fly at half-mast. He had enjoyed the look of horror and embarrassment on the man's face when informed of his lapse, after the service, of course.

"I have some business this afternoon," said Silva impatiently. He checked to see if anyone was close enough to hear him but there wasn't; fellow church-goers tended to avoid him unless it couldn't be helped. "I'll come back this evening when I have some free time. I can explain the finances for you then."

Lawrence walked up the steps.

"I'll be going into the city so I won't be requiring you after church, Lawrence, so go and do whatever it is you do when I don't need you."

There was no expression on Lawrence's face though Silva knew he must be angry. Lawrence had asked for the day off and had been refused on principle; his job was to be available at all times, twenty-four hours a day, seven days a week. He couldn't just go around asking for time off. The next thing you know, he'd want vacations. "Thank you, Mr. Silva," he said flatly and walked into the church. Silva immediately forgot him.

He nodded once to the waiting Mendax and went through the large oak doors.

The church was cool inside thanks to a wise investment in new air conditioners several years ago. There had been a fund-raising drive to get enough money to pay for the acquisition and installation of the machines. Unfortunately, none of the church members knew anything about doing electrical work or installing ducting; that was for the lower orders. If there had been anyone capable of doing the work, pressure would have been applied to do it as part of a congregant's duties, his service to his neighbors.

Silva had used his connections in the city—well they were O'Leary's connections—to get an extremely good deal on the units which he neglected to pass on to the church.

Silva strode up the center aisle to the seats at the back of the stage reserved for his family. He never got used to the changes that had been made to the interior of the old Anglican church after it had been purchased by the new Church of the Divine Word of God. The altar had been removed and the chancel covered with a raised stage from which church members preached. The pulpit was gone and replaced with an ornate wood podium at the center of the stage. The choir stalls had been expanded and seats installed along the back of the stage for important church officers. A huge cross still hung over everything, but Christ seemed to have rather a happy face for someone who had been nailed up.

It was an honor to be placed on the stage during the service, to be among the select that stood, like apostles, behind the pastor as he spread God's word. However, he hated having to sit there, exposed to the whole congregation, trying not to yawn. With no pew in front, everyone at the front of the church, the pastor when he turned around, the choir and organist, and any visiting dignitaries, had a clear view of him at all times. He wished he could just sit at the back and doze through the service or casually read a magazine tucked into a Bible. But being the most prominent citizen in Tyndale did come with its baggage, and it was only for a few hours once a week. It still put him in a foul mood. Woe betide any client who failed to have the proper payment ready on a Sunday afternoon.

The choir, supported by a pair of young men with electric guitars and a bass player, was droning on, some supposedly uplifting hymn about how Jesus was in all of us and led the way to God. *What a load of tripe. How can any rational being believe in such stuff?*, There were occasional nods of acknowledgement from people in the pews as he moved up the aisle. They were either trying to curry his favor for some scheme or trying to show their respect because he had them for whatever crimes and misdemeanors they had carried out. Silva wanted to strike them all down and wished, not for the first time, that all this religious claptrap was real and an avenging God would do his will.

When he walked up the stage steps to his seat, he was both surprised and annoyed to see a stranger sitting in the seat next to his. This seat was usually left empty as a sign of respect for the members of his family who had co-founded the church and since passed. The man was dressed all in black and his suit looked bespoke to Silva's experienced eye. Youngish looking, maybe in his mid-thirties, the man had wavy black hair that hung over his collar. After he sat, the man turned to greet him with a smile and a dip of the head. Silva's breath caught for a moment. The intruder was incredibly handsome, square-jawed, with large blue eyes that felt as if they were seeing into his soul. When he saw the smile, Silva could feel stirrings that he hadn't felt in years and wanted to grab the man, kiss him deeply then rip his clothes off and drop to his knees. With an uncontrollable erection straining to be free, Silva quickly crossed his legs before anyone could notice. He tried hard to resist turning and facing the man. *I'm too old for this.* He tried to think about finances, that swine on the hill, his treacherous wife, anything but the man next to him or that time in England with those three marines. He risked a glance and saw the man smile knowingly at him. A rush of desire swept from his loins to his head and he swooned a little, had to lean against the arm of the chair to steady himself. For the first time, he wished he carried a Bible like so many other churchgoers so

KING OF THE WOOD

he could read and take his mind off sex.

The man in black leaned over and with a lascivious grin said, "Hot, isn't it?"

He wanted to shout, "What do you mean by that?" Silva tried to respond but could only nod in agreement. He felt sweaty and uncomfortable, had trouble breathing normally, and couldn't get the image of the man standing naked over him out of his head no matter how much he tried. *This has to be gone before we have to stand and pray. What would the ladies in the choir think?* A Bible would provide cover for his lap, too. He heard a woman in the pews gasp and looked up to see what was happening, grateful for the distraction.

Deputy Schofield walked up the aisle, Bible in hand, back straight, jaw set, hooded eyes glancing left and right as if searching for someone to hit. His uniform was crisp; the creases in his trousers could slice bread. Silva was astonished to see he was wearing his service weapon. He'd never done that before, had obeyed an unwritten rule that guns were not permitted in the church. There must be some dire reason for this affront to the sensibilities of the congregation, none of whom were opposed to guns on principle because the right to bear arms was guaranteed in the Constitution, as was their inalienable right to live in a God-fearing nation. He'd have a talk with the man after the service. The deputy marched to the front of the church then took his seat on the other side of the podium from where Silva sat. Councilor Morisset was there and greeted his fellow in Christ with enthusiasm. As a deacon of the church, Schofield was entitled to worship at the front even though every member of the church was supposed to be regarded as equal. He sat and opened his Bible and started reading to himself. His lips moved as he read, something that got on Silva's nerves; it was worse if

J. Edwin Buja

he could hear them read. The deacon would be getting a stern reprimand later.

The pews filled steadily, the congregants eager to get out of the heat. Reverend Mendax pulled the church doors closed with a bang that made him jump. *He seems unduly nervous today. Is a meeting with me that daunting? I hope so.* The pastor moved up the aisle with small quick steps. He greeted those seated, touched outstretched hands like a movie star, and patted a few children on the head. When he saw Silva looking at him from his seat, he tripped but regained his balance almost immediately. Silva grinned.

Stepping up to the stage, Mendax raised his hand in welcome to the man in black then took his place behind the podium. He opened his Bible, checked the page, and fussed with some of the flowers that were arranged around the podium to give the congregation time to settle down.

Silva was momentarily curious about who this stranger was but then tuned out, not wanting to stir anything up now that his erection had relaxed. He was already bored with the show, and show it was, especially on his part. All this religious claptrap was fine for the uneducated who couldn't think for themselves, but men like him, the elite of the world, were above such absurdities. He was there solely to be seen as an important member of the congregation and a prominent citizen, to appear as part of the community, to garner support for whatever he deemed necessary to be done for him and the town. The other members of the Council, he knew, felt the same, except for Morisset, who was so caught up in this fundamentalist garbage, he actually believed God spoke to him every night while he knelt and prayed. Many times, he had tried to talk Silva into joining him in prayer before a Council meeting, assuring him that God would hear their prayers and ensure that their plans would be carried through. *My money and secret files do more to advance my cause than some tired old God.*

Silva prepared himself to suffer the service. He tried to focus on his plans for regaining his legacy from that usurper on the hill. So far, things had not gone well. The details of the trust had been mysteriously leaked—if he ever discovered the source of the leak, death would be too kind—and he had needed to back off. Bender now knew what he owned, and how, and would never sit back and let himself be thrown off the hill. Still, there were ways to remove such obstacles, and Silva had the necessary agents in Schofield and O'Leary. The councilors were proving to be utterly useless.

The choir mistress, a particularly large woman, whose print dress was far too tight and whose permed blond hair swept back from her forehead in a halo of curls, led the choir in a never-ending cacophony of worship to a God and Jesus who, if they existed at all, were probably sitting on a sunny beach somewhere sipping Margaritas and watching thong-clad women dance and cavort in the water. She banged away on a tambourine somehow in time with a bad note on the organ that the organist seemed determined to hit as many times as possible during the service. Silva regretted ever helping to raise the money for the thing. A decent CD player would have done the job just as effectively and no one would have to watch the moron with that beatific grin on his face who claimed to have studied at Julliard. And the constant idiotic smiles on the faces of the guitar players made him want to jump up and ram the instruments down their throats; electric guitars were meant for loud rock 'n' roll not this vapid pap they were performing now.

The current hymn ended and the choir sat.

Reverend Mendax adjusted the microphone on his lapel and softly said, "Welcome, Brothers and Sisters." He walked out from behind the podium, arms held wide, palms out, looking around the church and making eye contact with many of the people seated in the pews, all the time smiling. "God is *with* us today because His Kingdom is almost here. Please join me in *a* prayer." The congregation rose, many raised their heads and had hands to God in the sky; some clutched their Bibles to their chests and bowed. "Dear Lord, hear us," he boomed out; he was in full preacher mode now. "Today, your people pray *for* guidance in these troubled times. Your enemies are all around *us* and test us every *day*, but we are strong *in* our belief in the truth *of* Your Word and Your son Jesus Christ. Come *into* our hearts today and fill *us* with the knowledge that we may trample those *who* question Your mighty wisdom and raise *up* false idols. Hear us, oh Lord, in our moment *of* trial." He lowered his head and arms, panting from exertion. The congregation sat amid a chorus of "Praise the Lord!" and "God, hear our prayers!".

When everyone was seated, Mendax returned to the podium and picked up his Bible. He studied the passages for a while, though Silva knew the man had memorized every word in the book. It pays to be dramatic. Taking a deep breath, he said, "We live in *an* age of miracles. This is not surprising *to* those of you who follow the way *of* Christ; every day is a miracle given *to* us by God. But there is more. Just this morning, I learned that Evelyn Quayle's cancerous leg has been healed. And was *it* not written in Acts three, verse seven, 'And he took him by the right hand and lifted him up: and immediately his feet and ankle bones received strength.' Jesus heals the lame." There were sighs throughout the church, here and there a "Praise Jesus." Many were nodding as if what the pastor had said was an everyday occurrence, not the least bit surprising. Reverend Mendax waited until there was silence again. "And Ronald Symes has told me that in the last week he has been able *to* distinguish shapes and movement with eyes that *have* been blind for years. As we were told *in* Psalms one forty-six, verse eight, 'The Lord openeth the eyes of the blind.' Remember Psalms seventy-seven, verse fourteen, 'Thou art the God that dost wonders: thou hast declared thy strength among the people.'" He paused to let that sink in. There were more sighs and cries. He held the Bible high and walked to the edge of the stage and down one step, all the time surveying the congregation. Some had tears in their eyes; others held hands up in praise. Mendax nodded knowingly.

"You have all witnessed *the* amazing growth *in* your gardens and around town."

Someone at the back shouted, "It's like the Garden of Eden. Paradise on Earth." Others agreed. Again, there were shouts of "Praise Jesus!" and "God lives!". But Silva could see that a lot of the people didn't have a clue what the reverend was jabbering about.

Mendax said, "In one Corinthians three, verses seven and eight, we *are* told 'but God gave the measure. So then neither is he that planteth anything, neither he that watereth; but God that giveth the increase.'" He paused for effect then repeated, "'But God giveth the increase.' There are those *in* our midst who would say *that* it is not God that is responsible for this bounty." He paced back and forth across the pulpit. Gasps from the congregation. "Yes, they would give credit *to* another."

There were shouts of "Praise God!" from the congregation. Schofield cried, "Blasphemy!"

"Yes, these evil ones, servants *of* Satan, have committed the ultimate sin, *the* most unforgivable sin. As Jesus said in Matthew twelve, verse thirty-one, 'All manner of sin and blasphemy shall be forgiven unto men: but the blasphemy against the Holy Ghost shall not be forgiven unto men.' Jesus is telling us that to ascribe the wonders of the Lord to Satan is the most heinous of sins." He waved the hand holding the Bible in the air. "The one sin *that* God cannot forgive. And these sinners *are* amongst us now."

Silva looked over to where Schofield leaned out of his chair; his face was flushed with passion, his eyes wide and full of religious fervor. If there had been a sinner in the church, and Silva knew there were many, Schofield would have shot him on the spot. Morisset was feverishly making notes in the margins of his Bible. Silva wriggled in his seat. He desperately needed to go to the bathroom. Why did he break his own rule about too much coffee before church?

And he still couldn't get thoughts of naked men out of his head.

Mendax walked back to the podium and took a sip from a glass of water then went on, "God has *a* plan, and it seems to be unfolding in Tyndale. But be aware, God *will* not grant us paradise without *a* test."

Schofield leapt from his seat and joined Mendax at the podium. "He must test us to see who is worthy," he shouted then looked out at the congregation and added, "Who here is truly worthy?" Spittle flew from his mouth. "Who is willing to lay down their life for the Kingdom of Heaven? Jesus said, 'and whosoever will lose his life for my sake shall find it.'" No one spoke, their fear of Schofield as both deputy and deacon evident. Many dropped their eyes to the Bibles they held or carefully maintained their attention on Reverend Mendax who was clearly uncomfortable with this intrusion. Schofield had done this many times in the past, often when publicly calling for the expulsion of a congregant who had transgressed. Fired up now, he added, "In his first letter, Peter writes in chapter five, verse eight, 'Be sober, be vigilant; because your adversary the devil, as a roaming lion, walketh about, seeking whom he may devour.' Remember, 'He that is not with me is against me,' so says our savior Jesus Christ." Schofield smiled contemptuously and returned to his seat.

You are an evil swine, you self-righteous prig. Hypocrisy and hate rule your life. Silva stared at Schofield feeling hate welling within his breast. It was difficult enough to put up with Schofield when he was being used to further his blackmailing schemes, but to have to endure his endless smug superiority and Bible spouting outbursts here was a task that would test even the most tolerant person. *Why haven't you been murdered yet? Enough people hate you.* Not the first time Silva had that thought.

"Thank you, Deacon Schofield. I'm sure all here are worthy *of* paradise *in* the Lord's eyes," said Reverend Mendax with a hint of irritation. Silva was shocked that the man would be so defiant, would dare to stand up to Schofield in front of the gathered congregation. Though Mendax, as founder, was the nominal head of the church, Schofield was so fanatical, so absolutely convinced he was righteous that few dared defy him. The rare person that had confronted the deacon had found himself banished from the church and isolated from the remaining members.

"Now," continued Mendax, "while it may seem that all *is* right with Tyndale, there are devils in our midst." Silva risked a glance at the man in black who seemed to be ready for him and stared back directly into his eyes. Silva jerked his head forward hard enough to cause a twinge in his neck muscle. He slowly moved his right hand to his neck to massage the sore spot. "Heathens have come *to* our fair town and are infecting *it* with the lies of Satan," said the reverend. There were gasps and exclamations from the congregation. "So-called Wiccans are camped out *in* our fairgrounds, practicing their satanic rites, preaching their evil ways, and attempting *to* corrupt our pure and holy children." There were more gasps; someone exhorted, "Save us, oh Lord."

Silva wanted to scream, "Save *me*," at the fools.

When the congregation quieted down, the reverend said, "Some might say *that* they are merely poor deluded fools *who* mean no harm and sell fancy bangles with odd symbols. They do, after all, claim to worship the earth." He looked down at his Bible, took a deep breath and shouted, "Blasphemers." The congregants at the front appeared to be pushed back in their pews by the force of this word. "Deuteronomy twenty-seven, verse fifteen tells us that, 'Cursed be the man that maketh any graven or molten image, an abomination unto the Lord.'" He scanned the faces that were looking up at him. "Think *what* that means, 'An abomination to the Lord.'" He waited to let the congregation think. "I am sure *that* these evil doers, these spawn of Satan are responsible *for* the misfortune that has befallen Tyndale *in* the last two months. You know I refer to the disappearance of our brother, Gregory Wright. Somehow, and I'm sure God will reveal the answer *in* His own good time, this event may be linked to the murder *on* the hill and the other disappearance." He didn't bother to name names in this case; no one here cared about lowlifes like Gavin O'Leary or Billy Lush. "We must be prepared to fight the enemy *with* all our might. God is on our side. Our cause is righteous."

The congregation stood, hands raised in praise, as the choir began "Onward Christian Soldiers". The people swayed as they sang, eyes closed, heads held high. Quite a number had tears

KING OF THE WOOD

streaming down their cheeks. Many of the children were crying, probably out of fear that Satan or evil Wiccans were going to come for them in the night. *Even I wouldn't harm children. Unless the little harlot asked for it.* When the hymn was finished, with a flourish of guitar notes that would have made Eric Clapton wince, Mendax stepped to the edge of the stage.

"We *are* fortunate today to have with us an emissary of God. He brings us *a* message of good tidings and hope from the Almighty. His writings are known *to* be the truth, have proven *to* be the Word of God. Please welcome, from the Church of the Immaculate Brides *of* Christ, Brother James."

Mendax looked at the man seated next to Silva, smiled, and beckoned him to the front of the stage. The congregation erupted into thunderous applause, many standing and shouting, "Praise the Lord!" and "Praise Brother James!" Clapping the hardest and shouting the loudest was Paul Schofield. Silva, trying to blend in by standing and applauding, viewed everyone with contempt. He couldn't fathom how they could possibly welcome this man with such enthusiasm. Brother James, he was sure, was nothing but another phony soothsayer, preying on people too stupid to think for themselves, people who needed to be told what to do, who couldn't judge right from wrong without someone else doing the work for them. Sheep, the lot of them.

Brother James walked slowly to meet Reverend Mendax, waving to the congregation, smiling warmly. The women looked on him with open adoration, and in some cases, with naked lust. Even the men were taken in by him, most had beaming faces, but some looked shocked and uncomfortable. *I know how you feel.* Schofield had tears in his eyes, as did Morisset. The welcoming applause went on for five minutes until Brother James raised his arms and indicated that he wished everyone to sit.

Silva watched the man closely while he spoke, trying to see through the lies and religious rhetoric, trying to see how a man so obviously full of himself was able to win the hearts and minds of so many people. Trying to imagine Brother James naked.

Damn!

Brother James

Looking out over the sea of joyful faces, basking in the adoration, Brother James knew He had them in His clutches. They would do anything He told them. Here it was: the army He needed to defeat the Adversary, to bring about the glory of man and God. He couldn't help but grin, happy in the knowledge that His task would be so much easier. He scanned the crowd feeling for the women. It was easy to tell that they were all subservient to their husbands or brothers or fathers. The auras coming from them were of unfulfilled promise, unquenched desire, and unhappy life. He wanted to lash out at the men who treated their women with such contempt; how dare they defile what God had given them. Yes, it was a woman's place to serve a man, but that didn't mean she had to be treated with anything less than respect and all-encompassing love. Brother James could feel Himself getting hard at the thought of giving these women what they needed, what they desired.

Him.

"Thank you, Reverend Mendax," He said bowing to Mendax who had taken a seat near the choir, "for inviting Me to speak with your flock today. And thank all of you," He looked out at the congregation, "My brothers and sisters in Christ, for that warm and heart-felt welcome. It fills My heart with joy to know that there are so many devoted followers of the Lord in a small town like Tyndale. Where I live most of the time, in the center of the city, there is such godlessness as to make one despair that anyone of faith can survive. But We who know the truth of the Word of God need never despair or fear, for We know that God and Jesus Christ watch over Us and protect Us from evil."

He spoke without the aid of a microphone, His words thundering through the church so that even the people far to the back could hear Him clearly. Everyone was rapt, waiting for the words to flow and tell them what must be done in the name of the Lord.

"Your good reverend has spoken of the time of trial through which We are going and of those who have been sent by the Adversary to tempt you and sway you from the path of God and righteousness. What you see around you, growing from the very earth that God created in His wisdom, can be God's bounty and God's only. To claim, as these blasphemers do, that it is the spirit of the earth that is providing these gifts is such a grievous sin that not only those who utter the words, but also those who listen to them and are tempted will be taken up by the power of God and cast into the fiery pits of Hell for all eternity."

There were exclamations of "Praise Jesus!" and "Jesus saves!" from the congregation. Someone shouted, "Burn the heretics!" and a murmur of agreement went throughout the people.

"That's the spirit," said Brother James. "Be ready to kill My enemies in the name of the Lord but only when I say so."

He crisscrossed the stage while He spoke, catching the eyes of those sitting closest, boring into their minds with His will and binding them to Him. The women were the easiest and He longed to be worshipping with them, free from the conventions of society, naked in their fervor, spreading the seed of God where it might take root and be fruitful.

"But We must be cautious, for though God is on Our side in righteousness, the forces of the evil one are strong. Strike We must, but only when Our own strength is such that the evil will be overwhelmed with Our righteous fury and swept from the Kingdom of God.

"As you know, I, your humble servant, have been chosen by God to deliver His holy words to you. He speaks to Me at all times, counseling Me in times of trouble, guiding Me on the path to the salvation of mankind. I wish that all of you," He spread his hands and scanned the congregation, "could hear His words directly as I do. But know this: when you have proven yourself worthy, when you have defeated the forces of the Adversary," His voice rose steadily, "crushed his minions beneath your feet. Then shall you sit at the feet of God in the Kingdom of Heaven, with the angels, living forever in His glory, blessed and pure."

Dozens of congregants were standing now, arms held high in supplication to God. Few were the people who did not have tears in their eyes. Brother James was pleased and bowed His head in prayer, absorbing the intense emotional energy in the church. How could He lose now? The Adversary was sure to be destroyed along with all his acolytes. Nothing could stand in the way of the ascension of Brother James and God. Nothing.

He tilted His head back, eyes closed, and arms wide and entered the minds of all who were present. He felt the religious ardor of the believers, fed on it as He would bread, sustenance for His very existence. He felt the doubt leaving the few in the church who had not been wholeheartedly devoted to God before this day; who had gone through the motions of devotion but had been empty in their souls. And He felt the intensity of one who wished beyond all else to destroy the Adversary. This one would gladly see the end of humanity if it meant that the Kingdom of Heaven would arrive sooner. Slowly, He turned and gazed into the adoring face of the man Schofield. He was on his knees, hands clasped together in prayer, his cheeks soaked with the tears of belief. When Schofield saw he was the subject of Brother James's attention, he beamed and held his hands higher, offering himself to the service of Brother James and God.

"You will be useful in the struggle to come, can be manipulated easily to do the most horrific thing in My name." Brother James smiled. "I will be meeting with you soon, My devoted one."

The congregation streamed to the front of the church. Many gathered at the foot of the stairs, hands held out, aching to grasp the hand of their Savior. He stepped down to meet them, clasped the hands of the men, and accepted hugs from the women. None could tear their eyes from Him when He looked upon them; all felt the electricity when they touched Him. He loved them all, wanted to make love to them all but now was not the time. He knew He would see many of them later, in their homes or at the home of Sister Sarah. They would worship together and love together. It was all Brother James could do to resist the temptation to take someone right there, in front of the others, loving freely as He should, coupling with others, both men and women, as the whole assembly became a seething mass of naked bodies, spreading the seed of Him, and rejoicing.

In all the swirling sea of passion for God there was a rock, one who denied, one who did not believe. Brother James was astonished at the degree of contempt that radiated from this one. Unlike the woman, Ravenscroft, who had resisted Him in the swamp, this person was simply devoid of a soul. There was nothing in his heart but the blackness of the pit. It was cold, empty, frightening. He tried to single out the individual responsible for this outrage, this rebellion, but He could not, so overwhelming was the zeal of the congregation.

"You are so lucky, whoever you are. If I find you, no, when I find you, I will cut out your heart as you watch and feed it to the vermin that crawl in the dirt."

He tried to see if there was anyone in the congregation or on the pulpit that was an obvious suspect but there was no one. Someone was missing but He couldn't remember who it was. He had not been here long enough to know the faces and souls of every church member and there was too much to distract Him now. The choir was singing a hymn accompanied by the out-of-tune organ. Discordant guitar chords ripped across His mind as inspiration spread to the musicians and they let it flow into their fingers.

Brother James decided to root out the evil in the church later. There would be enough people to help Him. Someone would know who it was. And there was always that man Schofield who would be happy to do the deed, though in this case, He wanted to destroy the person Himself.

Frederick Silva

Crossing the road in back of the church, Silva felt sure that no one would notice his BMW parked in the hospital parking lot, though to him the large patch of rust on the front quarter panel made it scream for attention; he'd have to get that fixed, under warranty of course, the car was fairly new, as soon as possible. On the other hand, it would blend in with the rusting hulks in the lot belonging to patients and visitors. All this rust; must be the salt used for the snow, he guessed. To help hide the car, he had parked under a tree at the edge of the lot, far away from the main gate. Leaving wouldn't be a problem since there was no guard and there would be no record of his license plate. The road was clear; most of Tyndale's residents were at supper.

He didn't know where that fool Lawrence was, but that shouldn't be a problem because he had given him the day off. He's probably visiting that gimp daughter of his. *Anyway, I told him I'd be in the city, so he won't be expecting me even if he is at the house.* The man had rushed away from the church at the same time as Silva.

Unable to stand the fatuousness of the spectacle of Brother James and his so-called message, Silva had slipped out the back door of the church while everyone was distracted with bleating and insane adoration for the charlatan. Such a disgusting display of manipulation he had never seen. How could anyone with a rational mind fall for the patently ridiculous garbage that man was selling? About to unlock his car, Silva had spotted Lawrence hastily exiting the front door of the church shaking his head. The expression on his face was pure rage. At least the man had an iota of common sense. He had ducked behind a hedge until Lawrence climbed into his own car and drove off to whatever kept him busy during his free time.

Silva had gone home after church to check his files and compile something ruinous on the good Reverend Mendax before their meeting later. At least, if the man had in fact discovered his manipulations of the books, he'd be able to strike back and destroy the pious fool's reputation as an honorable religious man.

However, there had been nothing in the files. Mendax was every bit as honest and pious as he seemed. *Why must I end up with the one truly honorable evangelist? Why can't you be like all*

J. Edwin Buja

those others? Hookers, homosexuality, drugs, something. Not even fiddling the bingo. Silva had spent a couple of hours on the internet and was happy with what he had found. And planting the files on the reverend's computer would be easy. The downloaded pictures and stories would turn the stomachs of everyone in the congregation. Even that fool sheriff would get involved. Schofield would take out his pistol and kill the man without hesitation, true stories or not.

Silva now crossed the church parking lot and followed a path that led to the church's office door. He held an envelope with all the ammunition needed to stop the reverend's annoying accusations. He had a key, so whether Mendax was there or not, he could let himself in. Knocking quietly on the door so as not to attract attention from anyone who might happen to be passing, Silva waited for an answer. Reverend Mendax opened the door and invited his visitor in. The office was extremely warm and an old metal fan on the desk did nothing but circulate the hot air; the air conditioning had been for the church proper, not the adjoining offices and residence.

"Please have a seat, Brother Frederick," said Mendax as he sat behind the desk. "Can I get you something cold to drink? Some lemonade?"

The thought of Mendax's overly tart lemonade made Silva's stomach turn. He wanted a large glass of Lagavulin but more than that, he wanted to be away from this little man and his accusations. "No," he replied curtly; he wasn't used to being on the other side of a desk during a meeting. He preferred to be in command at all times. "What is this about the account books? You implied there was something wrong with them." When the man hesitated, Silva added, looking at his Rolex, "Come on, come on, I'm a busy man. You're already wasting my valuable time."

Mendax said, "I was going over the books to confirm the amount that was bequeathed to us when Brother Roger Whitcomb died last year. I had been talking with his widow, giving her comfort. The poor woman still misses him and just sits at home staring at the walls. I was hoping to …"

"Get on with it, Mendax. I don't care about grieving widows."

The reverend was clearly taken aback by Silva's lack of sympathy for a sad woman. "Surely, Brother Frederick …"

"Enough, Mendax. Call me Brother Frederick one more time and I will rip out your tongue. It's Mister Silva to you. Now, get on with it."

Reverend Mendax reached for the Bible on the desk and held it close to his heart as if to protect himself from unkindness while composing himself then continued, "When Sister Denise Whitcomb mentioned the amount of the bequest, it didn't sound right. It sounded like more than I was aware of. I wanted to double check the books."

Silva tried to keep his emotions in check. Whitcomb had left over three hundred thousand dollars to the church but fully a third of that had been diverted to his own pockets. Outrageous legal fees and assorted other expenses were the supposed justification, but Silva knew these wouldn't stand up to close scrutiny. "And what did you find?" he asked warily.

Mendax set the Bible down and opened a ledger that was on his desk and pointed out several entries. "See here, Mr. Silva. And here. They don't match up. Sister Denise gave me a copy of her husband's will. It contained all the details about the bequest." He unfolded a document that had been inserted into the ledger. "See here," he said as he placed the document next to the ledger entries. The entries were in Silva's handwriting. "The amounts don't match. I understand there are expenses involved with legacies and wills, but this amount is excessive."

Remaining calm, Silva said, "I wouldn't know. I'm not a lawyer."

The reverend went on, "And I checked some of the other entries. Accounts of weekly tithes. These seem wrong, also. I know for a fact that," he flipped the ledger open to a later page, "here," he turned the ledger so Silva could read it, "this week. Brother Thomas Chatworth received a large dividend on some stocks he owned. He mentioned it to me that Sunday, said his tithe would be almost quadruple the usual amount. It doesn't appear in the book. The amounts entered for that week, and I checked later weeks in case there was a delay, are all normal. No extras." He closed the ledger. "How do *you* account for this, Mr. Silva?"

Silva said nothing. *You've caught me, haven't you, you worthless piece of self-righteous trash. Will those pictures be enough to get me out of this one?* If it had only been something that could be passed off as a simple error, there would be no problem. Even the dividend payment could be ignored with the photos and printouts he had in the manila envelope. But the legacy from Whitcomb would be hard to explain. With time, and the acquisition of his rightful property, he could have paid back the money or, better yet, come up with more iron-clad reasons for the discrepancies.

"Am I going to have to call in an auditor?" asked Mendax. At least he didn't appear to be enjoying himself. That would have been too much. "I know you aren't an accountant and could have made some honest mistakes, but these larger amounts are too much. The church can't afford to be losing money, not in our times of trial. We have a real battle ahead of us with the forces of Satan. We need every penny we have."

"I would have thought righteousness and a firm belief in your God would have been enough to win. Since when did money become so important in a spiritual battle?"

"Mr. Silva," Mendax slammed his fists onto the ledger and stood. "I can scarcely believe I'm hearing those words coming from your mouth. God has given us a mission. We must have the funds to complete it." His face and ears were red. A strand of jet-black hair fell across his forehead, the first time Silva had ever seen the man's hair mussed.

"Has God given you a mission to defeat Satan or to gather as much cash as possible?" He picked up the ledger and waved it at the pastor as if it were proof.

Mendax's mouth fell open and he sputtered, "You can't say such things. You could be expelled from the church. Your very soul could be placed at peril."

"Shut up, you pious fool. I doubt that I have a soul," said Silva calmly. He dropped the ledger on the chair next to him and held out the envelope. "I've had to endure you and your kind for far too long." He was about to toss the envelope on the desk when he had a better idea. "Turn on your computer. There's something you must see." When Mendax didn't move, Silva shouted, "Now, Reverend." When the machine was running, he said, "Connect to the internet and find this site." He read an address that was written on a sheet he removed from the envelope. The reverend's eyes popped open and he began to sweat more but typed anyway.

While he waited for the site to open, Silva scanned the room looking for something he could use. The fan seemed to be the only thing of any size.

"What is this?" asked Mendax when he saw the site that had opened. His face registered both shock and disgust.

Silva moved around behind him and said, "What have you been looking at, Reverend?"

"I've never seen this before." There were tears in his eyes. "Those poor children. Why?"

"You disgusting man," said Silva when the pictures of the children began to download. "How could you?"

"What are you talking about? We must call the Sheriff."

"Really," said Silva as he emptied the contents of the envelope into the output tray of the printer next to the computer.

"What are those?" asked the reverend. Then he saw the image on the top. "What are you doing? Where did you get that filth?"

"You're an evil little man and a hypocrite. At least, that's what everyone will think." When Mendax tried to rise, a hand held him in place. "A member of your church, who discovers you with this is going to want more than your expulsion, isn't he? I'm thinking about that maniac Schofield."

The reverend reached to turn off the computer but before he could Silva seized the fan from the desk and brought it crashing down on his head. When it struck the man's skull, the guard flew off, bounced off the computer monitor causing the screen to crack, and clattered onto the floor. Mendax said, "Oh," and fell forward onto the desk scattering papers and pens all over. Silva brought the fan down again. This time, the still whirling blades bit into the flesh on the downed man's head. His long hair caught in the blades and when Silva yanked the fan back, a large hank of hair and scalp came with it. The reverend's hands moved, attempting to cover his wounded scalp. Silva smashed the fan into his victim's head again and again. He heard the skull crack and felt warm liquid splatter on his face.

KING OF THE WOOD

In a frenzy now, Silva beat the unconscious man until his head was little more than a mass of pulp and hair. One of the blades slashed the man's neck and severed an artery. The force of the blood spray sent papers flying off the desk and onto the floor. Brain matter covered the desk and computer, blood splashed all over the walls and ceiling. When blood stopped pumping from the gaping neck, Silva stopped hitting, chest heaving, gasping for air.

"Are you with your God now?" he asked through clenched teeth. "Are you happy? See what you made me do." Breathing hard, Silva set the broken fan on the desk and stepped away from the bloody corpse.

He leaned against a wall and waited a few minutes to let his heartbeat and breathing return to normal. He had his second erection of the day. When he felt calm again, he checked himself to see how much blood had hit him. Luckily, it was mostly on his suit jacket. A shame, this suit had cost two thousand dollars and fit comfortably. Oh well, it had to go into the furnace, no question about that. Silva carefully removed the jacket. As he was about to fold it inside out he remembered the fan. "My fingerprints," he said quietly and wrapped the jacket around the fan. He tied the arms together to be sure the machine wouldn't fall out then set it on the floor by the office door. "Did I touch anything else?" The envelope. This he folded and slipped into his pants pocket. "The computer might have mine, but they'd be under yours, you pathetic fool. Thank you." He looked around the office. "Nothing else." He went over to a mirror that hung on the back of the door to the church and checked for more blood. There were a few drops on his face that he wiped off with the reverend's jacket that was conveniently hanging on a coat rack next to the door.

As an afterthought, he took the copy of Whitcomb's will and stuffed it in the ledger which he then crammed next to the fan in his jacket.

Using his handkerchief as a glove, Silva gently opened the office door. There was no one about; it was still dinner time. He picked up his jacket with the fan and ledger inside and slipped outside pulling the door closed behind him. It was about a hundred and fifty yards to his car in the hospital parking lot. He walked calmly along the path at the side of the office, the fan under his arm. Sudden shouting made him freeze in his tracks. It was coming from down the road and when he turned to see who had discovered him, he was relieved to see it was only some drunks coming out of The Pub. They were stumbling away in the other direction. He was safe. Quickening his pace, he crossed the road and moved under the trees at the edge of the hospital lot. When he reached his car, distracted by that nuisance rust patch at the front, he dropped his burden in the trunk and got in the front. There was still no one in sight. He pulled up to the stop sign at the road but before he could turn, six rats ran in front of the car. He shivered in disgust. A few hundred yards away lay Cypress Road and the gates to the estate. In five minutes, he'd be home enjoying a nice glass of Lagavulin. Safe.

He barely registered the six crows watching from the roof of the church as he drove away.

CHAPTER THIRTEEN
THE CAMP

Lawrence Burke

Lawrence had attended the Church of the Divine Word of God for the last decade because his employer insisted. He knew this was not because of religious conviction; it was only the need to put on the proper face before the community. Hardly a religious man since the death of his wife and the tragedy of Luana, he had remained spiritual, believing that there was some higher power out there somewhere, but shunning organized religion. Where that power had been when his family had been taken from him, he didn't know; but he knew that it was not God or Jesus who had been in control. Born a Baptist, Lawrence had enjoyed the sense of community within the church and, more importantly, the sense of belonging. However, over the years, as he went through high school and then college, he had come to question the dogma that had been part of his life for so long. Eventually, he and the church came to a parting of the ways. He now followed a path with a personal moral code and set of ethics. This had done well by him and his life had been a happy one.

Then Frederick Silva had arrived on the scene and everything went south. He was preparing to take his family away from Tyndale and the Silvas, but catastrophe had struck in the form of a devastating car accident. Kindly old Horace had set up a trust fund to take care of his faithful secretary and his surviving daughter, but when the old man died, Frederick had used it to force Lawrence into a life of Hell. The threat that Luana's care could be cut off at any time kept him in service to a man he detested. Over the years, he had tried to find a way to free himself from the yoke of servitude and abuse, but always there remained the problem of Luana. There was no way he would ever be able to afford the kind of twenty-four-hour care she needed. Silva knew this and made sure to let Lawrence know every day that he owed his daughter's security to him.

Lawrence knew he had to warn as many people as possible about the imminent danger when that maniac Brother James started preaching hatred. *But why was I the only one? Did no one else hear what was being said? Were they all so mesmerized by all that other garbage he was spewing?* The sheer evil of what James said made Lawrence shiver. *And who is this adversary he was talking to?*

Mendax could wait; there was no way Silva would do anything foolish with the reverend. Tom Bender needed to be told the truth about everything, not just Silva but Marie and Belinda as well. And Marie was in danger. If Silva found out she was back in Tyndale, and he would eventually, he wouldn't hesitate to kill her or have that insane deputy Schofield do the job. Schofield's religious mania would help justify his actions.

With what he had read among the files in the hidden room, Lawrence could bring about the downfall of that arrogant swine and free himself and Luana, indeed, the whole county, from the grip of this madman. And madman he was. Silva had claimed to be going out of town for the afternoon but Lawrence suspected he was up to something. Deciding that Bender, the object of Silva's obsession, was in more danger than anyone else involved, he had driven straight to the house on Horace's Hill. But he was frustrated to find that the man was away. He hammered at the front door for fully ten minutes before giving up. While at the house, he marveled at the gardens, both front and back, at the amazing growth that was happening here. He had seen how plants and trees were growing early and at a rapid rate in town, but up here things appeared to have run rampant. Yet it seemed to calm him a little; there was still a sense of urgency in his mission, but he wasn't feeling quite so manic about it.

John wasn't home either, so Lawrence was left with no choice but to return to The Poplars and try to gather as much evidence against Silva as he could. However, when he got to the house, he discovered to his chagrin that Silva was already there, at work in the secret room, no doubt trying to find something to use against Mendax. Good luck with that. Lawrence had waited patiently in the house he shared with Luana and her nurse. From his second-floor bedroom room window, he could see into the garage where Silva had parked his car. No one could see the vehicle from the driveway, so the man must have felt safe with the lie about being in the city. When Silva had eventually left, very late in the afternoon, Lawrence wasted no time getting to the secret room to gather documents for the various people whom he felt were in the most immediate danger: Tom Bender, who stole his legacy; Marie, who had dared to defy him; John, the go-between and spy; and Sheriff Finnbrough, betrayer and bitter rival for control of the county whose file was surprisingly thin for such a public figure.

Documents in hand, he had left the Poplars a few minutes past six o'clock, and driven to The Pub. This was John's usual hangout and, though it was Sunday evening, Lawrence thought he might find his friend there having dinner. As he was going in, two men who had just exited the building got into an argument. He paused at the door to see if it would get violent but the men started to laugh at each other and stumbled off. Lawrence looked north along the street in time to see Silva dash across the road from the church to the hospital parking lot. *What's he up to?* John wasn't inside; and neither Eddie the bartender nor Nancy the waitress had seen him today. Nancy showed some concern when Lawrence had asked after John, which made him curious. The look on her face showed more than simple friendly interest; he'd have to pursue that with John later.

He was about to drive by the church on the off chance he would see something interesting to tell him what his employer had been doing there when he heard sirens. The Sheriff's cruiser roared by and screeched to a halt at the church. A few seconds later, an ambulance skidded to a stop and two attendants leapt from the vehicle and charged into the church after the Sheriff. This is not good. *Frederick, what have you done now?*

He'd seriously misjudged how desperate his employer was and realized what must have happened. If Silva hadn't murdered Reverend Mendax, then he certainly was instrumental in having the deed carried out. It was clear that the reverend had discovered Silva's manipulations of the church's finances; this much Lawrence gleaned from the secret files he had read and the second set of books that were being kept. No doubt Mendax had wanted to confront Silva with the crime. And there remained no question in his mind that Frederick Silva had gone over the edge.

Frantic calls to John and Tom proved they were still not at home, or at least not answering their telephones. The Sheriff would be busy with the events at the church. That left Marie.

Lawrence had not known Marie Watson before Silva got his claws into her. Everyone he had asked about her said she had been a vibrant young woman, happy with life and not at all spoiled by the millions she had inherited from her father. By the time Lawrence arrived at The Poplars, Marie had been beaten down by her husband, both physically and mentally, her once brilliant and out-going personality reduced to a mere shade of its former self. Whatever Silva wanted, he got, whether it was all her money or some disgusting game that further degraded her. Any opportunity, no matter how petty, had been used to humiliate Marie. Lawrence had been forced to watch as she became more and more a shadow, hardly noticeable in the background, never daring to express an opinion or thought of her own. He had seen one of the videos—involving Steve O'Leary—and had cried at the acts she had been forced to perform for her husband's enjoyment. He was sure it was no accident that it had been left among the papers he was working on that day. To make matters worse, he knew that the evil man had shared the videos with some of his closest associates simply to prove he was the master of the woman who had provided him with money when his family would not. Silva had effectively cut Marie off from all her friends and family, turned her into an automaton for his own devices.

The single thing that seemed to carry Marie out of her subjugated stupor was Luana. After the accident, she had been at the girl's bedside, cleaning and feeding her, reading her stories, and singing lullabies; this had meant so much to Lawrence who had no family and whose only other visitor was

John. It was as if the only way Marie could show part of her true self, the kind woman of her youth, was to the one person she knew could not respond. Lawrence had spoken to her many times during these visits to his daughter and found her to be an intelligent and bright woman who knew her situation but was helpless to do anything about it. Yet somehow, beneath everything she suffered, there remained a spark of optimism, a sure knowledge that things would get better someday.

When, a few months later, the chance to get Marie away from her imprisonment had been mooted, Lawrence had been only too happy to help Belinda with her plan.

And now she was back, for what purpose Lawrence didn't dare hazard a guess.

He turned the car right and drove to Hill Road. When he came to the entrance to the fairgrounds, he drove in and parked near the pavilion. A few teenagers were playing ball at the larger diamond while a number of girls watched and shouted out encouragement. At the smaller diamond, two men were playing catch. Lawrence got out of his car, made sure it was locked then headed for the back of the pavilion where there was a small campground. A shout made him look back; one of the teens had hit the ball far into center field and was sure to get a home run. It was then that he noticed the rust on the passenger side of his car. He had lovingly restored the sixty-nine Mustang Fastback, an extravagance to be sure, but he had loved the model since his father had owned one when he was a boy. And now there was a large area of rust just back of the wheel well on the front quarter panel. Bending to get a closer look, he saw that the rust ran all along the bottom of the car to the back. Duck walking around his prize, and feeling quite silly all the while, he was saddened to see that rust had taken hold in at least four other spots. *How I could have missed this, I don't know. I washed the car last Saturday and it was spotless.* "Damn."

His bad day had been made worse. Still, it was only a car. *But what a car.* Even Silva had grudgingly admired it once.

Walking along the pavement in the shadow of the pavilion, Lawrence could hear music. When he turned the corner, the music grew louder: fiddles and penny whistles, Celtic drums and accordions, and there was a harp; he loved harps. The Wiccan encampment had grown since they first arrived two weeks ago. Back then, there had been three or four tents and a trailer or two. Now there were dozens of tents, at least twenty trailers and Winnebagos of assorted sizes, and a couple of horse-drawn wagons. A canteen tent had been set up at the edge of the camp and was crowded with people eating and singing and generally having a good time. The musicians were set up on a small stage at the side of the canteen; children were seated in front of them, some with small instruments of their own and others singing along and playing games. It was a stark contrast to the service he had witnessed at the church this morning—all those people moaning and praying and afraid.

One of the men serving food saw Lawrence approaching, passed his ladle to another man, and waved him over. He recognized the man from a long time ago and was happy to see him again. Five feet ten and thin as a rail, Peter McDermott was nonetheless strong as an ox, due, he claimed, to the beard that had not been cut for over twenty years. The mass of hair was braided and tucked into a bib while he served food. The beard couldn't hide the huge smile on his face. Lawrence held out his hand and Peter took it and shook it vigorously.

"Larry, so wonderful to see you," he said with a soft voice. "What's it been? Eight years?"

Lawrence hugged the man and replied, "Yes, eight long years." When they pulled apart, he asked, "How's she doing? Marie?" He was concerned. The last time he saw Marie, she had been shivering and occasionally throwing up as she sweated out the drugs Silva had used to control her. Peter had assured him she would be alright with time but had urged Lawrence to leave. Marie had needed time to adjust and would contact him when she was feeling well again.

She had never called. Lawrence wasn't surprised. It would have been far too painful for Marie to maintain any ties with someone who reminded her of the hellish life she had escaped. And it would have been risky if Silva had found out. Still, it had hurt.

"She's fine," answered Peter. "But she calls herself Sybil, now."

"Come again?"

"Sybil," said Peter. "She found her Wiccan name and changed it."

"But why Sybil?"

Peter shrugged and laughed. "Who knows? Greek Sibyls were prophets. Sybil Leek was a famous witch. There was that Sybil that had all those personalities."

"Sally Field," said Lawrence.

"What?"

"Sally Field played Sybil in the movie."

"Right."

"So, can I see her? It's important."

Peter paused, looking into Lawrence's eyes. "This has nothing to do with that monster, does it? She doesn't need to be in contact with him. She's well now." He stepped closer as if to block Lawrence's way if he tried to run around and find Marie without permission.

"I'm sorry. It is about her husband ..."

"Ex-husband," Peter interrupted.

"Sorry again. Ex-husband. I think he's going to cause trouble. He's gone over the edge. I think he's really dangerous now."

"I can protect Sybil from him."

Lawrence shook his head. "No. It's not just him. There's a man, a so-called prophet named Brother James. He's been stirring up the local church congregation. Calling you heretics and blasphemers."

Peter laughed loudly. "Ha! We've been called worse. It's no big deal. We'll talk them round."

"No, you don't understand. He was talking about killing, about manipulating a psychopath to do his work. I heard him."

"Bah! Psychopaths don't scare me either."

Lawrence sighed; the man was so frustratingly upbeat. "This time it's different. Things in Tyndale have changed. And there's this insane deputy. He's the psychopath. I must see Marie and warn her."

Peter stayed silent for at least a minute then said, "Alright. But if you hurt her, if she gets upset because of you, I'll hurt you."

This time, Lawrence laughed. "No, you won't. You're a softy. You wouldn't hurt a fly. And besides, it's against your religion."

Peter's face went dark and he leaned close to Lawrence and whispered in his ear. "Just try me. Things have changed with us as well." He stepped back, his face expressionless, and waited for Lawrence to respond.

They locked eyes for a moment. Lawrence nodded.

Peter put his arm around Lawrence's shoulders, quite a feat since he was so much shorter. "This way," he said and led Lawrence towards a tent at the far side of the camp all the while giving him a rundown of who was here and where they were camped. While they walked, he checked the layout of the camp. There were trees that bordered Mott Street and Silva Avenue on the west and north sides. To the east was the pavilion and to the south was the large ball diamond's right field. There was no one watching the perimeter and, in any case, it would be hard to defend the camp here no matter how many guards there were. Enemy forces could come through the trees and pour across the ball field. The Wiccans could easily be surrounded; they needed to get to a more defensible position.

Lawrence stopped walking, watched Peter as he kept walking unaware that his companion was no longer with him. "What the Hell am I thinking?" he asked quietly. "Watching the perimeter? Defensible position?" Peter, suddenly aware that he was talking to no one, stopped and turned around to see where his guest had gone. He stared at Lawrence who was now gazing at the ground shaking his head. "What's wrong with me?" he asked the man when he drew closer.

"What do you mean?" asked Peter. "Why did you stop? What are you looking at?"

"I don't know," he replied. "I was walking, looking around the camp. Then I started to see how vulnerable it is. You could be attacked from three sides." He paused, looking towards the pavilion. "And the fourth side simply gives your attackers a place to round you up and kill you."

Peter backed away. "What are you talking about? Who's going to attack us? Why would anyone want to kill us?"

Lawrence rubbed his forehead with his hands and said, "I don't know. For some reason, all I could think about was defending this camp. I have no idea where these ideas came from."

"Were you ever in the military?"

"No, but I used to watch a lot of war movies on TV."

"That helps, I'm sure. Maybe Sybil will be able to figure out what's up with you." He walked to the tent where Marie was staying, knocked on a tent pole and said, "Sybil? There's someone here to see you." Lawrence approached the tent, nervous, wondering how Marie might have changed.

A moment later, Sybil/Marie came out of the tent. Lawrence gasped when he saw her. Eight years had worked miracles. Though he knew she was in her early sixties, Marie looked barely out of her forties. There were laugh lines around her eyes and mouth, and deep dimples in her cheeks, which were rosy red and free of makeup. The mousy brown hair that Lawrence remembered was now solid gray and tied back in a long braid that reached almost to her waist. Her eyes shone as he'd never seen them, free now of the unhappiness that had overshadowed her life with Frederick Silva. She was dressed in a tan waistcoat and white shirt with billowing sleeves. Her skirt, held at the waist with a wide leather belt, was hunter green and patterned with stars and moons. She was barefoot. The clothes could not hide the fact that she had a fantastic figure.

When Marie saw who it was, she leapt forward and embraced Lawrence, kissing his cheeks and hugging him tightly. There were tears in her eyes and a smile so wide it made his heart leap with joy. She was so different from the last time he had been with her, drug-addled and frightened of her own shadow, ready to be beaten for defying the man who had defined and confined her life for so long.

"Marie," he said softly. "Or should I call you Sybil?"

She leaned away from him and looked into his eyes. He could see a brightness there now where before there had been only

J. Edwin Buja

darkness. "I'll always be Marie to an old friend like you. How have you been? Are you still working for him? How's Luana?"

"Luana's the same. The doctors don't think she'll ever wake up. There are signs of brain activity but something's keeping her down. I live in hope."

A cloud seemed to pass over her and Marie looked away from him, her face suddenly red. "What is it?" he asked. She looked back at him then at Peter and said, "Would you mind leaving us alone, Peter? I have to talk to Lawrence about something."

Peter grinned and slapped Lawrence on the back. "Take care, my friend. I'll be at the canteen. Come by later and try some of my cornbread; it's magic." With that, he walked away.

Marie took his hand and led him into the tent where she passed him a camp chair to sit on. "Would you like some tea?" she asked.

"No, thank you. Look, Marie, there's something you must know."

She shushed him and said, "No, let me." She sat on a cot across from him and put her hands on his knees. The way she gazed into his eyes made him wonder if she was searching for something in him, some undefined thing that would help her say what she needed to say. She seemed worried, nervous now when before she had been so carefree.

"What is it?" he asked, placing his hands on hers, feeling the coolness of them. He remembered how she always felt cool before, no matter what the weather, as if she had an internal air conditioner. It had made life miserable for Marie in the winter months when her feet and hands were always cold. "What?"

Marie closed her eyes and said, "I have to apologize. I feel so responsible."

"Apologize for what? You have nothing to be sorry for. It's

that bastard husband of yours that should be sorry."

"Ex."

"Sorry, ex-husband."

"I knew what happened, you see. I caught them together, she was so innocent. But I couldn't tell; I was so afraid."

Lawrence gently placed a hand on her shoulder, squeezed and said, "Tell about what?"

She sat back, pulled her hands away and covered her face. "Even after all this time, it's hard." She looked at him, pleading in her eyes. "Please, Lawrence, don't hate me."

Lawrence got up and sat next to her on the cot. He put an arm around her shoulder, drew her close, and rubbed his hand up and down her arm. "How could I possibly hate you, Marie? You were always so kind. And what you did for Luana after the accident."

"It's what I didn't do for Luana before the accident that you should know about."

Lawrence backed off at the mention of his daughter before the tragedy that took her from him. "What do you mean?"

Marie stood and paced across the floor of the tent. Lawrence noticed that she wore several rings on her toes, and ankle bracelets that clacked as she moved. She stopped pacing and looked down at him. She took a deep breath and said, "I caught Frederick raping Luana."

"What?" His mouth hung open, his mind a tempest of emotions but most of all, hate—hatred for the man who had made his life miserable for so long, who treated him like some old-world slave, to be used as the master sees fit. "Is this true?" Looking at the floor, at Marie, at the tent walls, he tried to focus through the tears welling in his eyes. He felt himself become ill and turned to the side to vomit but he only dry heaved for several seconds. Turning back to face Marie, he went to her, took her by the arms and shook her. "Why tell me now?"

Marie wriggled free and fell to her knees, reached up and grabbed his hands. "Please forgive me," she begged. "I was weak and he threatened to kill me if I said anything." She was sobbing.

Lawrence stared down at her, angry at her for remaining silent for so long, but also understanding the fear that had motivated her silence. His hands balled into fists, wanting to strike out but instead Lawrence dug his fingernails into his palms. When his anger dissipated enough, he dropped to his knees beside her and hugged her again. "It's alright, Marie. I understand." He rocked her gently trying to control his emotions. *It's not her fault. It's not her fault.* He hoped he would believe it soon. "Now, tell me everything."

Marie wiped her eyes with a crimson handkerchief then blew her nose loudly. She looked at Lawrence again and he wiped another tear from her cheek with his thumb, smiling all the time. "It was a long time ago," he said. "It's alright." He nearly believed what he said.

He helped Marie to her feet and sat her back on the cot then returned to his camp chair. Holding her hands, he encouraged her to speak with a smile and a nod.

Taking a deep breath, Marie spoke, "It was the afternoon of the accident. I had just arrived home from a shopping trip and needed to tell Frederick how much I had spent—he was a fanatic about money, especially if it wasn't his. I searched all over The Poplars and couldn't find him. We were visiting Uncle Horace for the weekend and I assumed he and Frederick were off somewhere talking about money. Frederick was always after Horace for money. I miss the old man, he was nice. You had been sent to the city on some errand or other, and Celine was in the garden doing some weeding."

Lawrence winced at the mention of his long-dead wife. He still felt her presence at night when he was trying to sleep; and he was sure he could smell her cologne whenever he visited Luana's room.

"I was about to give up looking when I heard a noise in the greenhouse. I went in and that's when I saw," she stopped to gather herself. It was obvious to him that she was in a great deal of pain speaking about this. But it was nothing compared to the pain he felt everyday remembering the family he had lost. "I found Frederick in the greenhouse. He had Luana with him. He had a hand over her mouth and had her on the potting table and he was bent over her. He was ..."

"I understand," said Lawrence calmly. He closed his eyes, tried to banish the image that had invaded his mind. *I'm going to kill you, you son of a bitch. Forget the police, forget the courts. You're going to die.* He thought of ways to kill Silva, ways that would be painful and humiliating.

"Lawrence? Are you alright?" Marie's voice broke him out of his fantasy. "You went away there for a bit."

He looked at her sadly, sorry she had to hold this in for so long; feeling worse because he had to deal with it now. "What did you do?" he asked, his voice cracked a little.

"He saw me watching and jumped away from Luana and hit me. That's how I lost these teeth." She opened her mouth to show him the space on the left side where three molars used to be. "He started to strangle me, warned me that if I ever told anyone what I had seen he would kill me. I believed him. I was so scared."

Lawrence was silently crying now. "She was only five years old, my beautiful little girl. How could he do such a thing?" He sobbed into his hands. Marie waited until he was finished.

"That's not the end."

He let out a breath wishing he had never come to the camp, wishing he could go home and hold his daughter's hand and will her to be well again. He nodded for Marie to continue, dreading what was coming next.

"Celine heard the racket in the greenhouse and came in. When she saw Luana lying unconscious on the floor, with her dress all messed up, and the blood, she went crazy. She knew Frederick had done it. She rushed to Luana's side, covered her legs, tried to wake her up. The way she looked at Frederick, he knew she would kill him if she got the chance, so he hit her. The expression of surprise on her face, I'll never forget it. She fell back against the workbench, dazed by the punch. Then he picked up a shovel and smashed her forehead with it."

"No," said Lawrence through sobs. His face glistened with tears and his mind became confused. "I can't take any more of this. He killed my Celine, too?" He felt utterly defeated. There was nothing that could be worse than what he was hearing now. It had been eight years and the pain surged back. His bowels wanted to loosen but he fought against it, struggling to regain control of himself.

"I'm so sorry, Lawrence. If I had been stronger, I might have been able to save them."

"Save them?"

"Yes. They were both unconscious. Frederick got your old car and put them both in then drove off. I can only guess at what he did then, but I assume he set up the accident. He came back to the house several hours later, wet and disheveled, shaking like a leaf. I, to my eternal shame, was cowering in my room. I was terrified. I had seen what he did to Celine; I knew he would do it to me."

"You never told me," he shouted. "Why?"

"You were in so much pain already. To know that your wife had been murdered would have driven you mad. And there was Luana to think about. Horace had said he would take care of her forever and we all knew he was dying. I didn't want to risk it. Luana's help might have been cut off if Frederick was charged." She shook her head. "I don't know. I was confused and afraid. That's when he started using the drugs on me. Making sure I wouldn't be believed even if I did speak out. By the time you helped me get away, it was too late to do anything."

"But why didn't anything show up in the police records? Wouldn't they have noticed that Celine was hit with a shovel and hadn't hit her head on the steering wheel? And the rape?"

"Frederick had his own personal physician involved. He told the man what to say, paid him off. And that deputy, Schofield, was on the prowl, too. He helped cover up the details of the accident."

Lawrence's eyes lit up. "Schofield was involved?" *There's another one who's going to die.* He smiled bitterly at the thought. Then he screamed at the top of his lungs, all the hurt and frustration and anger boiling out of him. Sobbing loudly, he fell to his knees, his head resting in Marie's lap, letting it all pour out of him.

Pounding footsteps and bellows of alarm were followed by the tent flaps being thrown back and shouts of, "What the Hell is going on?"

Peter saw Lawrence and stopped. He looked questioningly at Marie who nodded in response and said, "It's alright, Peter. Lawrence has had some bad news. We'll be okay."

Peter seemed skeptical but said, "Okay, but I'll be close by.

Call me if you need anything." He peered down at Lawrence who was still sobbing then closed the tent flaps and left.

Marie helped Lawrence onto the cot and draped a blanket over him. "Sleep for a while," she said tenderly and went to sit in a chair outside the tent.

Half asleep, he could hear voices, thought he heard his name mentioned a few times, but could not understand what was being said. He drifted in and out of sleep, emotionally exhausted, drained of energy after what he had learned. But one overriding thought remained at the forefront of his mind: revenge on Silva.

Two hours later, groggy but feeling rested, Lawrence stumbled from the tent. Marie sat outside, knitting. Peter sat at her side reading a novel by the light of a lantern hung on a pole attached to his chair. When they saw him emerge from the tent, they put down what they were doing and stood. Marie looked hesitant, as if afraid he might strike out at her.

"One question: did Horace know anything about this?"

Marie shook her head as she said, "Not at the time. I think he may have suspected that Frederick had done something awful later, but by then he was so near death and didn't have the strength to do anything."

Lawrence smiled. "It's alright," he reassured them, "I'm not going to hit anyone except that bastard Silva and his lackey, the high-and-mighty Deputy Schofield. Do you have anything to drink? I'm a bit dry."

"Tea?" offered Marie. Lawrence looked blankly at her.

"Scotch?" asked Peter. He got up and took a small bottle from a knapsack next to the chair. He passed the bottle to Lawrence who took a long draught, nearly choked then returned it. Peter had a sip himself and returned it to the pack after Marie declined a taste.

KING OF THE WOOD

Lawrence sat in an empty chair a few feet from the couple, clasped his hands and said, "Thank you for telling me all that, Marie. You were right not to tell me back then. I would have killed your husband."

"Ex."

"Ex-husband and landed in jail for the rest of my life. Then where would Luana be? And no, I'm not going to kill him now. It won't bring back Celine and it won't help Luana. I have a better idea. It involves humiliation and financial ruin for him. I think that's far worse than being dead."

"What are you going to do?" asked Peter.

"He has a room full of information about people in this town and the city. It's the center of his power. But it won't be for long." He laughed. "Wait till he comes home and finds it empty. Oh, to see the look on his face." He thought for a moment. "And I think I will."

"Aren't you worried about Luana?" asked Marie.

"I've got that covered. Frederick's not the only one who knows how to manipulate ledgers," he answered with a grin. "Anyway, I came here for a reason."

"Yes," said Marie. "Peter told me you were concerned about our safety. Kept talking about how our enemies could kill us in this undefended place. Isn't that a little extreme?"

"No. You weren't at the church this morning. Reverend Mendax, who I fear may now be dead, stirred up the congregation with stories of heresy and Satanism."

Peter waved a hand to stop him and said, "We've encountered that kind of idiocy before. The organized religions think that because we're *not* organized with a hierarchy that we're a threat to them. We let people think for themselves."

"And then there's that horned god thing," added Marie.

239

"That always gets them going." They both laughed. "And don't forget the nudity and wild sex."

Peter leered at her. "How could I forget the sex?" He reached over and squeezed her knee. She giggled.

"Do you two want me to leave?" asked Lawrence, happy to see Marie having fun. He forced himself to lighten up, to push the sadness away, and let the pain dissipate.

"Sorry about that," said Peter. "She gets like this sometimes."

Marie looked shocked. "He always blames me when he's the one who can't get enough."

"I get the picture," said Lawrence, trying not to remember how Marie looked in the video. "On a more serious note, there was a guest speaker today, a Brother James. He's from the Church of the Immaculate Brides of Christ. Have you heard of it?"

Marie's face went white. The men stared at her while the color returned to her cheeks. "I've encountered him," she said. "I tried to rescue some friends from his clutches years ago but without success. The man claims to love all women but he simply uses them for his own gratification. All this word of God business is a sham. He's a charlatan, nothing more."

Lawrence sensed there was more to this but decided not to press Marie for details. "Whatever he is, he was at the church today. I've never seen the congregation so worked up. They were ready to storm over here and burn you at the stake. You've got to be careful."

"What about the police?" asked Peter.

"The Sheriff's not much use," he replied dismissively. "He's overwhelmed with the local murders and disappearances. And his main deputy is still Schofield, and he was foaming at the mouth to see you burn."

Peter looked over at Marie. "Maybe I'd better go see the

Sheriff, let him know what's going on, why we're here."

"Why are you here?" asked Lawrence.

Marie stood and said, "Surely you've noticed what's happening here. All this growth." She twirled around, arms spread wide, smiling. "The earth is trying to tell us something. We believe the Goddess is returning to guide us. We've come to welcome her. We're going to celebrate one of our festivals here Lugnasadh."

"Okay," said Lawrence. "Just be careful. Have someone stand watch at night. And be wary of strangers. It may not be necessary, but you never know what those crazies at the church might try." He stood and said, "I'd better be going. If I'm to bring down Silva, I don't want him to be suspicious of me right now." He hugged Marie. "You take care. And don't worry; you're forgiven for whatever you may think you did wrong. I don't know if I would have been able to stand up to him if I was in your situation."

"Thank you," she replied.

Peter held out his hand and asked, "Can I get a ride with you to the Sheriff's station? I think I'd like to see how things lie there."

"No problem," said Lawrence.

They walked to the car while four crows circled above.

Sister Mary

She watched them talk from her hiding place beneath the trees. Brother James had instructed her to watch the Satanists' camp and learn whatever she could. They were minions of the Adversary and would be dealt with in the most severe way. How she wished she could have been in the church when her Savior was at the front speaking. To feel the love and devotion of the assembled people would have made her heart soar. She would have remained at the back, unobtrusive but still able to hear her God speak. He had vetoed the idea, though, saying that it was too risky to expose her just yet. Feeling frustrated because she had to spend so much time in Sister Sarah's miniscule apartment, Mary surprised herself when she rebelled and insisted she would remain unrecognized in the church. Brother James's punishment had been swift and severe; her back was still sore from the flagellation. So angry had He been, He had refused to minister to her after the punishment. Instead, He had forced her to watch as He gave His holy communion to Sarah on the living room floor. Mary was sure there had been a hint of triumph in the woman's eyes as she stared over His shoulder. Sarah's fingernails had scratched Brother James's back bloody, so great was her ecstasy.

The morning and afternoon had been spent among the trees bordering the fairgrounds. To avert boredom, she imagined the scene at the church, the reverence with which the assembly would listen to Brother James's message. Oh, how she wanted to be there with Him, to support Him at His time of triumph. But He had deemed it necessary for her to perform other tasks, and now she knew better than to question His wisdom. To pass the hours, she mentally recited the messages from Brother James that she had transcribed. The only time she left her post was to relieve herself at the pavilion washroom; she suffered the leers and catcalls of the teenaged boys who were playing ball at the large diamond. She could endure anything for Brother James and God.

Then Lawrence had arrived at the camp of the Satanists. She was flabbergasted a man she had thought good would consort with such malign forces. Still, it was within all men to be betrayers. When she saw Marie, she understood the depth of

Lawrence's treachery.

Three hours later, cramped from hiding behind the tent in which they had gone to do whatever evil it was they did in tents, Mary concentrated on getting her limbs relaxed so she could follow the two men who were leaving the camp. They were headed for the parking lot; her car was parked in the high school lot across the street. She dashed from her hiding spot unafraid of being seen in the gathering darkness. Clambering into her car, she started it and drove on to Mott Street hoping to catch up with the men. She was astonished to see Lawrence's Mustang exit the fairground parking lot and come towards her. She quickly turned the car around and got to Silva Avenue in time to see the car pull into the Sheriff's office. It appeared that his passenger was getting out of the car. Quickly, she returned to the high school parking lot, turned off the engine then slipped out the passenger side door.

The Mustang was stopped at an angle in the Sheriff's office lot, so Mary was able to get close without being seen by either of the men. She crept behind a tree and listened while the men spoke. The passenger, the thin man from the Satanist camp, was out of the car now and had gone around to the driver's side. Lawrence had the window down.

"I didn't realize how close it was," the Satanist said with an evil chuckle. "You could have told me to cut through the trees."

"I wanted to have a word with you alone," came the answer from inside the car. Mary couldn't see Lawrence's face in the shadow of the interior but recognized his voice. "Just keep an eye on her. And be careful."

"Don't worry. I'll do what's necessary to keep her safe." Then the Satanist tapped the roof of the car and stepped away. It drove off.

Mary's mind raced. This man was a minion of the Adversary and he was going to see the Sheriff for some reason. She saw Sister Sarah look through the front window of the office and carefully caught the woman's attention. Making a slashing motion across her neck, she hoped her colleague inside would understand that she should not let the man enter the office. When the window blinds closed and the outside light went off, Mary knew she had been understood and thanked Brother James and God for granting her such a good companion.

The man went to the door and tried to open it. When it refused to open, he pounded on the door and yelled for someone to answer. Angry that what had a few seconds ago been an open Sheriff's office was now dark and apparently deserted, the man swore and kicked the doorframe.

But what should she do about this beast: should she stop him or report him to Brother James? She decided to act on her own but how to get the man away from the office?

He's a man. The way was obvious.

There was no one on the street and the nearest house was a couple of blocks away so she didn't have to worry about being seen by passersby. He was now standing at the edge of the parking lot looking in the direction the car had gone a short while ago. As quickly as she could, Mary tore off her tee shirt and undid her shorts. She was not wearing anything under the clothes, a preference of her Savior's. She let the shorts slide down enough to reveal the top of her pubic hair. She looked down and was worried that the hysterectomy scar would be a distraction. But it was dark enough so even she couldn't see it.

Mary stepped out and back from behind the tree to where she would be visible to the thin man. She coughed to get his attention. When the man turned to see who had made the noise,

Mary almost laughed at the expression on his face. It went from curiosity to shock to pleasure to lust in the blink of an eye. She motioned to him to follow and walked backwards towards the vine-covered fence surrounding the high school. The man followed; of course, he did. What red-blooded male wouldn't follow a half-naked woman? The grin on his face and the bulge at his crotch told Mary that he couldn't believe his luck: a beautiful woman was beckoning him into the shadows for who knew what. He'd soon find out.

When she reached the fence, Mary quickly turned to see if there were any openings. There was a break about twenty feet along where a dirt path exited a small wooded area behind an apartment building. It was probably a shortcut used by students who couldn't be bothered with going the extra twenty feet to the main sidewalk. *Lucky for me.* Through the fence, she could see that the area of the schoolyard near the break was dark. *Thank you, Brother James and God.* When she was even with the gap in the fence, she waved at the man and went through and crouched against the fence. He quickened his pace and followed her.

She was waiting for him. When he stuck his head through the break to see where she had gone, Mary rammed the knife hidden in her back pocket up into the man's throat. He stopped in his tracks, gurgled, and fell chin first in the dirt. The weight of his body forced the blade through his throat and out the back of his neck. His legs kicked a few times. Blood pooled beneath him. Then he was still.

Mary bent and retrieved her knife, wiped it on the man's shirt, and stuffed it back in her pocket. She went back through the break in the fence and grasped her victim's ankles. His thinness made her task easier and she dragged the corpse into the bushes next to the trail. There was a shallow drainage ditch not far from the path so she dropped his feet and kicked his body down the slope. Not far from where the dead Satanist lay, a culvert went under the street. Thanking Brother James and God for this gift, Mary dragged the man's body into the dark opening. It smelled foul but that was good because it would mask the smell as the body decayed. That is, if no one found it for a long time. There was a lot of debris in the culvert, probably from all that rain, she surmised. She used this to cover the body. Stepping back outside the culvert, she was satisfied that no one would see anything but trash from the path. It was too dark down there to check for blood along the path but the daily afternoon rain would wash away any that was around.

At the break in the fence, Mary panicked when she saw how much blood there was. She must have hit the big artery and veins. Quickly she scooped up handfuls of dirt to spread over the mess. When everything looked normal, she rushed back to retrieve her tee shirt. There was still no one on the street.

The lights went back on at the Sheriff's office. She saw Sarah through the front window and they exchanged knowing nods.

Thanking Brother James and the Lord for Their protection, and saying a prayer for her Savior, Mary drove her car away. Considering she had just killed her first man, she was remarkably calm. Though, how could a henchman of the evil one be thought of as a real man? "I am going to make You the perfect bride," she said to the image of Brother James that was always with her.

Six crows on the roof of the Sheriff's office watched her depart.

CHAPTER FOURTEEN
THE CUBBY

Tom Bender

"Hey John."

"Hey, Nancy."

Tom waved to Spanky from the cubby. Nancy met him there. He was astounded that she already had a drink in hand, ready for his friend before he had arrived. But that was Nancy; she was almost psychic when it came to serving drinks to the regulars.

When Spanky was seated and had drained half his beer, Tom said, "The oddest thing happened this afternoon. I was buzzed by a helicopter."

"That's *your* fault?" said Spanky. "I heard the thing flying over. They make a Hell of a racket. Couldn't see it through the trees, though. What did it want?"

"I haven't a clue. It hovered over the garden for a few seconds then moved to the side of the hill. I went out and waved at it but then whoever it was, flew off."

"Did you see who was in it? Some newshounds trying to find a story or something?"

"There is no story at my place, except for the birds and the green. No, there was sunlight reflecting off the canopy so I couldn't see in. Anyway, it wasn't a news chopper. I think it was one of those tour companies from the city."

"Odd."

"That's what I said." He drank some Guinness, eyed Nancy as she served the couple by the door, admiring her ankles. "So, you heard about the good Reverend Mendax."

"Yeah. Shame. He was a decent man even if he did preach blood and thunder gospel. I always got the impression that he honestly believed everything he said. Never came across as a phony like most of those guys on the tube."

Tom nodded in agreement and said, "I know what you mean. I never felt dirty when I heard him, as much as I disputed just about every word that came out of his mouth."

"How's Jay holding up? He's a member of that church."

Tom shrugged and said, "He's fine. When I asked him about it, his eyes glazed over as if he was bored or thinking about something else. Weird. But that's Jay."

"But what about the rumors that he had porn on his computer at the church?"

Tom said, "Why is it that, whenever someone dies, it comes out that they had porn? Like that isn't normal?"

"Not when you have as much as you do."

"Hey, I don't have anything like the collection Jay has. Have you seen some of his stuff?"

"Yeah, I've borrowed some."

"You, too? What, is the guy the local porn librarian or something?"

"Have you heard any more than what was in the paper?" asked Spanky, a little red-faced. "And I heard about that witch guy that disappeared, too. You've got that connection with Terry. What'd he tell you?"

"No. I haven't spoken to Terry for a couple of days, and the last time we did speak, he gave me the feeling that he was pissed off at me for something. I think the birds spooked him."

"You know, I spoke to Mendax a few days before he was murdered," said Tom. "He asked if I had anything he could use for tracking the church's finances and membership."

"Wow," said Spanky as he finished his beer. Before he could set the glass down, Nancy took it away and replaced it with a full one. She also took away Tom's empty Guinness glass. "That would have been some lucrative job if he'd hired you." He thought for a moment then said, "I can't believe I just said that. Thinking about money when the poor sod had his head bashed in. Who could do such a thing, Tom?"

"You've got me on that one. Hey, what took you so long? Couldn't find the dad?"

Jay sat down across from Tom, said, "Fuck off," and signaled to Nancy that he was now ready for a refill. "I shouldn't have eaten those tacos for lunch. As much as I love spicy food, it just doesn't love me." He tapped his sternum and let go a resounding belch that Tom was sure could be heard in the city. It felt like the walls had trembled, too. The cubby now reeked of onions.

"We really don't need to hear about your eating problems," said Spanky.

"Yeah, man," added Tom. "I was going to order food."

"Don't let me stop you," said Jay. He picked up a menu. "What's good today? Any specials?" He glanced over at the chalk board hanging on a pillar in the center of the main room; it was empty save for the faint traces of last weekend's specials.

Tom and Spanky exchanged meaningful looks. Nothing could

ever get in the way of Jay's appetite, even severe stomach cramps.

Jay put down the menu and said, "You know, I've been wondering."

Oh, no, here it comes. What disgusting thing must we hear now?

"Why don't guys talk to each other in the can? I mean, you're standing next to a guy at the urinal; you've got nothing else to do. Is there anything wrong with chatting with your neighbor?"

"He might think you're coming on to him," suggested Spanky.

Jay looked disgusted. "Hey, I'm not talking about trying to see the guy's dad and comparing it to the big one. I'm talking common courtesy. Shit, even if the guys know each other, came in at the same time, they never say a word."

"The French do," said Tom. "I was in Montreal a while back, and everyone in the toilet was talking. They never shut up. Couldn't understand a word they were saying, but they sure seemed interested in each other. One guy was even leaning against the wall next to the urinal, puffing away on a cigarette, tapping his buddy on the shoulder as he peed. It was the weirdest thing."

"Man, that's just sick," said Spanky.

"I know," said Tom. "I'd be afraid of getting splashed."

Jay appeared miffed that Tom had hijacked the conversation and said, "Yeah, yeah, but getting back to me for a moment. What about when you're sitting down? Just now, I was sitting there, and in walks Eddie—I recognized his shoes—and sits in the next stall. Does he say hello? Not a peep. He saw me go in; he must have known it was me." He sipped the last of his drink. "Quite the stinker, too. And you should have heard the sounds. I could scarcely believe they came from a human."

"This from a man who just a minute ago woke up half of Asia with a burp," said Spanky.

Jay ignored him. "And then, I heard hardly any paper come off the roll and he's outta there."

"Maybe he only farted and was checking for chunks," suggested Tom.

"No, no, I heard the splashes. Good old Johnny Skidmarks, you ask me."

Tom and Spanky looked through the cubby window to where Eddie was slicing lemons at the bar. Tom felt thankful that he didn't drink gin and tonics or tequila.

Nancy came by with Tom's drink and they ordered food. Not unexpectedly, Jay ordered extra spicy chicken wings. Then he asked, "Nancy, how can a salad be hearty?"

"What?" she asked flatly. She was used to his questions; they were usually irrelevant to anything to do with her.

Jay held up a menu and pointed. "See here, it says the chef's salad is hearty. Salad is just a bunch of greens. How hearty is that? Meat is hearty. An omelet is hearty if it has chunks of ham in it. Pork and beans are hearty. Salads are healthy."

With a sigh, Nancy said, "That's a julienne salad. It's got strips of cheese, ham, and grilled chicken in it. It's hearty. Perhaps if you learned to read you wouldn't make such an ass of yourself." She nodded at Tom and Spanky, said, "Gentlemen," and walked away.

After Spanky stopped laughing, Tom said, "Guys, can I ask you something? Seriously."

Spanky and Jay both put one elbow on the table and leaned forward chin in hand trying to look serious. "Go ahead, Tom," said Jay in his most teacherly voice. He adjusted his glasses so he could hear better.

Tom looked down at the table top then back at his friends. "This is going to sound kinda stupid."

"More stupid than the stuff Jay talks about?" asked Spanky.

"Hey." Jay smacked Spanky's arm.

Tom continued, "A while back, I was all overcome with melancholy. Feeling pretty sad for myself. It came on all sudden like, out of nowhere. Knocked me off my feet. Literally." Mouth dry and feeling a little uptight about revealing something so personal, he sipped his Guinness. "Anyway, I got to thinking about how I'm an outsider. I wasn't born in Tyndale. I felt like I didn't belong. For some reason, I figured you natives viewed me as an interloper and were only being kind instead of genuinely friendly. Stupid, I know. But the feeling was so strong."

His two friends were silent. "Shit, I was right," he said, joking. *Shit, I was right.* Hurt.

Nancy brought their food and they tucked in.

"Jerk," said Jay.

Between bites of steak, Spanky said, "I'm not from Tyndale. My parents moved here from New Hampshire when I was eleven."

"You're kidding," said Tom. "That does explain why you're so polite. But I thought you'd been born here."

Spanky shook his head. "Nope. I've been here about twice as long as you, but I'm a newbie of sorts, too."

"Me three," said Jay. "I got here in the middle of grade twelve. It was a bitch being the new kid in the last year of high school. Talk about feeling like an outsider. You ain't experienced nothin' till you've been ostracized by almost the whole grade. Steve O'Leary and Spanky here were about the only ones that were nice to me."

"You paid me."

"Did not. Well, not much."

Tom sat back, amazed. "You're shittin' me."

Jay said, "We shit you not. I even gave Spanky his name."

"Shut up, 'kay," said Spanky.

Curious, Tom said, "Continue."

Jay glanced over at Spanky who was looking around the cubby as if trying to find something to use to beat Jay to death, then said, "He was madly in love with Nancy in high school. I thought she looked like Darla from Our Gang so I started kidding him."

Watching Nancy serve a couple in the main room, Tom said, "I can see a bit of a resemblance to Darla. But why not Alfalfa? He was the one in love with the real Darla. Did you catch him doing something evil?"

"No! Shut up, 'kay."

Jay said, "Spanky was a fat kid in high school."

"I was not fat, I was stout."

"He looked more like Spanky McFarland than Alfalfa."

"Stout."

"Stout? You always drink ale," said Nancy who had silently come by to see if they needed another round. "Tom drinks stout."

"We were talking about Spanky in high school when he was a tub," said Jay.

"Stout, dammit."

"There was just more of you to love back then," replied Nancy and patted Spanky on the shoulder. His face went red and he tried to say something but his mouth only opened and closed like a fish. He drank some ale to hide his discomfort. Nancy went back to the bar where she helped Eddie slice lemons. Eddie had been slicing them for the last hour.

J. Edwin Buja

Jay continued, "He didn't become the svelte womanizer he is today until after graduation."

"I'm stunned. I can't imagine you big," said Tom.

"Stout. Like Brian Dennehy."

They didn't speak for a while as they cleared their plates. The Pub was quiet mid-week; hence Nancy's more-incredible-than-usual service tonight. The recent crime wave was also keeping a lot of people at home, not that there seemed to be any danger on the streets of Tyndale, only in Tom's back yard and the morgue and the church; and wherever it was that Wright was snatched. Okay, so a lot of Tyndale was dangerous.

"So, I guess Terry's from here," said Tom.

Spanky shook his head. "Nope. Arrived," he thought for a second, "about twelve, thirteen years ago. Wasn't that a little before you and Belinda?"

"Really?" said Tom. "That's incredible. I was sure he'd been here forever."

Jay piped in, "No. I remember my dad being pissed that this guy from out of nowhere showed up and became Sheriff. My dad wanted to be Sheriff but those rich assholes brought in Terry instead. Didn't even elect him. It was mostly Horace." He took a sip of his drink then said, "Fat bastard," with more anger than Tom expected.

"Fucking stout. He's stout."

"Whatever. The guy's never been elected. Always wins by acclamation. No one has the balls to stand up to him. Not even the rich guys anymore."

Tom said, "That would explain why he was able to force Silva to back down at my place. But how did he get to be so powerful? I thought Silva pretty much ran things around here."

"It wasn't that Silva," said Spanky. "It was Horace, just before he died. I found out when I was doing that research into Horace's will. Apparently, Horace made some deal with the Council to get Terry here and no one's ever been able to break it. Would cost too much and, anyway, Terry does a good job."

"For a fat bastard," said Jay, again with more anger than necessary.

"Stout. You've got a big chip on your shoulder about this."

"It's a stout chip. My dad was really bummed about not getting to run." Jay paused for a moment and gazed up at the ceiling, lost in thought. "He would have been a crap sheriff anyhow. No experience. I think he just liked the leather belt and the uniform. Turned him on. At least, that's what mom always said."

"By all that's holy, we don't need to hear that about your parents," said Tom.

Nancy came by to remove their plates. Tom said, "Darla, are you from Tyndale?"

She looked at Tom like he was insane. Spanky buried his face in his hands, mortified, and Jay was suddenly enjoying himself. "Who?" she asked.

Tom's eyes popped open when he realized what he said. "Sorry, Nancy." He pronounced her name carefully, making it three syllables. "We were talking about something else. I got confused."

She sat down across from Spanky and placed the empty plates on a tray. "You were making fun of John again, weren't you? It was probably you," she swatted Jay's arm, "you pig."

"Who, me?" asked Jay, all sweet and innocent.

Nancy looked at Tom and said, "Yes, I'm from here. Why do you ask?"

Tom shrugged and replied, "Just curious. I was asking these

guys about where they were from and it seemed like no one was actually born here."

Nancy wiped the table with a rag and said, "I was born here. So were most of those rich folks over at the estates. The O'Learys, Reverend Mendax—sorry Jay, Eddie, that swine Schofield, Billy Lush."

"I hated Billy Lush at school," said Spanky. "He used to bug the Hell out of me. Always trying to steal my lunch money and mooch answers during tests. I remember, this one time, he got caught with a note and the teacher believed him when he said it was for me and that he didn't know anything about it. I got sent to the Principal's office and got a detention. I didn't even know who the note was from. Something about meeting after school at the bleachers or something."

Nancy's face was red. She said quietly, "It was from me."

Spanky looked horrified. "You wanted to meet Billy after school? Gross. His lips were so wet. And he had bad zits. We used to call him Cave."

Nancy faced Spanky. "Not him, idiot. You. The note was from me to you. I had the biggest crush on you in high school. I finally got up the nerve to say something but that bastard Billy got the note."

Spanky went quiet and closed his eyes. Tom could see them moving around under his lids, as if trying to read something in his head. He fumbled with his jacket and took out a cigarette then wordlessly got up and went outside. They watched in silence as he left.

"I think you pissed him off, Darla," said Jay.

"You never said anything to him about it?" asked Tom.

"I felt awful because I got him in trouble. I thought he would hate me for doing it. Maybe think I was making fun of him." She reached over and grabbed hold of Jay's earlobe, twisted it. He winced, said, "Ow," and tried to get her to let go. She didn't. "Why'd you call me Darla?"

Jay explained the nickname and why he gave it to John.

"You know he's crazy about you, don't you," said Tom. "Every time you walk by, he goes all quiet and stares and gets tongue tied. It's all he can do most of the time to order a drink from you. It's worse because you keep coming on to me."

Nancy seemed shaken by what Tom said. Her eyes got a faraway look and she shook her head. "I was trying to make him jealous. You're not even my type, Tom."

Indignant, Tom said, "What? But, I thought. Wait a minute. Oh, man. You screwed up, Nancy."

She stood without a word, picked up the tray of dirty dishes, and hurried off. She disappeared into the kitchen and a second later, burst through the kitchen door. Eddie, surprised by the noise, looked up from his lemons. "Break," she shouted to him, and raced towards the front door. As she reached for the handle, Spanky came though. He was shocked to see her standing there and took a step back to get out of her way. Nancy followed and threw her arms around his shoulders, pulled him close, and kissed him. Stunned, Spanky looked around her head at Tom and Jay with an expression that asked what the Hell was going on. Nancy kept her lips pressed to his.

"Must be like kissing an ashtray," said Jay.

"No," answered Tom, "he always sucks on a mint when he's finished puffing."

"You're experienced?"

"Fuck off."

Finally loosening up, Spanky wrapped his arms around the woman he had loved for the last twenty years and kissed her back. The big man by the door whooped; his companion smacked his arm but smiled broadly.

Eddie, with a pleased look on his face, came over to the cubby window and asked, "What made them realize after all this time?"

Tom shrugged and said, "I had a bad day."

"Oh," said Eddie as if he understood and went back to slicing lemons.

Spanky and Nancy sat at a table by the far wall, deep in conversation. While they talked, they held hands as if afraid to let go after all this time. Tom felt a lump in his throat seeing his friend happy at last. He was, perhaps, just a little jealous.

At the window above where Spanky and Nancy sat, Tom saw a pair of crows looking into the main room. He believed they were trying to see the happy couple. While he thought this, nine more joined the pair. They paced back and forth on the window ledge, alternately looking through the glass and at each other, as if having a debate about what was happening inside.

CHAPTER FIFTEEN
THE TOWN

John "Spanky" McFarlane

He came up for air, felt the sheet move and looked up to see what Nancy was doing. She had the end of the sheet bunched in one hand, holding it up so she could see his face down there.

"It's been three days," she said lazily. "Don't you think we should see what's going on out in the world?"

Spanky thought about it for half a second, replied, "No," and went back to what he did best.

Nancy started moaning again and let the sheet drop.

Frederick Silva

Where was that imbecile Lawrence? For six days now, Silva had been hiding in the Poplars expecting the Sheriff to arrive at any moment with a warrant for his arrest. He knew the body of Reverend Mendax had been found within minutes of the murder and was sure someone must have seen him leaving the scene. Of all the bad luck: it must have been that moron of a janitor; he was supposed to have finished his work in the afternoon and returned to the hovel he called home. The man, Morrison, must have been in the church the whole time Silva was in the office taking care of his financial problem with the reverend. But if Morrison had seen him, why hadn't the police come around?

Silva paced back and forth in his bedroom clutching his aching stomach; his insides were a boiling mass of nerves that sent him to the bathroom almost hourly. His beard itched in the heat and humidity that was fast overcoming the power of the house's air conditioner. A small fan on a side table provided a little relief but made him nervous; the sight of the machine reminded him of how he had removed the nosy churchman. He scratched his unshaved face, unaware he had irritated the skin on his neck so much he drew blood with every scratch. His hair was greasy; he was afraid to go in the shower in case someone came to arrest him while he was helpless. The room reeked of his sourness.

"I should have left the county," he said to the stranger in the huge mirror that hung on the wall across from the bed. He tried to concentrate on the image there but his mind couldn't stop long enough to focus and every noise in the house sent him dashing to the door to listen for intruders. "No, I can't leave until I get rid of that man Bender. He's responsible for all this. Anyone with half a brain could tell. They just need to know the facts."

A noise from the hall outside his room startled Silva and he dove across the bed to get the pistol that was hidden under a pillow. With a shaking hand, he aimed the weapon at the door, ready to shoot his way out if he had to. No one came to the door and, after waiting ten minutes, he returned the gun to its hiding place and resumed his pacing, muttering his woes.

Lawrence was supposed to keep him informed but the fool

hadn't told him anything new for days. The man was too stupid to understand the seriousness of the situation and believed every word he was told. The story about being targeted by a mad killer who was out to get the Council was a stroke of brilliance, giving him reason to remain incognito in the house. Someone was killing off people though no one knew for sure whether Wright was a victim or not. The coward had probably run away with his tranny whore, was shacked up somewhere performing all sorts of perverted acts with that abomination.

He yawned, wishing he could get some sleep but his mind was alive with possibilities. Every time he tried to nod off, he acted out scenarios in his head where the police came for him and he tried to get away. Could he shoot it out with the Sheriff and his deputies? Would Schofield turn on his fellow lawmen and come to his rescue? Would he kill himself before allowing anyone to place him in custody? How could he get himself out of this situation? How could he get revenge on that swine on the hill?

There was a loud knock on the door and it opened. He froze. The gun was under the pillow on the other side of the room. There was no way he could cross the space before whoever was coming in caught him and dragged him away like a common criminal. And if there was one thing Frederick Silva was not, it was common. He straightened, took a deep breath and tried to regain some dignity. Maybe he could browbeat his visitor and talk his way out of the situation; he'd done it enough times before.

Lawrence walked into the room and glared at his master. The expression of contempt on his face was so plain that, for the first time in his life, Silva almost felt shame. *The man must know what I've done. Why else would he be so blatant in his disrespect? Well, there'd be no more of that.*

"What do you want? I told you not to disturb me. Are you deaf? Suddenly stupid? Has that pickaninny brain of yours ceased to function properly?" He was surprised that his voice was still bold and commanding. He waited with head held high while Lawrence groveled to find a reply.

But Lawrence didn't grovel. He stood boldly facing his better and said with a flat voice, "Deputy Schofield is here to see you." He gave Silva the once over, his face screwed up in disgust, something he had never ever done, and added with derision, "Sir."

Silva's bowels nearly evacuated at the mention of the deputy's name. Fortunately, he hadn't eaten for two days so he only passed gas. Lawrence grimaced at the sound, clearly impatient to be away from this room.

The time had come at last and that cretin of a sheriff had to send a lackey to do the job. He looked down at himself; his rumpled pajamas were soaked with sweat and stank. There were urine stains on the bottoms and he needed a pedicure. How could he, Frederick Silva, a man of dignity who commanded the respect of the town, have let himself go like this? He walked over to his dressing gown where it hung on a chair by the window. He put the garment on and tied it around his waist to hide his degradation then unconsciously straightened the tie he wasn't wearing; dignity: it was important to the Silva family.

The deputy strode into the room pushing Lawrence out of the way. Good, put the lowborn scum in his place. As usual, Schofield's uniform was crisp and clean. Lawrence huffed as the deputy passed and left the room without being told. Silva could not believe the insolence of his man. His job was done, trust fund be damned.

But all thoughts of his secretary vanished when he got a good look at the mass of scabs and bruises on Schofield's face.

Always ready to take advantage of someone who was obviously ill at ease or in pain, he asked, "What happened to your face?"

The deputy hesitated a moment then replied, "It was the minions of the devil. I was attacked while performing my duty."

"That tells me nothing." *If you can be distracted this easily from your mission to arrest me then I may be able to get myself out of this mess.* "Who did this to you?"

"It was that Jezebel, Ravenscroft. I was trying to arrest her and she resisted."

"If I remember correctly, she's not that big. Did she take you by surprise?"

Schofield looked uncomfortable but said, "As I told you before, it was the minions of the devil. The harlot called on her familiars to attack me. I am taking measures to see that it doesn't happen again." His face took on such a malign aspect that Silva wanted to run from the room. He had seen the deputy angry and vengeful before but this was something new.

I'd best to find out what's going on. He tried not to look at his visitor's face. The scabs and the scowl were making him feel ill, and one of the larger cuts on Schofield's forehead was weeping blood and pus. A wave of pain ripped across his stomach and nearly made him wretch. Holding back bile and trying not to show his discomfort, Silva asked, "What are you doing here? I'm a busy man." His nerves were frayed, anticipating the coming arrest and humiliation. Could he overcome this man in a fight? He was weak, hadn't eaten or slept in days, what chance did he have?

Schofield stared at him with surprising disdain. "I can see that." He wrinkled his nose and added, "And smell it, too."

Suddenly feeling a little like his old self, Silva bristled at the man's words and shouted, "Remember who's in charge here, Deputy Schofield. Do I need to remind you about your position within my business affairs?" He crossed his arms and waited for that to sink in.

Schofield seemed unfazed and replied, "Do I need to remind you of your position in everything, Mister Silva? I may know where the bodies are buried but I also know who said to put them there."

Refusing to let this subordinate get the upper hand and knowing that the fool had no proof, Silva kept calm and said, "Fine, Deputy. We understand each other." He walked over to the side table next to the bed and poured himself a measure of Scotch. The pistol was only two feet away, hidden from the deputy, his last line of defense. The amber liquid burned his parched throat and felt heavy in his stomach. With no food to absorb the liquor, its effects were almost instantaneous. His head became lighter and for an instant his vision blurred. When he shook his head trying to focus, the room swayed and he almost lost his footing. But years of experience being in charge and refusing to show weakness won out and he remained steady. With a pounding headache, he said, "Now, get to the point of this tedious visit." He felt immense relief, sure now that the man was not here to arrest him but had no idea what other business he could have.

Schofield sat in an easy chair, steepled his fingers and stared expressionlessly at his host. Silva sprawled onto the bed and gathered the pillows under his head and shoulders against the headboard. He casually slid the pistol along the mattress under the pillows so it was within easy reach of his right hand. Trying to look as relaxed as possible while his insides were burning both from the Scotch and anxiety, he said, "Well?"

The deputy started with, "We have a suspect in the murder of Reverend Mendax." Silva put every effort into showing no reaction but then thought he should show something. After all, the reverend had been a friend and fellow church member. He couldn't appear completely cold, that might arouse suspicion. He tried to show just enough interest and leaned forward in anticipation of the deputy's next words. He also placed his hand flat on the bed, ready to slip under the pillow and pull out the weapon hidden there. Schofield went on, "It's that junkie janitor, Morrison. He was seen fleeing the scene shortly after we received the call about the murder."

Silva nearly burst into tears and felt his bladder let go a little. Instantly, he felt relief then anger, then disgust. A week of hiding for nothing. No one suspected him. He wasn't seen. He was free and clear. Even if they caught Morrison, who would believe a drug addict? *But I can't seem too happy about this. I need to get rid of this fool, but how? If I rush him out, he'll be suspicious; and I can't stand up and let him see what I've done to myself.* As calmly as possible but with a hint of anger, he asked, "Why was I not informed of this sooner?"

Schofield showed no reaction and said flatly, "I was busy." His eyes never strayed from Silva's.

Trying to read me? I'll give you something to read. "I want to post a reward for information. We'll discuss the amount later. This killer must be brought in and punished to the fullest extent the law permits. What proof do you have?"

Schofield said, "We found his fingerprints all over the office and it looked like the place had been ransacked. He must have been looking for the collection money. Brother James's visit inspired much more giving than usual, praise His name."

You are truly repulsive when you get righteous. He could hardly stand to look at the man. "Reverend Mendax was a longtime friend of my family and a valued colleague. I want to see his death avenged."

"'Vengeance is mine; I will repay, saith the Lord.'"

"Quite," said Silva. "But He may need a little help from His faithful." *What an ass.*

"Thank you, Mister Silva. I do the Lord's work, as do we all. Still, I may need your help. The Sheriff is useless. He seems to be sick and can't take care of himself. I believe he's been drinking. You can smell the liquor on him despite his vain attempts to hide the odor with gum and mints." The deputy was patently enjoying himself talking about the shortcomings of his boss. "He is failing in his God-given duty to the people of this town and I feel I can no longer recognize his authority. It falls to me to keep this county under control. The murders and disappearances are but a distraction from the coming of the Kingdom of Heaven. Fortunately, we have one in our midst who has been anointed to guide us along the path to true righteousness."

Silva wanted to vomit. The Scotch was sitting heavy in his empty stomach and he knew he needed to get something to eat to stop the burning. His mind was still a little foggy, and this religious fool's scripture quotes and blind faith were not helping matters. He was curious about this supposed leader, though. "Who are you talking about?" he asked.

The smile that came over Schofield's face was radiant. His countenance softened and he relaxed into his chair. Silva had never seen the man so happy; in fact, he had never seen the man happy at all: glee at the misfortune and perceived weaknesses of others didn't count. Then it came to him, who the deputy was talking about. Before he could think the name, Schofield said,

KING OF THE WOOD

"Our Savior, Brother James." He clasped his hands together and bowed his head. Silva could just make out the muttered prayer. The man had surrendered himself utterly to the charlatan with the pretty face from the city and—Silva stopped himself. Thinking about the man in the black suit from the church last week was starting to arouse him. He could feel movement in his wet pajamas. This certainly was neither the time nor the place for that kind of thing. Perhaps later. No. He refused to succumb to such degenerate impulses. He adjusted his dressing gown to cover any telltale wetness or bulge. His throat was dry and constricted from his rising excitement but he managed to croak, "What is this Brother James doing to guide the faithful?"

Schofield stood and spread his arms wide. "Why, He's organizing a crusade against the unfaithful. There's a cell of Satanists in our midst and He's going to lead us in a valiant battle to eliminate them. And He says that there is someone powerful in Tyndale who is opposed to the coming of the Kingdom of Heaven, who is opposed to the magnificent presence of the Lord. Together, we will root out this agent of the adversary and destroy him and all those who sustain him." He strode back and forth across the room, his arms waving to emphasize his words. "And any who oppose our righteous cause, who have abandoned their faith, shall 'know therefore and see that it is an evil thing and bitter, that thou hast forsaken the Lord thy God, and that my fear is not in thee, saith the Lord god of hosts.'" As he quoted the Bible, he stared directly into Silva's eyes as if to say, "I know you aren't one of the faithful and I shall see you punished for it."

Silva grew nervous but was not about to let this man know about it. "When is this battle to begin?" he asked, trying to show interest but wishing that the blathering fool would leave him in peace. He felt foolish reclining on the bed while the deputy ranted, felt like some middle-eastern potentate waiting to be fed grapes by one of his many concubines. That was not such a bad idea but his shabby condition spoiled the image. He was distracted from his thoughts for a moment when he saw a shadow pass under the bedroom door. That traitorous Lawrence was trying to spy on them. *Soon you'll pay.*

The deputy broke Silva's train of thought when he said, "Tonight. There are preparations to be made. Our Savior will let us know the exact time. The Lord will guide His hand in this, as He guides all our actions. Praise Brother James."

"Quite." His mind was alive now; for the first time since he murdered Reverend Mendax, Silva was able to think clearly. *I have to ensure that whatever James and his followers do, it has to be to the advantage of one man: me. I can regain my legacy, destroy my enemies, and take my rightful place as the leader of the county. Perhaps I can go even further than the county; dare I think about ...the city? I must play this correctly, though.* He turned away from the deputy and got off the bed. Gathering the dressing gown around him, he quickly checked to make sure there was no sign of anything that would embarrass him or make the man think he was anything less than in complete control. He looked good. Walking around the bed to Schofield, he extended his hand and said, "Brother Schofield." *Appeal to the man's religious mania.* "I'm sure that with your capable help, Brother James will triumph over the forces of evil arrayed against us." *That's right; make him sound like a comic book hero.* He grasped Schofield's hand and shook it vigorously. "Go now," he said, leading the man to the bedroom door. "Tell Brother James I am at his disposal. For anything." There were those stirrings again.

At the door, Schofield was beaming. "Brother Silva, we shall triumph. Oh, it shall be a righteous affair. And the way will be cleared for the Kingdom of Heaven." He opened the door and went through then turned to say, "Take care, Brother Silva. Beware the influence of the Adversary. It is strong and only the most faithful can resist." A cloud had come over his face, the return of the Deputy Schofield he knew and hated.

Silva closed the door and immediately began to undress. He tossed the soiled pajamas in a heap on the floor and went into his bathroom where he planned to shower away the melancholy and foolishness of the last week. But first, a shave.

Frederick Silva, lord of the county, was back and ready to take over.

Sister Mary

Mary jammed the knife into the savage's stomach and twisted it up until the blade pierced his black heart. She watched as first surprise, and then then pain registered on his face. Slowly the light left his eyes and she let his body fall to the ground. She felt the orgasm quake through her body and had to lean against a tree to avoid falling. Her gratification was almost as sublime as it was with her Savior. And why shouldn't it be? She was killing in the service of Brother James and God, cleansing the world of those who would sully the glory of the Lord.

When she had returned to Sister Sarah's house last Sunday after preventing that evil creature from enlisting the aid of the authorities, she had feared that her Lord might be angry with her for acting on her own. However, Brother James had been overjoyed at her initiative, had taken her into His loving arms and rewarded her with a communion that had thrilled her to her very soul. His love had flowed into her for hours and later, when Sarah returned from her duties with those fumblers who were trying to solve the town's crimes, He had allowed her to join their blessed sacrament.

Brother James had been exceptionally joyous that evening. He told the sisters of the events in the church and how the assembly rose up to welcome and worship Him. And how could it be any other way for the chosen of God? The members of the church would be ready to lay down their lives for the promise of the Kingdom of Heaven and would destroy any who got in their way. One in particular would prove to be useful: the deacon, Schofield. Sarah shuddered at the mention of his name but Brother James comforted her and promised that she would be safe from the man. The deacon was doing God's work, to be sure, but God would never let him harm one as faithful as Sarah. If the man treated her with anything but respect, Brother James would deal with him most severely. With her newfound boldness, Mary wished that she might be the one to punish the deacon. She remembered how he had treated her when she was in Tyndale before. He was a humorless, soulless animal, no better than the beasts that crawl in the dirt. Whatever good he might do for the cause of righteousness today, it could in no way serve as recompense for his previous acts. She hoped Brother James and God would forgive her for such thoughts and said a silent prayer of contrition. For once, her Savior had been too preoccupied to read her thoughts.

She had been instructed to maintain her surveillance of the Satanist camp. If it was possible to remove any more of the enemy, then she had the blessing of her Lord. But the utmost care must be taken: nothing should be allowed to jeopardize the coming of the Kingdom of Heaven. If Mary was caught, it was her duty to remove herself from danger at whatever cost. She had longed to make the ultimate sacrifice for the Man who had saved her life and promised her so much. How could she possible balk now when paradise was so near?

After the second killing, the denizens of the camp went into a panic. Mary could hear their arguments from her hiding place in the woods. Some wanted to leave Tyndale before anyone else went missing. Others believed the men would return in time for their heretical festival the next week. The Sheriff had stopped by but had been unable to do anything more than talk. Finnbrough had always been clueless and now, looking diseased and tired, he was more pathetic than ever. She was confident that he would never find her or the bodies.

It had been effortless to lure the Satanist into the woods near the Good Eats diner and finish him off. This was her third victim and killing was becoming almost too easy. Discretely flash her breasts at a man and he was helpless to do anything but follow wherever she led. And because naked flesh promised pleasures that were best not shared, the men always came alone, never telling anyone of their destination. The woods up the hill across Mott Street from the camp were good killing grounds. The area was thick with bushes providing ample hidden places to exterminate the enemy without fear of discovery.

She wanted to get the woman who led them but knew this would be impossible. Too many suspicions would be aroused and the betraying bitch might intuit what was happening around her. It would be best to let her dangle, confused and frightened, while Brother James and His brides slowly destroyed her sickening horde. But did the woman know Brother James was here? Could she suspect anything? Perhaps the next man should be allowed to talk before dying.

Mary needed to pull the body of the dead man further into the woods. Someone walking by might notice the smell in this heat. There was a small deep cave a few dozen feet up the hill where she had hidden her second victim. She grabbed the man's ankles to drag him away, but something made her look up. Someone was walking by on Mott Street and Mary was almost overcome with anger and hatred. As quietly as possible, she crawled through the bushes to see who it was that was causing such strong feelings within her. Peering through the thick weeds she saw that it was that evil temptress who had hurt her Savior in the swamp. She tugged out her knife, battling the urge to jump out of the bushes and slash the life from this impure sow. Anyone who resisted the ministrations of Brother James deserved to die a horrible death. Ritual beheading upon the altar of their faith would be too good for this soulless whore. Unconsciously, she repeatedly stabbed the weapon into the ground.

But there were people on the road; it was Saturday, Éclair Day at the bakery, which had just opened. There was no way she could get to the woman without being seen. Mary followed her prey, keeping hidden in the bushes. When they had gone only a few yards, it was evident that the woman was going to the bakery. Seeing the crowds that were already there, Mary decided to return to the body in the woods and hide it. There would be enough time to return here then follow her target until an opportunity presented itself to rid the world of this worthless creature.

Brother James would rejoice.

Twenty minutes later, the woman exited the bakery and walked west along Hill Road. That could only mean one thing: she was going to the house on the hill.

The house of the betrayer.

Him.

Would there be a chance to kill them both? Would God smile

down upon her and grant this boon? She let the woman get a good lead then followed, staying in the trees that lined the road. All the way, she said silent prayers to Brother James and God, asking for guidance and a steady hand.

Revenge would be hers.

Steve O'Leary

Steve sat on a deck chair just outside the back door of his garage. The heat of the afternoon sun reflected off the asphalt, baking him. He concentrated hard to ignore the sweat rolling down his back inside his work shirt. Stringer the cat sat on a plastic sheet draped over his lap purring away as he stroked its neck. The latex gloves he wore were usually reserved for cleaning but he had noticed a nasty cat smell on his fingers a while back and didn't want to experience that again. The cat and the plastic added to the heat; he felt as if he was sitting in a puddle of sweat. He sucked on a mint and contemplated his situation.

Across the asphalt from where he sat lay the wreckage of his shed. Inside, smashed beyond salvage when the shed toppled and fell to pieces, was thousands of dollars-worth of hydroponics gear used for the growing of the best pot this side of Toledo Window Box. Worthless now. Also gone were half a dozen garbage bags full of market-ready product that had only needed to be divided into smaller bags for distribution to his salesmen in the city. He didn't want to think about how much money he had lost there.

At least there were no more rats. Stringer had gone berserk when the first rat appeared a couple of days ago. The little mouser instinctively wanted to go after the rodent but the rat was bigger than the cat and the feline had run and cowered under the hydraulic jack until Steve rescued it and gave the shaking animal some comfort. He wasn't pleased to see the rats either, filthy animals with their fleas and plagues. The rats had begun appearing when the fissures in the earth grew to be about a foot wide. They must have come from the caves below, frightened by the changes to their habitat, and seeking shelter up above. The beasts had poured from the fissures and run across the old highway to the crumbling box factory. They might have a battle there with the fat factory rats he had seen over the years but at least fighting other rats was something their vile brains could understand.

Shortly after the rat exodus, other animals began to migrate. There were long thick lines of ants burdened with eggs leaving their hills near the pit and heading off into the woods surrounding the garage. Beetles and spiders, grasshoppers and slugs, toads and voles, predator and prey, all were leaving the area. He hadn't heard a bird in weeks.

He wished he could understand what was happening.

When he had discovered the ... bump, bulge, whatever, a week ago, it had been interesting but not something to worry about. He had continued with his work, such as it was, and ignored it. Silva, his 'partner' in crime, had not stopped by with either money or instructions. That was unusual as the man almost always had some job that had to be done yesterday or the world would come to an end. The guy needed to relax, take some time off, maybe get laid; he wasn't too old for that and he could certainly afford it. Anyway, Silva wouldn't have cared about the strange thing happening to Steve's property. That Bender guy would have been interested but he was so honest and straight-laced, he would have insisted on calling in the authorities. That would have been fun: explaining a shed full of weed and a pit of toxic waste in the middle of a small town.

Maybe I could call John, my old friend. No, it's too late for that.

The only people to come by since then were the owners of the businesses eager to get rid of their toxic waste. The drums of waste sat next to the garage where the men had left them last week. They hadn't returned this week. Why not? They had been regular as clockwork. Why miss this week? It didn't matter because he wouldn't have been able to do anything with the stuff anyway.

Last Saturday, Steve had come to work early to dump the contents of the oil drums in the pit. He usually did the dumping as soon after the drums were delivered as possible to hide the evidence. However, the previous Friday he had been hornier than usual and had clocked off in the middle of the afternoon so he could get conquering sooner. The next day, when he tried to negotiate the path to the pit with the first drum, he had been stalled. The incline had become steeper. Strong as he was, and he was one of the strongest men in Tyndale, he had been unable to muscle the drum up the path to the pit. He estimated that the bulge was about two feet high now. A quick walk around its perimeter confirmed that the bulge had grown all over, not just at the path.

In the past week, the bulge had expanded and was now at least ten feet high. It still followed the line Steve had discovered a week and a half ago. The fissures appeared mid-week where the ground could no longer stretch. Two days later the rats started swarming out. He observed that the bulge was causing the shed to lean towards the garage. The creaking and groaning from the old wood was disconcerting but he had not thought it would get severe enough to knock the structure over. How wrong he was. Thursday, he arrived at the garage in the morning and found the building in shambles, the strain of being tilted and gravity proving too much for the shed to bear. Wood and glass had been strewn across the asphalt as if the thing had exploded with the release of tension. He'd spent most of Thursday cleaning up the mess.

An hour ago, Steve had gone exploring. He'd been forced to use a ladder to climb to the top of the bulge; its sides were almost perpendicular to the ground now. The ground on top was solid as a rock and felt alive. When he bent to get a closer look, he could see slight vibrations in the dust. He ran a finger along a small crack and was surprised when it split apart, spewing dirt into the air. The pit itself was popping out of the dirt around it. The cement foundation was now at least a foot above ground level as if something underneath was trying to push it out. The level of the waste had changed, too. When he first saw the bulge, the black mass had sunk a couple of feet, making him think that the foundation had sprung a leak. However, this morning the pit was filled near to the brim with the black liquid. When the ground vibrated, he could see ripples traveling across the shimmering surface.

When he reached the cave mouth, another surprise awaited him. Where the opening had once been in the side of the hill, now it was flat on the ground. He stood at the edge of the cave and looked down and saw some of the tires he had stowed inside. Steve shuddered and realized that he was standing in total silence. There wasn't a sound to be heard: no birds, nothing crawling, not even the warm breeze in the trees. It was as if the area was waiting for something. It was tense.

And what was happening to the trees? All around him, off in the woods, the trees were brilliant green with leaves. The ground was rife with growth. But on the bulge, it was as if there had been a blight. The trees were bare and dead like the life had been sucked out of them. The grass and weeds were brown and brittle as if they had been baked in a scorching sun. While he walked, he felt weaker, drained, and wanted to lie down and sleep despite having had a good night's rest.

He had returned to the garage and taken the deck chair out of the office. He set it up on the asphalt out back and sat to think. Shortly thereafter, Stringer had arrived. Since the time of the rats, the cat had been reluctant to leave the safety of the garage. Happy to see the cat, the only source of comfort for him in the last week—even his conquests were unsatisfying now—he went into the office to get the plastic sheet and gloves. No point in getting dirty while thinking.

He'd been here for three hours now. It hadn't taken long to run through all the ideas he had about what was happening. When it came to strangeness, his imagination was extremely limited. For almost the whole time, he'd sat stroking the cat, his mind a blank.

Brother James

Dennis Morisset's wife was stark naked, kneeling before Brother James who was seated on the living room settee. She was using her mouth furiously on Him while her husband watched from a recliner across the room, his face wrinkled with disgust. Brother James could not fathom why.

"So, you know Brother Dennis that we must be ready to fight at a moment's notice. The forces of the Adversary are amassing strength even as We speak. Their evil ritual will be performed soon. We must not allow this to happen."

Morisset nodded and said, "But what can we do? The Sheriff has given these heathens permission to congregate. If we protest, we may only get ourselves in trouble." He gasped as he unconsciously masturbated. "What can we do?" He was almost in tears.

Brother James said, "Tonight, We must gather the faithful at the church. I will preach a sermon that will fill them with holy power. Then they will arm themselves and march to the enemy camp." He concentrated on the woman between his legs. She was utterly beautiful, the ample folds of her fleshy body warm and soothing against his bare legs. How lucky Dennis was to be in possession of such a loving and giving wife. "The heathens are arrogant; they believe their false gods will protect them from Us." He could feel Himself reaching climax. "But they are wrong. Nothing can resist the power of the righteous. Nothing can stand before the light that is God. Uh." He felt Himself release and leaned back to relish the sensation as His seed flowed out.

Morisset's wife sat back on her heels and waited with a smile on her face. Brother James pointed at her husband and she obediently crawled across the room to him. She took his hand from his member and went to work. Morisset groaned and Brother James smiled, happy to see a loving couple enjoy each other.

"When our people march on the enemy camp, they will sweep away all opposition. If necessary, they will crush the so-called forces of law, though they should not be an impediment to our success. Brother Paul is fervent in his desire to hasten the coming of the Kingdom of Heaven." He could see that Dennis was not paying attention; the man was lost in ecstasy. Let him feel pleasure for he may not survive the battle ahead. There would be those who would fall in the name of Brother James and the

Lord and they would take their rightful place in heaven.

Meanwhile, there was the more mundane task of arming His soldiers. Many had pistols and shotguns; some had automatic weapons. A flamethrower or two would be nice and cleansing, appropriate, too, as a reminder of what happens to those who stray from the word of the Lord.

Dennis grunted as he came. James rose and crossed the room to join the couple in the warmth of their love. Soon all the people of the world would embrace the love of Brother James.

And God.

Lawrence Burke

Lawrence closed the basement door and returned to the kitchen. His house was quiet, had been too quiet for too long. He didn't know if he could stand much more of this. All those around him were coming apart, tainted by the evil that was growing in Tyndale. He must warn Marie about what he had overheard when Deputy Schofield paid his visit an hour ago. She had to get her people away before the attack. But would she believe him? And even if she did, could the Wiccans get out of town fast enough?

But before he did anything about Marie, he had to be sure Luana was safe. He looked back at the basement door praying Luana's nurse would not go down there and find his secret. Nigel Morrison had shown up at the house late last Sunday evening, covered in blood and in a blind panic. Reverend Mendax had been brutally murdered and the janitor had discovered the body mere seconds after the killer had fled. He had watched enough detective shows on television to know not to touch anything, but he lost his wits with fear and tried to find something to help the reverend. Nigel called the Sheriff but then realized that they would think he had committed the crime. He was an ex-junkie after all, and he had a police record in the city. He'd hidden in the bushes that bordered the estate until darkness could conceal his movements.

"I would never have hurt the reverend, Mister Lawrence," he'd said while Lawrence made him a cup of tea. "He gave me a chance when no one else would even look at me. I know some of his preaching went over the top, but he was a good man. What am I going to do?"

Lawrence had thought about it while the water boiled for the tea. He was certain that it was Frederick Silva who had killed the reverend but he knew that with men like Schofield on the force, Morrison was sure to be charged and probably found guilty unless he was killed resisting arrest. No one ever came to his house except Luana's nurse so Lawrence believed he could hide Nigel while he tried to find proof of Silva's guilt. The basement was comfortable enough, equipped with a camp bed and small bathroom. He took food down to his charge every day, brought him books to read. There was a black and white television set but both men thought it too risky to use it; Luana's nurse might hear something from the kitchen. The nurse had little reason to go into the basement, all of the supplies she needed for Luana's care were kept in a closet on the second floor. To be safe, Lawrence had told her he'd seen a rat down there and had set traps. At the mention of rats, the nurse's face had paled and now it was difficult to get her to go into the kitchen for anything. She had a microwave, hotplate, and kettle in her room on the second floor and the nurse used these exclusively now.

Since the murder, Silva had been secreted in his bedroom venturing out on rare occasions to visit his study. His treatment of Lawrence had become openly abusive with racial slurs a constant reminder of the man's true nature. It was increasingly difficult to endure the insults but he needed to stay just a little bit longer to secure his position and ensure that Silva's comeuppance would be as satisfying as possible. On the positive side, Lawrence had been able to enter the secret room freely and scour Silva's records for information that would help him get that revenge. Several times over the last few days, as he uncovered more details from the meticulously kept records about his employer's illegal dealings and the depths to which he would sink for a few dollars, Lawrence was amazed that no one had retaliated. The pettiness displayed by the man was beyond belief; a few hundred dollars here, a few hundred there, all from people who had done absolutely nothing wrong yet feared for their reputations lest a man of Silva's stature reveal his perverted version of the truth.

Lawrence had been tempted to find a pistol and kill the man who had murdered his wife and destroyed the life of his child. However, Luana was still alive and vulnerable so he held his emotions in check and worked feverishly to secure her future. What he could not contain, though, was his disdain for his employer. He was more defiant and less subservient than he had ever been but Silva was too caught up with whatever demons haunted him to notice.

What he had found in the secret room was proving to be extremely useful. Already he had been able to transfer stewardship of the trust to someone other than Silva with hardly any effort. As Luana's legal guardian, he'd been given that right by good old Horace but the nephew had kept this clause a secret, buried amidst legalese and mumbo jumbo. It would be unlikely that Silva would discover this manipulation as the money in the trust was not available to him anyway. The trust would provide enough revenue to finance Luana's care for the rest of her life. A city councilor had been freed from Silva's clutches with the return of letters that, while rather explicit in their content, were written at an age when experimentation was not unusual. The man's wife had been totally supportive, knowing that her husband loved her and that the follies of youth should not be held against him. His political rivals would not have been so understanding. Now the man was free to pursue the political career he deserved. The papers clearing the way for Tom Bender's outright ownership of most of the county had been couriered to a reliable attorney in the city who would see to it that the lucky man would soon benefit from the legacy.

The details of Steve O'Leary's involvement were also in the files. These Lawrence set aside. He wasn't ready yet to bring down the local crime lord. There was the intimation of Deputy Schofield's hand in some crimes but nothing concrete; the man lived a charmed life.

Lawrence decided to have a cup of tea while he mulled over the problem of the Wiccan camp. They needed someplace to go fast and he had an idea but it would require a lot of cooperation. He put the kettle on the stove then heard a commotion from above followed by the sound of stomping feet and shouting. Someone, most likely Nurse Cantor for there was no one else upstairs, was running along the hallway. He heard her heavy feet on the stairs and shouts of, "Mister Burke, Mister Burke, come quick." She always called him Mister Burke, even after eight years as Luana's nurse. Her one flaw was her overreaction to the smallest thing. He turned off the stove and left the kitchen to meet her in the hall as she reached the bottom of the stairs.

Cantor's face was flushed and she was panting. With shaking

hands, she grabbed hold of the banister to steady herself. When she saw him, she smiled widely and said, "She moved."

"Impossible," he answered. "Luana's been in a coma for eight years. It's not likely that she would move after all this time." His heart pounded in his chest. If there was the slightest chance that his daughter was waking up, he didn't want to spoil it by getting his hopes up too soon. But he knew it was only the nurse's overactive imagination; it had happened enough times before.

"It's not my imagination this time, Mister Burke," she said. "Come on and see." With that, she turned and sprinted up the stairs with speed that belied her bulk. Lawrence had never seen the woman move that fast. He raced up the stairs after her, mind awash with possibilities. This had to be a mistake like all the other times. Nothing had changed; nothing ever changed. His daughter was a captive in the bed and would never be free no matter how much he wished for it.

In Luana's room, his daughter lay there as she had for more years than he cared to remember. The sheet over her body looked a little rumpled and she was sweating from the heat. The small air conditioner at the window was having difficulty keeping up with the weather and he knew he would have to replace it with a new unit soon enough. The medical equipment all looked normal; there were no strange readings and only the steady beeping of the heart monitor. Not that he would have been able to tell if anything was out of order. The nurse had explained what everything meant many times but it never stayed with him.

Lawrence looked at his daughter, now thirteen, and marveled at how she had grown and matured. Nurse Cantor regularly exercised Luana's muscles and she was well-fed though he always wondered how nourishing food fed through a tube could be. She was beautiful, her face full of the innocence of a child. He choked back tears and damned himself for leaving his wife and child that day so many years ago.

The nurse stood by Luana's bed and looked down at the girl. "She moved a leg. Jerked it like she was having a dream. You can see where the sheet has moved." She pointed at the rumpled area he had noticed before.

"That doesn't mean anything. It could have been a spasm or something like that." He desperately wanted to believe the nurse but years of disappointment and doctors had drained any real hope from him. "It's happened before."

Luana's leg moved. He froze.

The nurse was about to say something but he shushed her with a stern look.

The leg moved again.

Nurse Cantor gasped and took hold of Luana's left hand; she looked up at one of the machines, something with a series of choppy green lines. He could hear his own heart beating. Lawrence looked at the nurse for an explanation and she said, "That machine," she pointed at the one with the green lines, "measures brainwave activity. You can see that there's more going on. That's happened before, but never like this. It's as if she's struggling with something inside, having a nightmare or something."

"Could she be remembering what happened to her? Please, no, don't let her relive that."

Nurse Cantor said, "The accident. I under …"

He cut her off. "No, it's worse than that. Never mind."

Then Luana's eyes opened. They swam around the room, found him and focused.

"Daddy, why are the old King and Spirit so angry? Don't they know their time has come?"

The nurse shrieked and let go of Luana's hand. She backed away from her patient, eyes wide open, head shaking. "She shouldn't be able to speak so clearly. Not yet." Cantor backed into a chair and sat. "It's not possible," she muttered over again.

His strength left him and Lawrence fell to his knees, sobbing silently, unable to speak. He reached for Luana's hand, squeezed it gently and for the first time in eight years, felt her squeezing back

Luana smiled the most incredible smile he had ever seen and said, "You must protect them, the lady and the man. Everyone wants to hurt them. You can't let that happen. It's your duty, daddy."

The King of the Wood

"You were quite beautiful," said the King to the woman's head. He sat naked on an old kitchen chair he had brought into the shrine. The rock ledges were hard on his backside and covered with dust, hardly befitting a creature of his stature. The battered old chair wasn't much better but it was all he could manage at short notice; carrying anything larger might have drawn unwanted attention. When all was said and done, the plastic of the chair seat was adequate for his needs at the moment. But when he was finished with his tormenter, oh would he have the finest furniture around.

This time, he had remembered to disrobe *before* the ritual disembowelment. A calmer head had prevailed though he still felt a twinge of panic. The sacrifices were not as effective as he had hoped. His power was considerably reduced and even after the extra victims, it had not returned sufficiently for him to destroy his enemies face to face. Regret flowed through him at the sheer number of people he was sacrificing now, and how many more would have to give their lives that he might live. Where once blood on the equinoxes would suffice, now he was shedding blood several times a week and would probably have to resort to daily slaughter fairly soon.

A tear escaped his eye as he looked into the face of his latest victim. A pretty red-head, he had found her hitch-hiking on Trinity Road out past the box factory. His kind face had assured her that she would be safe and it wasn't until they passed the bakery that she had begun to suspect all was not well for her. Her sightless eyes stared back at him from where her head rested on his knees. He gently stroked her hair and wished that he hadn't been forced to kill her.

The King leaned back and tried to see through the rock of the cavern's ceiling to the house above him. There, his rival was gathering strength though the fool didn't have a clue what was happening. "I'll have to take the fight directly to you if I get any weaker. No more sacrifices and playing by the rules. A bullet to the back of the head will take care of you." He coughed and a gob of phlegm hit the red-head between her blue eyes. "Sorry about that," he said and scraped the goo away with a piece of balsam branch. He'd had to bring many more branches into the shrine to cover the smell of decay. Natural as the odor was, it was still an affront to his nose.

Looking to the north, he thought about the other, the Spirit of Humanity. It was going by the name of Brother James now and was marshalling its forces for the coming battle. The King had not expected his ancient enemy to be so bold, but it must have sensed his weakened condition and, true to its now corrupt nature, decided to take advantage.

"Soon, my old friend," he said softly. "Soon we'll be facing each other for supremacy. I know that once we were part of a whole, united to make the world a better place. But that was many incarnations ago and you refused to stay in your place." He stroked the red hair and said, "It's his fault. He's forcing me to do this to you and the others. He thinks he has the answers but he doesn't know anything." The woman didn't reply and he felt sad and lonely.

"I suppose this is what I wanted Bender to feel when I tried to direct the despair towards him. Ironic that it's come back to me, don't you think."

The King closed his eyes and let out a long sigh.

And there was another force, familiar but small. He couldn't understand what this could be. Yet.

"If I can hold out until the autumnal equinox, I can beat them all. I must strengthen myself."

He let his mind clear and thought about the earth and the power it held. Ever so slowly, he began to draw some of that power into himself. His feet pressed into the rock and dust of the cavern floor, sending tendrils of root down to absorb whatever they could.

"Soon. Soon."

J. Edwin Buja

CHAPTER SIXTEEN
THE BASEMENT

Tom Bender

Tom watched Antoine Good negotiate the turnaround with his van and drive off to his diner. Antoine had been overjoyed to come up to Tom's house to pick up some surplus produce. Over the years, Eddie at The Pub had been the lucky recipient of some of the extra greens from Tom's garden. Eddie slipped Tom the occasional free Guinness in exchange for lettuce and tomatoes far fresher than anything he could get from his usual produce supplier. And, bonus, it was all organic. Tom always grew too many vegetables. He practically inhaled salads and plates of veggies on a regular basis—oh, was he regular—and made soups to freeze, but there was always plenty of green stuff left over. His friends, with the exception of Spanky who was strictly a meat and potatoes man, welcomed this free supply; they always tried to pay, which made Tom feel uncomfortable. This year, because of the weirdly accelerated growth on his property, Tom began dropping off bags of greens early. Eddie and Nancy were startled when he arrived at The Pub for his Friday evening get together at the beginning of June with bags of lettuce and Swiss chard, radishes, and beans. This year, being so early, Eddie had been sure it would give The Pub a slight edge in its competition for business with the restaurants in town; he'd been ready to take all Tom could supply. And he was right. However, even The Pub couldn't handle what Tom's garden was pumping out, hence Good Eats. The diner wasn't competition for The Pub, so Tom felt fine giving Antoine a call and inviting him over to stock up. The little man had jumped with glee when he saw the boxes of tomatoes and lettuce waiting for him in the garage on the hill. Before he left, Antoine assured his benefactor that his money was no longer any good at Good Eats.

Tom immediately called Ollie Knudson with an offer but the baker was too busy to come up the hill, it being Saturday, Éclair Day. Precisely, thought Tom when he volunteered to bring some herbs down to the bakery later that day.

Tom closed his front door and pondered how no one had thought it the least bit strange that everything was growing so fast so early. He'd taken the Falcon out for a drive yesterday to see what was happening with the trees and gardens down in Tyndale. All over, things were bright green and thick with leaves. Driving down some of the streets, he thought he was in a South American jungle, so thick was the vegetation at the side of the road. However, nowhere was the growth as accelerated as that on Horace's Hill. The lawns in town still only needed cutting two or three times a week, not daily like Tom's. *I'm so glad I got rid of all that grass and put in those flower and vegetable beds.* He pictured the tiny patches of grass that were all that was left of his once huge lawns. It was still a pain in the butt, though, dragging out the push mower every morning to keep the place looking neat. Perhaps letting the grass run wild would not be such a bad thing; it would hardly be noticed amongst the out of control flowers and vegetables. Speaking of which, don't daffodils and crocuses only bloom once, not repeatedly?

The townspeople he had spoken with about the weirdness took it all in stride or didn't seem to notice anything out of the ordinary. Almost everyone was so mellow about the whole thing. Except for some of the more fervent religious nutbags at the fundy church. *Maybe I am overreacting. What can be so bad about fast-growing food? It gives a whole new meaning to healthy fast food.* Perhaps the infection or mutation or whatever it is would spread. Plants would take over the earth. Tom had giggled at this idea and determined to check for triffids and any plants named Audrey when he returned home. He found none.

Tom stopped at the top of the stairs and thought about what he wanted to do today. The database project was in its final installation and testing stages and in a few weeks he and Spanky would start training sessions for the college's administrative personnel. His friend was the better trainer but when the two of them got together and began tag teaming the session it usually resulted in hilarity that never got in the way of the students learning what they needed. Good as Spanky was at coding, he really belonged in the front of a classroom.

The events of the past months—Gavin's murder, the growth, the disappearances, the birds and animals—had made it difficult for Tom to think about something as mundane as writing. He had a novel and screenplay to finish. And that chopper that flew over the other day; what was that all about? Plus, there was the call late Thursday from Professor Ravenscroft. Her voice sounded calm despite the Scottish accent, but something in its timbre made Tom think she was extremely anxious to meet him. It was rather nice having a woman interested in him, even if it was only for academic purposes. *Sorta makes up for being dumped by Nancy.* He laughed at himself for feeling at all put out because his best friend had finally won the woman of his dreams after so long. Now that he thought about it, he hadn't heard from Spanky since Wednesday. Could he and Nancy be ... "No, don't go there."

Tom decided to do a load of laundry.

The hamper in the bathroom was overflowing with clothes. Tom never put a pair of socks, a shirt, or underwear back on. The only exception was after sex, but since there had been none for more than eight years, it wasn't an issue. At least not as far as laundry was concerned. If for any reason the clothing had to come off, it went in the hamper. As a result of this habit, and because he had been doing a lot of gardening lately in the heat and intense humidity, Tom wore two or three sets of clothes a day. The laundry was piling up and he was running out of clean underwear. When he had it sorted into colors, whites, and towels, he was revolted not just by the smell of sweaty clothes, but by the fact that he had allowed so much time to pass without doing a load. One should never be too busy to clean up. He grabbed a pile and went down to the basement laundry room.

When he stepped off the bottom step and onto the basement floor, something made him shiver. He paused and looked around the room in front of him. Across from the steps was what he lovingly referred to as the big ass TV, a seventy-two-inch flat screen monster. On either side of the monster, shelves held hundreds of movies—nothing compared to Spanky's collection—and dozens of sets of TV shows. Arrayed in front of the TV were three overstuffed black easy chairs, each with its own table for drinks and munchies. This was Spanky's favorite spot in Tom's house. The third chair was for Jay on those few occasions he joined them. All seemed in order here and at the bar along the north wall.

As Tom walked across the cool cement floor to the laundry room, he heard a splash and recoiled when he felt cold water on his bare feet. He stopped dead and his mind raced. Water on the basement floor could only mean one thing: there was water coming from somewhere. "Brilliant deduction," he muttered, already angry at the idea of something new to distract him from the writing he didn't want to do anyway. He tiptoed through the water to the laundry room and put the basket on the lid of the washing machine, glad that he wasn't wearing socks. The thought of soggy socks made Tom shudder. Looking out the laundry room door, he saw a large puddle that stretched from the north wall across the cement floor almost to the small furnace enclosure. A quick check confirmed that the water heater next to him hadn't burst; there was no water under it and besides, he would have heard it if it had blown up.

Tom couldn't hear any dripping. That meant the water pipes were probably okay, but he wanted to check them to be safe. Next to the water heater was a small closet where he kept washing supplies and a small ladder. There was also a flashlight in case of blackouts. He popped up the ceiling tiles in the laundry room and shone the light along the lengths of copper pipe coming from the well room. Everything seemed fine, no drips, no spiders, and no mouse or bat poop.

No need to go into the well room. It was the one room in his house that he didn't like. The room was dark and musty and cold. A pump brought a steady flow of water up from the spring deep down somewhere in the hill. There was a hatch on the floor behind the pump that apparently gave access to the workings of the pump. In all the years he'd been in the house, he'd only had the pump checked once when it had stopped working. He probably should have it serviced again sometime. Just to be safe.

The water on the floor wasn't spreading; it was just sitting there waiting for him to step in it again. A beer refrigerator that sat against the wall next to the bar was surrounded by water. The refrigerator was laden Tom's beloved Guinness and Spanky's best ale and weighed a ton. Fortunately, Tom had put it on appliance casters that made it a breeze to move as long as you only wanted to go in a straight line. Tom unplugged it then struggled to pull it away from the wall so he could see if there was a crack in the floor behind it. When the refrigerator was far enough from the wall that he could get a good look, he found that the water was coming from somewhere under the molding.

"Oh shit," he muttered. Water pipes ran overhead from the well room to the kitchen and bathroom upstairs and to the wet bar, bathroom, and laundry down here. If they were leaking, that meant the water was dripping down behind the wall somewhere. And they passed directly over the wall of comic boxes and graphic novels. He got the ladder and checked above the acoustic tile but again could see nothing to indicate leaking pipes. That meant the water had to be coming through the foundation.

"Not the bookshelves," he groaned as he stared at the shelves lining the walls around him. The big ass TV room was part of one of Tom's libraries; he had six.

But how could there be water there anyway? Tom opened the blinds on the window above the puddle that looked out on the back yard from under the highest part of the deck. It had always puzzled him that old Horace had placed a window here where it would never get any sun, but he was happy for the convenience now. Outside, he could see a wooden rain barrel that had fallen on its side. He used a system of recycled wine casks as rain barrels at all four corners of the house to catch the runoff from the gutter. It cost enough running the well pump to bring water to the top of the hill without having to spend more money to get water for the garden. The barrels sat on small platforms so a hose could be attached to a spigot at the bottom for watering the yards. If there was a lot of rain, like there had been for the last while, the water ran into plastic pipes nailed to the fence about a foot above the beds. The excess water was channeled along these pipes and fell through perforations over the beds: a self-watering system. It had rained on the hill every afternoon for over a month, so the barrels were constantly full. Somehow this particular barrel had toppled, Tom figured the weight of the water must have weakened the platform; in previous years, the barrels had never been filled to the top. And now all the water that had been collected in the toppled barrel was in his basement. Tom made a mental note to check the three other corners.

The shelves looked okay, there was no water on them and the books were dry; it was seeping from under the plinth, so Tom went to the laundry room to get a bucket and mop. He sang, "Scrub the bottom and top," the McDonald's jingle from way back, as he sopped up the water. And he did a little jig with the mop, like the janitors in the old commercial. He never sang out loud unless he was alone, and dancing was definitely a no-no. When the puddle was gone, he dumped the water in the laundry tub.

After moving the books, Tom saw the wallboard behind the shelves was bulging slightly, and the screws were popping out, but there was no dampness on the wall itself.

"That's a relief," said Tom. He stood and scratched his head, not sure what to do. He thought for a few seconds then ran upstairs to put on his wellies—they'd be easier to pull on and kick off if he had to keep running in and out of the house. All his tools were in the garage. Tom returned to the basement a couple of minutes later with a heavy-duty utility knife, a wallboard saw, a level, a screwdriver, and a plastic margarine container.

After removing the shelf supports, Tom pulled away the plinth. The floor did not appear to be cracked. "That's another relief," he said. "At least I won't have to dig too far on the other side. I hope." He had learned never to be too confident about house repairs. Who knew how many times he had underestimated the amount of work? Well, Belinda, who graciously reminded him every time, but that didn't matter anymore. Now that *he* thought about it, he *had* underestimated every time: an hour-long job almost always took all day.

When he had put up the wallboard, Tom had marked the edge of the floor with the location of the wall studs. This made it easier to drill holes for the strapping along the wall to which the shelf supports were screwed. However, he didn't need the markings now. The nail pops visible on the wall clearly marked the line of the studs. "Damn. I'm glad they're behind the books." It was a real pain fixing nail pops where everyone could see them. At least this time they would save him some small amount of work. He gouged plaster from the tops of the screws and removed them, careful to place them in the margarine container for reuse. Using the utility knife, he scored the wall along stud lines about thirty-two inches apart so he would have plenty of space to work in, then began to dig deeper into the wallboard. It would also make repairing the hole in the wall easier when everything else was fixed. He paused after a few minutes then went to get the vacuum cleaner from the hall closet upstairs. Tom liked to work in a clean space and wanted to vacuum up the wallboard dust as he worked rather than letting it accumulate and spread all over the basement and the books.

When he had finished digging furrows in the wallboard along the studs, he used the level to draw two lines across the wall to join the furrows; might as well make the hole as neat as possible. With the saw, he cut along the lines. He had to use the knife again the cut across the stud between the furrows. When the second horizontal cut was complete, the wallboard slipped and tilted forward enough for him to get his fingers behind the top and pull it away from the wall in a shower of dust and chalky chunks. Setting the square of wallboard aside, Tom vacuumed up his mess.

The plastic vapor barrier was covered with so much condensation water was running down the inside. The yellow insulation appeared damp. Tom ran the utility knife along the studs to cut the plastic that hadn't already been sliced then removed it. He gingerly felt the insulation—as he had feared, it was soaked through—then yanked the two insulation batts from between the studs. They resisted a little but he tugged harder and, when they were free, set them aside for disposal; it would be best to replace them with new insulation. At least there didn't appear to be any black mold on the studs. *Thank you for small miracles.*

"Impossible," he said when he looked at the spaces between the studs.

At first Tom thought he was looking at thick spider webs and shuddered at the idea that the eight-legged bastards were infesting the space between the walls; it had taken long enough to get rid of the spiders in the basement after they had moved in. When he looked closer, however, he could see that the fine, yellowish-white strands were not spider silk but roots. Both spaces were tangled with tiny roots, some ripped and torn from

KING OF THE WOOD

where he had pulled away the insulation. The roots seemed to pulse. *I must be tired.*

Through the mass of roots, he could just make out the crack in the foundation. It started about a foot from the floor and went up not down. Tom was happy that he wouldn't need to repair the bottom of the foundation from the outside. He reached forward with both hands to part the roots and get a better look at the crack. As soon as he touched the mass, he felt something like an electric shock run up his fingers and the root mass quivered. Startled, he jerked his hands away from the moving things and sat back on the floor.

Tom was getting used to weirdness around his house, what with the growth outside and the birds. Speaking of birds, a pair of crows peered through the window above where he sat. "You're laughing at me, aren't you?" he asked. The crows nodded as if amused by such an obvious question. "Fine then, I'll show you I'm not afraid of no stinking roots," he said and scrambled to his knees. Very carefully he placed his hands on the mass of roots. There was no sudden shock this time; it felt more like the tickling sort of throb he felt when the shaft of the dentist's drill touched the side of his mouth. He slowly pushed his fingers into the mass above the dark line of the crack then gently pulled the roots apart. They seemed to separate of their own volition to reveal the concrete beneath.

There was dampness at the edges of the crack but water was no longer flowing. But what had caused the crack in the first place was what stopped Tom dead.

A single root, about half an inch thick, had broken through the concrete. It disappeared behind the mass of smaller rootlets that were clinging to the wall and studs. Tom knew this could happen with old sewer pipes, whether lead or tile, but he had

J. Edwin Buja

never seen it with eight inches of solid concrete. He remembered the weeping willows from back at his parents' place. For some strange reason, there were only two willows in the whole neighborhood, across the street from each other next door to Tom's parents. The trees' roots had been a problem for everyone on both sides of the road, breaking into sewer pipes and popping roots up in the middle of a couple of lawns. The asphalt had even begun to buckle between the trees. Eventually, after the trees had grown large enough to have trunks two feet thick, they had been cut down.

Tom didn't have any willows in his yard. There were some growing at the foot of the cliff by the river, but he had never heard of trees sending roots uphill and into someone's basement. He looked out the window where a third crow had joined its friends. The three birds stared at Tom expectantly as he cranked open the window. When he said, "I have no idea what you want," they took off over the back fence. "Let me know when you've figured it out," he shouted after them. The albino sparrows were gathered at the foot of the oak, their regular meeting place for the last few months. There was a new addition to the group; this one had the usual swatch of red on its breast and a small scarlet line on its head; it limped. They stopped their twittering to stare back at him.

Looking for the culprit responsible for the invasion of his basement, Tom surveyed the trees in his yard. There were fruit trees along the fence, apples, pears, and plums, but he didn't think they had roots strong enough to break concrete. The plum did send out a lot of suckers, but Tom cut these out as soon as he saw them. There was the oak, but it couldn't possibly be big enough to send roots forty feet to the foundations of the house. "Could it be you?" Tom asked the oak.

Before doing anything to repair the inside of the foundation, Tom wanted to check the outside to see how much damage there was and if it would be easy to fix. He changed into some old jeans and went out to the shed next to the garage to get a rake, a shovel, and a drop cloth.

Careful not to bash his head as he had done so many times before, Tom stooped under the deck. He tried to roll the toppled rain barrel out of the way but it stayed put. He tried pulling it away but still it refused to move. Getting his back into it, Tom crouched, grasped the ends of the barrel and yanked hard. The barrel came up so suddenly Tom fell on his back. Taken by surprise, he let go of the barrel and it rolled over his head and onto the gravel path. "Lucky for me you were empty," Tom said to the barrel, embarrassed and glad that no one except the birds was around to see him knocked on his ass by an empty barrel. "Luckier that I have a hard head. I've got to stop talking to inanimate objects. Anyone would think I'm nuts." The sparrows nodded in agreement.

Something on the barrel caught Tom's eye. He crawled over to get a better look. "The Hell?" he said. A piece of root about a foot long and half an inch thick was stuck to the side of the barrel. Tom tried to remove it but it wouldn't budge. Looking closer, Tom saw that tiny rootlets were digging into the barrel staves like ivy, except this wasn't ivy.

"Why would roots come out of the ground?" he asked the oak. As usual, it was aloof and didn't answer.

Stepping close to the house wall, Tom could see where the root had been broken away. A few inches of it were sticking out of the ground. "I need to eat something," he said when he thought he saw the root sway as if in search of the rest of itself. "Spanky's warned me about not eating. I don't want to fall off a ladder like he did. Shut up, 'kay." He looked around the garden, embarrassed that he was having an argument with himself, especially since he seemed to be losing. "I've got to get out more, see people. All work and no play makes me ... a lot of money."

Tom raked away the gravel under the window where the crack should be, being careful not to tear the landscape fabric he had laid under the gravel to keep weeds from growing. When he had a wide patch of gravel moved he saw the hole where the root had thrust through the fabric but there was no sign of the root itself. He had to cut the fabric to expose a large enough area in the underlying dirt to dig. There was a hole in the compacted earth that corresponded to the one in the fabric but again no evidence of the root; it could have been a worm hole, from a very large worm. He decided he must have torn the exposed length of root away when he raked the gravel.

Piling the earth on the drop cloth was hard work and the heat didn't make it go any easier. Within minutes, sweat poured from every inch of Tom's body. He had brought a couple of bottles of water with him and paused every few minutes to have a drink. The humidity was high and made him a little breathless, another wrinkle in the ever-changing weather.

It was difficult digging under the deck. Tom was six feet three and there was only six feet of space under the deck joists. Unable to stand up straight while digging, he was worried he'd throw his back out. It was already straining. He'd thrown it out a couple of times while shoveling snow off the driveway during the winter; he never did get that snow blower Belinda had wanted, a matter of pride more than frugality. The area was cramped, too, and a couple of times the shovel connected with one of the deck posts sending a spray of dirt onto the gravel path. When he had dug down about two feet, Tom paused to stretch and try to relieve some of the tension in his back. He looked down into the hole. There was still no sign of the main root that had sent its tendrils through the concrete into his basement.

After a few more shovels-full of dirt, Tom estimated that he was below the point of root penetration in the foundation. He knelt and scraped dirt away from the concrete with his hand, wishing he had remembered to wear gloves. Soon he found the hole in the concrete. There was a nub of pale root sticking through the hole but no trace of it or the main root in the dirt he had been digging. Tom was sure he would have noticed resistance on the shovel if he had cut through a root big enough to break concrete while digging.

He got down on his stomach and reached for the nub of root. As he touched it, he felt the now familiar prickle on his finger. Still, it startled him and he pulled his hand back, smacking it on a rock in the side of the hole. "Damn," he shouted. "Why am I so nervous? What the fuck is going on?"

He got up, shaking his injured hand where a welt was forming across the back just below his knuckles. Tom had a sip of water and sat cross-legged at the side of the hole, staring at the root sticking out of the foundation. A wild idea entered his head so he got up and ran back inside the house. Being wrong would be good but given all the odd crap he had experienced lately, he didn't think that likely. In a hurry to get downstairs to confirm his suspicions, Tom kicked off his wellies at the back door. One of them went skidding across the linoleum, sending clumps of dirt all over the kitchen floor. He ignored the mess though he could hear the ghost of Belinda yelling at him for dirtying her kitchen. Why did he still care about what she thought?

The ringing telephone went unanswered.

Tom's sock-clad feet slid off the carpeted steps and nearly

sent him careening down to the basement but he regained his balance by clutching the banister with his wounded hand and wrenching his shoulder. The pain almost made him faint. Then he misjudged the distance at the basement door and smashed hard into the jamb with his shoulder. More intense pain tried to distract him from his goal but he ignored it. He slid across the floor to where the foundation was cracked and fell to his knees and immediately went flying sideways on his back as pain from his knee overrode everything. An errant screw had escaped the margarine container. "Fuckity fuck fuck." His eyes watered and through the tears Tom saw blood oozing through the knee of his jeans. He scrunched his eyes against the pain and massaged his wounded knee. Carefully, he sat down in front of the cracked wall. Wiping tears from his eyes, he looked closely at the mass of growth there.

"Fuck me."

Using his finger, and prepared for the tingle, Tom traced the root from the hole in the foundation. The smaller roots parted as his finger moved along. When his finger touched a stud, it all became clear in his mind.

The root hadn't penetrated the foundation from the outside.

It wasn't clinging to the stud.

The root was growing out of the stud.

CHAPTER SEVENTEEN
THE GLIDER IN ARCADIA

Tom Bender

After the shock of discovery, Tom ran outside to the garden to get away from the freakishness in the basement. He sat on the bench at the back fence where the trellis above him groaned in the warm breeze from the weight of the clematis that twined throughout it. As soon as he sat, eleven crows landed at his feet and marched back and forth in front of him. The lead crow, slightly larger than his brothers—were they brothers, were some sisters, how could you tell? —kept looking over at him as if waiting for instructions. Tom's mind was too busy to try and figure out what the crows were telling him. And his hands were still shaking.

How could the studs, wood dead for at least twenty years, be growing? Okay, there was rampant growth in his garden, and all over town for that matter, but dead wood? No way. Tom had lopped branches from trees and, after he had jammed them into the ground, had seen some leaves sprout; the birch had done this a couple of times. But the leaves were always small and never lasted more than a few weeks.

"What's going on?" he asked the crows. They stopped their marching and stared at him. Two stepped away from the group and made noises that sounded a lot like laughing. He'd heard that crows could imitate various sounds and sometimes even people's voices. "Are you mocking me? Because if you are," he paused to think of something witty but only came up with, "then I guess you are and there's nothing I can do about it." *I will not sing that Doctor Doolittle song; I will not.* The albino sparrows were back under the oak, and for the first time didn't look frightened. They seemed to be playing, chirping, and bouncing around and charging at each other, flying up to a low oak branch then diving back into the fray.

Tom felt relaxed. The cavorting birds took his mind off the weirdness in the basement, made him laugh. Then he remembered the ringing telephone. "I wonder who called," he said to the lead crow. As he said this, the two laughing crows joined their nine friends and commenced marching again. Tom shook his head, said, "You guys," and stood. He gazed around the garden, soaking in the incredible sights. The apples were ripe and red and yellow, ready to eat or bake into pies. There were pears and cherries, plums and apricots. "I'm in a bit of a jam," he said; the crows laughed. And there were nuts on the chestnut; he'd never seen the tree bear fruit before. Cool.

He walked across the yard to the deck and saw that the wood was looking paler. He had noticed this months ago and had thought the winter's snow had somehow cleaned the dirty wood. But this was different, not the result of cleaning. He knelt on the lowest part of the deck and took a close look at the wood. There wasn't the slightest trace of green or gray or any of the colors pressure-treated wood took on after years of exposure to the elements. The wood appeared to be in its natural state, a yellowy-white. *Now what's going on?* Tom walked along the gravel path to the pile of dirt he had excavated earlier today. He carefully went under the deck, leaned against a post and examined the underside of the highest portion of the deck. Again, the wood was free of any indications of chemical treatment but the surface of the boards seemed nubby not smooth. So was the deck post he was leaning on; he refused to think what that might mean. When he was about to return to the house he saw a black puddle in the gravel near the post.

"Funny, I didn't see you before," he said to the puddle. "Are you one of the oily black pits of doom?" he asked, referring to nightmares he had as a child.

Bending closer to get a better view of the puddles, Tom smelled something familiar. Creosote? He stuck a finger in one of the puddles and it came out covered with oily black liquid with that long-forgotten odor. Looking under the middle part of the deck, he could see more of the pools. And nubs.

"This is just getting too fucked up for words. What next? Is the paint going to start melting off the walls?"

He went inside to check the phone and was pleasantly surprised to hear a welcome Scottish voice. Professor Ravenscroft, she had said her name was Cate, was coming for a visit if it was okay with him. Given what he had discovered today, it was more than okay. It was a damned relief that he would have someone scientific to explain everything. He had every confidence that the good professor would be able to tell him exactly what was happening and why he needn't worry his little head about it. The timestamp on the message said she had called about fifteen minutes ago. He didn't know where she lived or if she was coming from the college, driving or walking. He knew nothing.

He went into the living room and sat in one of his recliners to wait and think. Suddenly, he came over all tired. It felt incredibly relaxing as if all the tension was draining from his body. He went with the feeling, closing his eyes and reclining back as far as the chair would go. Within seconds, he was snoring.

And this is what he dreamed first:

He was walking along Main Street, distracted by the smell of the chip wagon. Though he wasn't hungry, he couldn't resist stopping for a bag of fresh-cooked fries smothered in malt vinegar and ketchup. As the cook was taking his order, he couldn't make himself heard because of the bus that had pulled up to the stop a few feet away. While the bus idled, he became more annoyed and agitated. Turning to glare at the bus, because that always helped in any situation, he saw the most beautiful creature on earth descend the rear stairs. The setting sun haloed her hair and his eyes began to water from the shine and the shock. She noticed him staring and smiled. It was as if she had reached in and clamped a hand around his heart. The coldness melted away, the butterflies began to dance, and he forgot to breathe. He tried to say hello but the lump in his throat trapped the word. She came closer, still smiling.

"Where is Arcadia?" she asked.

As he took in her vanilla scent, he knew he couldn't go back.

In the real world, the doorbell rang but Tom's dream mind thought it was someone on the bus pulling the bell cord.

He fell back into deep sleep and dreamed again:

He was sitting in his kitchen, thumbing through the day's mail when he came across a postcard she had sent:

Dearest Tom:

I have found Arcadia. It was not where we thought, but slightly to the left. You know what I mean. The quest is complete.
Join me.
                                                    Love,

The name was a blur and he couldn't remember her face.

They had been searching for years, together for months. She had come into his life by accident, a chance meeting at a bus stop. Her first words had been, "Where is Arcadia?" Tom, through the mist of love at first smile, had realized immediately that his life was over.

She had remained cool but friendly through the months of their search, while Tom's love for her had grown by the hour. He kept it all in, not wanting to scare her off, knowing such a distraction in her quest might turn her against him.

"Dearest." That had been unexpected, had made Tom's stomach flip and his heart flutter. "Join me." Perhaps his feelings were welcomed, might be returned. She had been single-minded in her desire to reach Arcadia and all that it held—riches beyond belief, knowledge lost to the world for centuries, answers that men and women had sought through the ages.

"Love." His future secure in a single word.

Now was the time for his test. Could Tom overcome his weakness and walk out the door to begin the journey to paradise? He sat for an hour, his mind in turmoil. Can I trust again? Can I face the risk? The pain?

He got up and walked to the front door, hesitated, then opened it and stepped onto the front porch.

"I knew you would come," she said, rising from the glider to his left.

He tried to see her face but was helpless.

The doorbell rang again but still didn't wake him fully; he was sure it was part of the dream. His heart was thumping in his chest and he felt excitement like he hadn't felt for as long as he could remember. But he also felt frustration because he couldn't see her, the one for whom he had been waiting all these years, the one who would take his hand and lead him up from the depths of despair.

He tried hard to influence the dream, to see the face of the woman waiting for him on the porch. But he didn't have a front porch, didn't have a glider.

The doorbell rang again and this time he did wake fully, sorry that the dream had ended, sorrier that he couldn't see her, smell her, or touch her.

A swell of anger swept through him for an instant and he hoped that whoever this intruder was, he had a good excuse for destroying his happiness. If it were someone seeking a donation, he'd send him packing. If it were some church person with the gall to search here for a convert after what he had been through, he would get far more than an earful. Tom wasn't in the mood.

Forcing himself to get out of the chair, he had a quick look in the mirror, saw that he was in decent shape, if a little dusty from his exertions trying to find the root of his problem in the basement, and checked his breath. "I may be rude but I won't be offensive," he said, picking a Scotch mint from a bowl on a side table and popping it in his mouth.

Something made him uncomfortable. Tom looked down and noticed a wet patch on the front of his jeans. He quickly unzipped and discovered the sticky mess. "Fuck, I had a wet dream? I'd better change first."

The doorbell rang a fourth time, distracting him. He shouted, "Okay, okay, I'm coming." *Fucking salesmen just never give up.* Then he remembered that in all the years he had lived here, no salesman had ever come to his door. Too far out of the way, he supposed. *Religious nutball then, anxious to tell me how much I need to believe to be happy. Oh yes, and don't forget the money it'll cost, too.*

Lawrence Burke

The closer he got to Tom Bender's house, the more he feared he was too late. Luana, dear sweet Luana, had told him that the man on the hill was in danger. Now! Hurry! He was still reeling from the sight of his daughter waking up from her coma after an impossibly long time. Nurse Cantor had regained her wits and was now taking care of the girl. No, she was a young woman now; the girl had been a memory, someone he had known a long time ago, before the evil had begun to dog his life.

Lawrence refused to question the miracle he had witnessed. Whatever had happened, he was glad of it, whether it was a gift from the god he had abandoned so easily all those years ago or something else. And despite the nurse's loud protests to the contrary, he did not think it impossible that his daughter should be speaking with such ease after eight years of silence. Whatever had revived her had strengthened her vocal chords for the warning she had given.

He had left Luana's side as soon as he had calmed the nurse. His duty was to obey the warning; tearful reunions and explanations would have to wait.

His car had not wanted to start and he wondered if the rust that was eroding the body had spread to the engine. When the motor had finally rumbled to life, he sped away showering the house with gravel. Silva had been at the front door of the main house trying to get Lawrence's attention as he drove past but had been ignored. The man was doomed; there was nothing to hold Lawrence back now.

But first, the hill.

When he reached the start of the turnaround, he slowed and parked the car. There was no one in sight, everything was quiet, the air was still. He walked the last few feet to the top of the hill watching the trees that bordered the turnaround to see if anyone was lurking there. While he quietly approached the house, a woman came from the side next to the garage and went to the front door. She didn't see him but he recognized Belinda Bender.

I knew I saw you a few weeks ago. What were you doing outside the Poplars that night?

Belinda sauntered to the front door like she didn't have a care in the world. Lawrence stepped off the asphalt and stood by a tree to observe her. She rang the doorbell and a moment later the door began to open. As it opened, Belinda drew a large hunting knife from her back pocket.

Tom Bender

He pulled the door open expecting to see the woman of his dreams to welcome her with open arms.

"I knew you'd come," he said before he saw who was standing there.

"Of course, you did, you betraying son of a whore," said Belinda. She looked down. "Disgusting pig."

The crows were making a Hell of a racket and he heard a

shout from somewhere far off then felt searing pain in his belly as the knife in Belinda's hand pierced his flesh.

Sister Mary

She saw blood well from the wound in the betrayer's side and pulled the knife back for the death stroke. Someone was shouting but she ignored it, intent on her glorious and righteous revenge. Brother James would be so proud of her.

Crows were fluttering about making an awful noise. She could feel the air moving from their flapping wings as they swooped in close.

While she batted them away, her prey took a few shaky steps to the edge of the porch. She followed and stabbed again. And again. And again.

Someone was running and she heard then felt something connect painfully with her skull.

She felt herself sailing through the air. There was a loud snap and more pain.

Her world went black.

Lawrence Burke

Lawrence leapt from his hiding place and sprinted towards the house. "No," he shouted but the woman didn't pay him any attention and climbed the steps to the front porch. He saw Tom Bender appear at the door with a happy expression on his face. The expression turned to horror and in the next instant Belinda plunged the knife into him. Bender stood for a few seconds then moved across the porch to the railing. His ex-wife kept stabbing.

A flock of crows was flying back and forth in front of the

house. It looked to Lawrence like they were trying to attack the woman but were reluctant to get closer.

When he reached the porch, he saw that Belinda was about to strike again. Without hesitation, he swatted her out of the way. Belinda made no sound as she flew across the railing and landed with a loud crack in a rockery by the path. He didn't bother to check and see if she was alright.

Tom slid from the railing and sat on the porch with a thump. He was bleeding from several wounds in his abdomen. Blood ran freely onto the porch then between the floor boards.

Tom groaned and opened his eyes. He saw Lawrence. "Hey, man, I think I fucked up. It wasn't her."

Lawrence knelt and tore Tom's shirt open. The blade had gone in deep.

He ran into the house and launched himself into the kitchen. He pulled open cabinets until he found some dish towels then rushed back to Tom who was slipping in and out of consciousness.

"Press these against the wounds," he said to Tom.

Tom blinked and asked, "Who?"

Lawrence placed the man's hand over the towels and pressed them against the dripping wound. "I'm Lawrence Burke, John's friend. You were attacked by Belinda. I hit her. She's somewhere. I think I may have cracked her skull and broken something. I'll see to her in a minute. Don't move."

"Okay," said Tom. He grasped the porch rail and went rigid with shock. Lawrence had his hand on the wounded man's shoulder and could feel the electricity passing through him. He fell back. When the spots cleared from his eyes, Lawrence asked, "What on earth was that?"

Tom grunted, "This house has been doing all kinds of weird

shit lately. The rail's made of wood. Nothing surprises me anymore." He winced and tears fell from his eyes. "Fuck, it hurts a lot. Who are you again?"

Lawrence held Tom's wrist and checked his pulse. It was barely there. Tom's skin was clammy and he was incredibly pale, and it looked like his lips might be turning blue.

"I'm so tired," said Tom. "I'll catch a few …" Tom's eyes closed.

Lawrence felt lost. He knew he'd failed in his duty. This man was going to die and there was nothing anyone could do about it. "Stay there," he said knowing it was pointless. Tom wouldn't ever be moving again. "I'll call for an ambulance then the Sheriff." He placed the calls. The ambulance was on its way and the Sheriff would be there when his deputy could find him. "I'll go see if your ex-wife is still with us."

Lawrence went out and saw right away that Belinda was no longer lying over the rockery.

Tom Bender

Tom had never felt such pain. He tried not to cry but the tears flowed freely anyway. The world spun. Tom tried to concentrate but failed.

Who is she? Why can't I see your face? It's not fair.
What happened?
Who's that man helping me?
Who's the King?
A sharp pain caused him to gasp. "Oh, fuck."
I'm scared. I need you.
Is this what it feels like when you …
Tom died.

The King of the Wood

The King couldn't stop laughing. Oh, the irony. His nemesis murdered by a crazy ex-wife. Oh, the joy.
"That'll teach you to be kind to your fellow man, you simpleton." The King took a deep breath. He giggled.
Nine rats stood on the path as he neared the entrance to his shrine. He walked in. The rats followed. Ten pairs of eyes stared at him from dark recesses in the cave wall. When he reached the main gallery of his shrine, twelve rats stood amongst the remains of his sacrifices. All the rats were silent and unafraid.
The King scanned the mess around him. So many corpses, so much decay. He clapped his hands. The rats all jumped.
"There's no time for rest. We've got lots of work to do. Lots of enemies to kill. A whole world to reclaim."
He stood silently for a few seconds relishing the feeling as the last little sign of life slipped away from the fool who thought he could take over.
"Good-bye, Tom. You're the final sacrifice. This feels so good. I've never felt so sanguine. You'll never know ... anything ever again."
The King grasped the roots of the oak from the garden above. He connected with the greenery of the town, of the world. He had the power. It felt wonderful. It felt ... incomplete.

Cate Ravenscroft

"Ferfucksakes.